STARFIRE

Warriors of the Elector Book 2

Featuring bonus novella

STAR OF THE FLEET

ISBN Print - 978-0-9954182-1-9

Contents

STARFIRE

Prologue   1
Chapter 1   5
Chapter 2   20
Chapter 3   38
Chapter 4   45
Chapter 5   57
Chapter 6   67
Chapter 7   75
Chapter 8   89
Chapter 9   99
Chapter 10   112
Chapter 11   121
Chapter 12   132
Chapter 13   145
Chapter 14   165
Chapter 15   177
Chapter 16   187
Epilogue   201

STAR OF THE FLEET

Chapter 1   207
Chapter 2   217
Chapter 3   219
Chapter 4   222
Chapter 5   235
Chapter 6   236
Chapter 7   246
Chapter 8   250
Chapter 9   258
Chapter 10   262
Chapter 11   270

Chapter 12   275
About Imogene Nix   285
Other Books   286

Acknowledgements

As an author, it's always difficult to know where to begin thanking those involved in the production of any book. But without all those involved, no book would ever be completed, so I must take a moment to thank Pamela at Beachwalk Press who allowed me the freedom to retain these print rights so I can release the entire series to the world.

Thank you also to my wonderful team of Sassie who ensured that the internal contents were perfect and Willsin who listened when I said no I don't like that photo. Without his forebearance, the cover wouldn't be perfect.

Thank you to JL who read the original manuscript and Tracey the worlds most super Beta Reader!

My family who have learned that when I say I'm writing mostly know to keep out of the way - yes and Super Pup, Cocoa Bean and Galilee too.

And of course, my readers. I wouldn't have this many titles without you being there to enjoy them. Thank you!

Imogene

STARFIRE

Prologue

The imposing white walls of the Earth Empire Academy rose like monoliths toward the sun, glistening with the quartz decorations representing the colonized worlds or those they'd formed alliances with. It was a symbol of both their might and drive that it remained standing.

"Get lost, Raven!"

Shocked looks shot in Raven's direction, and he jammed his hands into his pockets while a woman dashed through the shady quadrangle and paid the onlookers no attention. Instead, she muttered a litany of complaints, the sounds drowning beneath the crunching of many feet in heavy, black boots.

Her exquisite pink lips moved rapidly with caustic words that tumbled, and the knot of people gathered who saw the woman with the black hair and piercing blue eyes gave her a wide berth. Many a cadet had experienced her temper, already legendary in this corner of the Empire. They'd heard of her cold shoulder, and the jagged edges of her sharp tongue, while the rising red crest of fury washing over her cheeks warned them of the danger of crossing her right at that moment.

Raven stood under an awning at the end of the long building, watching her hurry defiantly away from him. "Dammit, Jemma." He had felt the heat of her tongue this day. The news he had brought, that she had to stay at the academy until she graduated, had enraged her further, causing an outburst that would have burned a lesser man.

Even as he exhaled heavily, he couldn't stop his gaze from roaming over her retreating figure. The plain black suit of an academy cadet did nothing to hide the subtle curves of her body or its suppleness. He was aware that many male students had already made the mistake of addressing this young woman with an offer of companionship. Some had compounded it by offering earthier suggestions on occasion. She'd cut them down, letting them know how little she thought of them and their self-confessed prowess.

He watched her with troubled eyes, knowing that the news he

would return to the Elector with would upset his captain further.

Touching one hand to his commbadge, he opened a channel. "Duvall? I've made contact."

"And?" The scratchy sound of his friend and captain's voice didn't improve his mood.

"She's not happy." The knowledge that she chafed against the strictures and the directive from the upper echelons of the Admiralty itself frustrated him. He remained forbidden to explain why or who'd made the decree. She assumed Duvall was to blame.

"Return to the *Elector*." Duvall's voice was weary, but there was little else Raven could do. He'd carried the Admiralty's wishes, but it didn't lessen his feeling of dissatisfaction in the errand.

Jemma rounded the corner, headed for the dorm tower, and disappeared from his sight. Raven turned and retreated beyond the walls.

✪ ✪ ✪ ✪

Crick Sur Banden sat in his headquarters on Sienna V, the frigidly cold planet nearest the border of the Earth Ru'Edan-delineated space. Dark and icy, the planet remained largely uninhabited except for the miners of the dark Juran metal. Highly toxic to most, its medicinal use in the drug Xeradax remained the only reason for the continued settlement of the planet.

He stretched on the lounger while women hovered around. "Get me another goblet of Dragorth's Blood."

They poured the shimmering red spirit into the metal cup and pressed it into his hands, as he waited for the chemicals to take effect. The crimson drink was native to the wastelands of the Alpha Star Colony, which he'd happily brought under his command, and he took a moment to reflect on how much his influence had grown since the abortive mission to Earth.

"Duvall, you haven't stopped me yet." A trickle of laughter escaped as he spoke. Duvall and the *Elector* had singularly failed to curb his expansion and soon… Soon he'd have a force strong enough to conquer the might of humanity.

The fire burning in the hearth was reminiscent of the destruction he had left behind at the colony. The fire he'd rained upon the colonists cleansed the dirt that should never have seen the infection of humans, he thought humorlessly. He had found an isolated pocket and wiped them from memory, burned their bones and taken their women for the comfort of his men. He'd only made a token effort this time.

He'd had plans for the Alpha Star Colony, but the riches he had found them mining had intrigued him even more. The activities nearly sidetracked him, until he'd remembered his goal—to annihilate the humans.

This time he'd accomplish it by blocking their access to the coveted Duschem Mineral, whispered to be used in creating the energy matrix of the stealth ships of the Earth Empire.

It was also said they were integral to the formulation of the shields of the Predators of the Ru'Edan. Such highly coveted resources would be his. That alone was the real reason he needed the Alpha Star Colony. He laughed. It would be interesting to cut off the supply and starve their shipbuilding, but he had bigger plans.

He stood, a sneering smile adorning his gray-toned skin. He raised a glass to the memory of comrades who'd died in the battle, then made his way slowly toward his desk screen. "Bring the girl and the maps. Let us see what we shall destroy and rebuild for our own purposes." Once more he flashed a grimacing smile, so feral in intensity that those around him gasped. Crick settled his mind and let the creation of plans begin. "Oh yes, Earth, you will rue the day you crossed me."

The crew of the *Elector* was on leave. Raven knew the last time this had happened had been well before he'd joined the crew and been sent through the Time Port. This time the crew had reason to celebrate. Their captain, Duvall McCord, had undergone the ceremony of communing to the lovely Mellissa, whom he'd saved on the *Elector*'s maiden voyage through the slipstream. The ceremony had cemented the link between them, even after the archaic wedding ceremony Mellissa had requested.

Raven, together with the rest of the crew, waited anxiously to see what their next mission would be. Each of them had a reason to want to be aboard the *Elector*, some history with Crick Sur Banden that spurred them on.

The stealth ship, the first of its class, had proven maneuverable and speedy, but there was consensus that soon they would join either a squadron or one of the fleets in order to fulfill its role.

The crew knew it was only a matter of time until they were once more deployed, and of course, they knew that with Crick Sur Banden, the surety of battle occurring grew closer. For now though, they celebrated, caroused, and enjoyed themselves.

"Jemma didn't come?" Chowd spoke behind him, and Raven considered it a failure that he hadn't been able to convince the young woman to set aside her rage for the day.

"No. She's still not ready to accept what was done."

Her transfer to the Earth Academy had been acrimonious, and she refused any contact with the crew and in particular Mellissa, who had always been her mentor and sister-like figure.

She accepted the position of Admiralty cadet under duress, feeling that she didn't need to be trained in the ways of the Admiralty, but her much younger age had made it imperative that she be appropriately educated and find some occupation.

Raven had been chosen as go-between for Jemma and the crew due to his parents' presence as professors at the academy, even though he knew it was unlikely that Jemma would have anything much to do with his parents as one ran the Science Exploration faculty and the other worked in the medical wing. Not that he had a close association with them. Their relationship had become strained when he chose active service, becoming a ship's engineer, instead of the more academic role they would have preferred he investigate.

Chapter 1

Jemma burned with anger and stomped her way back to the room the academy had allocated her. It was as bland as any other institutional building with off-white walls and large plate-glass windows, but she didn't pay it any attention.

Each footstep echoed down the hall. Oh yeah, it was right for everyone else to look like they knew what they were doing with her life. They weren't thrust into a new time against their will, she thought savagely. She had promised herself after the orphanage never to let *anyone else* make decisions for her.

"Never again." Thanks to Mellissa's betrayal, she was back to square one. After the orphanage, her life had been her own...for a while anyway. She muttered a vicious curse under her breath. "I hate the academy. The stupid clothing rules, enforced bedtime, and the food." Every aspect of her new life insulted her, because they treated her like some nameless, voiceless figure in some stupid institution. Just like she'd already survived once.

She slapped her palm on the reader, waiting only for the door to slide open enough for her to slip into the room. "Close door and engage locks."

Most of the kids here—and she privately considered them to be nothing more than kids— had never faced anything more difficult than cleaning their rooms or making sure they didn't exceed their budgets.

She threw the papers she'd crushed into her pockets, onto the small but sturdy desk that sat in the corner of the room. What would they know about the loneliness of not having a family? They didn't have a clue about making your own way in an alien world and culture. Yes, for all her humanity, the lifestyle changes made her feel like she may as well have been on Jupiter.

Before all this occurred she had always been able to talk to Mellissa, but now she knew the truth. You couldn't rely on anyone.

She didn't know where Mellissa was, either off with her husband on board his ship or still on leave for six weeks at the sumptuous spa resort on Mars. Their romance had captured the attention of the various media outlets. "Scum-sucking media hounds." Her chest ached at the betrayal that lanced her to the soul.

Mellissa had tried to explain why Jemma needed to attend the academy, including that she had age against her. Now that they lived until nearly two hundred, she was classified as a youngster. It didn't matter that in her time she was old enough to make her own decisions, the current thinking was she was young.

But the fact remained that there she sat, on her own again. When it came down to it, Mellissa had traded her in for someone else. She refused to admit it hurt.

She hated this place, and that any skills she did have were unable to help her find her place in this new reality. The fact that she *was* different to everyone around her angered Jemma.

Once again, she had to start over. She had done that before, after leaving the orphanage. She'd built a life for herself, but with the stroke of another's decision she'd lost everything she'd gained. "For fuck's sake, it's so damned unfair! How could this happen again? How did I lose control of my life?" She raged as she stalked around the small cubicle they called a dormitory.

Then the results she'd received for the exam passed through her mind, reinforcing her negative thoughts. A C-minus! For God's sake, she had only been there three weeks when she'd sat the exam! The others? They'd had months of tutoring and teaching. She'd managed that on almost nothing!

She heaved a sigh. How could her life have spun so totally out of control? One moment, she had been having this great affair with Andurs Feinstein. He had been very good in the sack—she grinned at that thought—and the next moment, she ended up on board some spaceship headed for the future.

Even her time on the *Elector* hadn't been that great. They'd been in such a hurry to get back to the future Earth, no one really had much to do with the person they probably thought somehow instigated the whole mess. Once Mellissa had been out of the SurgiTech, Jemma had seen she already had a place as part of the crew.

Jemma seethed. Her request for release from the academy had been returned, denied by Grayson, which really meant it was Duvall, in his usual highhanded manner, pulling the strings. He didn't even have the courtesy of telling her himself.

"Oh no! He sends the engineer. Whoever heard of an engineer acting as a bloody courier anyway?" Jemma threw herself down onto the bed. At least they'd allowed her a room to herself so she could have some privacy. No small mercy, she thought. She would have probably done something heinous if they had stuck her with one of the young girls in the classes she attended. "Twirling-hair, boy-watching babies." The snarl filled the air, and Jemma snorted.

She hadn't even had a freaking date in the whole time she had attended the academy. She felt surrounded with no one worth considering. Her choices, she acknowledged, were slim; either the professors—and no way would she let that happen—or little mama's boys. Those youngsters all considered themselves so grown up, but the only ones she had seen were namby-pamby wimps with nothing to make them appealing to a woman like herself.

Lying on the bed, looking at the ceiling, she thought over the courses set for her as mandatory. Basic self-defense, piloting—silently she acknowledged that was the best of all— and a make-up course on technical and engineering skills, basic self-sufficiency, and field medicals. Bah! They hadn't even let her think about the skills that she might have to offer, unlike Mellissa, who had slotted right into a researcher role on the *Elector*. No, she'd been dropped, like a good little girl, to learn her place. She let loose a roar of anger, throwing a pillow at the door.

"God! They won't even let me on an air-bike!" She had to attend testing so that they could deem her capable. The stupid thing was, just about every cadet had a license while she stayed stuck on her feet. They didn't even accept that she had a motorbike license in her time.

Nope. That didn't carry any weight in their eyes. Yet another sin to lay at their door. She shifted on the bed and continued to look at the ceiling. Back to the whole institutionalized mindset.

Jemma slumped down the steps toward the communal mess and wove through the lines of students, many of whom had seen her and moved away to allow her access. No one stood up to her and her already legendary temper.

She grabbed a meal and headed outside to the garden seats. Today she would be tested on an air-bike, having finally talked an instructor into letting her tackle the exam. Her spirits lifted a little, and she made her way through the meal. Jemma found it difficult to know what she was eating and since arriving had quickly learned not to ask. The one meal she had made that mistake with had been a Uranian Squirrel stew. She hadn't finished throwing up until the following morning.

Once she finished eating her meal, she disposed of the tray in the slot in the side of the refectory wall and headed for the large hanger where the cockpit simulator lay.

She hurried in to see Professor Anston, who had agreed to trial her and if possible give her the necessary documentation for a license. His grizzled countenance and white hair did not do justice to the sharp mind encased in an older body. He inclined his head toward her.

"Cadet Cardnew, come in. I was waiting for you." He motioned her forward with an easy hand. "I have prepared a holo-simulation for you to try. I believe you said that previously you had driven a land-based automobile?"

"Yes, Professor, we called them a motorbike in my time. It was just sweet, all chrome and blue and went like a shower of...umm, speed." She grinned awkwardly. Jemma found it difficult to remember sometimes not to be so unguarded with an answer. She backed up, reminding herself once more of where she was and with whom.

He smiled though, his blue eyes twinkling as if he knew what exactly the direction her thoughts took and the words she had nearly said. "Good. Good. Then we'll start you with the initial holographic sitting position—"

She opened her mouth to explain that something so basic really was not necessary, but he held up a hand.

"We need to work through the steps, otherwise there may be questions down the line. Queries as to whether we went through every aspect. It could cause them to rescind your license. And I know that you've been looking forward to this since arriving. We don't want someone taking it away because we didn't follow the rules, now do we?" He leaned toward her conspiratorially.

"No, Professor." Her spine straightened, and she felt her hands fist, the pressure on her palms from her fingers. She released the fists almost immediately. She might not like what he said, but she didn't want them to take away any freedom she managed to claw back. So she swallowed the ire that rose. *Suck it up, girl.*

"Right...holo-projectors online. Run scenario Alfa-Juliet-Alpha-Beta-one-five-niner." His voice carried a note of glee, and his eyes twinkled as he looked at her, and for just a second she could see beyond the aged body and white hair to the man he must once have been. Cheeky while he thumbed his nose at the system, she was sure. She felt a grin crawl over her face. *I could really like this professor.*

A small, red air-bike appeared in front of her, and he motioned for her to get on. She straddled the seat, sinking into it as it conformed to her body shape. She sighed, even while she still marveled at the wonders of instantaneous actualized holographic emitters. This was one experience she'd looked forward to since arrival, and by God, she'd make the most of it. Jemma moved a little and got her bum comfortable in the seat.

"Now depress the ignition button to start, and it should rise immediately."

Following the instructions, she felt a warm bubble of pleasure flare in her chest as the bike started to rise. Professor Anston handed her a set of goggles. "You'll need these in a minute, my dear," he said with a grin.

Taking them in her hand, she noticed that they were holo-glasses, which would allow her to see the rest of the holographic information she would need to complete the test, the bike the only actualized form in the scenario. She slipped them over her eyes and saw an open road. Her grin widened, and she breathed in, stretching her chest and neck in excitement and pleasure. *Oh, how I've missed this!*

Her hands grasped the bike handles, which conformed to the shape of her grip and became solid. Jemma moved them back and forth, getting the feel of the bike within her bones, making a connection on a wholly sensual basis as it thrummed beneath her body. *The pleasure of the open road once more, no longer cooped up...*

She noticed that the professor was talking again.

"In the next step, I want you to lap the bike on the road you see before you."

Lifting the glasses, she looked over at him and saw he wore an identical set of glasses to the ones she held, his white hair popping above the basic black goggles. He smiled at her. No doubt they had readouts concerning what she was doing as well as a visual feedback, she mused, but she felt a sort of kindred connection already and couldn't help smiling in return. She slipped the glasses back over her eyes.

"Go!" His word released her, and she let the bike go. Freedom, finally!

The bike flew into the air, and she leaned into it as she had with her road bike. She felt the wind blowing as she followed the track designated. The bike felt smooth beneath her, the satisfying hum rippling through her body. Jemma reveled in the sense of freedom. It took no time to speed around the track and return to the start.

He gave her further instructions, requesting she complete the track again, keeping a constant speed. Again, she did it almost instinctively, moving with the bike, leaning into the turns as if she was part of it. Lastly, he made her run a series of obstacles, which showed her ability to control the air-bike in wet, windy, and even dangerous conditions.

She inwardly rejoiced, knowing she showed him her preparedness for her license. She pulled the goggles off and felt that she had passed the routines more than capably.

It startled her when the professor clasped her hands firmly, praising her not just as a natural but talented at controlling the vehicle. "My dear, it has been many years since I've had the honor of licensing one so capable with an air-bike. I could only describe your performance as highly instinctive. I'll arrange the necessary documentation for you, and you should be able to utilize it within the week to borrow an academy air-bike."

She grinned. Here lay the freedom she needed. "Thank you so

much, Professor. You have no idea how much I've looked forward to this."

"Oh, I think I do, my dear. And to be honest, I look forward to teaching you on far more advanced vehicles soon."

Pleasure buzzed as he bowed her out of the holo-room with great ceremony. It startled her to realize she was drenched with sweat from the workout, but she felt elation at her achievement. She knew that most applicants for licenses were awarded at the age of twelve, but she had an inkling her test ended a little higher than the average.

Just before he closed the door behind her, Professor Anston leaned over conspiratorially. "While the initial test was meant for a youngster, I played a little with the schematics and scenario, including some military-grade exercises just to see how good you were. I had a feeling you'd acquit yourself creditably. Your reflexes are quick and sharp, my dear, and I was sure you'd pass them easily."

Jemma left him after those words, focusing on the positives in his message. She had achieved an air-bike license and would soon be able to have access to an academy bike—that's what mattered to her. Blessed freedom lay outside the institutional walls. Anything to escape, she told herself.

Quickly slipping from the area, she made her way back to her quarters. Along the way she sighted an electronic flyer. *Colonists needed for Alpha Star Colony* caught her eye. The bold type screamed out to her. She stopped and swiped her wrist reader over the barcode; she could look further once she reached her dorm.

She hurried onward as the thoughts danced in her head. Perhaps this was another new opportunity. After all, on a mining colony there would be opportunities, no academy, and most of all no annoying reminders of her past. She flew up the steps and along the corridor, her heavy boots beating a tattoo on the cold, unyielding floor. The small room at the end beckoned, and she palmed the door open.

"Engage locks." She headed to the desk screen, commanding, "Find all information concerning latest reader entries."

The screen threw up the image of the flyer she had seen. She read the sparse information. Support staff and miners required for Alpha Star Colony. Transportation covered with an indenture period of two years. That certainly gave her pause. Indenture was a big commitment, but it would only be for two years.

"Bring up all known information on the Alpha Star Colony, subsequent command, a list of all positions still to be filled on the colony and educational requirements."

The screen filled with information concerning the Alpha Star Colony, the harsh climactic conditions, the impassible mountains that no one had managed to climb, quickly changing landscapes and massive canyons, the Ice Fields to the north and the main continent to the south.

There was also a list of camps currently settled and a little information on the rare Duschem mineral they extracted, though the mineral's uses were rated as a level-nine clearance for information. She snorted at that. "Must be military use," she muttered.

Oh yes, this *could* be her future, but she needed to know more. It wasn't a decision to take lightly. Tapping once more brought up the information from the secondary search, and she browsed the positions. Mining didn't really interest her—something physical, yes, but not mining. Security officer caught her eye though. Basic skills in piloting shuttles, training in weapons and hand-to-hand required certified level-seven skill acquisition. Both academy and non-academy graduates welcomed. She smiled. Yes, this looked more and more promising.

A siren wailed loudly in the background, alerting her to shut the desk screen down. Yet one more reason to hate the academy—curfew. It interrupted her thought patterns all too often. She hadn't had a curfew since leaving the orphanage at sixteen, and there she was, twenty-three and back at square one. She snorted in disgust.

"Save all present data to personal files and conclude shut-down sequence."

Quickly making her way to the personal bathroom to complete her necessary preparations for bed, she then padded over to the narrow cot pushed into the corner of the small cell and crawled between the rough sheets.

Instead of sleeping, she played visions of the vast new world in her mind. There she could probably be herself, be mistress of her own future—after a period of indenture, of course. She smiled as she lay in the darkness. "This could be just the opportunity I need."

"Captain, it is good to see you back. Mellissa, it's great to have you back on board too." Raven looked at Duvall, a man he had never really envied before. He was relaxed with his arm around his chosen life partner. A satisfied smile flitted over Duvall's lips.

"It's good to be home. I know Mellissa wanted to get back too."

Raven looked at the woman beside his captain. She glowed in a way that spoke of good sex, relaxation, and something else. For a minute, Raven thought of a small dynamo with black hair and angry eyes. He thrust the thought aside for now.

"I need to update you on that small job you gave me." He looked at Duvall, waiting for his mind to click into gear.

Duvall straightened, running his fingers through his black hair as if he wanted to push the knowledge of what they were about to discuss out of his head, and turned to Mellissa. "I need to deal with this. You go ahead and find Elara. I'll be in the office as soon as I can."

Mellissa acknowledged with a brief touch of hands on his arm before heading off. They both waited until her footsteps died away.

He turned back to Raven. "What happened?" he demanded, his face hard.

"I passed on the message you sent through me, ostensibly from Grayson. I believe the term she used was 'pissed'," he said, watching for a reaction, knowing this whole mess upset Mellissa and as a result his captain.

"What do you mean?" Duvall's eyes narrowed as they zoomed in on Raven.

"Exactly that. She was exceptionally unhappy that you refused to consider that she should leave the academy. As per your instructions, I didn't pass on that the Admiralty was who made the determination." He shrugged. "But I did glean some useful information since then."

Duvall looked at him, waiting with a raised eyebrow.

"I made a couple of enquiries with some of the professors, since

I happen to be in a position to know most of them."

Duvall's eyes cooled slightly, but Raven couldn't summon up a smile to relieve his captain's tension.

"Helps that my parents were on campus at the time and it was the retirement party for one of the professors, so I was able to make the enquiries under the guise of social chit-chat. Keep the queries off the radar, if you know what I mean." He shrugged. "She has excelled in piloting and focused on weapons and hand-to-hand training. She has already shown an aptitude toward engineering, though it would seem she has not chosen to make it her primary subject."

Duvall sighed. "Anything else?"

"Yes, it seems she has picked up a statutes and laws course. She completed the basic self-sufficiency and the field medicals. She passed creditably well, from what I heard. She refuses to interact socially with the other cadets though. She has been categorized as not actively hostile, but certainly not an integrator. At the rate she's completing courses and units, she could leave the academy within months to work as station or dirtside security, or even law enforcement." He stopped for a moment and drew a breath. "In fact, her course choices don't seem random. It seems she is now licensed for the air-bike and is well on the way toward levels D and E shuttle tickets. Her current certified hand-to-hand is rated as a five. You know what that means."

Duvall grimaced. "She's well on her way to combat status or mining colony security rating."

Raven nodded. "Anston says she's a natural. He also believes she's standoffish with the other professors as a kind of passive aggression. He's been working with her after hours because he thinks she could even make fighter grade, if she can increase her skills. I've asked him not to tell her at this stage." He pushed his hands into the pockets of his ship suit. "I'm not sure that's enough to deter him from suggesting fighter school. I know you're worried about her and Mellissa thinks of her as a little sister, but perhaps you need to cut her some slack. Let her see what she can do."

"I would, but Crick Sur Banden has used her once and Mellissa... well, Mellissa worries about her." He looked up to the girders making up the spine of the *Elector*, letting out a sigh. "She refuses to talk to either of us, and so far, you're the only one she's seen since we made it dirtside. She refused to attend the ceremony, and Mellissa… She worries." He smiled. "And a man has to keep his woman happy. Keep looking around and discreetly asking questions. See what else we need to be aware of." He started to walk away.

"Why not get Chowd to take over?" Raven waited for Duvall's answer, fists jammed into the pockets of his ship suit and feet braced.

"Because there would be too many questions if he was seen on campus. You can come and go at will and no one will think twice," Duvall answered briskly, walking away and leaving Raven to ponder this for a moment before he turned back toward the corridor and engineering.

"Cadet Cardnew, could you stay behind for a moment? I would like to discuss something with you." Professor Anston made his request from below shaggy brows, a half-smile lighting his face.

Jemma stopped and looked at him. "Sir?" *What have I done wrong now?* But the professor had been good to work with, so she waited patiently while the students in the piloting program filed out, laughing playfully, chatting with the others in their groups.

"I'm not supposed to tell you, but I believe you should consider leaving the academy." It was a sucker punch to her stomach. Sure, she didn't want to stay there, but what the freaking hell had she done now? Her stomach roiled. If she had to leave, where would she go? She hadn't yet achieved the required ratings for the indentured security officer position on the Alpha Star Colony. She opened her mouth, but he held up a hand.

"Your skills are wasted here. I'd like to suggest you for the Combat Fighter Program."

Jemma stopped, startled. *What?* She felt excitement filter throughout her body. "But only the best of the students are able to get into that program. The scores needed to get in...well, I haven't achieved them, let alone done any kind of preparatory studies, and there is a waiting list as long as my arm. I know because I looked it up when I first came and discounted it." She looked at him, half-daring to hope. "My other scores are pretty basic across the board." She hated admitting that she hadn't worked to her full potential at other subjects, but honesty in this case would be the best policy. Besides, she would never get anywhere by deceiving herself. Her heart dropped once more like a stone. He'd most likely change his mind now that she admitted her scores and lack of preparation.

"I am aware of those things, but I have a wild-card entry to the program, and I believe you'd be the best one to use it with. I believe your natural ability would benefit the Empire." He stopped and waited for her answer, watching her intently.

The silence grew while she digested this information. Could she do it? Should she take this chance? Would she regret a wasted opportunity if she didn't take what was offered? *Hell yes*! She already had enough regrets in her life, and she didn't need any more.

"You really think I could do this?" It came out like an awed whisper. Her? A combat fighter pilot? Only the best of the best got that status. "But what about my grades and not having the sort of experience they claim you need to have?" she said, her words cold like ice. She was being wound up, surely. But the possibility...

"I know you could ace the program. However, you'd need to be committed to it. I'm happy to tutor you in the initial stages, but you need to give it everything," he replied, his voice stern but his eyes flashing with confidence.

For just a moment, the idea danced in her brain. *Take this opportunity and be someone.* The thought tempted her. "Oh God! I never thought about it. I mean, my scores..." Her voice trailed off. She looked up at him, and once more she questioned the opportunity. "You *are* serious, aren't you?"

"Never more so. But if you take this chance, you have to give it your all." His words were firm, filtering through to stun her once more.

She stood upright, letting the knowledge flood her system. She could do this. She would do it and be bloody successful too. "Oh, I want it. More than I ever thought I would. What do I need to do?" Her fingers rose to the front of her academy suit, shaking, and her heart hammered in her chest. Adrenaline coursed through her veins as they throbbed and hummed with excitement. She felt tightly wired, like a spring.

"Good. Just wait there," he said, and reached for his wrist chrono. "Perkins? I have my wild card in line. I want her moved immediately into the program."

"Really? Who did you choose?" The tinny voice echoed in the nearly empty room.

"Cadet Cardnew." He grinned at her, and she couldn't help but grin back.

I probably look like a drunken fool, but I don't care, this is the best thing that ever happened in my life.

"Cardnew? But she is barely scraping passes on some of her courses. We already discussed that, Anston. I really don't think she would be the best choice. Why not Elmhurst or Strachan? Even Jur Su would do better."

"No. Cardnew has a promise none of the others have. You've seen her scores already. Now I need her allocated to the program and re-housed. Today if possible." Anston touched his wrist chrono again, ending the connection.

She looked at him, amazed at the lightning change her life was about to undertake. Again, it meant a change, almost as big as coming into the future. Yet there were differences this time. This time she made the decisions. She controlled her own destiny once more. The world seemed a little brighter right now as new opportunities opened up, and she reached over to snag the professor's hands. "Thank you so much, sir. I promise I won't let you down."

"Come along, my dear, and I'll show you to the simulator." He led her through a door into another room, one she'd never entered before, filled with what looked like front ends of small planes. Here was her chance, her destiny. Time to grasp the future with both hands, she told herself as she moved forward.

✪ ✪ ✪ ✪

"Duvall! Need to see you in engineering. Now." Raven's voice echoed in the bowels of the *Elector*. He waited for Duvall to acknowledge the communication through his badge as he looked at the information that had just been thrown up on his screen.

"For *Eshra*'s sake!" The clanking of feet, swift but sure, on the decking had him lifting his head. He knew that rapid tattoo… Knew it could only be his captain.

Duvall clattered down the metal stairs and stopped beside him, a query on his face. He scowled deeply, knowing Duvall would be angry once he shared his intelligence.

"She's been moved to the Combat Fighter Program."

"What do you mean? You spoke to Anston!" Duvall's face tightened in time with Raven's stomach.

"Yeah, I spoke to Anston, but it never occurred to me that the heavies would be put on him to use his wild-card entry so fast. Apparently, she accepted and is currently moving to the training base outside Woomera. He kept it concealed from me until it was too late for me to head it off. Anston is continuing to tutor her in the basic flight processes for now, but that'll stop once she has integrated fully into the program. He thinks that could actually be within the next week or so," Raven said. Duvall opened his mouth, but Raven knew exactly what he'd ask. "I don't have any contacts in Woomera."

"*Barsha!* Once she's there, she is sequestered and beyond our reach until they are placed into a squadron. I have to tell Mellissa and make sure Admiral Elphin is aware as well." He said the words heavily, as if another weight descended onto his shoulders.

"Can we have her moved into the Alpha Squadron, do you think? At least then she will be within the same quadrant. Your contact with the Admiralty should be able to arrange that comfortably." Raven looked at Duvall hopefully, but he already knew he was grasping at straws.

Duvall shook his head. "I can request it, but you know they're highly sought-after positions. I can't be sure it would work anyway. Truthfully, we need to see if Jemma can make it through the program and which squadron is game to take her on." Once more, Raven noticed that Duvall looked strained. "I'll talk to Chowd though, see what contacts he has, then I will talk to the Admiral."

Chapter 2

Jemma grabbed the last bag. The past twelve months had been grueling. The combat flight training was both intense and fulfilling, and here she was finally, with the metal wings denoting her a fighter pilot clipped to her new unit uniform. The small data disk with the details of her first posting sat in her pocket, burning her with the knowledge that she had surpassed every expectation. Her future had arrived. She grinned at the whimsical thought.

Chatter echoed around the building. "Hey, were are you posted?"

"I got the posting I wanted!"

She snorted hearing them all. They were still green, but she had no illusions. She'd somehow managed to pull off a plum posting, but it wouldn't be easy. "I'm going to show them," she told herself, gazing at the press of bodies.

She trotted quickly across the asphalt and dumped her bags onto the anti-gravity bed ready for moving them to the *Star of Ishtar* transport. The *Star of Ishtar*, she thought with awe. The destroyer where she had accepted deployment as a member of the Alpha Squadron, the placement every pilot wanted.

She cast one more look back over her shoulder. Professor Anston stood watching her, his shock of white hair standing out visibly in the excited crowd of families. She would make him proud, this man who had given her the opportunity. She had invited him to the marching-out parade as her only guest, and to her delight, he'd accepted.

She hurried over to him. "Professor, I can't ever thank you enough for this opportunity."

His eyes twinkled. "You've already thanked me by proving me right." His gaze turned grave. "Take care, Cardnew. These are uncertain times, and you'll be right in the middle of it."

A grin wasn't appropriate, she understood what he meant, but thirteen months ago, she'd been sure there were no more adventures left for her. How wrong she'd been.

In her mind, the professor had become a symbol of opportunities that she wouldn't waste. "You take care too. The next time you get a hard nut like me… Tell them hi."

He laughed. "You're a good girl, Cardnew. I'll be watching to see you rise up the ladder."

An impulsive hug, she slid her arms around his still broad shoulders. "Thank you. For everything." Jemma tugged away and spun on highly polished boots as tears burned behind her eyelids. "I gotta go."

As she strode off she looked over her shoulder and saw him salute briefly before turning away. She flicked her hair, tied in a tight braid, over her shoulder, and followed the others to the shuttles.

"Cardnew, J. Step forward." The voice of the captain rang through the bay.

She stepped forward to meet Captain Thoray. He extended his hand, and her eyes flicked up to his face as she accepted the hand and shook it firmly.

"Welcome to the *Star of Ishtar*. You will no doubt want to see your craft. Commander Vors is your squadron leader. She was supposed to be here but was unavoidably detained." He dropped her hand, and she stepped back. He moved on to the next new member of the crew.

The hanger was full of new crewmembers, each waiting for their personal welcome to the destroyer that carried a full complement of two thousand seven hundred and forty-three, she'd read. From cooks to engineers, from fighter pilots to the lowliest crewmen assigned to sanitation control, each member of the crew would be personally welcomed before they would meet with their superiors. Her stomach quivered with nerves, and she stood there feeling like a fraud. *You achieved the rank of pilot because of your skill.* Somehow, though, the words didn't break through the nerves.

The newest recruits finally dismissed, she moved to the bay allocated for the combat pilots. Several others watched her approach, and as had become her custom, she ignored them, checking the roster to see her craft designation on the screen. AE-JK-423. What a name, she thought derisively. If it didn't already have a call sign, she would have given it one with a little zing.

A ripple of comments flowed through the others in the bay, and the sound of movements alerted her to someone entering. A tall, statuesque blonde moved in, perhaps in her thirties, but with a commanding presence nonetheless. Jemma saw her watching the pilots form a line with her deep-yellow eyes, and Jemma turned, joining the formation, aware that this was someone she should show due respect for.

"At ease." The voice was sultry.

A few comments followed while Jemma considered the woman. *Yellow eyes?* Ah, she must be Vors, her immediate superior. She had heard that she had certain feline qualities of the Te'Karans. At the academy, they said her mother was a Te'Karan halfling who had joined the Earth Empire after marrying a human. The story held legendary status in the flight program, telling how her father had been a combat pilot, rescuing her mother from an attack on the Te'Kar home world by the Ru'Edan.

"Cardnew!"

"Yes, ma'am." Jemma continued to stand at attention, watching and waiting.

"Welcome aboard. I see you have already found your designated craft. She used to be called the *Bitch*, but I'm sure you can come up with something more appropriate," Vors said with a hint of humor. She dismissed the other pilots and continued to stand in front of Jemma.

"Yes, ma'am."

"Come on, I'll take you to your cabin and explain what you need to know before we move off. We've been offering flight support to the *Ishtar* for about six months now. Raids in areas of the Phobos Sector have become an issue, and the captain thinks our presence helps to deter some of the incursions."

They were moving at a quick clip down the corridor beyond the bay, gunmetal gray with unrelieved metal flooring that echoed. The corridor was busy with crewmembers moving back and forth. A quick left turn took them to a long row of doors.

"We like to bunk down close to the fighter bays, as it allows us quick access to our craft if need be," she said simply. "New print, authorization Alpha-Gamma-Beta-four-four-niner," she said next, placing her palm to the plate. Vors indicated to Jemma to present her palm, which she did.

"State your name and designation," the automated voice commanded as the plate glowed green beneath her hand, reading the imprint.

"Cardnew, Jemma. Pilot."

The light on the pad flashed red briefly and a flash of heat warmed her hand. Just as it started to scorch, the light took on a green hue, telling her it had taken a complete read. The door opened swiftly, and Jemma noted the compact cabin, no more than a bed, workspace, and sanitary unit, but she felt pleased. This was her place. She smiled, knowing that sharing was something she did poorly.

"Right, Cardnew, drop your stuff and follow me to the *Bitch*. I want you on duty today. We serve five hours on with five teams running an overlap. There's fifty in the squadron, not including our techs and mechs. You, as the newcomer, unfortunately, also get the rear position with our friend the *Elector* until we're sure of your skills."

"Damn." The word slipped out and she wanted to kick herself. What bad luck to get stuck with the *Elector*.

"Problem?" Vors slashed her a piercing gaze.

"Oh no. None at all." Jemma reminded herself she needed to keep her thoughts firmly under control.

Once more they moved through the corridor. Vors grinned. "McCord is a bad-tempered asshole, but I hear you're good at dealing with those issues. Besides which, it isn't a bad position while you're finding your wings. The fleet we are working with consists of two destroyers, two frigates, one hospital transport, and the *Elector*, the newest stealth ship. But you know about that, don't you?" She stopped and looked at Jemma. "You *are* following this?"

"Yes, ma'am."

"I'm not a ma'am. I'm Vors. While in this squadron, you answer to Cardnew. We don't stand on ceremony here. Understand?" She motioned her back through the doorway into the bay. "As I was saying, we all have a designated craft to protect. You get the *Elector*. It's a single-pilot ship because it's got weapons you can only dream about. You're effectively on your own."

Jemma damned her cursed luck that brought her back to the *Elector*, but the excitement that bubbled outweighed the negatives of dealing with Duvall McCord and his officers.

They moved to the far side of the bay, and she could see the fighters as they downloaded them from their hanging racks above. They landed softly onto the plascrete floor.

Looking up, Jemma saw the other craft in storage containment hanging high from the rafters. It reminded her of an oversized wardrobe, the storage facility was obviously designed to keep the maximum craft in the minimum area. Each one was suspended by the nose, right next to the other. The large crane pulled the craft from their storage swiftly but in an orderly fashion.

One last ship was brought down. It was scarred with chipped paint and repaired seating, which she could see through the plas-glass shield. The panels were battered with age and wear. Vors indicated it to her. "Here she is. The *Bitch*. She got that name in the Ru'Edan wars, because while she sustained damage, she was never brought down. The *Bitch* is about thirty years old but has been a sterling fighter. In fact, she still is. She's also all yours. There are a few fiddly things about her, but at least you'll have time to learn her foibles before we enter an area of aggression. Coverall and helmet are stored within the cockpit. Anything else you need, fill in the appropriate paperwork and flick it to me." With that, Vors turned, walked a little way off, stopped, and turned back. "I look forward to hearing her new name soon." Then she was gone.

Jemma quickly clambered up the side of the craft. It was small and reminiscent of the old fighter planes she had seen pictures of. She pulled the plas-glass top back. She fished out the coverall and tugged it over her clothes before she climbed in and pulled on the helmet that lay within. The new hard black plas-mic helmet slipped down over her hair, conforming to her head even as the smell of the new material filled the cockpit.

She looked over the wing, seeing others do the same as Vors's voice sounded over the mic. "Okay, boys and girls, time to rock and roll. We have a combat virgin in our midst— Cardnew. You'll be with the *Elector*, so you're first out of the bay."

Jemma heard the rumble of welcomes, and the pilot in the craft next to her acknowledged her with a wave. She returned it as she toggled the engines for ignition. The muscles of her stomach tightened as nerves took control. She focused on the mic, squinted her eyes, and mentally counted to ten while releasing the tension in her body.

"Roger that, Vors. Engine engaging now." She pushed her finger into the ignition button, and it rumbled to life, the hum beneath her reassuring in a strange way. "Do we have a green for go?"

"Green for go on my signal. Go."

Jemma heard the purr of the engines winding up. She moved the throttle forward enough to make a minimal ascent and slowly, carefully, moved her craft out into the black, feeling the excitement of knowing this was her first flight into the dark that wasn't a training exercise. Taking a deep breath, she increased the speed.

She speared the craft toward the end of the fleet, dodging and weaving to get a feel for what the craft could do. She moved past the *Star of Ishtar*, dodged the long gray freighters and even the brightly painted hospital ship, and soon, within view, was the gray hull of the *Elector* looming in the dark inky horizon of her screen. Once within hailing distance, she toggled her comm.

"Captain McCord, this is Pilot Cardnew on your tail. I'll be running interference for you. Do you have any specific requests concerning my position?"

"Jemma? Duvall here. Good to have you with us. Fly to our right wing, thanks."

"Roger that, Captain McCord."

No way was she going to call him Duvall. He was the captain of the ship she was escorting. It would be a difficult assignment as it was; she already had enough issues with just knowing him and the decisions he'd taken with her future. Thankfully it would have been inappropriate to use any other address while she was on duty.

She reached for a toggle, catching her hand briefly on a shard, obviously left from a previous sortie or pilot treating the craft roughly. She flinched and shook her hand. She noticed a drop of blood and wiped it away.

"Jemma..."

"Can I help you, Captain McCord?" she returned. Her voice was firm. She congratulated herself on that, knowing it left him in no doubt that she was there with a duty to perform.

"No. Safe flying."

"Captain."

"Cardnew? Vors here."

"Yes, Vors?"

"We keep a radio silence if possible. I take it you're in position?" There was a bite now to the voice.

"Yes. Position achieved and waiting orders." Damn, first day on the job and already catching trouble. She'd have to ensure this was the first and last time.

"Boys and girls, it's party time. The captain has called for engines full ahead. See you in five."

The voices of the other pilots filtered through, with Jemma answering, the last to call in. "Cardnew acknowledging. Out."

One by one, the lumbering fleet took position and moved off, the flash of their engines bright in the inky darkness.

✪ ✪ ✪ ✪

The doors of the ST suite slid open, and Raven strode through purposefully. His black ship suit whispered along his muscular body shape, which he worked hard to achieve. He felt the pull of the material as he wandered toward Elara, the resident SurgiTech.

"Hey 'Lara!"

"Hey yourself, Raven. How's it going?" She smiled at him in a sisterly kind of fashion. The *Elector* was more like a family, especially the senior crew, he thought. "We haven't had a bump or chug from the matrix in some time, so that isn't the reason you're here."

"Yeah, I have the engines running pretty sweet now. Any chance you might offer me a cup of coffee?"

"Sure, help yourself." Elara gestured toward a carafe that was sitting on her desk and folded herself into her seat. "Have you made contact yet?"

He started at the query, the coffee he'd just poured sloshing in the cup. He knew what and *who* she was talking about.

"No, I doubt Jemma even thinks about me like that. While she was aboard, it wasn't the right time to be interested in her. There were problems in engineering and the wash-off from bringing her forward." He sighed. "Since then, the opportunities have been a little hampered, you know? I think she saw me as Duvall's messenger, so that struck me off her interest list pretty quickly."

"Now that she's the assigned combat escort pilot for the *Elector*, I'm sure some opportunity will come along. A chance for you to meet with her." Elara stopped and waited just for a minute. "Don't let your sense of chivalry get in the way of the possibilities."

"Yeah, I know. But the last time I spoke to her, she was so bitter and angry." He shook his head ruefully. "I just can't help feeling that the chance was gone before I could do anything about it." He stopped, looked at the coffee in his hands, and took a sip of the dark, rich brew. He looked back at Elara. "But by *Eshra*, if the chance shows, I will take it."

The firm words were met with a smile. "That's the way. Now tell me you have an idea for increasing the capacity and efficiency of the regen units."

He sat back in his seat, pulling out a palm screen, and within minutes, they were deep in conversation.

Raven stood in engineering running tests on the energy matrix when the first shudder hit, knocking him toward the console. "*Barsha*! What was that?"

Showers of sparks appeared near one of the mounts, raining down on the gray metal floor. His crew scurried to shut down whatever they could to minimize the possible damage, as per Admiralty guidelines, and he heard their comments as they communicated with each other, a sense of urgency invading the work area.

He quickly made his way toward the source of the sparks, hissing as he came too close and was caught by a stray spark.

"*Basha*!" He swore again as the heat forced him back. He reached for the extinguisher, pulling off the cap and starting to lay down the inhibiting foam, hoping once he'd created enough of a barrier he could get a look at what had happened.

Once he was sure there was no further chance of danger, he crouched down to inspect the damage. He noticed the shear's pattern. "Likely caused by wear." It was in a position no one would have noticed, he thought while he considered the jagged edges.

This was the first major issue in engineering since he had taken over upon the death of Corbin Jard, traitor to the Empire. While he thought none of his crew would have been able to create the damage's pattern, he needed to be sure.

He touched a grimy hand to the commbadge. "Captain, we have a problem in engineering. There looks to be a shear on one of the matrix mounts."

"What? I'm on my way." The voice that answered sounded distracted, as it had been for the last few days since they had entered the Phobos real space.

Raven continued his assessment, the foam on the floor dissipating slowly, allowing him to clearly note the striations' shape now. He grabbed his desk pad and made notations on it with quick, steady moves, and with his handheld computer system, he started to take measurements and test the depths of the damage.

Duvall McCord appeared in the engine room. "What happened?"

"It seems from the pattern of shear this weld was badly done, causing instability in the metal." He pointed with a penlight in the direction of the damage and Duvall crouched, squinted, and gave a grunt. "We'll need to go to a full stop to make sure it doesn't stress the mount further. Then we need to do a running repair." Before Duvall could speak, Raven shook his head. "We need to clean the mount first and make sure it's cold. That'll take us two to three days."

Duvall frowned. "Two to three days?"

"Yeah. The actual repair will only take several hours, but we can't be sure it's going to hold unless we take the right precautions." He sighed. "It'll mean pulling out of the fleet long enough to get it fixed then catching up. I'd estimate anything up to seven days depending on how it goes once we've cleaned the structure."

"Are you sure? No other way it can be fixed?" Duvall looked tense, rubbing his hands through his hair.

"No, not if we're going to do it safely, and if the mounting breaks we're effectively a dead ship in the middle of nowhere. Then our only option will be to catch a tow back to home base. Further damage will destabilize the rest of the mounts and possibly, worst case, a malfunction or total breakdown of the matrix."

Duvall was clearly weighing the options.

"Yes, it needs to be repaired immediately, Duvall." Raven looked at Duvall. He could feel the rivulets of sweat and grease trailing down his arms and face, plastering his hair against his face and neck.

"I'll inform the *Star*. Take us to a full stop now." Duvall walked away, and as Raven watched, it was clear the weight of the command was heavy as he rubbed his neck. With a tight voice, he gave commands through his commbadge.

Once Duvall had left engineering, Raven clambered up off the decking and headed for the engine's controls. One by one, he started shutting them down while he alerted Grayson, Duvall's second-in-command.

Jemma had been in the cockpit for nearly three hours of her shift after resting on the *Ishtar* when the call came through the communications system. "Cardnew? We have a problem. The *Elector*

has developed an engine issue and needs to come to a full stop. You're required to stay with her as protection for the period of time it takes to get her safely back to the fleet. We can't spare any further fighters, but the *Elector* is well-equipped in terms of weaponry, so it should be just a formality. This is a normally safe location anyway, with no known incursions or issues and a general fleet-shipping zone. Even so, remain on your guard and keep that bird flying." The voice of Vors came through tinny then chuckled. "Good luck! Vors out."

Jemma toggled the comm. "Acknowledged," she said, then once she had turned it off, she muttered, "Un-freakin-believable. God? You seriously have so much to answer for." Up until now, she'd been lucky, limiting her interactions with the crew to Duvall and Grayson for the last week since she arrived in the squadron.

"*Elector* here. Cardnew, bring your craft into the bay and I'll brief you on the situation," Grayson said.

Jemma winced. Damn, if she could just hold off a bit longer before docking, and anyway, if there was anyone monitoring the military channels, this would be the perfect time for them to have a sniff around and make an attempt at a strike.

"Commander, with all due respect, I think this is a perfect time for an incursion, given that the Phobos pirates are known to intercept transmissions on the military bands. With your permission, I'll remain out here for a little while longer."

"Permission denied. Get your arse in here!" Duvall's voice came through the comm. She closed her eyes briefly. If only he hadn't been listening, but she was out of luck.

Jemma acknowledged his command with a brief "Yes, sir" and brought her craft around, running scans, looking for something, anything that would give her a reason to ignore the command. Fate is a funny thing though, and for all her scans, she could see nothing on the radar as she carefully pulled her fighter into the bay.

Once the engines wound down and she could see the bay doors close, Jemma opened the plas-glass screen and climbed out. The door at the end of the bay beyond the small shuttle craft they kept on board opened as she reached the plascrete, and Duvall came storming in.

"Damn you, Jemma! I don't care how pissed off with me you

are, don't you ever disobey my orders. I'll bust you down to a bloody sanitation officer if I have to. Is that clear?" He growled the words at her between clenched teeth, and she saw the nerves jumping in his cheeks. His anger washed over her like a hot tide. She knew she deserved the reprimand, but that didn't change the fact that it still hurt to hear his words.

Jemma's cheeks grew hot. "Yes, Captain. I apologize, Captain. It was inappropriate," she muttered, standing rigidly to attention. Her eyes stung at the dressing down.

So few words, but they'd cut her like razor blades, sharp and stealing her breath. Raven Fraser entered and took position behind Duvall, and she wanted a hole to open in the floor. His eyes settled on her, piercing and cold as their gaze raked over her. None of them had seen her in the flesh since her placement in the academy except him. She scowled. As God was her witness, she so didn't want to be on the bloody *Elector*.

She was stuck there though, and she knew she would suck it up any way she had to until this torturous period was concluded. Whatever it took to get her through this purgatory. She railed against fate that brought her full cycle back to the *Elector*, into contact with Duvall and Mellissa. With the added problem of her physical attraction to Raven, one she'd fought against from the moment she had first seen him.

It really felt very unfair. In a different time and place, she would have marked him as a potential partner—for however long the feeling pulled at her. Right now though, she didn't need or want the problems of a physical, let alone emotional, entanglement that she sensed she could experience with this man.

"*Barsha*!" Duvall whirled away from her, muttering under his breath. "I don't know why Mellissa worries about you. You don't give a damn about her." With that, the captain left the bay, striding through the doors, which shut behind him.

"Well, you certainly handled that well." Raven's voice poured over her.

"I don't give a flying damn whether you think that or not. Where is this bloody briefing to be held and when?"

"Captain's office. 1000 hours. You do remember where that is, don't you?" he enquired in that silky voice that felt like pure sin.

She checked her wrist chrono. She had an hour. "I need a kit for the *Raptor*," she said, indicating her craft.

His eyes quirked at the name, and he grinned at her. "Why? Something wrong with her?" He cast an eye over the craft critically. She could see him inspecting the panels sporting chipped paint.

"No, just general maintenance. As there's no combat tech here, I'll do it myself," she said, hoping he would just find her what she needed and go. Preferably as quickly as possible. "I'll also need details of the fuel stores you carry for her." She turned away, her expression lightening as she looked at the now renamed *Bitch*, hoping he would get the message fast.

"I'll get you what you need," he said, and left her in the bay.

Jemma was checking the last of her indicators when the comm system chimed. "Cardnew, you're late to the captain's office. Your immediate attention is required."

She sat up with a hurry. Damn, she'd lost track of the time while running through her post-flight checks. It didn't help that Raven had come back with details of the fuel stores and waited until she had completed her maintenance work.

She dumped her equipment to answer the hail. "Cardnew here. On my way."

She closed the plas-glass, jumped down to the deck with a resounding thud, and headed to the door, palmed it, and moved at double-time toward the captain's office. The clanking of her feet on the decking encouraged others to get out of her way. Just what she needed—more shit. She sighed.

Once she reached the office, she palmed the door and noted the streaking of oil and grime on her hands. Damn, he'd probably carpet her for that too. She was wiping some of the mess onto the rag she kept in her pocket as the door opened.

"Nice of you to join us, Cardnew. Grab a seat."

"Ugh, if you don't mind, I should probably stand, Captain. I have grease all over me from mech checks." She hoped like hell this would be quick, because she really needed some downtime, and to be honest, she didn't want to be there any more than he wanted her there.

Raven stood up, moving toward her. "This is going to take a while. We've found a structural fault in the energy matrix that needs immediate repair. All engines need to be taken offline in order for me to get into the area and make the necessary repairs. I believe it could take up to a week before we can rejoin the fleet." His words were placid, but she remained rigidly at attention. In front of Grayson and Duvall, it was necessary, she told herself.

She glanced toward Duvall but remembered to be quiet, pushing against her instinctive reaction to argue. A week? Aboard the *Elector*? Oh, joy of joys. She seethed silently.

Duvall stood and looked at her. "As our designated combat pilot, you will of course be bunked down nearest the bay, and we've taken steps to ensure you have whatever you require during your time aboard the *Elector*. We have a backup generator set to ensure that your access through the bay will not be disrupted. I believe you've been running a five-hour watch cycle? Normally that would be acceptable, but as we will effectively be dead in the water for the next few days, we'll limit your rotating watch to three hours to conserve your flight time, but you'll be on call at all times. Any questions?"

"No, sir. I think that would work, although I'd rather take the bunk in the bay if I may. That way I can be immediately there should the need arise."

"Fine, if that suits you best."

"Sir."

The scarred, red-haired lady—Elara, she remembered—spoke up. "You will need to attend the mess hall for meals too. During this time Mellissa and I will be hand cooking to conserve our stocks until we can rejoin the fleet. Meals will be at 0600, 1200, and 1800."

"Yes, ma'am." Damn, she'd need to join them. Perhaps she could figure out a way to miss that too. But one look at Duvall's face told her that was unlikely to be acceptable to him.

The meeting continued, and she followed it absently, noting that Raven never once looked at her since his opening address. His hands illustrated points on the holo-construct of the matrix supports, showing the damage and what needed to be done.

His voice was mesmerizing, she decided, deep and smooth. His hair shined in the subdued lighting like spun gold, and his eyes were oh so blue, like a deep-water pond. For a moment she fancied she could almost drown in them. She mentally shook herself out of her fanciful notions. She didn't need any kind of physical intimacy with a member of the *Elector*'s crew, she told herself sternly, but her body continued to heat, listening to the cadence of his voice.

She noticed that they had moved on and the discussions were desultory. She'd lost track, never a good sign. She sighed inwardly, wishing she could move. Her legs ached from standing.

"Meeting dismissed," the captain finally said. Jemma turned toward the door, but he called out, "Cardnew, please stay behind."

Jemma closed her eyes. Well, when things went bad, they really went bad with a thud, she reminded herself. She turned back toward Duvall. A wave of exhaustion washed over her, and for a moment, she felt a spurt of vertigo. She locked her knees, opened her eyes to focus on a point over Duvall's shoulder, and hoped like hell she could keep it together for a little longer.

The rest of the crew filed past her.

Once the room was silent, she focused on Duvall. "Captain, how else may I help?" She kept her voice neutral.

"Jemma, while we're stuck together, you're going to have to deal with Mellissa."

She closed her eyes, wishing for some kind of stay of execution.

"She's worried about you, Jemma, and to be honest, after over a year, it would be helpful if you'd grow up a little and act like the person your wings say you can be."

She opened her eyes, ready to give him a piece of her mind. She swallowed the words though. *He's a senior officer. If you open that mouth, you better be prepared to face the consequences.* She took a deep breath and contained herself.

"With all due respect, sir, I am here as your combat pilot, not anything else. I will treat your wife—" She emphasized the word "—with all due respect according to both her situation and her role within the Empire and aboard the Elector."

"Dammit! You're not twelve, so stop acting like it!" he bit out.

"If that is all, Captain? I would like to retire." She waited for the slap down, knowing her mouth had run off again. Her head pounded to the beat of the blood pumping in her veins and her body felt seared all over. Far too warm, she knew.

"Dismissed." He bit the word out.

She inclined her head and retreated from the office. It was definitely going to be a long week.

The first meal in the mess hall was difficult. Jemma sat at the end of the furthest table, ate quickly, and removed herself as fast as she could, avoiding all contact with the crew. Mellissa wasn't there at the time, and for that, Jemma was grateful. Her head now hurt significantly, her stomach roiled with nausea, and all she wanted to do was crawl into her bunk and sleep.

She quickly made her way back to the bay and entered. Raven Fraser stood waiting for her, and she wanted to scream at the unfairness.

"Sir, how can I help you?"

"Actually I think it is I who can help you." He cocked his head to one side, and for a minute the sizzle of awareness thrummed through her body and a pulse of heat washed over her. She pushed it down brutally.

"Really? And how would that be?"

"I put together the kit you needed earlier," he said, holding out a toolbox filled with an assortment of wrenches and spanners. Even a sonic knife had been included. She felt a spurt of disappointment that he hadn't come just to see her.

She raised her aching head. "Thank you."

"You're welcome." He smiled, and that flash came back to hit her. "I'm just heading up to the mess—"

"I've already eaten. I need to get some shut-eye as I'm back on duty in less than six hours," she said quickly, ensuring he got the message and waiting for him to leave her alone in the silence of the bay. Peace and quiet called, and she wanted to close eyes that were hurting and lay down her spinning head.

"Right then. I'll leave you to it." He nodded and turned away.

She sat down on the bunk, watching him leave with a feeling of self-disgust. Here he was—a seriously sexy man, and one she'd love to have as a lover. Some sixth sense told her he'd be amazing. But he was a friend of Duvall and Mellissa's, and she was on his ship on her first deployment. Better to let him go than think about sex. But when she closed her eyes her mind played images of the most gorgeous and well-proportioned chest. Her blood quickened even as she fell into the well of exhaustion.

Raven stood outside the bay for a minute, just breathing. She was a hard nut, but he thought perhaps there was something more to her than she let people see. He also remembered seeing the white lines around her mouth and the bruising under those haunting purple-blue eyes. Oh yes, she was gorgeous, but unless he missed his guess, she needed sleep. Even more, she needed a friend. He could be that. But it wasn't enough and that drove him.

Her frame had been slightly rounded last year; now he would describe her as spare, bordering on thin, her long, black hair tied back in a braid, and her cold, violet eyes distant. Her bow lips pulled tight, and her skin, if it was possible, was paler than before. The uniform hung looser on her body than he remembered, and that disturbed him. A powerful wave of desire pulsed through him even as he fought the concern.

He'd been attracted before, but now, in close quarters, this woman made him want to grab her, to taste her lips, to find out if her body would fit him as perfectly as he suspected it would. "You need to control your libido, Raven."

They had a week, and by the end of this deployment, if he didn't have her in his arms, he knew it would be all the more difficult to achieve. She'd be on guard, and he needed to grab this opportunity with both hands. He just wasn't sure why he needed to hold her. It wasn't her sweet countenance; he nearly laughed out loud at that thought. He had a sneaking suspicion she practiced that persona to keep everyone at bay, with the real Jemma hidden beneath layers, far from view.

His body was tight from just being in the same room as her. He'd been constantly aroused around her from the first meeting on the *Elector*, and nothing had changed. She'd been given time, but now? Well, he would only wait so much longer. He turned and walked away.

Chapter 3

The wail of sirens woke Jemma with a start. She jackknifed up, thankful she'd slept in her uniform. She reached over and hit the commbutton, shivering from the cold in the bay. She shoved aside the grogginess that invaded her mind while she spoke. "What's up?"

"Incoming, looks like five unfriendlies."

Fuck! Grayson's voice was tense but controlled. She wouldn't have expected anything less. She jammed her feet into her boots, which were waiting by the side of the cot. She swayed but with determination battled back the unfamiliar sense of vertigo.

"Right, suiting up now!" She hit the commbutton and ran to her fighter, scrambling up the *Raptor*'s side and pulling on her helmet as she clambered into the craft. A quick depression of a small button on the console engaged the door-open sequence she had synchronized earlier on. Once more she toggled the communications button on her suit. "*Elector*, ready to deploy." Her hands moved over the controls instinctively as she prepared for take-off.

"Acknowledged. Deploy." Grayson was still at the command, though she knew he would have alerted Duvall. Right now, though, she needed more information. The shield from the *Elector* played havoc with the scanner range.

"Location of incoming?"

"Hard to port, looks like spooks."

Damn. New and sleek, they belonged to the Phobos pirates. They could now afford the newest and fastest of interstellar fighters after the successful raids they had been pulling off.

Dropping the helmet's visor into place, she allowed her craft to rise in the bay and punched the *Raptor* through the opening in the shields. "Commander? Close the shields. I'm on track to rendezvous with the spooks."

She controlled the thrust until she had the craft safely beyond the *Elector*, then turned a tight spin over a wing and arrowed toward the side of the *Elector* she knew they were approaching from. *They have probably scanned the Elector and know that we're running on aux generator power only. God dammit!* The thought ripped through her system while she worked on what she thought they would be thinking. Sitting duck? At the very least, they no doubt thought this too good an opportunity to let pass them by. But it also confused her. Wouldn't they expect some kind of defense on this type of craft sitting out here in space?

She ran a perimeter check, waiting for the spook ships to enter range, checking that the shields were in place and nothing else incoming. The beep of the console told her when they finally arrived, and she considered their V formation as she held position.

"This ship is taken. Find your own." For an opening gambit, it was probably a bit short, but they would get the message. She hoped so anyway.

"Ahh! The empire sends us a little girl! Move aside and allow us to access the ship. We have rights in this sector to salvage." The voice started initially in the sing-song pattern of the Phobos inhabitants before settling in hard and cold.

"Sorry, boys, no salvage opportunities here. Move along." She let her hand hover over the laser button, just in case she needed a quick shot across the bows to run them off. "Now!" She put everything into that one word.

No movement. *Damn!* They hadn't flinched, but she really wasn't surprised. Time to show them she meant business. She depressed the button, the laser fire coming within a breath of the leader's wing. *Fzzt!*

He tilted away from the streak of light, just as she expected.

"What in *Eshra*'s name are you doing, Cardnew?" Duvall's voice came through the headset. *Damn.* Pissed at her again.

She growled back into the headpiece. "Captain, I am letting them know you are not dead in the water. Now with all due respect—" The ship returned the shot. She spun to avoid contact. "—I'm a little busy here."

"Interesting game, little girl. Maybe we should just...grab you too. We could always do with new and talented pilots."

She growled. This bastard had no idea how pissed off she was getting as he commented to her in his sickly sweet voice.

"Back off. I won't hesitate to put a hole between your eyes if you don't break off now."

"Cardnew! Jemma! Break off the encounter! Now!" Duvall demanded, his words coming through the secure commlink, and she clamped her mouth shut, breathing deeply as anger washed over her. His voice was firm and grim, matching her current mood.

She reined in her emotions, knowing what she needed to say. "With all due respect, Captain, I'm here to keep your ass safe. In this instance, my judgment overrules whatever you might want," she answered through gritted teeth. *I'm gonna catch hell for this.* Too damn bad. She had a job to do, and she'd do it the best way she knew how.

God knew the last thing she needed right now was an all-out confrontation with anyone. Here she was, with a dead-in-the-water stealth ship, exhausted and getting more and more pissed by the moment, but she had to hold on to her temper. She narrowed her eyes, considering the ships in front of her. They had no intention of moving, so they were now at an impasse.

She had one new trick up her sleeve though. Although still experimental, the multiple acquisition program might just give them breathing time. Her mind debated at lightning speed. *If you threaten it, you have to be able to use it, but once it is used, they'll know you have the technology.* The outcome could and probably would be more pirates next time.

She took a deep breath, flicked the cover off the tab, and depressed it. She knew the minute the targets realized their ships were tagged. They held firm for a just a moment, hanging in the dark inky blackness long enough, she guessed, to confirm they were all targeted, then as one they turned a tight spin, backing off. She let out her breath.

The one that baited her tossed his final comment, "We'll be back!" at her. She watched them, breathing slowly in the silence as the ships disappeared from her radar screen.

This was just the beginning, and she knew they would be back in bigger numbers. A sense of urgency roused her. Time to get back to the ship and get an estimation on how soon they could move, or at least restart some of the engines. The longer they were there, the more dangerous their situation would become. The spooks would be back soon to find out the capability of the multiple acquisition—something she couldn't afford to have happen without making sure she was ready. Her stomach heaved, and another wash of pain filled her head as the adrenaline slid from her system. With a swallow, she beat the nausea away but nothing shifted the ache in her skull.

She ran perimeter checks a little longer, putting off the minute of docking until she really needed to head back in, her fuel alarm beeping softly. She spun *Raptor* on its wing and headed for the temporary base.

Jemma powered down the *Raptor* and sat with her head inclined toward the control panel, her eyes burning. Her head throbbed, she shivered with cold, and the waves of nausea once more threatened to swamp her. She knew she had done what she had to but was worried that she had once more exceeded her authority and would have to face Captain McCord's coldness. Sure, she knew that it had to be said, that her authority to protect the *Elector* overrode Duvall's wishes, but she certainly didn't expect him to take that well. She sighed heavily, disengaging her safety restraints.

She crawled out of the cockpit, slowly drawing off her helmet. She shook out the hair that had come undone in her sleep and groaned as dizziness assailed her. She wished she'd had time to tie it back before getting into the *Raptor*. She slid down the cold side of the craft and looked around. Duvall stood in the corner, a scowl on his darkly handsome face, like an avenging angel or grim reaper. Either description seemed appropriate. Behind him stood Mellissa, white-faced.

Jemma staggered briefly. For a minute, she remembered when she had first met him, sitting with Mellissa, the one person she had considered her friend and confidante.

She noticed how tense he was and dropped her helmet to the plascrete with a dull thud as she made her way toward him. Stopping just steps in front of him, she came to attention, knowing it was expected.

"Sir, with all due respect, I have a job to do and that means taking any and all steps necessary to ensure the safety of the *Elector* and her crew." She waited tensely at attention, ready for the outburst of anger.

"*Barsha*, Jemma. Mellissa is beside herself, and you're risking yourself too much." He looked at her with sorrow in his eyes. Suddenly, a lump formed in her chest, growing larger and larger. She certainly hadn't expected that.

The words shocked her, and she stood fighting the pain they caused, her stomach rolling with black waves of sickness. The lump lodged in her chest grew and threatened to suffocate her, stealing her breath. Her body burned again, and her head felt like it would burst. Her eyes filled with hot tears, the itchiness increasing. She raised her hands to her chest, pushing hard at the padding of her flight suit.

Duvall spoke again. "Jemma, we want you to be part of our team, and family. You're Mellissa's sister in every way that counts. Don't continue on this path of self-destruction." His expression softened, as did his voice.

She wanted to reach out, to grab what he offered. The fear grew though. What if she trusted them and she was let down again? A hiccup-sob escaped as a hot tear trickled down her face. She clamped a hand over her mouth, trying to hold it all inside her, but the floodgates had opened.

She couldn't cope. No more. Her body gave in.

A tear rolled down her face, then another, coming faster and hotter. Unable to stem the tide, she was consumed as another sob racked her. Knees giving out, she folded to the floor, clamping her head between two shaking hands.

She felt a movement, but her strength fizzled away, raising her head now so far beyond her consciousness as the well of pain and despair overcame her. She felt arms move around her. The paroxysm of grief drowned out the crooning even as she soaked up being rocked back and forth.

Raven's feet beat a heavy clanking on the decking as he entered the cargo bay. Jemma was on the ground sobbing while Mellissa rocked her back and forth, panic evident on her face. He made to move forward and stopped as he saw Duvall hit his commbutton.

"Elara, I need you in the shuttle bay, now."

Jemma continued to cry, her slender body shaking, her pale face tinged with the red of a fever.

"What happened?" he demanded hoarsely, taking in what he could see of the situation and starting to move forward once more. Duvall held up a hand, and while Raven wanted— needed—to be sure she was all right, he saw something in his captain's face that stopped him

The thud of feet moving down the decking with speed filled the air. Elara and Grayson burst into the bay. She carried a SurgiPack in her hands, her face tense. She pushed past Raven, heading directly for Jemma. Crouching down beside her, she flicked open her diag-alyser. A few seconds later she shook her head, lifting it to look at Duvall and Raven.

"Jemma needs rest, decent food, and a cabin, not to be sleeping in here." She gestured toward the small cot by the wall. "If I don't miss my guess, she's also running a fever caused by a localized infection. We will need to find the wound site and deal with that. We can use my body scan in the SurgiTech suite, though I think that's overkill. It's something simple in most cases. We can treat this with a spectrum hypo-biotic. She's also unfit for any missions at the moment."

Her words were soft, but Raven heard them as clear as a bell ringing through the quiet sobs of the woman on the ground.

Elara stood slowly, motioning to Grayson and Raven. "We need to move her to one of the cabins. I don't think the SurgiTech suite will be necessary at this time, unless her condition worsens. Is the shuttle pilot's cabin vacant?" She cast a look at Grayson, who nodded. "Right, that's about all we can do for now then. Move her in there, carefully. Be careful not to jar her, as with the infection her body will be achy and sore. We don't want to make her feel worse. I'll start a hypo-biotic, and we need to ensure she gets enough fluids while it takes effect. After that, she needs at least twenty-four hours rest." Her mouth tightened.

"Chowd has been trained to fly these babies. I'll get him to take over from her until you give her a clean bill of health." Duvall's face was grim, and Raven looked at him before moving to crouch before Jemma on the ground.

"I'll take her." Carefully slipping his hands under her hot body, he cradled her softly before turning with her in his arms. Mellissa stood, reached out, and touched his arm. He stilled until she nodded and let him carry the woman in his arms out of the bay.

Chapter 4

When Raven reached the cabin, he laid Jemma carefully on the bed, easing a sweaty strand of hair from her skin. He stripped off her boots and flight coverall, leaving on her crew uniform, his eyes ranging over her body.

Raven had time to spare. The matrix supports were still being cleaned and cooled, and a couple of his crewmembers could do it, leaving him free. Soon they would be ready for him to complete the repairs. The tricky point was, it would take a day for the area to be ready to start working on the mounts. Knowing there was really only room for one or at most two crewmembers to work had him concentrating on busywork. He rocked back on his heels as he mind spun in small circles of concern. No matter how he tried to block it out, it sat there, at the back of his mind, gnawing on any sense of well-being he'd garnered.

Elara came to apply the hypo-biotic, which would kick in soon, he hoped. The IV line was in place, but before Elara left she told Raven that Jemma would only need it for a few hours and then they could dispense with it. Mellissa and Duvall had both been needed on the bridge with Grayson, and Raven offered to stay and keep watch over this slight woman. His mind rolled back to the first time he had seen her, spitting all sorts of curses while he and Grayson had escorted her to another cabin.

"You were so angry and yet so beautiful at the same time." A memory of her face, red with both shock and fury, rose before him, as did that of glittering violet eyes. Of course, that was nearly eighteen months ago now, and he'd seen her briefly at the academy several times since then.

He was aware she had no clue as the full ramifications Duvall had faced with his decision to bring her to the future. Raven knew that Duvall had been officially reprimanded for his actions and he'd come seriously close to demotion for bringing back extra people. He'd broken the rules to save Mellissa the hurt of knowing Jemma would die.

No, Jemma did not need to know that then or even now. It would be just one more weight on her slender shoulders. The knowledge left him with a niggling sense of disquiet.

He knew that she thought they'd dumped her at the academy. Unfortunately, she wasn't allowed to be told the truth—that Duvall and Raven had needed to do some fancy footwork toget her placed there. Even Admiral Elphin had weighed in, ensuring she remained sequestered, just in case Crick Sur Banden ever decided she could be a chink in Duvall's armor. Raven shook his head as he pulled up the hard chair next to the bed and settled himself down to watch over her.

Crick Sur Banden continued to be a problem, growing more and more bold with intermittent incursions and daring raids. Both the Admiral and Duvall had agreed that the academy was the safest place for Jemma. It was fortified and essentially a military base. Raven had kept an eye on her, thankful that his parents' role there had made it easier for him to monitor her. His added associations with some of the professors had opened doors that should have been closed to him.

He knew she couldn't hear him, so he let himself say aloud some of the things he'd felt over the last long eighteen months. "If only you knew. We're so proud of you, Jemma. I'm damned proud of you. Very few could have been thrust into that kind of situation and flourished like you have."

Her commitment and work had rocketed her through the system at the academy and into the Combat Pilot program, an almost unheard-of feat. Then she had achieved her placement to the Alpha Squadron, the most highly contested placement, only offered to the best of the best. He was proud of her, so damn proud.

He reached out and touched her hair, feeling the softest of silk against his fingertips. She murmured and moved restlessly. He wanted to pull her closer to him. He wanted to soothe her restless movements. He turned his head away and drew a breath, settling deeper into the chair as he continued to watch her sleep. Her restless tossing and turning finally became peaceful as the hypo-biotic took effect, and she slid into a quiet, healing sleep.

✪ ✪ ✪ ✪

Jemma stretched, feeling better than she had for some time. Her head was clear, and she opened her eyes. She catalogued what she could see, knowing she was back on the *Elector*. The gray walls and impersonal cabin space surprised her. The bed felt comfortable though, and the light no longer hurt her eyes. She turned her head, noting that her muscles no longer screamed in pain. Jemma drew a cleansing breath. Then her actions stilled.

He was here. Raven. In the cabin. With her. His eyes were closed, and he looked soft and so appealing in that moment. She drank in his features as he rested quietly in the chair, his slightly rumpled clothes, the fine blond hair that lay close to his head, the chiseled jaw covered with stubble she wanted to run her fingers over, a mouth that seemed to call her to kiss it, and a high forehead.

She'd dreamed about him, not that she would ever admit that to anyone, and some of those thoughts had been seriously R-rated. The question that rose in her mind now was simply

Why was he there, with her, in this cabin right now?

She turned, groaning as her sore body protested slightly. She looked again, this time into his deep-blue eyes.

"Good to see you awake. How are you feeling? You gave us a fright." His eyes crinkled in the corners as his lips turned up in a small smile, confusing her with the warmth she detected from him.

"What happened?" Her voice croaked, surprising her.

"You must have hurt yourself and ignored it. It turned into an infection, which you also ignored...the wound on your hand?" He looked at her, questioning, and she remembered the cut on the jagged metal of her *Raptor*. "With exhaustion and everything else, your body had enough and you basically collapsed coming back from sorting out the pirates."

He moved forward in his seat, and she could smell his body. The musky scent of him rose in the still air of the cabin, making a slow heat begin to curl deep in her belly.

"How long was I out?"

He smiled, and God help her, she smiled back. "About twelve

hours. It's 1700 hours. I had arranged for your meal and mine to be delivered here shortly, but since you look and seem to feel so much better, we can go to the mess hall. Do you want to clean up a little?"

Levering up on one arm, she took a deep breath. "Yeah, that would be great." She closed her eyes briefly then flicked her gaze back to him. His rumpled ship suit told the tale that he had been with her for some time. "Why aren't you in engineering, doing the thing with the matrix?" she asked as she rose.

He reached a hand toward her, offering support. "My crew is clearing the area, getting it ready for me to start tomorrow with the weld patches. Just so you don't worry, Chowd is flying the *Raptor* for you, so there's no need to rush at the moment."

He smiled, and she itched to reach her hand out toward him to touch his skin, but she stopped herself before she could follow through and stood carefully, pleased when no vertigo or nausea assailed her.

He threw her a clean ship suit and pushed her toward the sanitary unit, closing the door after her. "I'll wait here in case you need me."

She closed her eyes. For a moment, she made a mental check of her body. Her temperature seemed back to normal, her head had definitely improved, the thumping headache was gone, and even her stomach had settled. She felt a little shaky still, but a quick shower would help.

Stripping out of her underwear, she engaged the shower, stepping into it. The feeling of well-being rose as the water ran over her body. She lathered her hair and body, smiling as she imagined Raven with her in the shower. Briefly, she wondered how he would react if she just opened the door, but she quickly cut off the thought, castigating herself mentally. Not a good idea, she sternly told herself.

The image of Mellissa in the bay rose in her mind. She knew she had to make peace there too. A modicum of understand had dawned and she wondered if maybe she didn't have all the facts. That shook her. What else could she have been wrong about? "No, Jemma. Don't go fooling yourself." It didn't change anything though.

Jemma turned off the water and reached for the towel she expected to find on the hanger. She discovered there wasn't one there. Damn. Now that was an oversight. She looked at the discarded underwear. At some point, someone had stripped her down so she didn't even have a flight suit to act as towel.

She couldn't see anything that would do the trick. She sighed then firmed her shoulders. "Nothing to do but ask, Jemma."

Slipping behind the door, she opened it a crack, looked out, and caught his eyes. "There's no towel in here. I don't suppose there's one out there?" She felt more than naked without her flight suit to act as a barrier between her and Raven.

His eyes gleamed, and she could see a burning emotion present. It could be desire; his eyes narrowed and started to glitter in the dim lighting, and the heat ramped up a notch in her belly, curling like a living thing and calling to her. His face tightened, and he stepped toward the cracked door. He advanced slowly, snatched up the toweling cloth from the chair beside the bed, and stepped closer—like a predator—clutching the towel in his strong hands.

She swallowed as he reached out.

"Want me to dry your back?" he said with soft words that seemed to argue with the heat in his eyes.

"No. I think that should be sufficient." She grabbed the towel and held on, watching his eyes for a moment longer until he let go. She watched a minute longer.

"You'd best get dry quickly. You don't want to catch a chill." His voice was deeper, and she dragged in a breath then slid the door shut.

Jemma leaned back against it while her heart thudded in her chest. She shuddered, closed her eyes, took one breath, two. She opened her eyes then, shaking her head, started to dry and dress.

Raven watched the door close. Oh yes, she felt it too, the consuming passion. The way her eyes had darkened and the flush that rose on the inches of pale skin had told him that. He felt his heart rate increase. He could imagine her right now, her eyes glazed with her hot passion, her skin rosy, and he felt his body grow hard.

He wanted to push into the room but didn't. She needed careful wooing. Strategy was something he did well, and he knew that his instant action might get him a short-term bit of sex, but that wasn't what he was looking for. She wouldn't believe him if he pushed hard and fast now. It could only be temporary, and that wasn't what he wanted.

It had taken all his willpower not to look into the mirror behind her. He knew the reflection of her body's curves would have been on show, but it would have made it more difficult, so he'd resisted the temptation and continued to focus on her eyes during the challenging exchange, but his sweating body and the thumping of his heart continued to remind him of his arousal. Her beautiful body called to him, the silken skin arrayed for him to see if he just shifted his gaze. No, he would wait until she wanted him as much as he wanted her.

He puffed out a breath, listening to the rustling sound behind the door. Now he'd taken the first step, and he just needed to get her to realize she wanted to join him on the long walk he associated with relationships. He sat down on the bed and waited for her, fighting his body and subduing it—for now anyway.

When Jemma slowly emerged from the sanitary unit, he was waiting for her on the bed.

"I contacted the mess hall and said we'd come up. " His voice and mannerisms were casual, but she could sense a tension in the air.

"Why?"

"Because you have something you need to do, and now, before anyone else is there." His eyes were kind, but she didn't want his pity. She just didn't want to have to do this.

"Maybe I don't want to," she countered, knowing what he was alluding to.

"Maybe you don't, but you're not a coward or a quitter. You need to do this. Clear the air and move on. You know you can't move on with your life until this issue between you and Mellissa is dealt with and fixed." His voice was soft like his eyes. She could see the understanding in his face.

He was right, of course, just as Duvall had been, but facing it was harder than anything she'd had to do. She nodded jerkily.

He raised a hand and touched her face. "I'll be with you, all the way. In your corner." Raven grabbed her hand in his, and the shock of his touch was electric. She looked at him and saw he had felt it to. He smiled at her, winked, and pulled her out of the cabin.

She stopped as they stepped into the corridor. "Thank you." She took a deep, shaking breath and steeled herself.

"What for?"

"Just for being you. For staying. For…" She waved a hand in the air, hoping he'd understand.

He smiled and her knees took on the consistency of jelly.

With a nod, she signaled her readiness, and they started up the corridor along the metal decking toward the stairs that would lead to the mess hall and to the room where Mellissa waited for her. She'd have to confront her behavior and the demons of her past.

But once they stood outside the mess, her feet refused to move. Panic rose in her chest. *Damn! Why did I let him talk me into this?* The only answer waiting for her was the truth.

Because he promised to stay by your side.

The honest thought flashed through her mind and calmed her agitated emotions a little. She took another deep breath, trying to settle the racing of her heart and the ragged jumping of her nerves. He was watching her, waiting for a sign she was ready.

She squared her shoulders and nodded silently. This was it—she was there to do a job. "Ready?"

"As I'll ever be, I guess." One step took her through the doorway. She glanced around. Nothing much had changed since she'd last been aboard the *Elector*, except maybe her...for the better? Well, she wasn't sure about that either.

The gunmetal gray of the walls offered her no relief from the pounding of her blood through her system. All it did was make her relive the memories of her previous time on the *Elector*. The color and feel reminded her of the fright and anger that had filled her system then— something she had no intention of reliving.

Jemma looked around. The seating was still rudimentary, as the *Elector* was a stealth ship—it was built for battle, not for comfort. Her gaze landed on Mellissa, and she took another deep breath to steady herself.

"Want me to come with you?" His voice was soft. "No, this is something I need to do on my own."

She stepped forward, one foot in front of the other until they had carried her across the room. Elara, who'd been serving others, stepped across the room to sit with him at a table, giving Mellissa and Jemma some privacy.

She looked up into Mellissa's eyes. "Liss? I don't really know what I should say." She stopped, feeling the heat rising in her face. She dropped her gaze.

"I know. It's confusing, isn't it?"

Jemma looked back up. Mellissa's eyes glittered with sadness, and Jemma realized she had been one of the reasons it shined in her friend's eyes.

"I understand. Really I do." Mellissa's voice was soft.

"Liss, there's so much more, some things I just can't... You know, after you left..." Jemma stopped and gulped. Nerves jittered around in her body. "I can't tell you everything. I just felt...unwanted and abandoned. I guess I should have known better. But you weren't there and you said you always would be." She shrugged as she looked at the woman she considered not just her friend, but her sister. A lump welled in her throat, threatening to choke her, and her eyes burned. "I don't know what..." She stopped, lost for words to describe the loneliness and abandonment she had felt, not to mention frustration and fear.

Mellissa stepped forward and opened her arms, and Jemma moved toward her. She felt the reassuring warmth of Mellissa's arms around her, just like she always had. They embraced.

"I know," Mellissa said. "I missed you so much though. I wish you could have been with us for the wedding."

They stood quietly for a moment, together. Realizing that each now had a different role and status, and accepting the changes, they slowly moved apart.

Jemma saw that neither Elara nor Raven were watching, but she was sure they knew exactly what had happened. Heat rose in her face again, burning her cheeks. Mellissa cleared her throat and handed Jemma two plates. "For both of you," she murmured, and started to load them up with enticing-looking stew and bread.

Once the plates were filled, they shared a quick smile before Jemma made her way toward the table where Raven waited. Elara rose, quickly patted his arm, and went back to Mellissa.

"Sit down and I'll grab some forks and spoons." His voice slid over her like silk. She sat down and waited for him. She watched the way his body moved and felt her nipples tighten in response. She had to work hard to subdue the arousal that bubbled inside her.

Once back, he sat beside her, and every move he made heightened her awareness of him.

Their arms brushed against each other as they ate, and she nearly jerked away in response. They ate their meal in silence as an awareness thickened and swirled around them. At the end, they sat there, watching people make their way into the mess hall. After a few minutes, she glanced toward him to find him watching her. A small smile lit his face.

She rose, and so did he. In silent agreement, they left the mess hall together. He reached out and grabbed her hand, and she felt a zing run through her system. Awareness of him moved up another notch, and the fire in her belly roared just a little higher.

They stopped, and he looked at her. His eyes turned smoky in the dim light. "Come with me."

But instincts of self-preservation kicked in. "Where?"

She could tell he wanted to say "my cabin," but he seemed to think twice. "My office. I want to show you something."

Hesitation warred with desire. Should she? Could she? She let go of his hands. "Why?" "I want to show you the most amazing thing of all. The energy matrix." His face screwed

up, and she blushed once more. Dear God! She had thought he meant to seduce her. She was so dumb!

She shook her head. "I don't think so." Her voice was low.

"Sweetheart, don't get me wrong, I do want you."

Oh my God! He's either a mind reader, or I just totally gave it away. She wanted to die, or at least be swallowed up by a big black hole in that instant.

"But you aren't ready, and neither am I. Let me show you a little of my world." His face was close to hers, his breath brushing her face. His voice was low and throaty, and for just an instant, she could see his desire for her blaze. "Come." He gripped her hand again and led her to engineering.

She was surprised. The engineering section of the *Elector* was much larger than she had expected. Several bodies clustered around a large glowing cylinder, which rose from floor to ceiling. She wasn't sure quite what she'd expected—turbines? No, she knew that there was no way they could generate the amount of power needed to propel this ship forward.

She wasn't disappointed though with the grease and equipment lying around. Two crewmembers were actively cleaning an area around a metal structure. They had a tiny vacuum-like machine and another that was blowing any debris away.

"That is the arm of the matrix structure that needs to be repaired," Raven said, pointing toward the two working men.

Another crewmember, small and dumpy with blue hair, sat at a machine, tapping and pushing on buttons and tags. There was a grace to her movements, and Jemma watched her for a while, mesmerized, until the woman turned and she could see that she was a full Te'Karan, with the elongated incisors and glowing yellow-gold eyes. She stood and stretched, and Jemma was surprised to find she wasn't dumpy but pregnant.

"That's Saynara El'Fasa. She's here until we reach the Alpha Star Colony. We're to transfer her back to a Te'Karan Cruiser and receive my second, Blade Snyder, back. He's been on an enforced exchange with them for the last five months while we train recruits and specialists across the Empire." He shook his head. "Saynara is extremely talented, but she needs to be with her mate in time for the birth of their baby. She will transfer once we reach the Alpha Star Colony, if it's safe to do so. You know that only the full-blooded Te'Karan females give birth, don't you? With hybrids, it's usually the male, and the males do the feeding."

She started. "Umm, no. I didn't take the courses on advanced physiology, just the basic field medicals unit. All men, whether hybrids or not, feed?"

"Yep."

"Okay." Yet another piece of information she would file away.

He grinned playfully at her, obviously at home in the calm atmosphere of the engineering section. Slowly, he led her around the section, introducing her to his crew, explaining concepts she didn't understand, and listening to her insights. At the end of the tour, he led her to his small office and offered her a coffee.

"Amazing, isn't it? Not six hundred years ago we had no idea about what was out there or even what we could achieve. Today, we don't even blink at what we see." He smiled expansively, and she settled in, cradling her coffee as she considered her own experiences. "But the most amazing thing of all is that we can travel through time. Meet intriguing people, and of all things, I can meet someone like you." He stopped again and looked at her.

She flushed. "Come on, you've met so many people in your role. Me? I'm just a girl whose circumstances have allowed her to experience the fantastic worlds of the future. I don't think I could go back though. Not now. I've changed too much to be satisfied with the past." She smiled and slowly finished her coffee. "And, on that note, I think it's time for me to retire to my cabin." He grinned, and she grinned back. "Alone." But as she rose to leave, she stopped, her hand gripping the architrave, and bit her lip as uncertainty assailed her. "You said Chowd was out in the *Raptor* while I was ill?"

"Yeah. He's been trained to fly just about everything. As security officer, Duvall felt he was the natural choice to fill your role in the short term. Don't worry, your *Raptor* will be in perfect condition when he returns. He's anal about those sorts of things. Oh, and you're expected to report at 0900 tomorrow morning in the bay, ready to fly again."

"Good," she said, although she privately wondered if she was ready to go back out there. Sure, the physical symptoms were gone, but something strayed at the back of her mind.

She inwardly shrugged. She'd wanted to become a combat pilot when the chance arose, and now here she was, and it wasn't that she regretted her choices in becoming a fighter pilot at all, but maybe what had led up to that decision. With a final fleeting smile, she left the room and Raven.

Chapter 5

Once more seated in her *Raptor*, Jemma moved it through the bay and out into the black inkiness of space. It had been three full days since her collapse, but she was feeling good. Well-rested and alert, but watchful nonetheless. She'd been pleased to be back in the saddle, and she wondered if this was why she'd never felt settled in any aspect of her life. Because she hadn't found the vocation that fulfilled her.

"Cardnew to *Elector*. Everything's silent out here and I'm catching a blank on my radar. Anything showing on yours?"

"Negative there, Cardnew. Run the perimeter and check in again soon. McCord out." She plotted an elliptical path allowing her to stay within a reasonable distance of the *Elector* and ran through drills in her mind. In the time she'd been flying, she'd learned, very quickly, that it could be lonely under these conditions, and it helped to have something to keep her mind active. She'd discovered during her time at Woomera that running through drills and management techniques for her craft kept her sharp as well as focused. It also had helped her to achieve the high marks she strove for.

It was while running through drills for ditching that the alarms started bleeping. The comm unit bleeped at the same time she turned the vehicle, ready to spear through the darkness toward the ship.

"Cardnew here, *Elector*. What are you seeing?"

"Jemma, we got spooks. Lots of spooks. Looks like upward of fifteen heading in our direction." Duvall's voice came through the secured comm interface clearly. In her mind, she could picture him looking grim and running a hand through his short, black hair.

"Shit! Why didn't we pick them up before?" Jemma demanded.

"We would have, but we shut down the long-range sensor to check some schematic issues we've been having. How soon can you get back here?"

She hit the turbo boosters, moving quickly toward the ship. "I'm on my way, *Elector*. Hang tight." Something of the strain from maneuvering her ship must have shown in her voice though, because next she heard Raven's voice.

"What's going on, Jem?"

"Err, negative. No issue, just a touch of vertigo in spin."

"Stabilizers?" his voice demanded through the comm.

"They're currently offline to get enough oomph." She sighed. Not that she wanted to broadcast that kind of information, but he'd asked as though he needed to know and she'd instinctively answered. Thank heavens this was on the secured commlink, she told herself. It was something that required attention when she landed back on the *Elector*, but she'd make do for now.

"Chowd here. Need another set of hands out there?"

"Howdy doody, Chowd. You sure would be welcome, my friend." She kept the ship moving and quickly took position in front of the *Elector*, watching as the small, retrofitted shuttle launched through the bays.

She'd spent time last night working with Chowd to prepare for this event. Both of them had considered the odds of the pirates not coming back as highly unlikely, and they'd agreed that any incursion would come sooner rather than later.

Looked like she was right again, she mused. They knew that there was only one single *Raptor*, and that had concerned her enough to seek out Chowd to ensure there was some kind of backup. But oh, how she hated being proven right in this situation.

She sent a ship-to-ship message to Chowd. "Stay out of sight, behind the ship. You're my backup if anything fails, Chowd my man. But for now, let me rock and roll."

She grinned, putting the *Raptor* into position. "Morning, boys. Back for another lesson?" She dead-eyed the lead spook as adrenaline coursed through her once more.

"Ahh! It's the little girl with a big attitude again," came the sing-song voice she had heard before. "What are you doing with some broken ship? Why not join us and fly a spook? They're new and so good to fly." There was a bite in the words.

"You know what? I prefer to stick with friends who won't knife me in the back. But thanks anyway, not that I appreciate the offer." She poured as much syrup into her words as possible. It wouldn't help smooth the situation, but they looked like they weren't in the mood to negotiate anyway.

"Then move aside, little girl, and let us at the prize. We have salvage rights and we intend to use them." The voice was much harder this time, and her hand tensed on the thruster in response. It was her job to protect the *Elector*, one she took seriously. She would do whatever it took to keep them safe. *Anything.*

"You know, this is getting a little old. If I've told you once, I've told you twice—nothing here to salvage. Now move along." Her voice was hard and she tensed, fingers on the toggle of the multi-acquisition button. "I'm giving you the count of five to turn around and get out of my face before we find out just how many of you I can attend to at once." It was sheer bravado. She couldn't take them all at once, but she shrugged mentally. All they had to do was hang on tight until she'd done enough to encourage them to leave. Or died. Whichever came first.

A burble of laughter filtered through the comm unit. "Little girl, do we look that gullible? The multiple acquisition tool can only take on so many at once and can only be used once with the lasers before requiring a hard reset."

Shit! He knows about the fail safe settings! Her stomach soured with that knowledge. "Now, given there are so many more of us than you, perhaps you should consider joining us as an alternative. Think of what you could do if you joined us."

Righteous fury flared and she hissed. "Get lost, you lump of camel dung. There's no way I'd join you and the other scum you call allies." She knew Duvall was listening, but the time for talk had passed.

She pressed the switch once more and watched with narrowed eyes as the lead ships started to turn, splitting into two groups with the secondary group behind them. A new ploy. She considered her status and decided it was time to play them at their own bully games.

She squeezed off a quick round, clipping the wing this time of one of the spooks. "That should be enough of a reason to leave us alone, you asshole." She murmured the words quietly to herself, watching as the craft spun in space, turning and heading back where it came from.

One down, about fourteen to go. She wasn't going to use her best tool until absolutely necessary. Somehow, the thought that she had this tool didn't settle the butterflies that were flying around in her belly. Maybe it was because she wasn't sure, deep down where it counted most, that it would be enough to save them.

"Now that wasn't very nice, little girl. Time to play rough, I think."

Forewarned of an impending shot by the alarms that started to blare, she took evasive action with a hard swing to the left. Once more, she used the multiple acquisition targeting setting.

"Right, you moron. This is where you need to back off. I have you all targeted, and I won't hesitate to put a laser shot through you."

"Jemma, we have a problem. More incoming, and this time I think you need help." Grayson's voice was tight as he ground out the words.

"Damn, Grayson, how many coming our way now?" She was beyond worry and descending into panic. Control came after long puffs of air and a quick tally of the numbers appearing on her screen.

"By my count, looks like another dozen or so. Chowd, get out there now."

"Grayson, even with the retrofitting, I'm not sure we have enough firepower between us to make this work." Chowd's voice filtered through the lines, sharing information that Jemma had already grasped. Thank God the spook pilots couldn't hear the secured line. Chowd had instituted a level-three scramble on certain frequencies and insisted they use them only for this type of communication.

"Jem, Chowd. The weld is completed. I think I can have this bird in flight within the next hour or so. Can you hold them off until then? In the short term, I can move everyone into the four main isolation areas and divert the aux generator to shields and weapons."

"Raven, I'm not sure I can hang out for an hour, can you make it sooner?" She waited, her mind trying to keep track of the movements of the ships.

"Negative, Jem. That's as soon as I can get them back online."

"Okay, shift what you can, because our situation is precarious."

One ship broke away and she tugged the *Raptor* to the left, cutting of their access to the *Elector*. "Captain? Duvall? Do you agree?"

"Yeah, we need to get out of this safely. Do what you need to, but stay safe. McCord out."

She gave orders to Chowd to once more assume a position behind her *Raptor* and with a final flair opened communications with the spooks. "My captain and I agree...there is nothing to salvage here of interest to you."

This time a different voice echoed through the headpiece. "So, we meet again, my dear. My name is Crick Sur Banden, and I see you have met my colleagues from Phobos. Alas, I can't be with you at this time, as I'm a little busy right now. I wish to extend an offer to you to join us. A lovely and talented young lady like you would be properly appreciated and thanked. And of course, there is a certain something or someone I am hoping to retrieve from the *Elector*." The voice was oily, and she shuddered.

"You know what? I don't like your rules, so I'm going to decline. Thanks, but no thanks," she bit out, feeling quite sick about the exchange. *Fuck! What could he possibly be after on the Elector? Or more to the point, who?*

"Very well then. Of course, it is such a shame. You're supposed to be incredibly talented in more than one way. Paros? Do as you please."

Suddenly the beeping in the cockpit got louder. "Shit. Chowd, get ready for incoming," she called as the first burst of laser slashed close to the wing.

She managed to spin away, and another fired. Jemma returned fire, strafing the lead ship so it spun wildly away into the blackness. Another ship fired laser cannons, and she waited until the last minute, sure she felt the rush of wind disrupt her trajectory.

One by one they took turns at trying to push past her defenses. If she didn't know better, she'd say the captains seemed to be toying with her. As she emerged from one spin, another would shoot and the spinning would begin again. After the fifth spin, she reached for the multiple acquisition and keyed it in.

"McCord, I need a Go to—" Another spin. "—use the lasers on

multi-acq." She quickly pulled the nose of the *Raptor* up, and a spook dropped the first of its missiles. "Any time now would be a great time."

"Go to green." Duvall's tight voice filtered along the lines.

She could see Chowd was in a similar position, the shuttle making heavy weather of the tight spins and movements. "Chowd, prepare for green light on multi-acq!"

She hit the button. The lasers misfired, and she swore savagely, re-engaged the setting as she'd been taught, and fired once again. This time it worked. She scored multiple hits, effective but not enough to damage more than six or seven. She swore loudly and powered up the phasers. Three spooks exploded, scattering debris and adding an extra hazard to fly through. "Geez…"

A ship snuck up behind her and she had to turn a tight spin to avoid the laser fire. She noted several other spooks were damaged, but not enough to ensure the *Elector*'s safety or to ensure that they'd back down.

"Chowd, I need you to advance and take some of these suckers out. I need space to move!" Her voice was hard, and she was sweating, her hand gripping the thrusters as she toggled the comm. "McCord? I need air cover! Like now! Get your weapons online and hot, because I can't hold them all off like this!"

Once more, she was spinning out of the way of fire. She felt the jolt as the *Raptor* took a hit on one of the wings. Thankfully, from what she could see, it was only a glancing blow, but her stomach clenched tightly. Chowd returned fire at the same time she depressed the button again. Another couple of spooks retired, but she and Chowd were still seriously outnumbered. It wouldn't matter how good she was, they could keep taking a beating and she'd eventually find her luck running out.

Jemma was running low on firepower, her phaser banks sitting at just under thirty percent and laser missiles almost gone. Her shielding had also taken a battering, and she rerouted whatever she could to them.

The front of the *Elector* started to glow, and she realized it was the shields and something else. *Ah, they have the weapons online.* She smiled grimly; that would even up the score some.

The *Elector* shot off a guided rocket, hitting another spook and clearing the scene a little more. The glow intensified. She fired the phasers again, but this time, Raven's voice came through the headset. "Jem, get me another half hour and I can be ready to move. Can you manage that?"

"Raven, I don't know that I have that much left in the tanks." She was now concerned but was determined it wouldn't show in her voice.

"Chowd?"

"I am also running low, Raven, but can hang on, I think. They're more interested in neutralizing Jemma at the moment." His voice was muffled, as if he was doing something else.

"Jemma? I think that we need to get further away from the ship to allow for any safety margin. Draw them away. I would suggest we head toward that small planet." Chowd's words rang through the cockpit.

A tiny dot of blue-gray hovered before her and Jemma nodded in agreement, even knowing none of the men could see her. Being in a huddle made the battle even more dangerous, as they dodged debris and flew close together. Right now any advantage and freedom to maneuver was welcome.

Close quarters had worked out fine for the beginning of the engagement, as it had given the ability to pick of numerous enemies at once. Now with laser banks running low, she needed to change tactics, draw them out, while securing the safety of the *Elector*.

"I agree. Time to boogie, Chowd. Follow my lead." She accelerated the *Raptor*, taking the pirates by surprise.

She knew the *Elector* would be fine, with their shields and weaponry online. In the back of her mind, she worried about her own ship. It had sustained heavy damage and would need to dock soon, otherwise…

"Don't go there right now, Jemma." She swung over and around the spook ships, dodging and weaving up and down, avoiding contact. They were little and light looking, which meant their shielding was probably less effective too. Jemma spun a sharp turn again and snuck up behind one.

The pilot worked hard, hopping around and trying to throw her off its tail, but she stuck like glue. The targeting computer beeped when it had the small craft in optimal position, and she fired two shots with the phaser. She felt no thrill when the ship exploded in front of her, spewing hunks of metal and catching her ship as she raced through it.

Chowd was also dodging fields of debris, but while the larger body of the shuttle offered a larger target it was also far more flexible, turning tighter and moving faster. She had to push that thought away as she targeted the next craft, hopping in behind it. She pulled into their blindspot and hit them fast.

"Jemma, get moving toward that planet. I think we can get them down into the atmosphere. Their craft are light and with less efficient shielding. They aren't for dirtside, and I'm sure we can pick a few more off."

"You think?" The words slipped out and she nearly cursed. "Jemma? What's wrong?"

A red light had started beeping softly on her console, but she ignored it. "Nothing. Do you—"

"Grayson sent me the coordinates. He's been plotting out a possible course that's defensible." That was the kind of excellent teamwork she'd expect from the *Elector*, she thought. Yet even as her mind seized on it, she wondered if her own craft would survive what lay ahead.

"Okay. Good thinking, Chowd. Let's give that a go." They started working toward the planet, zigging and zagging from side to side while other ships jerked and shuddered.

A tremendous crack sounded and her ship heaved to one side. Jemma tugged and pulled it back upright. "Fuck!"

"What's your status?" Chowd demanded fiercely. "I've sustained some damage but am still in the air."

He didn't need to know that the damage on her wing could potentially be a killer for her. At this point, it would only exacerbate the situation if anyone else knew.

Something would come up, she hoped once more, spinning tightly to avoid laser fire, but the ship was now sluggish to react and she bit her lip. "I'm heading for the planet and going to try a dead drop through the atmosphere."

The closer they came, the more determined the spooks seemed to become, as if they'd worked out the plan and saw their death on the horizon. It was harder to get past them, and it occurred to her that perhaps they knew that once they hit the upper atmosphere they were in great danger of not surviving the re-entry pressures. Her misgivings about the *Raptor* moved up another notch as more alarms blared and flashed at her.

She entered the atmosphere, washing off as much speed as she could, with Chowd right behind her. The burn of the entry caused an orange glow to form in her viewscreen as she struggled with the aging and damaged craft. The spooks followed. She could see them shimmying wildly, but they remained on her tail. *Damn!* They should be ready to give up by now. One tried to pull up, but the pressure ripped it apart like a paper plane, wings and nose spinning out of control. She held on grimly, fighting her own ailing craft.

They were down to five and through the atmosphere when a single spook rose out of nowhere; the trajectory indicated from somewhere on the planet. Rapid fire hit the front of the *Raptor*; she saw the damage as the craft started to smoke in the thin atmosphere. Shit! They'd used her blindspot to target the Raptor. She pulled the ship upright, hard, so that a single wing took the worst of the damage, but it was too late.

"Chowd! I'm hit and going down!" she yelled.

Manually working the flaps, she tried to pull the ship up. It careened out of control, pitching from one side to another, and finally the wing detached, torn away as the ship shuddered wildly. The screaming of the engines cut to silence in death.

"Jem! Eject now! Eject!"

She could hear Chowd shouting the instructions as she pulled on the ejector lever, but it was stuck. She grasped her breathing apparatus and jammed it over her face, fastening it with one hand, the gravitational forces pushing her back into the seat. The ship gave one more shudder and dropped nose-down, twisting and turning.

A final massive heave on the ejector arm, and it gave, ripping the top off the *Raptor* as the plas-glass roof tore away, propelling her out of the craft as it dove toward the planet's violet surface. The parachute deployed, but she was too high. The fall and impact would kill her. She closed her eyes, breathing deeply from the mask as her heart thudded. The comm was still working, and she could hear Chowd screaming that he was coming.

"Raven?" she called one last time, knowing he could hear her, but unable to hear him. Her heart rate increased, and the wind whistled past her as she plummeted toward the surface.

"Jemma, I'm going to try to bring this about and get under you, matching your speed. I don't have much time..." Chowd was wrestling the shuttle into position, spearing downward, attempting to match her trajectory.

It was a risky maneuver and, if he pulled it off, magnificently flown. She feared it was a death sentence for both of them. The craft neared her, and she spied the surface of the planet speeding toward her. Suddenly the craft was edging below her, and an instrument that looked like a hook deployed.

"Jemma, let the hook grab the chute. Don't reach for it though. Let it grab you. I think we can slow you down sufficiently for the *Elector* systems to grab you and transport you."

She closed her eyes, hoping like hell this mad plan would work. Suddenly she felt a jerk, and inside her body she felt a tearing sensation. It sliced through her, stealing her breath and sight. "*Raven!*" The scream cut off as the tug of the chute disappeared, and blackness enveloped her.

Chapter 6

Chowd instructed Jemma swiftly, but there was no answer, and Raven's heart thudded harder than before. *Let her hear the instructions, and let it not be too late!* He watched the hook deploy via the video feed, praying as he worked that it would do enough, slow her enough for him to grab her.

The hook caught momentarily, and her descent slowed enough to allow him to grab her and transport her to SurgiTech. For a moment he stood, stunned, as the video feed showed she had been transmitted.

"Elara! Do you have her?" he called urgently.

"I've got her, but she's in a bad way, Raven." The voice cut off abruptly, and his heart dropped to his feet.

"I'm on my way!" he yelled as he pushed away from the console and pounded down the decking, not stopping to think. He had to get there. He had to make sure he had done enough to save her.

He ran to the door of the SurgiTech suite and pushed it open. The beeping of systems greeted him as he hurried toward the intensive care unit. He spied Jemma lying on the medi-bed and advanced, only to be stopped by Elara barring his way.

"You need to let me do my job, Raven. I know how you feel, but you can't be here now." Her voice was soft but firm.

"I need to be with—" His voice was hoarse with fear. She looked pale, abrasions clear on her face, as she lay so still. So white, except the trickle of scarlet at her lips. He gulped.

"She'll be fine, but I need to work with her while you do your job. Now go."

"I can't"

"You can. You must. I'll call you if something happens, but she won't be able to—"

"No. I have to be here." His eyes snapped to hers. "I have to be here, Elara. She needs me, and I need to be near her."

Elara sighed, frustration clear on her face as she turned away. "Fine, but you need to stay in my office. No matter what anyone thinks, this is still my SurgiTech suite. But if I say you need to go, you go. No arguments. Right?" Her eyes spat fire as she turned her head toward him. She turned back to Jemma, pressing points on her palm screen as she went.

She'd dismissed him, but he'd won this small concession. At least he could stay here, for now. He wandered into the office and sat down.

Another disturbance erupted in the SurgiTech suite. He rose to his feet, ready to be there for her, when he noticed it was Duvall and Mellissa. He saw Elara, her face dark with anger, as she gestured toward her office. He watched as the couple moved toward the door and opened it, Mellissa white-faced and trembling as Duvall ushered her inside. They looked surprised to see him there.

"Oh God! Raven, did you see her?" Mellissa's voice cracked. "I was listening to her. She nearly died out there!" Her voice rose toward hysteria, then she shook herself, found her center determinedly, and turned back to Duvall, who enclosed her in his arms.

Raven sat back down, resting his elbows on his legs, pitched slightly forward, and head in his hands. He noted that they shook slightly.

"Are you all right, Raven?" Duvall's voice broke through the fear that welled inside. His precipitous flight toward SurgiTech after she was transmitted here had obviously telegraphed some of his feelings and the shaking of his body told the rest of the tale. Right now, he didn't care. He was here if she needed him.

"Yeah. *Barsha*! I've never been through anything so nerve-wracking in my life. I wasn't sure I could get to her in time." He kept his head down. His stomach protested as the roiling continued. He was sure it wouldn't stop until Elara had determined the extent of Jemma's injuries and worked her magic. He scrubbed the heels of his hands over aching, dry eyes.

"Elara says she'll be fine."

"I know that, Duvall, but even so..." He stopped and centered himself once more. "I don't think I could do that again." He looked up to see Duvall and Mellissa watching him.

"Oh God, Raven. I never knew you had a thing for her. Are you okay?" Mellissa reached toward him with one slim hand, and he looked at it then her.

"I don't know if I am." He let the words, heavy with painfully brutal emotion, fill the air. Sure, he'd been proud of Jemma's accomplishments, but this had jerked reality out into the open for him. He never expected she would see any sort of combat, and certainly not like that. He wasn't sure how well he would deal with this in the future. That is, if they had a future, his head reminded him.

He shook his head. "I really don't know," he concluded heavily.

"Come on, Raven, she'll be fine in a day or two." The look in Mellissa's eyes told him that the reality of the situation had hit home for her too. He closed his eyes.

The sound of the door opening once more had him opening his eyes again. Chowd stood just inside the doorway. "I came as soon as it was safe to do so." His face, covered in sweat, attested the difficulty of the fight. Chowd may be some sort of security machine, but he showed not just great respect for Jemma, but also concern. "Elara said she'll make a full recovery." Raven just sat looking at him, seeing the concern in Chowd's intense eyes.

"Yeah, so I hear. Elara said she had quite a few injuries, but with a few days, the help of the regen units and physio systems, she'll make a full recovery." Mellissa's voice washed over him.

"I am pleased. She's a marvelous warrior and an exceptional pilot. To be able to maneuver that ship the way she did and to manage to hold it for as long..." His voice carried an emotion that Raven could only define as awe. A quick explosion of jealousy zinged through his system. He squashed down the emotion just as Elara pushed her way into the crowded office.

"Well, her injuries are numerous. She has several broken ribs, a severe concussion, extensive lacerations to her left arm, which I believe she had received in the ejection, and is already being healed. She also has a broken arm and leg and some internal injuries. Having said that, I believe she'll make a full recovery swiftly." Elara looked at Chowd. "You can see her soon. She was briefly conscious and said that she has some information for you."

Raven stood and made to head toward the door, but Elara stood in his way. "I need to see her."

"No, Raven. What she needs now is rest, and honestly, I don't think you're currently in the right frame of mind to see her. Give me a couple of hours—"

"No. I need to see her now." His voice was like shards of ice, and he attempted once more to push forward.

"Raven! Elara has said not now. You can speak to her in a couple of hours—just let Jemma rest for now." Duvall's face was closer than he realized, and he felt the hand on his arm. "Come on, man. Let's go back to my office, and you can fill me in on the repairs."

Frustration rose like a black cloud around him. He sensed that with Chowd and Duvall, not to mention Elara, pushing him further away from Jemma, there was no way he could currently get to her. For now, he conceded defeat. He would do what they wanted, but Jemma was his, and he'd be back.

He'd waited a long time for her, but no longer. Not while Jemma was aboard the *Elector*. He walked through the door and, without looking back, made his way out of the suite.

✪ ✪ ✪ ✪

Jemma cracked open an eye. Her entire body hurt, even her eyes stung in the bright light. She tried to move her head to the side and found it was immobilized. The sound of feet tapping on the floor caught her attention.

"So, you finally woke up, did you, sleeping beauty?"

The voice was familiar, and she trawled through her memories. Oh yes. Elara. *Damn!* Then she must be back on the *Elector*. Slowly, the memories began to resurface—Raven, Duvall, and Mellissa. Her sickness and the first attack of the Phobos pirates. The second attack on the *Elector* slid back into her mind together with her attempts to protect it, ending with her *Raptor* going down.

"Why am I in here?" Her voice croaked, and she immediately tried to push the weakness away.

"Well, after Raven and Chowd saved you and you were transmitted here to the SurgiTech, I've been working to repair all your lumps and bumps." She could hear strain in Elara's voice.

"Lumps and bumps?"

"Broken left arm and leg, some ribs, concussion, internal injuries, and lacerations. We're slowly getting you back together." Elara grinned weakly before she moved out of Jemma's line of sight.

"Ahh, I see. How long have I been here?"

"Fifteen hours, give or take. We kept you sedated long enough for the initial regen work to begin and alleviated some of the discomfort you would have experienced. We also had to do a little internal surgery, but that was successful."

"Surgery?"

"A few of your organs were compromised during the fall. But unlike in your time, we have techniques that allow us to fix that without needing to make an incision." Elara's face popped back into view. "Now I need to run some quick tests then a meal for you, I think."

The little handscreen was employed; the clicks as her fingers ranged quickly over it and the look of intense concentration told Jemma it was time to be quiet and let Elara do what she did best.

A couple of flickers of light and finally, after what seemed a long time, Elara smiled, the tension that had been evident on her face giving way. "Good. You're well on the way to recovery. Now Raven is waiting for me to call him and bring you something to eat. Do you feel up to it?" Elara looked at her carefully as she slid the diagnostic arm covering Jemma back into the wall.

"Sure, yeah, that sounds great." She smiled weakly as her stomach growled loudly. Nothing like having your body tell on you, she thought sourly.

Elara laughed. "Yes, I would say a meal must definitely be in order."

Elara left the room, already contacting Raven to head to SurgiTech with the meal she'd suggested. Jemma lay quietly on the bed, listening for the footfalls that would tell her Raven had found his way to her bedside. When he arrived, he carried a steaming bowl of soup and soft foods, setting them down on the movable table beside the bed.

"Hey, sweetheart. You gave me one hell of a fright." His voice was rough, and his sexy hair was standing up in spikes as if he had been pulling at it in frustration. His eyes were burning blue orbs of intensity, and she could see lines on his face that hadn't existed before.

"Rough day?" she queried as he spooned the soup into her mouth.

"You have no idea," he answered, his normally smooth demeanor gone, betrayed by the terse answer and jerky movements.

She gulped quickly, feeling the warm slide of liquid down her throat. "Want to tell me about it?" Another spoonful was thrust into her mouth.

"Not right now."

He closed his eyes, taking a deep breath, and she watched in fascination as his broad chest expanded. A tingle of awareness flickered through her. He seemed to need to do something for her, so she let him continue to feed her. It was nice to be cared for, she decided, even if he was a little rough.

She watched the play of emotions on his face, totally mesmerized. He might be sexy and all, but his attitude confused her, and right now she really did not need anything else to make life harder. Once the bowl was empty, he stood and took it from the room.

Jemma heaved a sigh. *So, what comes next?* The answer was immediate as Elara made her way into the room. Raven made to follow her, but she shooed him out efficiently.

"Go wait in my office," she told him, and Jemma noted his angry glance before he turned and followed the instruction. "How do you feel now, Jemma?"

"Like I got hit by a meteorite." She answered Elara's query dryly. You couldn't lie to a doctor, she supposed.

Elara snorted. "Well, I think your injuries are about on par with that." "When can I get out of here?" Elara quirked an eyebrow in her direction. "You don't want to keep me company?"

"Well, to be honest, it's nothing to do with that. Medical places like this give me the heebie-jeebies. I just want to… You know, be in my own cabin." She extended a shaking arm.

"Hmm. You did have quite a few injuries, but I think I can

release you now that you've eaten. The regen band has started the job of healing your bones, and most of the lacerations are closed. I think we can just attach regen tabs now." Elara activated the diagnostic device she had slipped onto Jemma's skin and slowly waved it to and fro over the left-hand side of her body.

"Is… Is there anything I need to know about… Dammit, the internal injuries?" "Are you planning on doing something strenuous? Like have sex?"

Jemma blushed. "No. Not exactly." She didn't want to look at the medic right now. After all, what kind of a question was that anyway?

"Good to hear. You aren't ready for anything like that. So lie back and let me check the rest of you over." A few *aha*'s and *hmm*'s later, Elara smiled. "Just let me fit a leg brace and you're free to leave." She rooted around in the cupboard beside the bed and came up with a lightweight contraption, swiftly strapping the metal to her leg. "I expect to see you first thing in the morning for a full check up though, and no gymnastics, right?" She smiled at Jemma.

"Sure thing, Doc. The high wire is a little beyond me at the moment."

She lay still as Elara retracted the last of the diagnostic equipment from around her, then she slowly stood up. It was only then that she realized she was still in her flight suit—or rather what was left of it. She looked down ruefully at the torn and filthy garment.

"Come on, Raven will escort you back to your cabin."

Jemma walked, her movements cautious as she ached all over. Raven held the door open, and Elara motioned for Jemma to make her way through. Her arm and leg throbbed, but not as much as she would have expected.

"You're letting her go? Now? What about pain meds?" He looked earnest. "She'll be fine. I administered pain meds via hypospray, which should be good for another fifteen hours or so. Bed rest is best at this point, and the regen has done its work very effectively." Elara smiled at Raven. "But *rest* is the optimal word."

Jemma blushed again and sighed. "Right then...off I go... Thanks, Doc." With those words, she slowly maneuvered her way through the door that led to the corridor. This could take a while, she thought as she felt a hand insert itself around her waist.

"Hey, what are you—"

"I'm getting you back to your cabin in one piece." Raven's face was close to hers, and she watched it, fascinated once more by the play of emotions. She sighed and leaned back slightly, trying to gain some distance. In response, he tightened his arm around her, pulling her closer to his body. "Then we need to talk."

Chapter 7

By the time they reached her cabin, Jemma felt utterly exhausted and just wanted to rest her aching bones. She turned at the door and balanced to swipe her palm over the screen when Raven swept her up into his arms, giving the order for the door override. She felt her body shaking in reaction to her weakness and cursed herself. Once the door closed behind them, she groaned slightly.

"You can let me down now."

"I rather like this."

She felt the rumble of his words and raised an eyebrow at him. "Yeah? Well, that's fine, but I bet you're busy, and I'm tired."

"Nothing much to do at the moment. The matrix is back online and my crew is running diagnostics." He smiled at her, and she wanted to melt.

"I hate to be the fly in the ointment and all, but I really think you should leave." Her tone was harder, fighting against the sensations that she fought to overcome. She squirmed in his arms, hoping he would take the hint, but he ignored the unsubtle suggestion, tightening his arms in response. Not what she expected, or wanted, she told herself.

"No, Jem. We need to talk, and this is the best place for it."

He put her down on the bed, propping a pillow under her leg, and immediate relief flowed through her system. Talking...talking was okay... She could survive that.

A red tide rose up his cheeks as he sat in the chair beside her bed. He looked down for a moment, and she got the impression he was trying to find the words, or at least the right ones, and she was intrigued. He had a silver tongue, and she'd never seen him at a loss for words. *For God's sake, Jemma, stop being so fanciful!* He was, after all, the right-words-every-time man.

"Jem, when I heard the transmission, I nearly died. I know I haven't really made any moves. My excuse was that I wanted you to have time to settle in to the changes. Now..." He stopped, taking a deep breath, and she could see the heavy rise and fall of his chest encased in the dark uniform. "I don't want to waste another minute with you. Standing back has nearly left me without you at all, and that's just not right."

She could see the uncertainty in his eyes. *Uncertainty?* The knowledge that he felt uncomfortable and uncertain stunned her.

"Raven? I don't know what to say. I mean, you've hinted but you never seemed ready to take that step. I didn't really think you were that interested in me." She gulped. "Don't get me wrong, I think you're tremendously sexy and all, but I'm not a keeper. Know what I mean? I'd love to be with you, but you need to understand going in, I don't know how to do the *long-term thing* in relationships." He opened his mouth, but before he could form any words, she laid a finger on his lips. "It's important to me that you know. I don't want to lie to you or give you some kind of a false impression."

She told herself it was better she told him clearly and upfront. No one else knew better than her that she wasn't a person other people kept. She was only ever a temporary thing. He had to understand that. For heaven's sake, even her own mother had written her off as temporary. She straightened in her bed.

"No. You're wrong. You've had a rough time, but Jem, I want forever."

She could see the earnest in his face. "Raven, I can't. This is hot and sexy, but short term. I can tell you honestly, I so want you, but it will only last until it ends on either side. Either you or I will grow out of this— " She waved her hand in the air. "—relationship, thing. That's all there is. For me that's all there can be."

"No, you're wrong. Do not limit us before we even begin. Give us a chance to be more." His voice was deep, his face tight, and her chest ached at the thought of causing him pain. "Let me show you."

"You're deluding yourself where we're concerned. Forever is for Mellissa and Duvall. One day you will find your forever too. But for now, yeah, I want in." She watched him intently. "I can be in for as long as this works for us. But I'm a no-strings-attached sort of girl." She kept her voice low and even. *If I were a forever kind of woman, this is the man I'd want.*

But she knew to take a good thing when it was offered and make the most of it. She smiled at him, pushing her hair to one side and lifting a hand. He moved closer, out of his chair and onto the side of the bed.

"Give it a chance, Jem. You might find it is forever."

"No, Raven, but I will give you me, for as long as you want me."

He shook his head. "No go, but here's a different deal. Don't write it off before it starts, right? Give it a chance to be much more than just a fling. Keep an open mind and it might just surprise you." He smiled at her, the sexy glint back in his deep-blue eyes.

She sat for a moment, her thoughts whirling, but the overriding feeling was that he wanted her. What could be simpler? She closed her eyes, taking a deep breath and feeling her lungs expand, held it, and let the breath whoosh out. She opened her eyes and smiled. "I'm game if you are."

He leaned in toward her, smiling, then stopped and looked into her eyes. "I want you, but you need time. And so do I. Time to learn about each other." He leaned in closer, and she squeaked when a twinge of pain in her back bit hard. "Time to heal from your injuries." His warm breath tickled her lips.

She licked her lips, and his eyes darkened. Her breathing slowed as the delicious scent of man invaded her senses, and languor spread. He leaned closer, taking great care not to crowd her, and lightly touched his lips to hers.

"But I do need to taste you," he whispered, so close to her that she could feel the words against her skin.

Her body ached for him. She reached out, but he intercepted her arms, pushing them down by her sides. Once more, his lips touched hers lightly, like the barest brush of butterfly wings, and her eyes closed. She felt him pull away but didn't fight it.

When she opened heavy eyelids and glanced at him, his eyes shined brightly. He smiled and leaned toward her.

His hands left her arms and pushed her back against the pillows. Jemma grabbed his hands. Always before, she had been aggressive in her passion, but with this man, she was slow and unhurried. She let her lips part just as they reached his, and this time she softly placed her lips against his, flicked his lips with her tongue, and waited for him to open them. She felt the rumble of his laughter against her mouth as he moved to pull back. She really wanted his arms wound around her, but instead he merely leaned down and plunged his tongue within her mouth.

The kiss turned red-hot, scorching her in its intensity as she surrendered to him. She moaned against his lips and reached for his shoulders, tugging him closer to her. For a moment, she felt she would burst into flame, then once more he pulled back. Her breathing had accelerated along with her heartbeat, and when she opened her eyes, she was gratified to see that he was almost as unsteady as she was.

He rested his forehead on hers as they both caught their breath. Finally, with a sigh, he moved away awkwardly, rising without his usual grace.

"Jem, you need to sleep, and if I stay, this will go so much further than either of us is ready for. But don't think I don't want you, because I do. Very much, as you can now see."

His eyes were smoky with passion, and his voice a deep rasp. He watched her for a minute then turned toward the door.

"Elara says you're off duty for the next few days, and so am I, so I'll swing by at 0800 hours. Be ready. I have vids in my cabin, and I think a quiet, relaxing day is in order. Now sleep, my sweet Jem." He turned, opened the door, and just before closing it, looked back and said, "Dream of us."

The door shut behind him, leaving Jemma in a state of arousal, reclining on the bed, considering his actions and words. *I am so in trouble.* The thought worried her as she lay in the half-light.

It took a long time for sleep to come.

Jemma was just getting out of bed when the door opened, and in walked Raven. "Good morning, beautiful. I thought you would need help, so here I am." He grinned at her as he made his way over to the bed to help her up. She looked at his twinkling eyes and broad smile.

"I need to see Elara before anything else," she groused, watching him pull fresh clothes from the pile that had been deposited on the desk.

"I know that, but you're going to want to shower first, so grab these clothes and off you go. I'll wait here in case you need help." She made to reach for the clothing he offered, but instead he gripped her, propelling her forward into his arms as his head dipped. "But before you do, I need my good-morning kiss."

His mouth settled over hers, his lips soft and the kiss passionate enough to cloud her mind. She moaned deep in her throat as his tongue explored and tangled with hers. She clutched him closer, needing to feel his hard body against hers.

Slowly, he pulled away, and she lifted heavy lids to see that he was not unaffected either. They stood together for a minute, then— regretfully, she could see—he pushed the clothes into her arms and gently propelled her to the door of the bathroom. His actions confused her. He claimed to want her, but each time he ratcheted up the heat, he left her dangling.

"I'll be right here if you need me to wash your hair, or back, or...." His words held a promise as he shut the door behind her.

She couldn't control the laugh that echoed in the tiny ablution room.

She showered quickly, her body aroused from his nearness and the scorcher of a kiss, while thoughts of what he was up to raced around in her head. She closed her eyes as the water sluiced over her naked body, leaning into the stinging spray. With a sigh, she reached over and turned it off. The precious supply required her to be sparing, and for a moment she clung to the fond memories of long, hot showers in her past.

Thank goodness the frame around my leg is waterproof, she thought as she toweled and dressed. Once she'd slipped into the ship suit he'd handed her, she turned to the mirror, running a brush through her hair and taking the tablet that would clean her teeth more efficiently than a brush had ever done. She grinned. Another chore that didn't need to be dealt with, she told herself.

Absently, she noted the circles beneath her eyes and the paleness of her skin. She'd certainly lost some weight lately, she thought, turning to the side. However, even without a bra her breasts were still high and firm, though on the small side.

Casting a last look at her face, she grimaced. Well, for a woman who always dressed for passion and an eye on the main game, the ship suit really did not do much for her, but it was as good as she was going to get. She thought longingly of the jeans and skimpy tops she had in her closet and the lacey lingerie she had amassed before her transfer to the future. *He hasn't seen anything yet. Wait 'til he gets a look at me in a demi-bra and thong. They always tipped the balance in my favor.* The thought put a smile on her face. Wait until she got back to the *Star of Ishtar*.

"How in hell am I going to write my report telling Vors I lost my ship?" Shit. Her arse was so cooked when that report was received. Once more, she had managed to mess up a good thing. "Damn!"

She shook herself. There was nothing she could do about it right now, and Raven was waiting outside. The longer she lingered in here, the sooner he would walk in and start asking what was up, and that was something she didn't want to have happen. Not yet. She wanted the atmosphere to be just right. Time to put on that happy face, she reminded herself. *Remember, you can rely on you and no one else.* She pinched her cheeks lightly and was amused to see the color rising in them. Jemma put on her brightest smile as she reached over to open the door.

✪ ✪ ✪ ✪

"Good morning, Elara. Where would you like us?" Jemma said as she and Raven walked through the door holding hands.

"Raven, you can wait in my office. Jemma, come through to the consulting room please." She indicated a small doorway, and Jemma breathed a silent sigh of relief as she followed the petite Elara. The door closed behind them, and she sat on the diagnostic bed. "How are you feeling this morning?"

"Not too bad, thanks. Still a few twinges and aches, but I guess that's to be expected. Those pain meds worked the trick, but I suppose you already knew that too." She watched as Elara picked up the diagnostic palm screen. Once more the band extended over her, but as she waited quietly all she could hear was *hmm*'s and *yes*'s.

"Your results are looking good. I think we need to keep the regen units on you for another day, but the healing process is coming along nicely. Also, we can dispense with the supports for your leg now." She smiled at Jemma as the band retracted back into the wall, and Elara removed the supports around her leg. Jemma sat up on the diagnostic bed, ready to get down, when Elara placed a hand on her arm. "But I do want to have a quick word with you before you leave and Raven comes in."

"Sure, what can I help you with?"

"It's more a case of how can I help you. I need to know if you're planning to use any contraceptive control. I'm not trying to pry. This is one of the aspects of being the ST, and I ask everyone who joins the crew. It is something you need to consider if you plan on engaging in activities with someone. I can see here that you don't have anything on file." She tapped something on her palm screen.

"Umm, that would be because I'm not currently involved with anyone. However, that may change." So what if Elara reported back to Duvall?

"Have you considered conception control though?" Her words were level and quiet, and for just a moment, Jemma wanted to ask what if she didn't chose to use any contraceptive. But reality reared its head, and she subsided. She wouldn't jeopardize her future. Couldn't. Besides which, she wasn't cut out for motherhood.

"Well, yes I have, and no, I'm not using anything currently. I do need to do something about contraception, I guess." She didn't want to discuss this with Elara—after all, she was a member of the same crew as Raven—but it was a fact that she needed to consider it as she had previously in her own time.

"So do you want to go ahead and start on a course? I can have the implantation completed immediately if you like, but only if you are happy with it. Do you understand how it works?"

"Yeah, you implant using transmission technology. It's good for six months, unless I want it removed before then. I get that. Side effects?" Jemma rattled off what she had learned in the academy.

"Not many. The odd double vision, some nausea, but they're rare and the hormones were updated in the last few months, so we have minimal issues now. But if you do experience any side effects, you need to return to me and I can remove the implant."

"How long until it takes effect?"

"Pretty much immediately. In some cases the hormones take up to forty-eight hours, but that's rare, and we can check to see if you're one of the unlucky ones with that susceptibility."

"Sure, get it done then," Jemma answered.

She liked sex, had no qualms about her sensuality. A fling was one thing, but a baby was something completely different. It sure didn't figure into her lifestyle or plans. She remembered the old adage—there are bold pilots and old pilots, but very few old and bold pilots. If something happened to her, her child would be alone, left to fend for itself, and that she would never do.

Just for a moment, she had considered the possibility of parenting, but not with any real dedication or conviction. That was never meant to be her future. As she had told Raven, she didn't do forever.

The testing complete, Elara administered the implantation, letting her go join Raven and leave for the mess hall with the injunction to pop back in the following day.

They left the SurgiTech suite, walking side by side in companionable silence up the clanking deck, stairs, and finally to the mess hall. They served themselves and found an empty booth as Mellissa and Duvall walked in. They both seemed so happy, Jemma noted, looking at the sparkle in Mellissa's eyes and Duvall's arm around her waist. Wistfulness lanced her quickly through the heart.

"They look really happy." She turned to Raven, who was watching her.

"Yeah, they do, don't they? That's what I'd like, one day." He smiled, and the corners of his eyes crinkled. Before she could say anything though, Mellissa and Duvall had served themselves and, having caught sight of them, joined them at the table.

"How do you feel this morning, Jemma?" Duvall asked. It seemed odd, this softer side of Duvall that she'd never seen before, and it made her feel a little uncomfortable.

"Not too bad. A bit stiff and sore, but otherwise alive, which I guess is a good thing. I think that's one of the benefits of living in the future. It doesn't take too long for the body to heal." The words were casual, but she watched him carefully.

"You gave us a fright." Mellissa leaned forward, grabbing her hand and holding it lightly. "I'm pleased it all ended okay though." She smiled at Jemma with watery eyes.

"Yeah, I gave myself a bit of a fright too." Jemma laughed nervously. "So, how long 'til we catch up with the rest of the fleet?"

"Ahh, there has been a slight change of plans, but we don't need to discuss that today. You've three days sick leave, so pop by my office Friday and I'll fill you in. 0800 hours, ready to resume duty. You too, Raven. I will need you and Chowd."

She understood that meant the discussion had ended and bowed her head, picking at her oats slowly, thinking about what it could possibly mean. Under the table, she felt Raven grab her hand, and it steadied her. She refused to give the rush of support any extra credibility though. With great care, Jemma pushed away thoughts of any disciplinary action for the loss of the craft.

After a while, she pushed the bowl aside, and Raven looked at her. She nodded in silent agreement at the question in his eyes, and they rose together. She wished she'd somehow missed the enquiring look Mellissa and Duvall shared. Jemma and Raven deposited their bowls at the service point and left the hall together, heading back down to Raven's cabin.

He slid his hand over the palm-print reader, and the door whooshed open. She took a second look and was surprised to see it sported a color so different from the rest of the ship. The door shut, and Raven walked behind her, winding his hands around her. Slowly, he pulled her back against his body. She soaked up the heat from him. She turned her head, and there was his mouth, calling to her somehow, and she had to taste it. She turned in his embrace as their mouths met and clung, soft and filled with a promise she so wanted to accept. He deepened the kiss, and she started to drown in the emotions that rose within her.

His hands had moved down her back, cupping her bottom and

pulling her, molding her to him. His erection nudged against her belly, and she felt her body heat in response. One hand released him to touch his face. He lifted his mouth from her lips and traced soft kisses over her jawline and down under her chin. She lifted her head back, allowing him better access. She burned in his arms and tried to breathe, but the sheer heat of him stole the oxygen from her lungs, and she panted. Oh God, he was so good at this lovemaking gig. He lifted his head as she gulped for air.

"*Barsha*! But you're so beautiful, Jem. I just want to touch you, to be with you." His voice was gravelly, and his eyes glittered.

He laid a hand against her face, and she noted that it shook; his breathing was as ragged as hers. They waited a minute with an arm around each other until they settled once more. He lifted her and carried her to his office and sitting room off his cabin. The blues he'd used to cover the functional gray calmed her, and she realized with a start that the rug, and even the picture frames, were the same blue-violet as her eyes.

"Wow! What a great room."

"Yeah, I find it relaxes me." He smiled as he sat her on the sofa, pulled a crocheted blanket down over her legs, then muscled in behind her. "Vid screen, play options."

The unit ran through a number of choices as they sat together, his hand holding hers. When they decided on a movie, he gave the command, and the movie began. The whole time, though, she was aware of Raven sitting so close beside her. He held her hand, and she sat uncomfortably aware that this was the first time she had sat like this with a man, in harmony without the focus on sex.

Most of her previous relationships had been quick with lots of immediate passion, but with her no-forever policy, she'd kept them very basic and essentially unemotional. This was uncertain territory, and she was at a loss as to how to deal with it.

After the movie finished, they sat for a while in silence. During the movie, he'd managed to wind his arms around her middle as she leaned against him. She lay back, savoring the closeness and warmth, all the while her mind reminding her heart not to get too involved. It was hard to forget the safety she felt in his arms.

"The first time I saw you, spitting fire and throwing a hell of a tantrum, I never would have imagined this," he whispered into her ear. He laughed, and the rumble of his chest was shockingly sensuous. She turned to look back at him.

"You know, I wasn't exactly at my best."

"Perhaps not by your standards, but by *Eshra*, you were certainly sexy in that get-up you had on. Those heels made you look like you had legs up to your armpits, and the red made you look so hot." He grinned.

She swooped in, did not even attempt to check herself, and kissed him hard. His mouth opened to accept the sexual kiss, lips and tongue tantalizing them both. Each laugh had sent shocks of emotion zinging through her body, and she just needed him—now. She stretched further upward, increasing the pressure, and the kiss turned wild.

His hands shifted between them, moving up to cup her aching breasts, and she pushed into them. A throb began low down in her belly, the hard curl of heated desire flowing through her body as the need grew. He kissed her, grace forgotten, as he roughly thrust his tongue into her mouth as if seeking everything in her soul until he pulled away, panting.

She gripped his hands, still kneading, arching into them, then let go of one to lift her fingers to his face. "More" was all she said, her voice low and throbbing, and he gasped.

He tore his hands away from her. He got up and moved away from her reach. The redness of his face and the tightly curled hands told her how hard he fought.

"No, Jem. You aren't ready yet, and neither am I." His voice was hard, gravelly with the desire he warred against.

"Well, I would certainly beg to differ there." She cast a glance toward his groin. "Jem, don't make this harder than it is."

"Do you reckon it could? Get harder, I mean?" She knew her eyes sparkled as she grinned, and the flush of her skin had to let him know exactly what she wanted, how she burned for his touch.

"Jemma, please don't push this now. I want to build a relationship with you. But we need time to let it grow." He moved forward and reached an entreating hand toward her. His eyes told a different story though. He wanted her, and now. She could see it in his face and the way he held his body tightly controlled.

She rose from the seat gracelessly. "Raven, I want this and you want this. Here we are, with time we wouldn't normally have. I don't want our first time to be rushed and hurried, with you going one way and me the other. Right? Please?"

"Come with me." He scooped her up and strode to the darkened room beyond.

Jemma didn't look at the bedroom, instead she moved toward him with her hands outstretched, and it was as if a switch turned. He groaned, moved forward and grabbed her, pulled her closer. His mouth descended hard—demanding—hot. Devouring her with his passion.

She twined her arms behind his head, grabbing his hair and holding him there. She opened her mouth to his. His hands grabbed her bottom, molding her so close to him.

God help her, she moved against him, matching his body plane for plane while the tingles within her became a roaring fire. His hands shot to her suit, ripping open the buttons as hers reached for his, tearing at the cloth. Soft pops sounded as his buttons flew to the floor, tearing from his uniform. Once she had his suit open, she touched his chest, and he stilled, ripping his mouth from hers, sucking in a deep breath.

She smiled. "Like that, do you, grease boy?"

"Oh yeah. But not as much as you're going to like this," he countered. His hands found her breasts through her serviceable white cotton bra and pushed away the cups.

He touched her skin, and it was her turn to gasp at the sensation of his hands against her bare flesh. Her nipples tightened almost painfully, and he cupped her breasts, flicking them with his thumbs. His mouth found the sensitive skin at her neck and nuzzled. Her head was thrown back as she lost herself in the whirl of emotions that zinged like lightning through her body.

"Oh God, Raven," she moaned.

She pushed blindly against his chest, once the bed dipped below her. She needed to feel the warmth of his body, rubbed her hands up and down his chest. Jemma was pleased to find it smooth and hairless, while she slid her fingertips over his exposed flesh. He muttered a curse against her skin while letting go of her and stripped the rest of her clothing off her.

He kissed and laved each inch revealed with his magic mouth. She was mindless by the time he had her naked upon the bed. She writhed beneath his knowing fingers as they trailed over her nude body.

He sat back on his heels as she opened her eyes, reached for him, and pushed the open jacket off his shoulders. She reached down and opened the snaps on his pants. "My turn," she whispered, slowly crawling to her knees. Her fingers fumbled, and he brushed them away and looked at her, the blue of his eyes so deep she felt she would probably drown.

"Be sure that this is what you want with me, Jemma, because *Eshra* knows if we go any further I won't be able to stop."

She stilled at his husky words. Once more she reached toward him.

He stopped her fingers. "I love you, Jem. I have since the first moment I saw you, but I won't settle for anything less than forever. I want everything with you." His voice was filled with an emotion she shied away from.

"Raven, I want this now, with you." She looked at him and watched his face cloud with disbelief and hurt.

"Do you, Jem? Do you want the emotion or just the sex? If you want everything with me, then I want to be here with you. However, I get the feeling you just want the brief, quick high. That isn't enough for me." He looked at her, and she got the uncanny feeling he was reading her mind, seeing the truths she tried to hide from herself.

"Raven...I want what I can have with you." She faltered, seeking the words to tell him that she wanted the emotional experience for the short while she knew this would last. An ache started somewhere in her chest. Couldn't he see she was giving him everything she had in her? Her heart splintered, realizing he was going to leave her. *You're such a coward. Give in and you might find forever.*

"No, Jemma. It isn't enough for me." He backed away and turned around, his face and eyes distant. "I'll leave you to get dressed." Then he left her naked and empty in the cold room.

Chapter 8

Raven waited for Jemma in the sitting area, listening. His heart beat like a drum as he thought over his actions in the bedroom. The one woman he had dreamed of lying naked on his bed and he'd walked out.

Barsha! He wasn't sure if it was his not-so-hard-earned reputation that made her wary of a commitment to him or something deep within her throwing up the walls, but at this stage, it was taking every ounce of his willpower not to go in there, stop her from dressing, and throw her down on the bed to make delicious love to her.

His mind told him that showing her exactly how much he wanted her would only reinforce the temporary nature of their connect. "I won't do that to us." He stood still, straining to hear the sound of footsteps entering his living area.

The leash he held tight, the determination to do the right thing, was the merest thread— fragile and ethereal. If he gave in to his desire, then he'd never be sure that the commitment to him was lifelong and enduring.

No, he needed to wait for her to catch up to his level of devotion to her. Still, his arousal hurt, his body aching with unfulfilled desire. His heart beat in his chest hard and fast, his body warm from hers— not to mention the taste of her on his mouth lingered, reminding him of what he'd walked away from.

He looked at his wrist chrono, all the while listening for the rustle of clothing, straining...*nothing. Silence.* The time increased, and he broke, turning in the direction of the sleeping area, cracking open the door. Knocked. No response from within.

He knocked again, and this time his pulse rate increased, but not due to arousal. He entered the room, and instantly he knew it was empty. She'd left. He checked the sanitary unit, but it was also empty. *Barsha*! She was gone. She'd found the other door from his suite.

He kicked the bed in frustration. "This was not how I planned for the day to go." He'd wanted to show her that they could be together, get to know one another, without sex getting in the way until they both wanted the same thing—the lifetime commitment he craved with her.

He wanted her to enter into communion with him. He knew she understood the concept; after all, not only had Duvall married Mellissa—and what an archaic concept that was—but they had also communed, the accepted contractual understanding that was lifelong and binding.

He stalked back into his sitting room, throwing himself upon the seat where they had sat in companionable ease not so long ago. *Now what do I do? How will she react if I go after her? Should I give her time to think the relationship thing over?* He dropped his head into his hands as his eyes closed.

He sat there a long time.

✪ ✪ ✪ ✪

Jemma hurried back to her cabin, thankful that she didn't see anyone she knew on the way. She was upset, stomach churning over what had transpired in Raven's cabin. She knew he didn't understand that she wasn't a keeper. *Why didn't I just think before opening my mouth?*

The minute she thought that, though, she answered herself. Even a short-term relationship deserved honesty from the outset. Sure, she hadn't intended to hurt him—there was a quality to Raven that she couldn't help wanting to be close to—but he wanted forever, and she just couldn't do that to him.

"I told him up front." Why didn't he see?

Her leg still hurt as she moved quickly and silently down the corridor. At her cabin she palmed the reader and was grateful that soon she'd be returning to the *Star of Ishtar*.

"I'm such a failure!" Her life was one disaster after another. Right now she'd fucked up any chance of a relationship with Raven and had to account for her missing craft.

She sat down to begin tapping out her report for Vors, who would no doubt carpet her for losing her ship. Jemma didn't query her need to get busy, all she focused on was the activity which kept her mind from dwelling on yet another mistake. The words blurred before her, so Jemma closed her eyes, letting the silence balance her, but for once, it didn't work.

The silence stretched, and the bone-deep loneliness she worked hard to ignore seeped into her pores. "I have a lot of experience of that." The ache in her chest was sharp, and biting her lip, she stifled the sobs that wanted to erupt.

Perhaps she should start thinking about what options would be open to her, in case Vors decided she was a liability and the disciplinary action included a discharge. Her throat clogged, but she'd never been one to ignore reality, so Jemma kept on considering her choices. Better to prepare for the worst, she told herself, and went back to working on her report.

She unwound fingers that had instinctively curled and noted the crescent-shaped indentations that her nails had left in her palms. *Deep breaths, close eyes, and think! Concentrate on what you are, how you're strong and resourceful.* The mantra didn't work as it usually did, but she opened her eyes, straightened her shoulders, and forced back the tears.

Over the next few days, Raven tried many times to engage Jemma through meals, appointments with Elara, and even going so far as to appeal to Mellissa for help. Nothing worked. Each time he contacted Jemma via desk screen, he found she either dodged the contact or had already eaten, been wherever, or was busy completing a task.

By the end of the third day, he was climbing the walls in frustration. He had reached his last chance, the day before she returned to active duty, and he needed to find some sort of resolution to the empty limbo he inhabited. He trudged up to Elara's office, formulating plans as to how he could breach the wall Jemma had built around her heart.

The door whooshed open ahead of him, and he looked up to see Jemma leaving the office. He watched as she bade Elara goodbye and turned. She obviously hadn't seen him, and he waited quietly until the door closed behind her.

"Jem, is everything okay?"

"Raven! You startled me!" Her hand rose to her throat as she stepped back.

"Sorry about that. But I'm glad I ran into you. Join me for a coffee?"

"Well, you know, I'm trying to put the final touches on my report before the meeting..." Her voice trailed off as she looked at him.

"We really need to talk, and sooner is much better than later. Come on. We'll go to my office, where we can't be disturbed." He grasped her arm, not giving her a chance to argue as he propelled her forward. The muscles of her arm tensed beneath his hands, and he thanked every deity he could think of that the chance to fix this mess had come his way. The whole time he was aware that she had not answered his first question.

"I really don't—"

He steered her toward the door of his office and swiped his palm. "No, I know you don't, but we can't continue like this. This is such a small ship and we need to be able to work together without you feeling the need to avoid me."

He worked to keep his voice calm. The words he'd practiced in the last twelve hours slipped easily from his tongue. Jemma relaxed as she moved away from him, nodding. She looked pale and listless, as if she hadn't slept or eaten well since their interlude. Perhaps she had felt the effects as much as he had, and that gave him hope.

"Look, Raven, I don't want to hurt your feelings. I did tell you that forever isn't something I can do, and I meant it. Whatever you're seeking in a life partner... It's just not in me. I don't know the first thing about forever relationships and what you see is exactly all there is."

His gut clenched, but he had prepared himself for whatever she said. He'd let her get it all out, then he'd explain his feelings. He just hoped he wasn't reading all of this wrong.

"I never lied to you, Raven. Not once. If that causes you an issue, I can't fix it, because it isn't about me." Her brittle voice told him just how much she suffered, and a pain shafted through his chest.

He rocked back on his heels, listening to what she was saying. In that instant, he understood—she didn't think she had value or worth. Her abandonment as a child and the thought that she had been abandoned again as an adult at the academy had reinforced the concept that she was valueless. Rather than take the chance of further abandonment, she chose to be alone.

Barsha! This was going to be more difficult to overcome than just explaining his feelings to her. He needed to talk to Elara. A black pit of despair filled his belly. How could an amazing woman like this not see? How could she not know that her value was above the moon and the stars to him?

"Jem, let me arrange dinner. We can just have dinner and see where this goes. Can we do that?"

She looked surprised at the change of tack, the suspicion on her face hurting him, but it occurred to him that if he wanted to go forward, he would need to slow it down, accept the small steps. Not push any kind of a physical relationship right now.

He made a mental note to talk to Elara about the best way to proceed. She had access to information that would make this so much easier to deal with.

"Only dinner?" she queried, those beautiful eyes looking at him warily.

He wanted to laugh. He accepted the step forward—a small one, but he felt like he had won the most amazing prize.

"Just dinner, and we can see what happens next." He watched her intently. The stiffness in her body seemed to melt away slightly. He wanted so much more, but his head told him to slow down. "Come on, sit down and I'll make you a coffee if you want. No strings," he reassured her quickly.

She smiled, and once more the flash of beauty made his throat catch. He clamped down on the emotion. Slow was the key, he reminded himself.

"Yeah, that would be great."

He eased away from her and reached for the carafe, pouring them each a mug of the strong, hot brew.

⭐ ⭐ ⭐ ⭐

Jemma pulled on her flight uniform, feeling like a fraud. Whoever heard of a combat pilot without a ship? God damn!

What would happen now? The day that Duvall had met her and Raven in the mess, he'd said there was a change of plans. What could go wrong now?

She ran a hand through her hair and noted the trembling. Damn! She should have been able to pull the *Raptor* back up rather than focus on ejecting, then she wouldn't be in this position. Well, there was no time like now, she reminded herself, knowing that she had to be on time to Duvall's office.

The door pinged, and she started. "Identify," she commanded of the unit tersely. "Fraser, Raven."

She puffed out her cheeks as the computer gave the identity of the man waiting on the other side of the door. She gave the "open" command. Her stomach flip-flopped as she thought about the coming dinner date. She trembled at the thought but thrust it aside, wondering why Raven would be at her door right now.

"Raven, what are you doing here? We're due in the captain's office in less than ten minutes." Her voice was firm as she queried him.

"I thought we should go together. You know, first day back and... Well, I just wanted to say good morning." He looked almost innocent with a bland expression on his face, wearing a freshly pressed uniform, his face clean-shaven, and his wonderful blue eyes twinkling.

Suspicion rose inside her. He leaned in, and for just a minute she thought he was about to kiss her. She leaned away as he turned to drop a quick peck on her cheek. Her heart dropped.

Jemma told herself she wanted this disappointment—forever wasn't on her list of things to do or expect, and he was a forever kind of guy.

"Well then, let us 'once more unto the breach' go," Jemma quoted from memory with a small smile before indicating that he should lead the way. Never before had it occurred to her that she would need or use a Shakespearean quote she'd learned in school. She shrugged her shoulders at the odd turn life had taken.

Raven shook his head with a confused smile then moved into the room. They walked together, neither seeming to be in a rush, so she relaxed slightly as they moved down the metal planking. The cold air raised goose bumps on her arms the closer they came to the door—or was it the nerves she refused to acknowledge? She raised her hand to the palm print, and the door slid soundlessly open.

Captain Duvall McCord sat waiting in his office. Elara, Grayson, Chowd, and even Mellissa already filled the conference table in front. She looked back to see Raven was as confused as she was. *Why was everyone here?*

"Good morning, Jemma and Raven. Come join us. I am about to take a direct link from Admiralty."

Jemma started. Were they going to court martial her for the loss of the craft by Interspace Link? Surely that wasn't normal? Panic rose in thick, oily waves, leaving her stomach clenching. Raven placed his hand on her shoulder; obviously, she'd been radiating her discomfort, and the hand upon her shoulder not only grounded her, but gave a measure of reassurance.

"I don't…" Jemma couldn't help the weakness, and she leaned into Raven, seeking his touch. His warmth and nearness supported her, and she soaked up his strength.

"In a moment. You two grab a seat, and we can begin." Duvall indicated two empty seats at the conference table, and Jemma gingerly made her way over and sat down, with Raven taking the seat beside her. The glances their way betrayed interest in their togetherness.

Reading each face, she was sure they weren't hiding some negative emotions. *How can you be so sure?* But there wasn't any answer to be gained.

The screen at the head of the table flickered briefly, then the face of Admiral Elphin filled the area. "Good morning, all. We're here to discuss the issue of Crick Sur Banden making attacks on the Alpha Star Colony. As you would be aware, Captain McCord was originally required to travel with the fleet through to ASC, offering firepower should the fleet be challenged. However, in the last several months, the attacks have not only increased in frequency, but also in severity."

He paused as if waiting for someone to interrupt.

"In fact, we've received intelligence that causes us great concern," he continued. "It has been suggested that Crick Sur Banden has achieved a foothold on the planet. We believe the Alpha Star Colony is his preferred target for a number of reasons, including the current boom resulting from the mining of the Duschem mineral. We believe he has decided to focus on the mining sectors initially to slow down the Earth Empire's ability to use the raw mineral in the energy matrix, as well as the use by the Ru'Edan in a refined form to increase shielding capacity of their ships. As a result, the War Council has met and your mission has now changed. You are required to travel with all due speed to the Alpha Star Colony. I believe, Captain, that you have recently had a run-in with them?"

"Yes, sir. There was an issue with the energy matrix supports, which required us to drop out of the fleet and undertake repairs. Pilot Cardnew sustained serious injuries in the defense of the *Elector* and her craft was lost in the battle with the Phobos pirates. Furthermore, we have proof that Crick is working with them and actively attacking ships, most likely to damage our ability to transport goods and equipment to the various sectors along this route. We've forwarded a copy of her report to Commander Vors, and I ensured a copy was sent to you as well. We have managed to hold on to the shuttle, though it also sustained damage in the skirmish."

"You've lost your fighter? I will need to check that report, Captain." Elphin's gray, bushy brows narrowed together as he digested this information. His tone was terse.

"Yes, sir, although I would like to point out that only her exceptional skills kept the *Elector* from direct attack and an attempt at boarding by the Phobos pirates." Duvall looked uncomfortable with this, sparing a quick glance her way.

Jemma sat a little taller in her seat. If the Admiral and council were going to carpet her, she would accept whatever they threw at her.

"Fine, I'll review the report and contact you from there." His tone became dismissive of the information presented. "Your new mission is to infiltrate Crick Sur Banden's base on Alpha Star Colony, retrieve our operative, who I believe has been compromised, and if possible get me a couple of the spook ships the pirates are using."

He dragged a hand through his shaggy mop of hair.

"I also need you to clear out the Ru'Edanians that continue to cause us issues. You have authorization to do whatever it takes to make the area safe for the incoming fleet. Destroy their transmitters and sweep the area of ears and eyes. I need this completed before the fleet arrives, and time is running out. We have a senior diplomat traveling within the fleet who also needs to enter into final negotiations for the final cease-fire agreement between the Empire and the Ru'Edan. This must go smoothly, Captain."

"Yes, sir," Duvall answered quickly.

"In addition to those orders, Duvall, no more visitors are to be brought back with you." His voice betrayed a hint of dry humor. "It played hell with the council and my digestion last time. Thankfully, the last time you brought back people who have committed to the Empire. I'm not so sure next time will be so positive though." He grinned with this final comment, and Jemma was perplexed.

Raven looked at her with something akin to worry on his handsome face. What was this discussion about? Did Duvall catch hell for bringing her and Mellissa forward in time?

"Sir, I have a few questions," Duvall started.

"Yes, I thought you would," Elphin responded, and not for the first time, Jemma wondered about the unspoken relationship between McCord and the Admiral. It had been whispered at the academy that Elphin had personally chosen Duvall to become his protégé.

"How will we know the infiltrator?" Chowd was the first to question.

"Chowd, good to see you. I have sent a coded intel briefing through to the captain. It has all the information you will require for making the identification, including codes that will override certain information sources. However, it's likely he'll have jammed any ability to transmit direct to the planet, which means you'll need to find an alternative method until you can turn off the jamming device. Duvall, we need Chowd and Raven on this expedition. You are personally to remain on board the craft at all times. We will need your steady hand working with Grayson to pull this off."

Duvall frowned and Jemma sat forward, looking for any subtleties and nuances that would give a hint as to why the *Elector* crew were being given such a high-level mission.

"Yes, sir," Duvall replied. "We'll need to make alterations to the shuttle to ensure it gets in unseen."

"I have specifications for some modifications that'll be required to stay under the radar, as well as the holes in the radar that can be utilized. Cardnew, do you think you could handle flying a spook?"

"Admiral, I believe I could bring one back for you, if that is what you are enquiring about." Her words were stiff. Under the table, she felt Raven grab her hand.

"Right. Duvall, I'll leave you to brief your people. Once the mission is underway, you know to keep radio silence. I'll need confirmation of mission commencement. Other than that, I don't want to hear from you until the mission is completed. Be on guard. It'll be dangerous, and while your team is the best, things can still go wrong. Our information points to Crick Sur Banden personally overseeing this operation. Look for the encoded transmission in the next hour. Elphin out." With that, the screen darkened.

Chapter 9

The room was silent as every member of the crew in the office thought about Admiral Elphin's parting words.

Jemma spared a quick glance around the table, noting Mellissa and Duvall both grimacing. Never had she been privy to such a briefing, and she knew that the Admiral's parting words were not the norm. As nothing more than a lowly combat pilot, her briefings had always taken place in the flight room, given by her commander, Vors. She had met the captain of the *Star of Ishtar* only when she joined the crew and since then, the captain had kept his distance, a distance appropriate for those of the junior officers and pilots. She understood and accepted the privilege of involvement in a briefing of this type.

In the back of her mind, the knowledge that she could die on this mission bloomed. For the first time, she felt a stirring that maybe there was more out there for her, more than being disposable to the world, and that unsettled her. She pushed that to the side to concentrate on the briefing.

"Grayson, how soon can you plot the new course?" Duvall, his face as hard as granite, pushed his chair out from the table, standing purposefully before striding around his office, the plush carpeting swallowing his footsteps.

Palm units were now open and in use by Grayson, Chowd, and Duvall. Raven let go of her hand as he picked up his small unit from where it lay on the table. His blunt fingers flew quickly over the screen as he pulled up schematics and logistical algorithms.

"Captain, I believe within the hour we should be able to set course," Grayson muttered as he flicked a setting. "It may necessitate traveling through the beta hyperspace though. I believe it would be the fastest route, but we need to check that the weapons arrays were fortified sufficiently during the building of *Elector* to make that safe."

Duvall stopped. "Yes, the last ship that tried to use that beta hyperspace found that the arrays were totally destroyed, and they were the lucky ones. The ones that didn't make any preparations…"

He spread his hands expansively, and Jemma knew exactly what he alluded to. They'd been told in training that the remains of those ships littered the hyperspace channels.

"Check the specs and get back to me." Duvall looked at Raven. "I take it the repairs to the matrix will be able to handle hyperspace?"

"Captain, you couldn't tell it wasn't the original work," commented Raven. "The only thing is I need to check is that there is sufficient backup power should anything go wrong with the matrix. The last thing we need is a power outage either on entry or exit to the channel. Those transits must be clean transfers to protect our arrays."

Duvall nodded. "Chowd, when we're finished here, I need you and Jemma to stay behind to look over the information we have on the Alpha Star Colony. Jemma needs to find the most practical orbit for us and plot the entry of the shuttle, ensuring we stay under the radar. I need your help planning the raid into the base."

Jemma had heard the terrain of the Alpha Star Colony made flying difficult under normal conditions. She looked forward to the challenge of flying without detection.

Duvall stopped and looked at everyone at the table. He took a deep breath. "People, this is the most difficult mission for the *Elector* to date. Everyone needs to remain focused. I need you all back here at 1700 hours tomorrow, when we'll conduct a full briefing." He paused, spearing each member with a hard look. "This is the next step in shutting down Crick Sur Banden. We'll only have one chance, and we need to make it a winner. Dismissed."

Jemma felt Raven's hand grab hers and give a squeeze, then he was up out of his seat and gone. Suddenly, she felt very exposed. Jemma looked up to see both Duvall and Chowd watching her. She swallowed. Now it was time to prove that she could do this on her own. She sat up. "Okay, where do we start?"

Raven knew the members of the crew were wondering what was going on between him and Jemma. Hell, even he wondered right now. He strode purposely through the door and moved to the side, out of sight, waited for Elara to wander through the door, and quietly signaled to her. She gave him a wary look, and he motioned for her to join him.

The others walked by, casting glances in his direction, but he ignored them. He had something he needed to find out, and the sooner he started on an appropriate path, the sooner he could start his renewed campaign with Jemma.

"Elara, I need to talk to you, privately." He motioned toward the corridor that led to his office.

She looked at him with a narrowing of the brows, but she followed him without question. Once they entered his office, he said, "Door, engage locks."

"Locks engaged," the disembodied computer voice confirmed.

"Please, Elara, sit down. Would you like a coffee?" A flick of his wrist indicated the carafe he reached for.

"Yes, a coffee would be lovely. What is this about, Raven?"

He reached over and placed the cup into her outstretched hands. "It's about Jem." Elara opened her mouth, and he waved a hand before she could go any further. "I know, patient confidentiality and all that, but seriously, I've been thinking about the issues with her anger. I think she has a problem with self-esteem." He watched as her eyes widened. "Hear me out, okay? It's been rattling around in my head for the last few days."

Raven gulped down some coffee, needing something to engage his mind while he struggled to find a way to begin.

"She engages in risk-taking activities, cuts herself off from everyone who cares about her, she keeps telling me she doesn't know how to do forever." He sat down heavily. "I think she thinks she's even expendable." He looked down and breathed heavily.

"Ohhh." The way Elara dragged out the words betrayed her surprise. "Well now, that certainly is an interesting conclusion. Here I am the SurgiTech and yet you're making a diagnosis based on your...what? Gut instincts?" She cocked her head and he waited, fingers tapping on the tabletop. "This isn't a diagnosis to take lightly, Raven. This is something we usually notice in the early school years. We screen and engage in therapy before it becomes a problem."

He watched her face screw up as she pulled out a palm screen unit, tapping information into it. He waited quietly as her face clouded. "Damn. You could be onto something there, but if that's the case..." Her voice trailed off.

"Yeah. It's a big call. But if that is an issue for her, then what do we do? How do we work with this?"

"I don't have experience with this. I mean, I'm a SurgiTech, not a PsychTech."

"I know, but it makes sense, right? She's a loner, doesn't trust anyone easily. She likely even has abandonment issues."

"Abandonment? Was she?"

He nodded slowly. "Yeah. Left in an orphanage as a baby, then compounded by the way she was left at the academy. It makes sense, doesn't it?"

Elara swiped her hand over her brow. "Yes, it does."

Raven gulped down the sick feeling that rose. "Even when she was sick, she didn't alert anyone. Elara, I love her, but I don't have the skills to fight this on my own." She blinked at his words, but her forged on. "I need your help to make her see that she's beautiful, worthwhile, and worthy. That she can be loved and have forever. I did some investigating of the known indicators. But I don't know what needs to be done. I know with children, we have therapy groups and drugs, but obviously, we don't have that here, or even the knowledge. I was hopeful that even if you didn't have experience, perhaps you could find appropriate treatment."

"Raven, firstly she has to understand that there is an issue. Accept it. Until she does, it's just a waste of time." She screwed up her face. "Look, leave it with me. I'll see if there is some way to engage her and research the indicators and treatment. Until then, say nothing to her.

Nothing I can do will help if she is expecting some kind of interference by me." Elara reached a hand over and placed it on his.

"Yeah. Sure." There didn't seem much else to say.

"Leave this to me, and I'll get back to you. Without details though. Patient confidentiality and all that." She smiled, took a deep draught of the coffee, then handed the cup back. "Time you made another pot, I think. This one's a little bitter, even by your standards."

Elara rose and started to leave.

As she reached the door, she turned. "You know, if it's any consolation, I think she loves you too. She doesn't understand that just yet, but I'm pretty sure of it. Just hang in there, okay?"

"Thanks, Elara. Let me know if you find anything or if I can help. Door, unlock." Elara left the room, but Raven sat for a few minutes pondering the assurance she had given him. By *Eshra*! He certainly hoped she was right.

With a sigh, he rose and moved toward his desk screen, engaging the comm system. "Fraser to engineering. I'll be in my office for some time. If you need me, ping me through the system. Fraser out." He sat staring at the screen, knowing it would take some time for him to focus and concentrate on his role.

✪ ✪ ✪ ✪

1700 hours the next day came around mighty quickly, Jemma thought as she lowered herself into the seat at the conference table. She noted that Raven was missing and wondered where he could possibly be.

The door chimed, and he strode in. For a moment she saw nothing but the handsome man she desired. Sure, he was a little grimy with his hair plastered to his head, but even with that, he looked so good she just wanted to hold his hand and accept what he was promising. She was scared though, she finally admitted to herself. What if it didn't work out? What if she opened herself and it failed? Could she survive that?

She shook herself mentally; this wasn't the time or the place. She turned swiftly and focused on Duvall as he sat down.

"Now that we're all here, let's get started. As you're aware, we need to get to the Alpha Star Colony as early as possible. Raven, how did you get on with looking at the effects of the hyperspace on the array?" Duvall asked.

Raven looked up from his palm screen, which he'd clearly synchronized with the screen in Duvall's office. He flicked up some schematics of the *Elector*, showing the areas under discussion.

"I went back through the specs and ran a couple of simulations. We should be fine as long as we remain at a constant speed and within the central trajectory. I would be concerned, though, if something slowed us down, or an anomaly caused us to deviate from this narrow corridor. I had Grayson check the charts for possible issues."

"Thanks, Raven. Yes, I investigated the hyperspace route and I believe we can set a course that is clear of interference." A star map flickered on the screen so that they could see the proposed route. "It'll take an extra day to allow for that, but we can cut our travel time to a week by taking this route." Grayson used a pointer to track a path on the screen. "Under normal circumstances, traveling in clear space, we would expect to arrive in two weeks."

He shook his head and gazed at the people gathered.

"My major concern with this route is that we'll be using the hyperspace corridor that skirts past a known black hole zone," Grayson continued. "There are a few more projections I need to check, but I believe we can traverse it safely, although as Raven has indicated, we will need to remain in the center of the corridor." He cleared his throat. "I have also been talking with Jemma and Chowd about the amount of time it would take to run the modifications on the shuttle to increase its speed and stealth capabilities in order to complete the dirtside portion of the mission." Grayson looked in turn at both Jemma and Chowd.

When Chowd indicated his willingness to allow Jemma to deliver the vital information, she was uncomfortable with the responsibility, although sure of her facts.

"We looked at the range of modifications that are required." Images once more flickered on the screen as she held a small palm screen, flicking the images up. "We'll need Raven in on these modifications, but we believe that a week is sufficient time for us to complete the necessary retrofitting. They aren't large additions...just a little fiddly. We'll need to reconfigure the shielding harmonics and remove the extra fitout we put in place to deal with the pirates. Once they're removed I can be sure we'll stay under the radar during the entry sequence."

She took a breath and looked around. Everyone seemed comfortable with her report. She continued. "There seems to be a blindspot at about twenty-five thousand feet in the schematics of the radar used at the base, according to what we've ascertained. We ran a couple of simulations, and it seems that as long as we can remain in that range, give or take say twenty feet, we should be able to sneak through without them marking us. It'll require some difficult flying though to make that work, and most important of all, it will have to be manually flown. To get in, I'll need a narrow entry profile and it'll mean at a speed most ships couldn't manage."

She swiped her hand over her eyes, knowing exactly the risks she was going to be taking. "No computer auto-flight program could manage with the constant changes of the landscape and the safety protocols would kick in, moving us up or down, depending on the terrain. We'll be flying outside the acceptable parameters, but I'm sure..." She stopped and drew a breath, calming herself. "I know I can manage it. The biggest issue will be if they get a visual confirmation from a ship or watcher."

Jemma looked at Raven, and he smiled slightly.

"We also need to fit transmission and communications dampeners to the shuttle so that, should we be seen, they can't alert those at their base via any known electronic or digital interface system." Jemma finished her report and felt Raven's hand once more on her thigh. She accepted his support gratefully and released the tension she had built up during the delivery, clenching and unclenching her hands.

"Sounds like you have that organized," answered Duvall. "Do you have all the equipment and resources you require?"

Raven answered in his quiet but firm voice, "We'll know shortly. I have my staff running through the requirement lists now and they'll have a report, I would imagine, within the next half hour."

"Once we're underway, there'll be no further chance for requests of equipment, so be sure to finalize it quickly. If I know within the hour, I can send a requisition to the Admiralty and they should arrive by morning on the intercepting shuttle from Mino. Any questions or queries?" He looked around at the members of the crew. "No? Then moving on to the next aspect of the mission—Meredith Gentry will be joining us in the morning."

Duvall looked at Jemma.

"You may not remember Meredith. She was with us on that mission when you joined us, as Communications and Encryption Support, a position she'll be filling again. I expect her arrival at 0600 hours. Apparently, the Admiral thought she would be best with us, to continue with her work as the most skilled encryption and decryption professional dealing with Crick Sur Banden and in the Ru'Edanian techniques. She'll be invaluable in offering backup support, tracking the usual transmission channels to and fro. The Admiralty is giving us every resource they can to ensure we get this bastard.

"Mellissa will research into exactly what has been going on in terms of the attacks on Alpha Star Colony, their frequency, and patterns to extrapolate. We need to know where the attacks have taken place, how many mining operations have been compromised, and to what extent and exactly what firepower has been utilized. We can collate that data to help us finish the rogues, hopefully once and for all."

Mellissa nodded at the instructions.

"Elara, it's difficult to know what will be needed on the ground in terms of medic support, so you'll be providing support after the mission is complete to the populace, the companies on Alpha Star Colony, and the medics. Meredith is bringing a range of SurgiTech items with her and medications, which we feel will be the most necessary. You'll triage as necessary until the hospital ship and the rest of the fleet has arrived. Once the mission is complete, we can transport any emergency cases that need attention to the hospital ships."

Duvall's face shined with the light of battle, and it was clear he looked forward to the task ahead.

"Now then, I suggest we run an update briefing at 1100 hours tomorrow. By then we should have started our tasks. Requisition lists need to be on my desk screen within the hour. If they aren't here by then, you don't get anything." He quickly looked around the room. "Dismissed."

Everyone filed from the room.

Raven was waiting for Jemma outside the door as she left

Duvall's office. He held out his hand, and after a quick pause, she accepted it.

"You did well, Jem. Good. You were focused and knew what you were talking about." He smiled at her, and while she wasn't sure where this was going, she felt the muscles in her face smile in response.

"I was so nervous, but this is a great crew that Duvall has around him. It's no wonder Mellissa feels comfortable here." She ducked her head, and Raven placed a finger under her chin and quietly pushed it back up. He looked at her intently.

"Do you? Feel comfortable too, I mean?" His voice was low, and a curl of heat started in her belly.

"Yeah, I do," she whispered.

"Good. I want you to feel that way." He smiled softly, and she felt like she would melt into a puddle at his feet. He looked at her for a minute longer, his gaze dropping to her lips, and just when she was sure he would close the distance and kiss her, he let go, stepped back, and smiled. "Join me for dinner?"

She paused for a minute. Doubts chased around in her mind, but ultimately, the time had come to take a risk. She knew it. She could protect herself and her heart and push this man away, or she could take the chance and see where it led.

"Yes, I'd like that very much," she whispered.

His eyes widened slightly, then a triumphant expression crossed his face for just an instant. If she had blinked, she would have missed it, but she was so pleased she hadn't. He controlled the expression into a grin.

"Great, I'll be by your cabin at 1900." He paused as if he wanted to say something, but he didn't. He just gave her a wink and turned.

She slowly turned to make her way back to the cabin. The day seems much brighter, she thought, with a soft smile on her face.

Jemma reached her cabin, and the high remained. *Raven.* He remained an enigma to her mind. He wanted everything, and now the rules had changed and she was at sea. What was his tactics and how the hell was she supposed to deal with this?

She needed advice, but not from Mellissa. That smacked of talking to the boss's wife, not to mention the fact that she wasn't ready to resume their old friendship just yet. She felt it would be unfair and awkward to Mellissa, who owed her first loyalty to Duvall, to be burdened with Jemma's confusion about another officer.

Jemma sat slowly, thinking. The only other person was Elara. No other person came to mind and she needed someone, anyone, to talk to. She took a deep breath and reached for the comm, hand hovering over the button uncertainly. As the SurgiTech and a doctor, she seemed the best option when there was no one else. It made sense to go to her for advice. Jemma depressed the button and waited for the screen to blink and show Elara.

"Hi, Jemma. How can I help you?"

"Umm, I've got a problem and need some advice. Are you free now if I pop up to your office?" She could hear rustling in the background. "I mean, if you are busy, I can arrange a different time."

"No, Grayson and I were just looking at some details, but he's leaving now. Give me, say, five minutes?" Elara said.

"Sure, sounds good."

The screen winked off, and she sat looking at it. Well, that was the first step. She stood uncertainly and headed to the sanitary unit, freshening up then making her way to the SurgiTech suite.

Leaving her cabin, she moved along the decking, listening to the tap of her feet on the metal. Before she knew it, she stood outside the SurgiTech suite. Jemma swiped her palm, not allowing herself time to think. She felt confused and uncomfortable, and heat rose in her cheeks.

"Come in, Jemma!" Elara called to her as the door silently slid open, and she could see her sitting at her desk screen quickly tapping commands. "Make yourself comfortable and tell me what I can do for you today."

She sat and for a moment just wondered what to say. *Where do you begin these types of questions?* "I have a problem. I don't know what to do." The words just tumbled out in a rush. "Raven...umm... wants a permanent relationship, and I just don't know...how to do it, I guess. I mean, I don't know anything about families and..." She stopped. *How do I say no one ever wanted me?* She struggled to hold herself together, because she realized she was shaking.

"You don't think anyone would want you? You don't think you know how to be a member of a relationship?" Elara finished the thought quietly, her face so full of understanding. Jemma was damn pleased there wasn't a trace of pity showing, just an understanding of her fears.

"Yeah." She blushed deeper and hotter than ever before, her skin radiating heat. "I mean, not that I want anyone to feel sorry for me, or anything like that. Because I've enjoyed the majority of my life..." She grimaced, realizing that sounded more like she expected to die.

Jemma hunted for her emotional center, settling the emotions that roiled in her gut. "It's just I don't know anything about long-term relationships and how to keep them alive." Her voice dropped to a whisper. "My relationships have always been hot and wild, but they burn out quickly. It's the way I've always lived my life. I've encouraged that even, but now? I want more, but don't know how to make that happen." She dropped her head into hands that shook, and her eyes burned.

"Jem, this is understandable, given your background. Can you tell me, did anything specifically happen, maybe when you were a child, that you think may have influenced this belief? Before you say anything, I have to explain that I'm not trained in this area, so this can only be one friend to another. Are you okay with that?" Suddenly Elara hunched down onto the floor next to Jemma, having moved silently from the other side of the desk. Elara touched her hand gently. "Jem?"

"I'm just feeling really silly." She sniffed. "Yeah, I'm fine with that. I didn't know who else to ask. I couldn't go to Mellissa, you know?" She raised her face to Elara. "But I feel something I've never felt before, and I don't want to hurt him." She gripped the arms of the chair, her heart thudding so loudly in her chest she was sure Elara could hear it. "I've always known what to do before. Whatever it takes has been the way I have lived and the consequences were usually pretty immaterial. But this time it's different. This is too important."

"I think knowing that you need help is a big step forward. But was there something that happened to you that made you feel you had no value?"

"The nuns knew who my parents were..." She stopped and

settled herself once more. "My parents were a nun and a priest. They had an illicit relationship, and I was the result." She whispered the admission, never having told anyone else that fact.

Her eyes burned, and she dipped her head to hide the liquid glint she knew Elara would see.

"They made sure I knew that what they did was wrong, that I should never have been born." God! How it hurt to share the most secret and worst thing she'd ever known about herself. "Mother Superior in particular used to make sure I never forgot. There was one time, I'd forgotten to do something—I can't even remember the infraction—and she lost it with me. Told me I was just as feckless and irresponsible as them."

She shook her head, trying to clear the emotion from the memory.

"She made it clear that they'd learned their lesson and didn't want anything to do with me and that I was only there because they'd begged, otherwise I would have been left in the streets. That was where I belonged, she said, not with God-fearing women. She knew every button and pushed them with great skill." There were traces of bitterness in her voice, and she looked away.

With her head dipped, she couldn't face the pity she expected to see, but Elara grabbed her face and pulled it back, her fingers digging into the soft flesh of Jemma's face. "She was wrong. Everyone counts. Everyone."

Jemma looked at Elara, beyond the scarring she could see on her face and hands and into the green eyes. There was no pity there, but a hell of a lot of anger.

"Nobody has the right to do that to a child. No matter who or what the parents were or did. No child should pay for the mistakes of adults."

She could see Elara struggling with her fury over the way she'd been treated.

"Jem, can we arrange a time, say tomorrow? I want to do some research and reading and we can discuss this in detail then. See what we can come up with? In the meantime, take it slow. See where it leads. Sometimes relationships burn hot and bright but disappear quickly because that's all they're meant to be. Others build slowly and are foundations to the real passion hidden from view—a bit like buried treasure."

Jemma blinked and watched as Elara grinned.

"Grayson and I took years, but Mellissa and Duvall's was quick, yet they're both working on making it last. Each is different with lumps and bumps along the way. But remember, if Raven wants a relationship with you, he sees the treasure hidden from everyone else."

"But what about all the other women from before? I heard there were lots of them," she whispered.

"Oh honey, you're going to have to talk to him about them. But I will tell you, he hasn't been around as much as he likes to make out. And you need to tell him about your history. Be open. Talk to him about everything, including the bitch Mother Superior. The only way a relationship can grow and bloom is with honesty, working together and sharing your weaknesses and strengths."

"What time do you want me here?" Jemma wiped away the few drops that had escaped her eyes with a quick swipe of her arm.

"Pop along here, say, 1200 hours, and hopefully I'll have some sort of an idea. Does that work for you?"

"Sure, that sounds good."

Jemma rose from her seat and was surprised when Elara grabbed her and gave a quick, hard hug. Jemma looked at this small woman who had experienced so much pain already herself and wondered at her capacity to give empathy and friendship.

"Maybe one day I can be like you, Elara." She certainly hoped so.

"Jemma, we all have our scars. Mine are visible, because that's what Crick Sur Banden did to me. Yours are hidden, emotional. They're just as debilitating in their own way though." With that, Elara released her and stepped away.

"Thanks, Elara. I'll see you tomorrow." She left the room quickly, mulling over what had been said.

Chapter 10

The door pinged, and Jemma started. It was Raven. She knew it in her bones even as she demanded the computer identify the person on the other side of the door.

"Fraser, Raven," the disembodied voice of the computer relayed to her.

She wiped sweaty palms down her legs and brushed her hair back as she stood and headed for the door. Jemma depressed the button that would open it and smiled uncertainly at Raven. Her breath fled though. He waited in his formal uniform, which molded to his chest and strong arms like a second skin. She felt untidy in her borrowed flight suit.

"Should I have worn my formal uniform? I don't have it—"

"You look beautiful just as you are," he assured her. "Now come with me. Dinner on the holo-deck is in order for us."

He took her arm as the door behind them whispered shut, and together they walked toward the small entrance at the end of the corridor. This man bemused and confused her. Every time she thought she knew what he was doing, he surprised her. They entered the room, he engaged the locks with a command, and she raised her brows.

"I don't want us interrupted. I asked Mellissa where you always wanted to go. She said Paris, so here we are." He indicated for her to look around, and to her amazement, he had recreated the most amazing aspect of Paris, the Eiffel Tower, just for her. The Eiffel Tower of the past, not the carefully shielded version that still exists in the future, showing the stresses of age. A table sat below it.

She turned surprised eyes on him. "How did you manage this?" she breathed.

"I'd do anything for you, Jem. This was easy. All I had to do was get the correct code from the holo-library and tell it what aspect I wanted. Arrange the dinner. Simple really, but I did it to show you, to let you know, I love you. I won't pressure you though. I know you need time, and we can take this as slow as we need to." In the dim light and breeze of a Paris evening, candles glittered, illuminating the glow in his eyes.

She leaned into him, and he opened his arms, holding her tightly to his body, letting her feel his resolve, she thought. It felt like home, or what a home would be like. She breathed in his scent, male and musky.

"Now, what would you prefer? Dinner first or dancing?" He grinned at her, and her heart flipped over as she moved away.

"I think dinner first might be a good idea," she responded huskily, and knew in her bones that tonight she needed to show him that he was different from all the others. Tonight, she promised herself, she'd tell him that he meant everything to her. She didn't know for sure yet if it was love, but she hoped so. *God, how I hope it is.*

He showed her to a chair, pulling out the white lacy seat for her, and she sat down, feeling clumsy in her flight suit once more. He looked so handsome in his formal black uniform that she practically melted right there.

The conversation that flowed was desultory. He told her stories about his time at the academy. He talked about his training as an engineer with the Empire. She learned that he'd served with Duvall and Grayson on the *Star of Ishtar*, together with Elara.

"I left the *Star* a couple of years ago, for the position of Senior Engineer on the *Vehemence*. Of course, when the Admiral contacted me about the *Elector* and explained everything concerning Corbin Jard and that he'd committed treason I wanted the position. I was grateful that Duvall offered it to me."

"Did you know him? Jard?"

Raven shook his head. "No. He came on after I left." "Oh." She couldn't think of anything else to say.

"During my time on the *Vehemence*, I got involved in the designing of the energy matrix system, helped with the prototype testing, which is why I was considered for the *Elector*."

"It's a marvelous technological breakthrough. Mind you, every day I'm still learning of new things and how to use them. Things you must think of as old hat." She took a sip of wine.

"I can't understand how you managed in the past. I mean even the most basic, ablutionary tasks, like cleaning your teeth, were hideously manual."

Jemma laughed. "Yeah, I have to say, using a pill to achieve that is a time saver!"

"What about school and growing up?"

His quiet question rang out like the peal of a bell. She bit her lip. "It wasn't half as much fun as yours. Tell me what you were like as a boy."

Jemma wasn't sure if she welcomed the change of subject at her marked evasion of his question, but she was grateful. She knew the time would possibly come when she would have to tell him everything, but for tonight, she needed to avoid those truths that hurt with each thought. She pushed that away and once more forgot herself in the charm of this handsome and impossible man who stole her breath with every heated glance.

He plied her with the finest Arturian wines then laughed at her first sight of the purple Bulois'Ja he had imported from Sonoran himself. The dishes of exquisite flavors and tenderness, which they took from the small heater box she hadn't noticed before. The Coq au Vin that evoked her senses and Creamy Vuvoltan fruits covered with the finest Gorvan creams, so light they almost disappeared from the tongue, dazzling the palate. The meal ended with them sharing a glass of Cerberus Port that had taken years to obtain and get through customs. Each drink had a tale, and he told them with laughter until her sides ached.

During the meal, he touched her arm from time to time, making a point or increasing her awareness of his closeness, and the gazes he let fall upon her warmed every cold part of her soul. By the end of the evening, she felt mellow in a way she had never been before, and when they stood, he took her in his arms.

Music swelled from all around, and she moved in his arms without qualm. Slowly they swayed from side to side, and it was natural that eventually her head would dip to his shoulder as his intoxicating scent filled her senses. He pulled her closer and rubbed a light hand up and down her back, his lips touching her skin briefly, scalding her with his heat.

"One day, I'll take you to Paris and we'll dance together under the Eiffel Tower," he whispered into her ear, "and make love in a little hotel overlooking the Seine."

His hands continued to move up and down her back. Each touch set off sparks of electricity that shocked her, and as the strains of the song died away, she pulled back just a little so she could see his face and could see herself reflected in his gaze. His eyes were soft, and she reached up, pulling his head down toward her mouth and lightly touching his lips with hers. It was a whisper of a kiss that melded their breaths into one. This time when they drew back from each other, their hands clasped.

She looked into his eyes. "No one has ever done something like this for me before." Her voice was soft and low.

"Then more fool them, sweetheart, because you deserve the best." With that he swooped, lifting her into his arms and striding to a chair to sit down with her on his lap.

Their mouths fused and tongues danced with each other's. Her hands reached up to clutch his hair and hold him close. His hands softly kneaded her flesh through the flight suit. She trembled as the frisson of excitement speared through her body.

Jemma pulled back slightly and caught her breath. "Raven?" Her voice was husky. "Raven, will you stay with me tonight?"

"Oh, Jemma, you have no idea how much I want to. But I don't think it's time just yet." He closed his eyes and trembled beneath her.

"Please, Raven. Stay with me. I want us to be together. I want to see where this goes." She waited, tense, hoping like hell he would understand what she was trying to say. It had taken everything she had in her, and if he said no, she just didn't know what she would do. Her stomach clenched with nerves.

He looked at her hard and long. Finally a smile worked its way to his face, and his eyes shined with a triumphant gleam. "You have no idea what you do to me. I will stay with you. Now and for as long as you want me."

He echoed her previous thoughts on their relationship, but her heart sang. He crushed her to him, his arms like bands circling her, holding tight. She could feel the thudding of his heart, and she closed her eyes.

"Are you ready to go then?" His voice was soft, but she caught the underlying question.

"Yes." She nodded as she said the word, her heart full to bursting as it beat a wild tattoo in her chest.

He eased her to the ground, took her by the hand, and headed to the door. "Holo-program end. Door open." His voice was gravelly, but he smiled at her. His eyes, so blue in contrast to the dull gray around them, glittered in the light of the corridor.

He led her quickly through the open door and along the corridor toward her cabin. They saw no one along the way, and she was grateful for no interruptions. They didn't need to go far and reached her cabin quickly. The shimmer of desire ran through her hotter and wilder than before. He pulled her into his arms and kissed her. She felt hot all over and scorched from the passion of his kiss.

"Are you sure?" he whispered against her lips.

"Yes." She palmed the door, and it whispered open, closing behind them once they stepped through. Before he could pull her back into his arms, she gave the command, "Door close and lock." Then there she was against him and the passion that rose, igniting within her.

His lips touched hers as his hands rose to frame her face. As he held her close to him, her eyes closed and the burn that licked at her insides seeped through her body. She moaned low in her throat, and he tore himself away long enough to shed his black jacket. Her eyes watched through narrow slits, her breathing hard as she reached out for him.

He grabbed her hands. "Sweetheart, you have no idea how sexy you are standing there watching me." His hands circled her hips, drawing her closer. "Feel how hot I am for you. Just you," he purred into her ear as he angled toward her jawline.

His lips touched the sensitive skin, feather-light and oh so arousing, and she shivered. She moved in his arms and felt shocks of electricity through her whole system. Her hands splayed over his shoulders, holding on to him as she angled her head back to allow him access to the flesh below her chin. Her mouth was open and eyes closed. She could feel his every touch and burned where their bodies connected. She let her hands run down his arms to his fingers, dragging them up to her breasts. She sucked in a breath and heard his gasp. Jemma raised her gaze to see his face tight with passion. His eyes glittered with desire.

"Raven, I want you. I need you," she whispered brokenly.

He covered her mouth with his. His tongue entered her mouth, smooth and warm, while her arms moved down his body to grasp his buttocks in her questing hands. She needed him and pulled him closer, so much closer. His erection jutted against the softness of her belly, and wet heat pooled between her legs. His hands left her breasts to find the buttons of her flight suit. Slowly he released her from the confinement. Raven pushed the suit down her body, touching his mouth to every inch of skin that he bared. She gasped and burned, standing in just bra and panties before him. Raven was on his knees in front of her, one hand inching slowly up her legs.

She backed away. "No, I want you naked. Now."

He stood and moved closer, and she swooped in, hands furiously tugging and pulling on his buttons. His uniform shirt gone, she tackled his pants next. Finally, dear God, she thought, he was totally naked and pulling at the clips of her bra, and it too was gone, flying over his shoulder to land somewhere in the dark recesses of the cabin. Her nipples puckered in the cool night air.

She hooked her fingers into her panties, trying desperately to get rid of them.

The drive of her body pushed her faster for the intimate connection. She needed to feel his naked body against her own. Raven moved, and they touched, skin to skin. Every glorious inch of his body warmed hers. Mouths met and clung once more. Hands moved up and down, touching skin.

Warm. Naked. All of him was arrayed for her to enjoy. The thought splintered as his hands cupped her breasts once more, slowly kneading the bare flesh and heightening her need. She reached between them and captured his length in her hand.

Then she pulled back from their kiss with a gasp. Jemma looked into his eyes, stroking him at the same time. "Come to bed with me and be mine."

Together they shuffled to the bed, and she noted he was shaking. "Jem, I don't think I can last much longer." His voice was hoarse with desire, his eyes closed as his breathing labored. "I need to be in you, now." His hands traced a path down to her core, and a finger pushed aside damp curls, explored, touched, and she cried out.

She tensed, the flesh hidden within pulsing with need. "No! I want all of you," she cried as the finger slid within her wet flesh once more.

"So ready. So wet," he muttered.

She caressed him harder and faster, her hand pumping him, and it was his turn to gasp. His hands moved away and grabbed the hand touching his erection, stilling it, his body bowed low, and he panted.

He pulled her hand away, threading his fingers through hers and pushing them above her head. His kiss now was furious and bruising, and she met it force for force. He moved over her, nudging her knees further apart. His tongue played with hers furiously as she felt the head of his erection at her entrance, and she whimpered.

The feel of him touching her so intimately set nerve endings singing with pleasure. *God!* She nearly came from the sensations he aroused, and finally, slowly, he slid within her, and she moaned into his mouth. They moved together. Faster. Harder. Their skin now glistened with perspiration, hands gripping each other tighter.

"Raven!"

Moans filled the air, and the scent of sex was pervasive. It heightened their passions to fever pitch. Her nipples brushed against his chest hairs, rasping the sensitized nubs further. She tore her mouth away and gulped air while she thrashed below him, head thrown back and totally lost in their shared passion. Once more he thrust, and lightning streaked through them. She tensed, feeling the throb of his release, and she lay there in his arms, shattered.

Once more the woman screamed, little more than a groan between crusted lips, and Crick Sur Banden grinned in glee. His work on the pain threshold of humans was coming along nicely. She had now lasted a full week, and though he knew she was weak, with a few days for recovery, he'd be able to continue his delightful work. His scientists had deserted him, thinking this aspect of his work untenable. He needed to know just how far he could punish those sneaking humans for the infraction of invading *his* space.

He turned to his second-in-command. "Make sure the staff have the girl fed and rested. I want to find out more about her abilities and skills when I am ready to work with her next time. Then meet me in the office. We have some planning to do." He turned and walked away. His softly shod feet were almost silent in the cavernous room.

He'd dallied here for several days longer than he had planned, but it was time for another incursion into the mining operations of the Alpha Star Colony and to capture yet another camp. He knew that would be the best way to draw out Duvall and the motley crew of the *Elector*, not to mention upset the plans of both the Ru'Edan traitors and humans. Once they had no access to the Duschem mineral, they would be weak. Then it would be time to make the final attack.

He would delight in that, in making them suffer and pay for the treachery they'd wrought —in particular, the one who was a traitor to his kind and to his house. His hands fisted at his sides. Who would have thought that the one he'd raised would betray him with the humans? Never mind, he'd see the error of his ways, and if not...well, he was expendable. Perhaps he should consider another concubine, someone young and fertile—maybe another Earth girl like the one he had taken before. The thought raced through his head, exciting him as he reached his office.

He poured an Arturian wine, sweet and full-bodied. The smell filled his nostrils. Truly, if those traitors had not sided with the humans, he would have enjoyed a regular supply. Such a shame he would need to repopulate that planet with his own people. Perhaps he would take one of the vineyards for his own base on Arturia IV and keep the owners as slaves so he could continue to enjoy the fine-quality wine.

His desk screen bleeped as he sat down, and the information waiting for him made him smile. The update from the Phobos pirates stated they had seen the *Elector* make for the hyperspace column. That was fine. They were probably already on the way to Alpha Star Colony. He smiled. His plans were coming together quite nicely.

His second-in-command made his presence known as he waited in the doorway. "My Lord? What would you have me do?"

He looked up. Now here stood a worthy warrior who completed everything the way he wanted it. He'd ordered him to kill his family as a show of loyalty, and it had been done. Obedience. Faithfulness. He would be rewarded.

"Prepare the shuttle. It's time for another incursion to Alpha Star Colony, and this time I want to lay a little trap for our Earthly friends. Make the girl ready to travel with us. I have an idea on what we can do with her." He slipped a small capsule into his mouth and smiled.

"Sir." He inclined his head, then raised again, waiting for further orders. "When do you wish to depart?"

"Tonight would be best, don't you think? Four days to arrive and enough time to prepare a welcoming party." He thought about it for a moment. "Yes, I think that would work. Go do it. Make sure you bring some medics for the girl and our warriors."

"As you decree, My Lord." The Ru'Edan warrior bowed his way out, and Crick Sur Banden sat nursing his wine.

He watched the rainbow of colors form in the wine, cast by the flickering light of the fire. "Time is coming, my son. You'll need to come home and make reparation. Learn to be obedient and faithful." He grinned at the picture he brought up on screen. His infiltrators had caught the image at the Communion celebration for Duvall McCord and the girl he had brought back from the past. In the background stood his son. In Crick Sur Banden's own mind, there wasn't any doubt that his son would return to him.

Chapter 11

Raven lay back, listening to Jemma sleep. The rhythmic sounds reminded him of her spirit; strong and steady despite everything she'd experienced. He hoped that sleeping with her was the right decision.

He flung an arm over his eyes. He had never been so ready or turned on in his life. He'd wanted her from the moment he had first met her. When he'd kept a watch over her while she attended the academy, staying away from her had been one of the hardest thing he'd ever done.

Now the Admiral had decided she should remain a member of the *Elector* crew, even if just for a short time. What would she do when that was over? The Admiralty frowned on relationships within the same ship, or more correctly, on battleships and the like, but in their instance, he was concerned that she might get deployed to the opposite end of the known galaxies. He huffed out a breath as the thoughts churned in his mind.

She moved in her sleep, and he spooned in behind her. He put his arm around her sleeping form, knowing they would need to get up in the next couple of hours. There would be no rest once this mission began, but for now he would take the lull to make this amazingly beautiful creature see her value to him and the other members of the *Elector*. Failure is no longer an option, he thought, closing his eyes.

✪ ✪ ✪ ✪

Something rubbed along the back of Jemma's head. "Go away," she grumbled, trying to pull the covers over her cold shoulders.

It rubbed again, and this time she batted it, her eyes still closed as she fought to recapture the erotic dream that fizzled away. The covers seemed to be slipping off, and the chill touched her skin. She tugged, but instead of covers, she found a hand.

"What..." She sat up quickly, opening her eyes. There in his glory was Raven, naked and grinning at her, hair rumpled and sleepy-eyed. "Oh my God! My dream has come to life...or I'm still asleep." The mumbles escaped from surprised lips.

Raven leaned forward, and she realized she too was naked. The events of last night filtered into her brain. He dropped a kiss on the end of her nose. "Good morning, my sleeping princess. I think we slept in a little and now we have a grand total of ten minutes to be dressed and, if not fed, then at least coffee'd before we have to meet Chowd at the shuttle." He smiled. "But before we do, you're beautiful, and I really hope we can recreate the magic of last night again later. Put on your thinking cap, because I'm leaning toward dinner in my office then maybe a nightcap in my cabin?"

She watched speechless as he stood up. *Tonight? Recreate last night?* The cataclysmic passion that had zinged between them was a one-time deal, wasn't it? Was what he suggested even possible?

"Now I'll use the sanitary unit before you and get out of here, because I need to change back into my flight suit and I didn't bring it with me." One last lingering kiss and he turned, disappearing into the small room beyond.

She lay back for a moment, listening to the sound of him showering then dressing. As soon as the sanitary unit door opened, she was out of bed, and she saw his gaze roam over her naked form hungrily, making her burn once more.

Jemma chuckled. "Tonight."

She knew there was a smile on her face as she dashed into the sanitary unit and closed the door behind her, his rumble of laughter filling the cabin.

She might want to think about the amazing night just gone and even follow through on it, but she knew they would likely be late, so she pushed the thought aside. She slid into the shower, scrubbing her hair, then dashed back out, hastily drying, and dressed in another flight suit. She quickly arranged her hair in a messy ponytail and spied the steaming coffee beside the bed. His thoughtfulness touched her as she grabbed it up, palmed the door open, and headed to the shuttle bay.

Jemma arrived out of breath to see Chowd waiting for her,

smiling. "Glad to see you made it, pilot. I don't know where Raven is. Do you?" He waited, a ghost of a smile on his face, which seemed almost at odds with his usual somber demeanor. His eyes were usually serious, and he rarely smiled. She'd noted a sadness about him too, a loneliness that she could read and understand because she too had a similar empty space inside her.

She was uncomfortably aware that now, though, he was teasing her. Jemma blushed, ducking her head. "Um, I think he can't be too far away." She moved forward. "What do you want to start on today?" She thought perhaps changing the subject might deflect any further discussion, and the sooner they got started, the better anyway. "It looks like you took a bit of damage in the firefight. How about I run over her to see if I can find any issues with her integrity?"

"That sounds like a wise idea. I'll start looking at the removal of the extra armaments, and when Raven arrives, I'd like to consider how we can increase the shielding without causing any inefficiencies or glitches in other areas."

They moved to the tool racks, each snatching up the items they'd need. "Yeah, that sounds good," Jemma agreed. "We'll also need some other tools, which we can probably get from engineering."

She climbed into a pair of grubby coveralls and started to pull them over her flight suit, her mind whirring into the day-to-day tasks of a fighter pilot, then started checking the hull integrity. Schematics of the shuttle were not her strong area of knowledge, so she pulled the palm screen from her pocket, bringing up the information she would need. Jemma had started running her hand over the front cone of the shuttle when Raven arrived.

Coffee in hand, he looked fresh and ready to work. He raised a hand to Chowd. "I know I'm late, but I've ordered extra tools and equipment to be transferred down here, and I also ran an update on the schematics we needed to look at." He walked toward the shuttle. "I had engineering run a break-down with a range of options factored in. I've come up with some interesting ideas I want to run past you both."

He motioned to the table that had been set up and laid the hard prints on it. They grabbed chairs, and within minutes, the three of them were deep in discussion about the best way to amend the harmonics.

Jemma had stretched out under the shuttle when the sound of another body slipping under surprised her. She tilted her head to see Raven. "What are you—"

He cut off her words as he zoomed in for a brief, burning kiss. "I just needed to kiss you before I head back to engineering to check on what's happening down there. Remember we're supposed to be meeting with Duvall and the senior staff in his office in about thirty minutes. You should go grab a shower, and I'll meet you at your cabin in say fifteen minutes. We can walk over together." He smiled wickedly, swooping in for another quick kiss, then he was gone.

She lay on her back for a minute longer. With a sigh, she shimmied her way out from under the shuttle.

"You know, kissing under shuttles isn't exactly the safest activity." Chowd delivered this comment with a dry tone.

She blushed. "Chowd? I know, I shouldn't, but I just..." She shrugged. How could she explain to him she was lost and trying to find her way through a path when she had no idea where it would take her? That she didn't even have a clue where to start with the whole relationship gig? She shook her head.

"Jem, when I first met you, you were brash and loud. But it hid something that was broken inside you. I can understand that, because I've been there too. If this is what you want, then take the step with him. If you need a friend, know that I am here." He smiled and laid a surprisingly soft hand on her arm.

Chowd puzzled her. She knew he was the senior security officer. At the academy, students spoke of him in hushed tones for his amazing skills in combat and as a security officer—not that he ever visited the academy, but his name was raised in stories of conflicts used as teaching exercises. She didn't know why he never visited, but it was something that had been hinted at a few times.

He looked normal, yet there was something about him, something she couldn't put her finger on. Could it be in his eyes? Was it the slant of his cheeks and his almost feminine features, or something less visible? It could be the quiet way he held himself apart from others, except for those few moments when he broke his shell to offer humor or comfort. Though he was accepted here on the *Elector*, she always felt there was more to his story than anyone knew.

"Thanks, Chowd. I'll definitely remember that." She gave him a quick hug then stepped back. "I'm heading back to my cabin to grab a shower and change for this meeting. Maybe you should do the same. I won't be back in here tonight. Will you secure the bay or will I?"

"You go. I'll arrange the security. See you in Duvall's office."

It felt like a kind of dismissal, and she took it at face value, slipping out of the bay and making her way back to her cabin. She palmed the door and hurried inside. "Lock. Access allowed, Fraser, Raven."

She quickly stripped out of her soiled clothing. She caught sight of oil smears on her face in the mirror in the sanitary unit. Grimacing, she let herself into the shower, turned it on hot, and began to wash. Her hands were in her hair when she heard him.

"What a beautiful sight I spy right now." She turned her head to see Raven watching her.

She reached for the taps, and when she turned back, he was holding a towel open for her. She stepped into the embrace, and he wrapped the towel around her.

"Raven, there's no time..." Her body began heating even as she told herself there was no time for sex.

"I know, but I can wish. Come on, get dressed and we'll go to the briefing together." She made her way into the cabin, pulled the spare flight suit out of the cupboard, and noticed, with dismay, no underwear anywhere. Her cheeks heated.

He noticed the blush and saw her dilemma. Then he winked. "Less to get off you later."

She rolled her eyes, but they were out of time, so she pulled on the flight suit over her nude body, bent down to pull on socks and the flight boots she'd worn earlier, and then rose. Raven extended his hand. She grabbed it, and together they set off for Duvall's office.

When they arrived at Duvall's office they found the other members of the senior crew already there, ready for the briefing. Jemma grimaced, knowing that they'd been noticed entering together. She was going to have to talk to Duvall about this and wasn't looking forward to it. For the moment though, she focused on the job at hand—getting to Alpha Star Colony and completing the mission.

A younger woman, dark-haired and slight, sat next to Duvall. Jemma had a vague recollection of this woman aboard the *Elector* over eighteen months ago. Jemma felt uncomfortable—Meredith no doubt had heard about her tantrums and pity party on the way to the future, and she hoped it wouldn't color any association they might have. Jemma sighed inwardly.

"Raven and Jemma, now that you're here, let's get started. You all remember Meredith Gentry? Meredith will be our cryptologist on this mission. She has vast experience with the variant strains of encryption that the Ru'Edan, and in particular, Crick Sur Banden, uses. Meredith, you have the floor."

"Thanks, Duvall. Okay, getting right to the bottom of the job at hand, we've been intercepting messages between the Phobos pirates and the rogues of Crick Sur Banden. We believe there is a splinter group but don't know too much right now about their role. Anyway, we believe Crick Sur Banden has been using the pirates to create havoc in and around space in this area."

A map displayed on the viewscreen showed where they had come to a dead stop.

"We hadn't broadcast the information that they were there, so when the Elector came to a dead stop, no one here or on the Star of Ishtar had that information—that was a dangerous oversight on the part of the Admiralty and nearly resulted in the loss of both Pilot Cardnew and the Elector." Meredith sighed heavily, frustration evident on her face. "Now, it's somehow leaked out that the pirates are in this vicinity, and freighters have become aware that anyone getting supplies and assistance to the Alpha Star Colony must first run the gauntlet. To date, they've attempted to intercept freighters, hospital ships, and even lone private craft. The Admiralty are now offering fleet assistance to ensure that the lanes remain open. We've sent the

Vengeance into that area with a squadron of fighter pilots, hoping to clear out the pirates nest."

Meredith paused and looked around the room.

"We have also had incursions in several different locations, including in and around the Alpha Star Colony. We believe they've been receiving donations, help, and even training, from Crick Sur Banden, which is how they've acquired the fleet of spooks. They've effectively starved the Alpha Star Colony, which has ultimately endangered the mining planet. We need the mining to continue, as we are reliant on the Duschem mineral for the matrix of the stealth ships. The Ru'Edan, we understand, have also managed to find their own uses for the mineral in the shield structure of their current generation destroyers, or so our intelligence leads us to believe."

Meredith stopped and waited, allowing the group gathered at the table to absorb the details.

"The Diplomatic Corps had a high-ranking security officer disappear just as we began receiving credible intelligence that Crick Sur Banden is starting to ramp up his campaign to overthrow the ruling Senate. If that's true, then the treaty's in danger of collapsing and we will be back to a full-scale war."

Jemma got the impression the next statement would be important, as Meredith's face tightened.

"Neither the Senate nor the Empire wishes that outcome." Meredith's face and voice were hard as she delivered the information. "Our diplomats have agreed to a joint task force at the end of this particular mission. The *Elector* is to become a central player, but this mission must succeed. To this end, I will be continuing my work on the *Elector* for some extended period in order to intercept and decrypt transmissions in and out of the Alpha Star Colony and Ru'Edan space initially, and at a later point as translator as required. I've delivered extensive information to Duvall on behalf of Elphin and the Admirals Conclave. He'll be apprising you of the contents in due course. Each of you here has an integral place in this continuing mission."

With a nod to the members at the table, Meredith resumed her seat, her face now a mask of serenity, and Jemma wondered what was going through the woman's head.

"Thank you, Meredith. Grayson has informed me this morning that the final course settings are now in place. Grayson?"

"As you're aware, we've been previously unable to use the beta hyperspace technology due to issues with the communications arrays being compromised. With some effort, the engineering department has been in contact with the designers, and we believe we've managed to rework them in order to utilize the hyperspace corridors. We must remain in the central trajectory, which raises some concerns, as we have a minimal ability to maneuver in the case of anomalies."

Grayson brought up schematics of the corridors.

"We've also tested bouncing the signals off planetary systems since the last briefing. I believe that we can minimize the risks to the *Elector* by using sonic return technology to accurately find the center of the corridors. So far our records indicate no anomalies that would cause deviations, but use of this technology will give us time to make course corrections as required. The course has therefore been plotted and we should be getting underway within the hour, with your permission, Captain." Grayson looked to Duvall, who nodded firmly.

"Good." Duvall stood and wandered around to Raven. For a moment he was silent then looked directly at Jemma. She started in her chair. "How are things coming along with the shuttle?"

"So far we've removed the majority of the retrofitting. There are some issues with the outer plating of the shuttle from that, but within the next day or two, plating sections can be removed and replaced as required. Some of those sections also sustained damage in the encounter with the pirates. I should be able to finalize repairs to those areas, if not tomorrow, then the next day. Chowd has been working on the harmonics, and I believe he has a workable solution underway."

"What about plotting the course once we reach the colony?" Duvall's words cut through the air.

"Well, it will depend on where we make entry, as to the particular route I'll take. I intend to sit down with the new terrain mapping as soon as the shuttle is ready to go. It means I'll need that information within, say, two to three days so I can go over the maps allowing for the necessary calculations." Jemma waited for a further information request, but there was silence in the room. All eyes were on her.

"Grayson?" Duvall looked to Grayson for some sort of confirmation of their plans. Grayson nodded his agreement. "Right, as soon as the shuttle is ready, you'll meet with Grayson to undertake that area of plotting. Raven, have you looked at the schematics we were sent?"

"I did, and I believe that the transmitter frequencies can be blocked without difficulty. I already have my crew working on creating a blocker. We can then fit a larger version within the shuttle and will create a number of handheld versions to be manufactured for the ground mission members." Raven's voice was decisive, and his report sparse. She felt his hand seek hers under the table.

"Fine, I believe at this stage everything is going to plan. Remember, though, any information that impacts this mission slows down our ability to shut down Crick Sur Banden. Anything I need to know, alert me immediately. Within the time available to us, I am sure we can make arrangements. Jemma and Raven, can you please stay back? The rest of you are dismissed."

"Damn, we are so dead," Jemma whispered, then hoped like hell Raven didn't hear her words, or anyone else for the matter. She closed her eyes, listening to everyone else filing out of the room. Raven let go of her hand, and she opened her eyes.

The sound of the door shutting was loud in her ears. She fought the urge to hide her head. Never before had she shirked bad news, and she wouldn't now. She raised her gaze to Duvall. He sat down just beyond Raven, and she felt distinctly uneasy.

"So, are you an item, and if so, what's the long-term viability of your relationship, not to mention plans, if it falls in a heap?" Duvall looked at Raven with hard eyes, his cold voice cutting in the silence.

"It's none of your business, Duvall."

"Raven, if you believe that, you're whistling in the breeze. Any relationship on my bird is my business. So, what is it?" His voice and his eyes were brutal as he asked Raven the question.

"Duvall, please. It isn't his fault. I instigated it." Jemma winced as she heard her voice, thin with distress. "If anyone should be carpeted, it's me." She looked at Duvall, urging him to accept what she was saying.

"No, it isn't, Jemma. I wanted you from the first moment I saw you. I want forever, you know that." Raven flashed a look of anger at Duvall.

"Don't do this, Raven. Don't ruin your relationship with Duvall over me." Jemma gulped, her eyes seeking his, wanting him to accept the situation so she could spare him. She knew they were like brothers and felt the fury in the air sparking between them. She'd save them both the time and energy and remove herself. She'd been foolish to even *think* that she had a place either here or in Raven's future.

Duvall pinned Raven with a glare and her own fury ratcheted up a notch. "Fine, so you go for the forever. What happens if it doesn't work out?" Duvall's voice was harder and more cutting than before, pulling them back to the issue at hand.

He knows I'm no good at forever. Oh God! Let him take it to me, not Raven. Never Raven. The worried thoughts circled in her brain.

It coalesced in her mind; there was only one way to deal with this. Remove herself from the frame totally. Her heart splintered as she rose and screwed up every ounce of pain that radiated. "Then I'll be gone and your ship is sacred ground once more." Jemma pushed away from the table. Tears burned their way from her eyes, coursing down her face. "I go and you all go back to being one big, happy family without me. Just like it's always been. Start my transfer now, and after the job is done, I'm out of your hair."

Duvall looked at her, shocked, and Raven made to stand up.

"Sit down, Jemma. I'm not quite finished yet," Duvall said, his voice bitterly cold, and a chill swept through her.

She swiped angrily at the tears rolling down her face, mortified that Duvall had cut right through her argument. Raven grabbed her hand, but she pulled away, refusing to look at him.

"Sir." Her voice was a shaky whisper. She dropped her gaze so she would not see the contempt she expected in either man's faces.

"Jemma, you've been assigned to the *Elector* for the duration of the mission. Admiral Elphin read your report and watched the footage from your encounters with the pirates. That fancy flying and the fact that you were prepared to do something outside the box, including the retrofitting of the shuttle, impressed the hell out of him. He needs you to get at least one spook to use against the rogues. But you need to focus on the mission right now, not a romance." His voice softened toward the end of the statement. "I can understand that sometimes it sneaks up on you. But I need to be sure that you two will keep it straight. If it does go wrong, we can't afford to have the two of you at odds with each other. So whatever you do, just keep it straight." His voice hardened with frustration, and Jemma flinched once more. "Jemma, you're dismissed."

She nodded miserably and turned. The excitement she should have felt at the unexpected placement had been drowned by the misery of Duvall's reaction to her and Raven—a relationship she'd finally taken the plunge into. Yet the sense of security she craved was ripped out from beneath her as soon as it began, and she realized that she couldn't do this to Raven. She would end it. Now.

Without looking at either man, she left the room.

Chapter 12

Raven shook with rage as he listened to Duvall and his rant about forever, commitment, and the crew of the *Elector*. He had cringed when he heard Jemma stating it was her fault. For all the work he had done with her in the last few weeks, his patient waiting for months, he felt it had all been lost in one ham-fisted attempt by Duvall to work out what his intentions were.

"You're a bastard, you know that? She has issues that you never even stopped to consider. You ran roughshod straight over her. Didn't let either of us explain. I've been working with Elara to try to get Jemma to see that she's a worthwhile person, because she sure as hell doesn't think so. In one stupid outburst, you have torpedoed everything I've achieved with Jemma. *Barsha*, did you even stop to think before you opened your mouth?" The rage spewed forth hot and angry, and his fists curled like claws as he fought to control them.

"Shut up, Raven." Duvall attempted to talk, but Raven was too wound up. He advanced on his friend and captain.

"No, you shut up and listen. She has the most fragile self-esteem I have ever seen. She thinks she's worthless, and your thoughtless words have probably undone hours of thought and planning on my part and work with Elara. For *Eshra*'s sake! I care for that woman, and you've put her back so far... I can't even think..." Raven growled, throwing up his arms in rage. He gritted his teeth as he fought to control the snarling, angry beast that rampaged within his chest. He wanted to grab Duvall and shake him until his brains rattled, so he grabbed the back of the chair and squeezed.

"What do you mean?" Duvall stood up, pushed the chair out of the way, and toed up to Raven.

Raven knew his face glowed red; he could feel the heat he radiated. "She has bloody self-esteem issues. That's why she acts like she does. That's why she took those chances in her craft to save the *Elector*. She sees herself as expendable." He slumped back down in his seat, putting his hand over his face and letting the rage wash away until bone weariness replaced it. *Barsha! She'll retreat now and I'll be back to where I started.*

He heard the creak and groan of the chair as Duvall sat down as well. "Hell, I didn't realize. For *Eshra*'s sake, if I'd realized..." Duvall's voice tapered off, frustration with himself now clear in his voice. "But we test for those sorts of issues."

"When they're first assigned to the academy as well as while in the educational system, yes. But she wasn't exactly a normal intake or had what we'd consider a normal childhood, did she? They missed the psych eval."

"*Barsha.*"

"Yeah, well you should've asked me first what was going on. You've known me for more than a dozen years, you should've trusted I knew what I was doing. I've got to go check on her." Raven stood up slowly, but the fear and anxiety remained in his chest, making him feel like an old man who'd lost everything. "I'll see what I can do to sort this out. But I have to tell you, you ever treat her like that again, and I will gut you, friend, captain, or not. Got it?"

"I'm still your senior officer, the captain of this ship."

"Then act like it. If you've an issue, ask before you jump down our throats!" Raven pointed at Duvall. "No one said a word when you brought Mellissa into the fold, or even Grayson and Elara. I'm not asking for special dispensation here, just the same courtesy as you lot were afforded."

"Damn! Do you love her?"

The words surprised Raven, who stopped short and looked at his friend, then dropped into a seat. "What? Of course I do. I want everything, babies and houses and forever..." His voice tapered off.

"Then when were you planning on telling me?"

"As soon as the mission was over. I was hoping to ease her into a relationship then go from there. Natural progression for us, I thought."

"What about all the other women though, Raven? She'll hear about them."

"Oh, that's rich coming from you, Mr. No Commitment." The words dripped heavy with sarcasm. "There hasn't been half the women everyone imagined, and since I met her there's been no one else. No interest. Now, sir, if you will excuse me, I have to go scrape my girl back together and see what I can salvage of our relationship. Working and personal." He hoped his voice, so full of anger and rage, would find a target in Duvall's conscience. With that, Raven stood and stalked from the room, leaving Duvall watching the door shut.

Duvall sat heavily in his chair.

"Well, that went well, didn't it?"

He swiveled in his chair to see Mellissa standing in the doorway to their cabin.

"Duvall, sometimes you just have to leave things alone to make it work. Seriously, that was pretty harsh the way you brought it up. Raven was right, you should've asked them first." Her tone was in line with the tightly bunched brows, and he felt the dissatisfaction with him settling on his shoulders like a tangible weight.

"Yeah, I just learned that." A long, deep sigh issued from him, and Mellissa moved forward.

"I never realized that Jem had all those troubles, but even so, I wouldn't have handled it like you did. That scene was like a hammer on a porcelain cup. I mean, I know she's always so out there, with both her attitude and the way she lives, not to mention the men." Mellissa shook her head, her face screwed up. "Damn. I wish I'd known."

He felt the frustration right down to his toes. He didn't want to regret anything he did with Mellissa, but there it was, staring him in the face. "So…"

"You're going to have to do something about what you said and did. You can't leave the situation as it is."

"You're right, as usual." He sighed, accepting that Mellissa was making her point without being angry. But rarely did she lose her temper; massaging him into realizing he'd made an error was more her style. "I should've seen that there was an issue. That is my job. To lead and encourage my crew and keep things smooth. *Barsha!* If only I'd done what Raven suggested. I was concerned he was only toying with her and she him. I can't afford for the ongoing crew dynamics to be compromised." He let his head slip to the headrest, for just an instant the responsibilities of captain-hood overtaking him.

"So, diplomacy is an art form you've never really mastered. I guess the next thing you need to work on is how to sort this out? You can't leave it, otherwise it'll fester and that only makes things worse. You need to be honest with both of them, tell them that you regret the way you handled the situation. Tell them that you were wrong."

He closed his eyes, and she moved forward until she was equal to his chair.

Leaning toward him, she opened her lips over his, kissing him softly. "I can have a talk with her tomorrow, if you prefer. Let her get today and the upset out of the way first."

He considered letting Mellissa talk to her, but as quickly as that occurred, came the shame. That would be wrong. He wouldn't ask that of her. It was his responsibility to make the situation right.

His eyes opened and he could see the rise of desire in those gorgeous pools of forever. "No, you're right. If I leave it, the problem will be bigger." He let the words whisper against her lips. "I guess I need to talk to Elara, find out how to deal with the situation and get her help. Then I need to make my peace with Raven. Try to find a way to undo the damage with Jemma and generally get the ship's senior crew back to some sort of equilibrium."

He leaned forward and grabbed Mellissa around the waist.

"But before I do any of that, I'm going to make love to my researcher, who also happens to be my wife, partner, and a very clever author. Yes, I saw that your manuscript was finished." He pulled her forward until her knees touched either side of his seat. He pulled a little more and she moved in, straddling his lap. "Just. Like. This." His mouth crushed hers on a moan as he pulled her more firmly into the embrace, his hand already working on the buttons of her ship suit.

"Well now, my girl, one more stuff-up in a lifetime of them. You're batting about one hundred percent currently." Jemma looked at the mascara streaks on her face and her puffy, red eyes. No way was she going back out there looking like a drowned raccoon. If she had nothing else left, at least she still had her pride.

Grabbing a cloth, she quickly scrubbed her face clean and carefully reapplied her makeup. She tackled her red and swollen eyes, applying the camouflage as best she could, so that several minutes later she looked under control, or as good as could be expected. It was hard to avoid thinking about how badly her chest hurt. One hand extended up and rubbed the region of her heart where a crushing ache lay. Knowing that she and Raven couldn't have any more of a future had destroyed something within her.

Focus on the task. Do what needs to be done, but keep it light and keep it clean. The internal monologue didn't soothe as it usually did. She straightened up, looked one last time in the mirror, then smartly turned on her heel to walk through her cabin doorway and out to the corridor. With swift strides, anyone passing her by would just think she was in a hurry, not running from the biggest disaster of her life.

Jemma reached the shuttle bay and authorized the opening of the door. Pleased to see it was empty, she entered, giving the command to shut the door behind her. As if the hounds of hell were nipping at her heels, she hurried over the plascrete, clambered into the shuttle, and closed the doors. She'd rather no one saw her there; she could do her work on the weapons panel as efficiently inside as outside. A quick crawl under the captain's chair and she started working on removing the patched-in weapons systems that Chowd had fitted.

The wires and cords she and Chowd had retrofitted reminded her of her own temporary status on the *Elector*. Oh, she'd heard Duvall saying she was to stay with the ship, but seriously, the need to distance herself once more from the crew in order to do her job and make sure she didn't jeopardize Raven's now took on a much higher priority with her. His job was so much more important than hers, and so was his place in the Empire.

All she had to do was blow as many out of the sky as she could before they got her. Simple. Her work slowly filled her mind. Her fingers moved quickly—remove this cable here, replace the original cords there. Some leads needed a full replacement, as the originals were spliced to allow the extra cords to be added. She worked feverishly, letting the tears run down her face. Bit by bit the job continued. The ache in her chest grew with the mountain of wiring that littered her feet.

Slowly, the sobs came, shaking loose. Her eyes unable to see for the flood of tears, she stopped and rolled into herself.

That's how Raven found her, sobbing and cold, hidden in the shadows below the captain's chair in the shuttle. She didn't hear the door of the shuttle open or the footsteps. His voice slashed through the air. "*Barsha*! Jemma! Oh, sweetheart, I'm so sorry. Duvall is a ham-fisted idiot and didn't realize that I love you, or that I was committed to us. I didn't want this to happen."

He reached for her, but she shrank away from his touch. His face tightened, and she just wanted to disappear at the hurt that was clear in his expression. She swiped a hand over her eyes and wanted to die of embarrassment when streaks of black eye makeup appeared on the palm of her hand. She stared at them and refused eye contact.

"No, Raven. He was right. I shouldn't interfere with your work. What you do is so important. That's why they wanted you on the *Elector*, and I understand that. It was right that he said those things." The words flowed out of her mouth before she could stop them, and she tried to lift her head, but it was so heavy, and she just *couldn't* show him the depths of her despair.

Once more he reached forward, and she shied away again.

"You need to concentrate on your job, just as I need to concentrate on mine." She raised her eyes to his. "It really is better this way. For you. For me. For everyone."

Jemma took a deep breath and held it as she tried to control herself and the sobs that robbed her of breath. She exhaled.

"Please don't come looking for me again. We're colleagues and can never be anything else. Now you need to go and I need to finish my task." With that, she turned her head and started removing the old wiring again.

She controlled her breathing, holding in the sobs that wanted to escape, but they filled her chest once more to the bursting point. She waited, listening for the sound of his feet on the decking, but instead, the sound of him sitting in the co-pilot's chair took her by surprise. Gentle hands captured her around the waist and lifted her from the cold floor.

"No, Jemma, he wasn't right. I won't let you disappear again like you did at the academy. I need to be with you, as much as you need to be with me. We're each other's perfect half, matching together forever, like a key and its lock. I love you too much to see you alone and hurting."

Her chest fractured one sob, then another escaped. She curled into his arms, needing the warmth and reassurance she was coming to rely on. Her hands made their way up to his neck and clasped behind it, uncaring of anything except the need to be in his arms and accept the support he offered.

"Oh God, Raven! I'm so sorry. I never meant to make it difficult for you." She cried the words against his flight suit.

He held on tighter and whispered into her hair. "It's not your fault. There is no way in this lifetime, or any other, that I'm going to let you go again. Not ever."

Jemma lay in his arms and shivered, as the worst of the emotional outpouring was spent. Now all that remained was an exhaustion of the body and spirit.

"I'm never letting you go. I've loved you since the first time I saw you, and even more now that I know you. The person that you are is just too special to me." He kissed her forehead, cheeks, and finally, softly, her mouth. "Let's get out of here. My cabin is near, and you and I need to be alone." He lifted her, and while she protested, he just hefted her higher, tight against his chest, and strode out of the shuttle bay, down the corridor to his office. Jemma hid her face in the curve of his neck, holding on tightly, saying nothing and drawing on the power he exuded. He palmed open the door, entered, and gave the command to lock once more.

Raven stalked through the office to his bedroom. He deposited her gently on the bed and pulled up the thick, satiny-blue covers. He disappeared back toward his office only to reappear a few minutes later with warm drinks for both of them and a steaming face washer to soothe her sore eyes. Jemma accepted both gratefully. Hiccupping softly, she focused on wiping her face clear then holding the clean side across her upper face.

"You know, I wouldn't normally do that. It's not who I am." She was so embarrassed he had seen her sobbing like that and the face she'd presented.

"I know, sweetheart. But maybe this time you can let go because there's someone you can lean on." Raven sat down on the bed beside her. He gathered her in his arms, and God, how she wanted to accept that strength. "Maybe it's time to let go of control and hold onto me."

"But Raven, I'm scared. What if I do that and it goes wrong? I mean, look at what happened this time—"

Raven cut her off swiftly. "Jemma, sometimes in life you have to take a leap of faith. Yes, it could go wrong. We don't know what'll happen in the long term, but maybe, just maybe, what we have is the real thing. Are you prepared to hide from an opportunity like that?"

He turned her in his arms to face him. "I know how I feel about you." His eyes blazed, and she sat looking at the wonderful man who kept saying he wanted to be with her. "There are no questions left for me. But you need to work out if it's right for you."

He pulled her close, just holding her in his arms. There was nothing sexual in the way that he held her, and she stayed still. The comfort spread through her like a warm haze on a summer's day, and she soaked it up, letting the cold that had seeped into her bones disappear.

✪ ✪ ✪ ✪

Jemma woke with a start, her stomach rumbling loudly, and she heard voices beyond her line of sight. They sounded angry, yet quiet. She sat up, trying to orient herself and listen at the same time. The soothing blue of the room, the large bed, and the smell of Raven all around her reminded her of where she was. She'd fallen asleep in his bed after that conversation.

Jemma felt woolly-headed and confused, but she pushed the

covers out of the way and rose slowly. She stretched and padded through the doorway.

Raven stood facing Duvall. "No. She's having dinner with me. After the way you ripped into her today, there's no way she's going to have dinner with you and Mellissa on her own, not without me there, and to be frank, I wouldn't eat with you right now even if you were the last people in the universe."

"For *Eshra*'s sake. What do you think I'm going to do? Run off with your girl or make her cry? Mellissa already carpeted me, straight after you left." Duvall's voice sounded frustrated. He inhaled deeply, then continued. "We thought dinner in our cabin, maybe the eight of us, will help to break the ice after my outburst. I still need to talk to her, though, and let her know I was out of line."

Jemma hooked the stray stands of hair behind her ear. She felt grubby and disheveled, and in no way ready to deal with the emotional fallout, but she refused to allow Raven to take all the heat.

"Duvall, you were way out of line. I've no intention of upsetting the ship, but what's between Raven and I...well, it's our business." Jemma moved silently through the doorway and into the room. Both men looked shocked to see her. "I can tell you that we have no intention of letting things get out of hand, even if it doesn't work out." She watched Duvall's face intently. "After all, we're all adults aboard this ship, and I'm only here until the end of the mission."

Could he understand and accept what she was saying? For the first time, she felt like maybe she was in some way equal to the others, as if maybe she did have a place here. It was only a whisper-thin feeling of belonging, but it was more than she'd felt in a long time.

"I'm sorry, Jem. I didn't mean to wake you." Raven looked cross with himself and Duvall. The hard look he gave Duvall indicated that she'd read the situation correctly.

Duvall continued to look upset that he'd found her there and that she'd overheard what he'd obviously been meaning to say to her later, in private. This was, after all, a man who didn't like to be taken unaware or proven wrong, Jemma reminded herself.

"It's okay, Raven." She moved around him soundlessly. "Duvall, you had no right to attack me the way you did, but I can understand that you felt uncomfortable about the whole Raven-and-me thing. For now though, I think we should just let it go. If we don't, things might only get worse between us, and to be frank, until we get through this mission, we don't need any more angst."

She smiled, hoping to smooth out any bite from her words. She waited for his response. For some reason, it was important that he understood what she'd tried to say. Her body tightly clenched as she waited for his reaction.

"Good then. Right, Mellissa wants you both to join us for dinner. I think the eight of us, something fun before we get into the meat of the mission. Say 1800 hours, my office." He turned and headed toward the door, stopped, and looked back. For a moment, the discomfort at being so wrong showed in his face, together with the dismay he felt. "I am sorry for what I said. It was very wrong of me. It certainly wasn't my intent to wound you, and if this relationship works for you, then that's terrific. I just have to consider all my crew and the way it could impact if things do go wrong." A brief nod of his head to Raven, then he palmed the door and was gone.

"It's not okay at all," growled Raven, looking fiercely at her. "We should have said we were skipping the dinner."

"Now probably isn't the right time for a bloody fight. We need to be on our game, and taking this on right now means we're not concentrating on the important things. Like staying alive. Like being together. Now, I don't know about you, but I think my eyes are puffy and I need a shower and makeup."

She walked back to his bathroom, stripping off her clothes as she went. Sure, she wasn't over it. She felt frayed around the edges and battered by emotions she never really wanted to experience. In some ways, Duvall was right. They needed a circuit breaker before the battle ahead.

As Jemma reached the doorway, she turned and was startled to see Raven right behind her. He had also started removing his clothes. "Just what do you think you're doing?" she asked.

"Well, I find I have a hankering for a shower with the most beautiful woman in the galaxy." He leaned in and kissed her softly.

"I'm sure you need a slave to wash your delectable back." He grinned wickedly at her.

"No, Raven. You shouldn't." Her arguments grew weak as he cupped her bare breasts. "Yes, I should. Nothing you don't want, and no sex involved. But you deserve tender loving care and I want to give it to you," he whispered into her ear, and God help her, she melted against him. He pushed her into the shower. "Hot shower, wide flow."

The water started through the head of the nozzle, which pushed out enough for both of them to fit under as he pushed in behind her. She could feel him, every inch, against her body.

He hefted the soap and lathered his hands, which he gently transferred to her wet body. She closed her eyes, feeling his supple hands sliding over her flesh, warming her wherever his fingers touched. His insistent erection burned into her from behind. She sighed.

Hands gripped her shoulders and turned her toward him, and she opened her eyes. His eyes blazed down, his face flushed with exertion as his chest rose and fell.

She wanted him, here in the shower, right now. She burned for the touch of his body against hers. She felt his shaft jutting against her belly and moved closer. He stepped back as much as the small stall allowed. She stood watching him, feeling the delicious, sensual flow of water sheeting over puckered nipples. Waiting. Aching.

He lathered his hands again, and this time the sliding touch over her breasts made her writhe beneath the soft touches. She moaned low in her throat. His hands left her body, and she let her eyes open.

"Nothing sexual. I promised, and I mean it." His voice was rough. "Shower off." She watched as he reached for towels, wrapping one around his waist and moving forward to rub her dry. It had never been like this before, as she mutely accepted the tribute, still confused but feeling cherished in a way she had never experienced. She mentally shrugged her shoulders as she reached for her clothes.

Raven watched as Jemma dressed her magnificent body. He was still aroused from the shower. He wanted to touch her, but he knew in his gut that if he rushed her, everything he'd regained would be lost.

"What is my makeup doing here?" She speared him with a glance and his face heated. "I knew you'd want it, so I grabbed it while you slept."

Her expression softened. "Thank you, Raven. You really are the most thoughtful man I've ever known." The tender kiss she gifted him with didn't help his urgent desire, so he stepped back as a trickle of sweat wound its way down his back.

He knew that she would want to cover her face with makeup. It was a defensive shield that she hid her true self behind, and he understood her need. For now, he would be patient.

Together they left his cabin. He itched to grab her hand and proclaim to the world that she was his, but he restrained himself. His fingers curled into fists.

They reached the door to Duvall's cabin, and he made sure he went in first. It was instinctual, he knew, to protect the woman he loved. He knew she could protect herself on a physical level—he'd seen her scores from the academy—but emotionally, he knew she had few defenses. Those that she'd used as barriers were seriously depleted right now.

He sighed inwardly as she entered the room. Mellissa made her way over to Jemma, and he watched Jemma tense. He wanted to step in but knew that this was necessary. He would be here in case she needed him though.

"Jemma, I'm so pleased to see you. How are you feeling?" Mellissa enfolded her into a hug. So far so good, he thought.

"Thanks, Liss. Yeah, I don't feel too bad, all things considered." "Now, that outburst from Duvall..."

Raven braced himself, ready to cut into the conversation as he watched Jemma stiffen slightly.

"He was so out of line, and I told him so. He was wrong. You're entitled to a personal life. I have to say, you've got good taste. If I wasn't married to Duvall, I may just have been interested in Raven. Good thing you got him first." She whispered loud enough for him to hear, and he had to work hard to keep his embarrassment from showing.

You never hear what you want to hear when you eavesdrop, he reminded himself. Over the next few minutes, the others joined them. Elara and Grayson. Chowd and Meredith too.

As the company gathered Duvall strode into the room, and Raven felt his body tensing. Duvall moved toward Jemma, and once there, he stopped. "Jemma, I owe you an apology. My outburst was wrong, and in front of everyone, I want to welcome you to the *Elector* officially." His words sounded stilted, and Raven could see his discomfort. *He never did like to apologize.*

Jemma reached out toward him, briefly touching his shoulder. "Thanks, Duvall. I really do appreciate it."

She smiled, but he could see the wariness in the corners of her eyes. She hid it well, but *he* could see it was still there—a distrust of what Duvall had said. He waited silently to see what would happen next.

Mellissa sat down at the converted conference table, and the rest of the senior crew— Elara, Grayson, and Chowd—found spots, as did Meredith. Raven reached for Jemma's hand and led her to a seat. His awareness of the watching audience made him weigh and measure his actions. It buzzed through his system, but he ignored the interested looks. He was going to enjoy the night with his girl.

Chapter 13

They touched down, and Crick Sur Banden made his way out of the hatch, turning to watch the pallet following him. His future consort lay supine on it. Since considering her as a possible mother of his offspring, he'd felt it appropriate that she be treated as such. An infiltrator in his ranks should be punished, and what better way than to impregnate her and make her incubate his young? He felt some distaste at the smell of her, but that he could ignore as he used her body. After all, she was only needed to bear his child.

He was surprised that, this time, the girl was taking longer to heal. Perhaps he should have found another specimen for his scientists to conduct their research on. He would have to ensure she wasn't used again in the short term, at least until his young was born; after that, he really didn't care what happened to her.

A flash of interest flared. "It will be interesting to see how quickly she heals this time and the effects of bearing a Ru'Edanian child."

"Sire?" The healer must have caught his low words.

"Nothing." With a wave of his arm, he dismissed the medic and flicked his gaze around the barren landscape. The purple grass waved softly in the breeze under an azure sky, but the walls of the red-striated canyons rose in the north, making this an ideal location for a bunker. He watched as his second-in-command made his way toward him.

"Are the defenses in place? I'm expecting them to arrive soon. "

"Yes, sir. The pirates confirmed that they entered the hyperspace corridor, and I would expect them to arrive within days. They encountered resistance when the ship was powered down, and they lost a number of pilots in the skirmish."

"How careless." His mind conjured images of a damaged *Elector* running from its foes. "However, we still don't know the reason why the ship stopped. We know they have a combat pilot aboard of great skill."

His second bowed low as he relayed the information. "I've arranged enough markers to be set in place so they can find us, but not so easily that they'd consider it a trap. But sir, I have to ask, is it so important to neutralize Duvall McCord? What if they bring in this pilot? We know they lost the fighter plane, but if they can find us with something smaller, they will have had time to make amendments to a ship, placing our defenses in danger. Could we not seek his destruction after we take control of the Empire?"

"What?" The word burst out of stiff lips. He watched as the officer backed off, dropping once more to a servile bow. "He took what was mine and turned him against his own! He must pay, and the sooner the better. The lost needs to return to the fold, and if that means removing the one who stole him, all the better."

A film of anger overlayed everything and his hands shook. With great effort he forced the vicious bite of fury away. They were fodder not strategists… Only he knew and understood.

"He will be by my side when we triumphantly walk through the corridors of the Empire Chambers." He spat out the words, and he could see that he had cowed the officer once more. But the seed of concern had been sowed—if his second-in-command was questioning his authority, then perhaps he was not the one who should be at his side. It could damage his role as leader of the rogues.

But who else was there at this point? It should be his son. *It will be my son.*

He smiled, a feral lifting of the sides of his mouth, showing razor-sharp teeth. "Now come, you're my second-in-command. It is right that you should ask these questions." His words were silky, but in the back of his mind, he considered what he needed to do. Keep this one only until he had his son back within the fold. *Yes, that will do nicely.*

The point was made for now—don't question why things must be so. He would see his actions and orders carried out, and as an act of faith, once he had his offspring back under his command, he would have his son kill this worm. After all, they were all dispensable, no matter how much they may have done in the past. They were all no more than cockroaches beneath his feet. They may once have seemed compliant, but he knew what they did behind his back. Did they think he didn't know?

Once he had control, then he could do away with the Senate and install his offspring into a position of power. The thought stabilized his emotions. He smiled once more. "The girl. When do the medics believe she will be ready for her new role as my consort?"

"They say that there was more extensive damage sustained during the last session and that they are looking at her spine. They have also mentioned the possibility of reproductive damage. They will hopefully have her ready within a week, sir." The younger Ru'Edan shook before him, his gray face taking on a red sheen and his yellow eyes flickering nervously from one side to the other.

"Good. I want to know as soon as she's ready. She will need to then be cleaned and dressed appropriately for her new position." With that, he turned and entered the underground bunker. Most of the Earth creatures that had been there had been eliminated, but he could still smell the stink of them. He screwed up his face in distaste.

The bodies had been removed and placed into piles, ready to burn. Those that they hadn't killed would remain, especially the women. They would make excellent slaves, preparing their food and warming his rogues' beds. That would settle any mutiny for now.

He nodded to himself. Yes, everything was going to plan. He would have his showdown with Duvall McCord, and he'd have his son very soon.

Jemma stretched sore arms above her head. Days in hyperspace had passed by, and they expected to exit within the next few hours. The removal of the fittings on the shuttle were finally completed. She had worked for many hours with Chowd and Grayson to find the most defensible points for their entry into the atmosphere and the best place to hide the stealth ship from detection. She was quietly pleased with her efforts.

The relationship thing still caused her the most disquiet in the time they had traveled through hyperspace. Since Duvall's outburst, she had remained doubly careful to keep businesslike and distant when she was on duty, but in her private hours...well, there was no escaping Raven.

He'd insinuated himself into every aspect of her role aboard the *Elector*, in discussing the issues involved in forming a shield over the shuttle that made it undetectable, even in the route they would take from insertion to touch down and in what part she would play on planet—he was there.

She sighed and reached for the door of the shuttle, running one last check to be sure everything was in place, that every aspect of the retrofitting was removed, then a quick check of the exterior. Time had run out. Once satisfied, she wiped her hands down the soiled flight suit, then headed for the door. She and Chowd had decided that, given the level of preparation they had just completed, full security systems would be in place now on the bay.

She placed her hand over the reader. "Level four security clearance only." She turned away to see Raven walking up the corridor toward her, his feet clanking on the decking.

"Done?"

She nodded. "It's as ready as it will ever be. Have I got time to change before the briefing?" She looked at Raven and noted he looked as soiled as she felt.

"Yeah, we have about an hour. Come on, we'll use my cabin." He grinned.

"I don't have a spare uniform in your cabin. Remember?" Her voice was teasing, but she still felt uncomfortable knowing that most of the crew were aware that she and Raven were sleeping together. She nearly passed out at the word *involved*, but there wasn't another term she could think of that came close to describing their situation.

"Well, I did offer to let you move in with me." He leered, and she laughed.

"Yeah, like that would be the right thing to do. No. We need to keep separate cabins, even if only for us to tag-team between." She stopped, feeling the giddiness subsiding, and looked at him. "We need to keep our own areas. You know that. Duvall is right—if it goes badly...well, we each need somewhere to retreat to." She reached out and grabbed his hands. "You know I don't mean to be difficult, don't you? I just don't know how to do this yet, but I promise, I'm working on it." Her voice caught, rough and uncertain, and she watched his eyes soften.

"I know you're trying, and I love you for that." He dropped a quick kiss on her nose and looked into her eyes. "I can wait for it to be right." Then, winking, he grinned. "So, when do I next get to check out your gorgeous body? Now or later?"

Jemma laughed, and his eyes crinkled in the corners as he too smiled. She knew it was exactly as he had planned, and she couldn't help the bubble of mirth that rose.

"Come on, I need a quick shower and change." She dragged him toward her cabin, pulling him by the hand.

"I already dropped a fresh suit into your cabin, so I can join you," he whispered into her ear. She stopped and turned, and he cannoned into her from behind.

"What? When did you do that?" She hadn't expected him to be so close, so she brushed against him when she turned.

"This morning. I knew it was likely to be a hands-on day, and I wanted to be sure that we could get the maximum time together before the mission started. Knowing that you refused to keep a spare suit in my cabin, I dropped it in before starting my shift." His shining blue eyes looked intently into hers. "It doesn't mean I'm moving in, just making it more comfortable for both of us."

She felt he was trying to get inside her mind to see where the problem existed. "You're right. It's not like you're moving in. Come on, time is getting is wasting and we need to get ready." She turned again and palmed the door open.

Raven released a breath. Jemma was still so skittish, and he needed to take it slowly. But every word he spoke to her was the truth. He could wait, no matter how difficult it was for him. He watched her shimmy out of her flight suit and felt his heart rate speed up as it always did when she was around. She was truly a beautiful woman, an amazing pilot, and had a super quick mind. He wanted her with him forever.

Raven reached for the clips of his uniform and started to divest himself of it. They had a limited amount of time before the briefing and he wished there was more. He closed his eyes, knowing his responsibility to the crew, the Empire, and Duvall had to come first.

Jemma climbed out of the unit, and he passed her the towel he had snagged as he climbed in. The water sluiced over him.

"When this mission is over, I'd like to talk about maybe leaving some items in each other's cabins. Not invading each other's space, just to make it easier." Her voice echoed, and for a moment he was stunned. Elated. Excitement fizzled along his nerve endings, setting his entire soul aflame.

Not now. Don't get ahead of yourself, Raven, otherwise she'll back off at a million miles an hour! He stopped and turned toward her. "Water off. I thought you didn't want to do that?"

Her eyes glittered, and a faint blush sheened her skin. "I know, but I was thinking about what you said. You're right. It isn't giving up our space, and it certainly isn't a deep commitment. But it'll make it easier for both of us. I do want to make this work, Raven. I know it's difficult for you, and I am trying to... I don't know..." Jemma's voice tapered off.

Her blush deepened, and he could see how hard it was for her. He also knew she needed to say the words as much as he wanted to ease her discomfort.

"I really want to make whatever this is between us work out right. I know you keep saying you love me, but I still don't know what to say or do. You let me take the time I need and do it my way, and I know this is hard for you too." Her head dropped, and she was looking at the floor again. If there was one thing she did that he could decode, it was her deep discomfort from her dropping her head.

He reached out and placed a hand on her shoulder. "I'll do whatever it takes for you to understand I love you, and whatever it takes to show you that I value you above all things." His voice stayed soft.

Her head snapped up. "But what if I don't think I'm worth it?" Tears swam in her eyes.

"You are, but if this is too much, too fast, then talk to me and we'll work it out together." Stepping forward, he opened his arms, and she stepped into them. He savored the feel of her against him, close, skin to skin, taking and giving strength. His eyes closed, and he let the scent of her calm and quiet him. One day soon he hoped she'd see the value of what they had, and then they could plan a future together. He just needed patience and time.

✪ ✪ ✪ ✪

Jemma grabbed a seat at the conference table, looking around. The people at the table were now familiar to her, only Meredith remained an unknown factor.

A palpable air of excitement hovered as they prepared for the showdown. It was there in the vibrations of the table as feet and fingers tapped and the subdued chatter. Duvall had a meal prepared as they ran through the tactical aspects of the assault.

"So now that we're all here, let's run through the last information we have at hand." Duvall nodded to Grayson who reported on the arrangements he'd made for the *Elector*. Her fingers twined in Raven's as she listened intently. When Mellissa gave her report, she slid her hand free.

"Okay?" Raven's soft question caught her off guard.

"Yeah. I just want to take some notes." She tugged out her handscreen and started tapping as the information on known impact zones and possible areas for future attack were shared. Then came the sobering statistics of known deaths and losses.

"Well, since the food is here, let's take a break and eat." Duvall waved to the large platters that had been placed in the center of the table.

In almost silence the gathered filled their plates. The smells of the meats and vegetables wafted up from her plate as she ate, the knots in her belly loosening until she remembered she'd soon be called on to add to the reports.

After the dishes were cleared, Duvall called them back to

attention. "Chowd?" Chowd's report was just as sobering. "We've made all the preparations for entry into the atmosphere. Jemma and I have ascertained that there's a dark zone in their scanning. It only gives us about twenty feet of flyable space where we'll be off their radar, but I'm confident that with her skill, we can remain in the zone. The greatest threat will be if we meet any traffic, as that will interfere with our flight plan. We've also created a small device which would allow us to jam their comm. systems, but it'll be touch and go as it has a limited reception area."

Jemma straightened in her chair and glanced at the gathered crew. "We fitted it to the front of the shuttle, and all the retrofitting has been removed. With some judicious work, we've altered the tail and wing configuration to get maximum speed out of the shuttle. I've also preset coordinates, so that on my signal, it will fly itself to a small settlement hidden here, just in case something happens." Jemma pointed to a small area on the holographic construct of surface of the planet. "I've also added a cloaking screen, where it'll assume the image of its surroundings. It's a bit like having a monitored parking zone, and we'll know exactly where it is. But my plan is to get out with at least one spook ship."

She looked around the table, assessing each participant. Duvall nodded slowly in agreement with the planning.

Jemma continued, "Chowd also raised some concerns that, even with what we know about the spooks, there could be some issues with the controls. He has asked that Meredith be available in case there are issues. At this point, I don't think we'll need her on the planet for that, but I'd like her on standby."

Meredith looked up, her dark eyes questioning, and nodded slowly. Duvall's mouth tightened, and she could see Mellissa place her hand over one of his.

"I know she's your sister, Duvall, but she is also a trained member of the Admiralty. Chowd has informed me that she's more than able to protect herself, but that's an aspect of our job. We take the risks for the Empire. We keep the citizens safe and protect them, however we need to. You took that oath, I took that oath, and so did Meredith." Jemma's words were carefully spoken as she watched him, his gaze on his sister. His eyes swiveled to meet hers, dark and angry. The room was silent, and she felt her back itch and prickle. Finally he nodded, and Mellissa shot her a grateful look. The feeling retreated.

She exhaled, letting the pressure wash away. She'd initially been unsure when Mellissa had asked her to raise it in this forum. But she'd said what needed to be said and he hadn't jumped all over her.

"I know Mellissa appreciated your speaking out," Raven whispered to her.

She turned to look at him. "I just hope he takes it in the manner it's intended."

The meeting continued and she held on to Raven's hand, listening to the rumble of his voice as he gave a short report. When Duvall requested any further information, Chowd spoke up.

"Duvall, there's some conjecture as to the safety of the Empire infiltrator. I've been working on a plan to get to her and free her if possible. I believe now would be the appropriate time to share some of the information I've gleaned over the last six months. I have contacts within Crick Sur Banden's camp, some very long-standing connections." He turned to face the questioning gazes of the newer crewmembers at the table. "Duvall has been aware of this for some extensive period of time, together with my full identity. Most of you know me as Sturat Chowd, but my full title is actually Chowd Sturat Sur Banden. My father is Crick Sur Banden, and my mother was a slave he took as concubine."

A ripple of surprise and consternation filled the air, and Jemma found herself tensing slightly at this information. She kept her eyes on his face as he waited, calmly shuttered against the reaction.

"I was considered a lesser son, not being full Ru'Edan, but after his other son died, my mother was concerned that he'd try to brainwash me into thinking that the Ru'Edan was the superior race. She died trying to get me to the Empire. When Crick Sur Banden found us, she injured him, giving me time to take his personal shuttle. He killed her. My mother was half-sister to Admiral Elphin, which is why my identity has remained hidden until now. That's why I've been working covertly with a range of operatives within the Empire to get information to the Admiral." He paused, and for the first time Jemma noted the slightest gray tinge to his skin. "Grayson and Elara have known for some time too, as it has been necessary for both medical and service reasons to have others understand the situation I have been in."

He glanced around to those sitting at the table, and Jemma would have described the air as thick with tension.

"My friends have indicated that the infiltrator has been watched for some time, as Crick Sur Banden knew she was slipping information through diplomatic channels to the Admiralty. What he didn't know was that I was the one receiving the information. The last update I heard, before we left Earth, was that he had plans in mind for her and that his use of Xeradax, a Ru'Edan drug, has been increasing. Xeradax is highly addictive, with side effects that include paranoia, hallucinations, and eventually the closing down the nervous system with prolonged use."

He paused again, looking around almost ruefully.

"It's understood that he has been becoming increasingly unstable for some time and that there are, within his ranks, dissidents who regret their choices in joining the rogues and fear him. That, and the fact that his dependency on the drug has increased markedly in the last six months." His voice had become heavier, and now he looked and sounded exhausted, something Jemma had never seen from him before. "I believe that I can get her out of there, but it may necessitate me doing things that seem incomprehensible and leveraging a number of my contacts. It may necessitate me going under cover with him for a period, though we won't know until we get there. I've spoken to Duvall about this eventuality and he agrees, we may need to do whatever works by the end of the mission." He looked at Duvall, who nodded.

Meredith raised her head and said, "They know you're tied to Duvall. I intercepted a transmission from the Admiralty. There's an infiltrator there too, on the Ru'Edan side. We've been working on that since Duvall destroyed their plans to stop the Earth Empire formation. I hadn't had time to work out who it was, but they knew who you are. I believe that they'll try to take you, as Crick Sur Banden thinks you're coming back to the fold. So that would work in our favor if need be."

"Shit! Are you sure, Meredith?" The words erupted from Duvall.

"Absolutely. It was the last transmission I intercepted before leaving for my mission." She looked grim. "I've already made the Admiral aware of this and they're seeking the infiltrator using information from the transmissions I've intercepted and decoded." She stopped and looked at the rest of the crew. "I believe he may be within the hangar crews. To the best of our knowledge, he's male, possibly thirties or forties, and trying to hide in plain sight. He has knowledge of the comings and goings that only the hanger crews would be privy to. We believe he's been in place for some time, as we've been watching the information dribble through, so we can stay abreast of his plans. He knew when you came in with Mellissa, Duvall."

Duvall scowled at the piece of information, and she nodded in understanding.

"He also knew where Jemma was initially placed within the academy and when she was deployed to the Alpha Squadron. I would imagine they also now know that she's with the *Elector*."

Jemma sat up and looked at Duvall, who nodded.

"They've been following you for some time. That's why we sent you to the academy. Of course, you had to learn how to survive in your new time and we couldn't keep you on the *Elector* at that point. However, we did have crewmembers keeping an eye on you. Particularly Raven." Duvall spoke quietly.

"What? What do you mean Raven kept an eye on me?" She swung quickly to look at Raven. A red tide rose over his cheeks, and she narrowed her eyes.

"The Admiralty thought it might be safest to put you somewhere secure, but have someone watch over you. I volunteered, Jem. I wanted to make sure you were safe. Actually, to be honest, I needed to know that you were safe and I had good contacts in the academy. Chowd wasn't able to work there, given his background, and if it had been Duvall...well, you would have refused to see him."

"Oh God!" Her voice became strangled as the truth was revealed, making her feel shallow and self-absorbed. His hand squeezed hers, and she examined how she felt. Sure, she wished she'd known earlier, but she felt pleasure that he felt her important enough to protect. She squeezed his hand and heard him breathe a sigh of relief. They would need to discuss this later, and she gave him a tentative smile.

"Okay then, we believe that they know we're coming," Duvall stated.

"Yes, but I think that we can use stealth in our favor. We need to draw their attention to the *Elector* while the others go in." Meredith's voice was steely. "If we can get their focus there, it will mean Jemma can fly the shuttle and arrive at the base before they realize it, then neutralize their security systems. Once that's complete and the fleet arrives, they'll be ready to deploy the ground troops they have on standby. The Admiral has authorized whatever means are necessary to shut down Crick Sur Banden. He personally would rather see him taken alive, but if necessary, a body will be sufficient for the rogues to surrender. At least, that's what all our intelligence has pointed to."

"Right. We need to prepare a plan for the *Elector* to act as decoy long enough for the shuttle and crew to do their job. Let's get another look at the star chart." Duvall hit the button, and the chart rose above the table.

✪   ✪   ✪   ✪

"0100 hours and just dragging in. Reminds me of my past and partying, but this time I'm just plain dead on my feet." Jemma yawned loudly, raising her hands into the air. "But you know what? We need to talk, and I'd rather get this cleared away right now." She kinked her neck to the side and back as they stood in his quiet, blue office.

"Yeah, I can see why you think that. Duvall, Grayson, Chowd, and myself...well, we all thought he might come after you. You were so angry, with your refusal to talk to any of us. Chowd, unfortunately, is banned from all those areas because of who he is, Duvall was too close to Mellissa, and you were refusing any contact there. We thought Grayson would be too close as well, which is why we all agreed I was the lucky candidate. Didn't you ever wonder why I was around at the academy so much?"

His eyes shined in the half-light as he stood on the other side of the room, as if trying to let her reach the conclusions she needed to without any suggestions from him. Watchful and waiting, he jammed his hands in the pockets of his flight suit, his eyes hooded.

"Not really. Initially, I was too focused on my anger, then trying to come up with a plan for my future." She shrugged. "I knew you were there, but you always seemed to be doing something, so I guess I never put two and two together." She felt defeated for a moment. "Remember, I thought I had been left there. Pretty much abandoned. Again."

Her shoulders slumped, and her voice was thready with exhaustion and remembered loss. She dragged a hand through her hair, letting him see the inner turmoil as she thought carefully through what she said next.

"I'd been in that position my whole life, but this time I was out of my depth. I didn't just not know anyone, I also didn't know anything. Everything was so...alien. I was lost." She looked at him with tears in her eyes.

He swallowed. "I would never let that happen, Jem. You know that, don't you? There wasn't anything I could do to show you, but I was there. If you'd been in any danger, any at all, I would have acted. I had people watching out for you the whole time."

His eyes blazed hot, and she accepted what he said. She could feel the honesty in his voice winding a path through to her heart. God help her, she did believe him, and that terrified her as much as it reassured her. Unconsciously, she took a step forward.

"Yes, I believe you. I just wish I'd known earlier." Her voice was quiet.

She took another step, all the while watching those beautiful blazing-blue eyes of his. "I do love you too, and do you know something? I don't feel alone anymore. Here, with you? I feel safe. Safer and more cared for than ever before." She took a step, then another, and somehow he met her and enfolded her in his strong arms.

"God knows I needed to hear that, Jem, but be sure, I still want forever with you. I know you aren't ready to give me that, but some day you will. When that day comes, I'll be the happiest man alive. But for now, just being with you is enough." His voice was rough, and his eyes glittered. She had the uncanny feeling he was looking into her soul, and she shivered.

"Why me though? I mean, it's not like I'm anything special. I come with so many problems. How can you possibly want forever with me?" Her voice dropped to a broken whisper.

"Because inside, you're so beautiful, in every way that counts." He pointed to the region of her heart. "You would give up everything, even yourself, for someone you care about. You would give your life for your friends. I've seen you in action, and that amazes me. It draws me to you in a way I've never before experienced." With that, he leaned forward and kissed her softly on the mouth. His hand skittered up until it rested on her shoulders, grounding her as nothing else could.

She took a deep breath. "I want forever with you too." The six words she whispered fell from her lips, and he smiled. "But tonight isn't the time to talk about that. Tonight I just want to be with you, to feel your body against mine and to know you need to be with me." Her hands twined once more behind his head, pulling it closer, and her eyes slid shut.

"Then I'll be satisfied with that for now, and when you're ready, we can talk about what comes next." His voice was muffled, and she could feel the movement of his lips against her hair. The warm whisper of his breath on her skin sent shivers of anticipation through her.

"I don't want to talk now. I want to show you what I feel." Her lips met his, and the shock that jolted her system was electric. She opened her mouth to his.

He grabbed her waist and crushed her to him. The muscles of his chest moved, hard against her frame, as her fingers tangled in his hair. She pulled him closer toward her as the kiss deepened.

Then his hands were on her fasteners, ripping and tearing at her uniform. The air in the room heated as their passion grew, overwhelming them both. Breathing grew ragged. Hearts beat faster than before.

His mouth tore away from her lips and skittered down to the pulse at her throat, which beat hard. She thrust her head back wildly while her hands found his suit and tore at it. Buttons flew to the ground.

Breathing raggedly, she whispered, "Raven, I need you to fill me. God, I love you so much."

Hands grabbed her around the waist with her ship suit caught in bands of warm iron. He carried her to the bed and carefully placed her down. The dim lights in the cabin reflected the glitter of passion shining in his deep-blue gaze.

She stood quickly and stripped down to her bra and panties, which offered little protection from his heated gaze. Then that divine mouth of his, tightening with passion and need, descended once more. His long fingers trailed over the straps of her bra, toying with it as she reached for the clasp at the back.

He stayed her hands. "No, tonight I can do that."

She could hear the grin in his words, and she stilled. His fingers continued to trace up and down slowly until an ache grew. His fingers brushed the cups lightly, tripping over taut nipples, which jutted out against the fabric, then back up. Her breathing grew more ragged.

He first played with one side, then the other, up and down. He toyed with her breasts as they grew heavier. Unconsciously, she moved in time with his fingers, pushing into his touch. Up. Stroke. Down. Stroke.

She was panting with need when he finished his down stroke, but this time instead of starting back up, his fingers stroked around her nipples then continued down under the weighted flesh and around the band to the back. He leaned forward to unclasp her and lightly licked her lips with the tip of his tongue. She gasped against his mouth, so tightly wound with passion.

Panties wet with need, she hooked her fingers under the elastic, but his hands were there too, pulling her fingers away. "My turn again." His voice was gravelly and his eyes bright. The flat of his hands pushed down her flanks, hooking thumbs under the elastic and pulling them away to leave her stripped bare to his gaze. The heat and passion in his eyes burned her. Her panties slipped to the floor, and she stepped out of them. He reached for the remnants of his clothing and tore them off.

By the time they were both naked, they were once more fused

at mouth, chest, and hips, hands moving over the other's already passion-slicked skin.

The touch of his lips this time was electric, and the thrill of his caress was like nothing she had ever felt before. It shocked her to the core like lightning pulsing through the sky, pulling the breath from her body. Her body was boneless, yet energized. Moaning low in her throat, the feeling of his arms tightening around her, pulling her closer, she stood within the cradle of his body, ratcheting her need to a higher point. Hard muscles met soft, feminine curves as she moved her damp body against his.

The air in the cabin grew close. He pushed her up against the wall, and the feel of the coolness on her skin made her shiver. His body crowded against hers.

"Tonight I'm going to love you like no one else ever has or ever will." His voice echoed through her system.

His fingers touched and caressed every inch of her skin as they moved lower, each move scorching her. A trail of fire licked at her skin as she tossed her head from side to side, his lips at her throat, sliding downward, ever downward, his tongue flicking and darting until he reached one peaked nipple. He licked it, teasing it with his hot tongue, then when she was ready to cry out, her hands clutching his hair, he opened his mouth and sucked.

Firm. Hard.

She bucked. His hands found her most intimate skin and touched the downy hairs that grew there. He traced the lips of her sex lightly, and her hips moved once more, the torture ripping heaving gasps from her body. Her heart beat a wild tattoo as she moaned.

He released one breast. "Perfect. Oh, so perfect," he muttered against the skin of her belly as he slid further down her length.

His lips found her stomach, and his tongue toyed lightly with the indentation. She pushed into him.

"I'm going to feast upon your delectable body."

Her eyes flashed open, blind with passion, as his tongue found her. "Oh God!" she whimpered.

His fingers opened her to the invasion of his mouth, and she felt the tightness in her belly as she shook. A screaming orgasm roared through her, and she clenched. He sucked harder, and her body tensed then slowly subsided. Her legs wobbled, and she was caught up in his arms.

"But Raven, you didn't..." Her words died away as she felt his erection hard against her. "Not yet, but we aren't finished." His voice was hoarse, and she could see the sweat shining on his skin and feel the tremors of his body as he carried her to the bed, laying her down. His lips found hers as they lowered to the bed, his hands once more on her breasts. She reached for him, rubbing lightly on his shaft. He moved against her hand.

"Wait." He groaned the word, held himself taut for one moment. Then another.

He opened his eyes, and in them, she saw not just lust, but also love. She reached out, once more pushing him back toward the covers.

"My turn." Gripping his hands, she pushed them up and out so that he was completely at her mercy. She nipped the side of his neck then blew lightly, touching the spot with her tongue, and he moved. "Not yet," she said.

He moved below her, his body betraying his aroused state, but he held himself in the position she'd requested. She nibbled her way down his chest, pale and hairless, just as she liked them. His muscles flexed beneath her touch and below her hand, the rapid beat of his heart, the dampness of his skin, and his panting breaths pushed her onward.

Reaching his flat nipples, she stopped, toyed for a brief moment, then quickly licked as she moved down his body. His nipples tightened in response to her ministrations. His trembling grew beneath her hands, and his groans escaped tight lips. She smiled wickedly at him.

"Stop bedeviling me, woman." His voice was hoarse.

"I'm not finished yet, Raven. I still have to get to the best part." She widened her smile as he reached for her. "No, it's still my turn." With that, she lowered her head. She found the indentation of flesh and dipped her tongue in and out in a parody of the act of passion. "I'm going to drive you so mad," she whispered against his stomach, continuing to trail down his body once more.

Her mouth had opened over his erection when he jackknifed up. "I can't...*Eshra* help me...I need to be in you." His hands gripped her shoulders, pushing her over and down onto her back, his mouth zeroing onto hers, and his tongue speared into her mouth as his cock drove home.

Her legs wrapped around him as she undulated beneath him. Their movements grew wilder, faster. Hands slipped and firmed against flesh; cries of passion filled the air as their bodies slapped against each other. Her head was thrown back as she cried out, her body quivering as she orgasmed in his arms, feeling him thrust once more, firmly pushing himself home within her body.

"Jemma!" His hoarse shout echoed through the cabin, and he then held himself against her. Their hearts beat in time as they heaved, locked tightly around each other. "I love you," he whispered into her ear.

As he shifted both of them slowly, their bodies cooled. He tucked her into his arms as they both drifted off to sleep.

❂ ❂ ❂ ❂

Morning came all too early, she mused, stretching as she woke, then turned to pat the bed. His spot was cool, indicating that he'd been up and around for some time. She scanned the room. There was no sign of him.

Rising slowly, she made her way to the small bathroom, wincing as the bright light assaulted her eyes. "Lights dim thirty-five percent," she said, climbing into the shower. "Water on high, medium spray." She waited for the blessed touch of water on her sleep-fogged body. She closed her eyes and cleared her mind.

Finally, feeling free of the last of the fogginess, she opened her eyes to see Raven standing outside the shower, slumped against its side with a slight smile on his face.

"Water off," she said, taking the step out of the shower and toward him.

He lifted one hand, holding a towel. A fierce emotion rose in her gut, and she shook her head to dismiss the feeling of dizziness that rose in her.

"Come on, let's get you dried and a coffee into you before we head to the mess. We have about fifteen minutes." He pulled away from the wall with a slight smile on his face and turned toward the door. "Don't be too long," he called over his shoulder, and she watched him saunter away.

She hurried through drying off and made her way into the cabin, dressing as speedily as she could as the smell of coffee wafted through the open door. Her stomach rumbled, and she grinned. "I hope you have that coffee ready for me?" Jemma called through the door, dragging a hand through her hair.

"You need to come and get it. I'm not bringing it in to you." His voice was light, but there was a grave undertone in it.

She stopped short as she entered the room. He stood in the center of the office holding a parcel, a particularly somber look on his face.

"Jem, I know you can protect yourself, but... *Barsha*! I'm making a hash of this." The uncertainty on his face caught her. "Look, I know you know how to take care of yourself, but training is nothing like the real thing." He looked at her, eyes piercing, and she saw his worry.

Her heart dropped to her stomach.

For a moment, she felt a burn in her stomach. *He doesn't want me to go?* "I'm going. It's my job."

"No, it's not that you shouldn't go."

A wave of dizziness swept through her once more.

"You need to be there, probably more than me." He stopped and dragged in a ragged breath. "I need you to be careful, because you mean so much to me. I had this made for you." She reached out as he awkwardly shoved the package into her hands. His hands shook, and her eyes flew back to his. Carefully, she shook out the parcel to find a protective combat jacket within.

"I can't make you stay behind, but I can find a way to protect you. Please wear it for me." His words touched her deep inside, and a crack opened in the wall around her heart.

Jemma reached up to Raven. "What about you? What will you

wear?" Her words were soft. She extended her fingers to his face and touched his lips. "What about your safety? Without you, my world is gone." She leaned toward him and kissed him on the lips. "Forever is something we are going to discuss when we get back here, right?" Her eyes burned, and she hoped he could see what she felt in them.

His arms swept around her. "I love you so much, but I need you to come out of this alive. Okay? No heroics, no saving me at the cost of your own life. Do you understand me? Promise me, Jem." His voice was taut with emotion, his lips against her ear, and she felt the shake of emotion in his body.

"I promise, so long as you do too. I haven't committed just to lose you now." She was fierce, turning in his arms. "I will wear your jacket, so long as you have one too." She pulled away, knowing that they had just minutes before they were due in the mess with the others going on the mission.

His crooked smile made her heart beat faster. "Yes, I have one, and yes, I'll be wearing it."

She released a pent-up breath. "Good. Now, where's my coffee?"

She broke the tension, stepping back from his embrace. Her chest was still tight from the emotions that churned inside, threatening to overwhelm if she let them. A bubble of love and commitment that she'd never felt before filled her, and she embraced it fully.

He handed her the coffee, their hands meeting and the spark of awareness flickering through her. Their eyes met. Silently, they finished their drinks, then put down their cups on his desk.

"Leave them there," he said gently, the warmth in his voice washing over her. "We can clear them up when we get back from the mission."

They locked their hands together and left the cabin.

Chapter 14

Jemma clambered into the pilot's seat, running through the pre-flight checklist, her face impassive and tight with concentration. Raven watched her work, mulling over the events of the morning, especially those in the office when he had surprised her with the jacket.

He'd nearly broken his silence, his worries over her safety overwhelming him for a moment, but his greatest hopes crystallized the minute she had said they would talk when they got back from the mission. Now all they had to do was get in, do the job, and get out. His role was simple—go in, disable the systems for Chowd, then get the shuttle back to the *Elector*, or if not that, then at least have Jemma get him back.

The suit might protect her body from most gunfire, but it had taken him only seconds to realize it wouldn't protect her if they transmitted her somewhere else. For insurance, he'd had a tracking tag inserted into her suit. His crew had worked around the clock to ensure the suit was completed in time for the mission.

He shook himself. Time was short, and he needed to run a final check of the systems he and Chowd had created to keep the Ru'Edan systems jammed, hiding their entry into the area. He ran through each point, checked and double-checked, and finally satisfied, he turned to see Jemma watching him.

Her face glowed with excitement. "You know, if it wasn't so dangerous, this could almost be fun."

He knew she expected him to rise to the bait. He felt the smile climb over his face and laughed at her comment. This woman brought out the best in him, he mused, watching her climb out of her seat and move toward him.

"Sure, and you just live for the adventure, don't you?" He winked at her, and her beautifully-shaped eyebrow arched up. She reached him and laid her hand softly upon his shoulder. He covered it with his, giving her a squeeze.

"Don't you know it, grease boy!" For a moment, he heard a glimpse of the carefree girl she should have been, then her hand pulled free of his. "I'm ready to go here. What about you?" She sobered in readiness to begin the mission, and her eyes cooled as she changed gears, the shimmering violet turning flat as she became all combat-pilot before him.

"Yeah, I'm ready, and Chowd gave me the all-clear on the secondary checks. Let's get him into place. Once we exit hyperspace, we'll have only seconds to launch so that we're using the disturbance from the gate to mask our movements."

"Right. Do you want me to page him, or will you?" Her words were cool and professional, and he marveled that a woman with so little experience in combat could be so professional already. He'd known many experienced pilots who could react like this, but very few new ones.

"You do it. I have a couple of things I need to grab, and we'll rendezvous back here in, say, fifteen minutes? That way our window is about twenty minutes to launch."

A quick nod and she withdrew from him and headed out of the shuttle to use the intra-ship communication point. He watched her go and turned back to finish his task.

❂ ❂ ❂ ❂

"Exiting beta hyperspace now. Shuttle, be ready to launch on my mark... Mark!" Duvall's voice filtered through the communications system of the shuttle. Jemma eased the throttle forward as the craft lifted from the shuttle bay floor.

"Ready for launch. Drop the shields around the cargo bay." She spoke as her gaze darted around, checking and double-checking the surroundings. "Bogey check?"

"All looks clear, no emissions or radar showing." The voice filled the cockpit as she waited for the final confirmation of clearance. "Shields are down, and you're good for go." The words were hard, and she felt the excitement thrum through her system. Jemma punched the throttle, and they shot through the opening.

"Chowd, get that blocker on line," Jemma muttered, and frowned.

"Raven, keep an eye out for any unfriendlies. I'll need as much notice as possible to maneuver this craft. We should be out of here before they can scan for us, but we can't afford to take anything for granted." Her words were tight and controlled, just like her movements on the controls. "*Elector*, we're going to silent mode now. We'll catch you on the other side. Cardnew out." She clicked off the communications system. "Right, we're on our own now. Hang tight, I'm about to run the tight elliptical path, then we're going to take the dive."

She hit the thrusters, and they whined as she started the tight turn, the forces involved pushing them back against their seats from side to side. She could feel the safety belt holding her in position, cutting into her skin as it fought against the centrifugal forces. Her heart pounded.

Not two years ago she wouldn't have felt the rush of pushing a shuttle beyond its design specs, yet now here she was, spearheading this part of their mission.

"Jem? Still no bogies that we can see, but it seems too easy. How quickly can you change trajectory once we're committed to entry?" Chowd's voice broke through her thoughts.

"Yeah, I was thinking something similar. Grab the helm while I try something on the simulator."

She moved awkwardly out of the pilot's seat, moving aside to let Chowd in, waiting until he was settled, his long legs stowed in front, the straps raking over his shoulders and clicking into place. Then she gave the voice command to transfer all piloting systems to him.

Weaving around Raven's legs and making her way to the small workstation located at the back of the cabin, she strapped in and started running simulations, her head running calculations even as she started the system. Watching the proposed trajectory for entry on the small holo-screen, Jemma turned the simulation results this way and that, looking for viable alternatives.

They had descend into the canyon, then fly through it. That was the biggest tactical advantage they had. It was perilous to traverse under any circumstances, more so at the pace they'd need to travel, but nothing better flashed into her mind—no entry spots that would give them the opportunity of stealth, except the entry point she'd located initially above the largest body of water on the southern continent.

She shook her head and rolled her shoulders, releasing as much tension as she could. "There have to be alternatives," she muttered under her breath, and her hands started to fly over the keypad once more.

"Jemma? We have a problem. I think we have been visually scouted." Chowd's grim voice broke her concentration. She swung her head around to look at him. She had thought him beautiful in the past, but in full warrior mode, he was scary. His eyes narrowed as he swung his head back toward her.

"Are you sure?" Her voice was steady, calm even. Her hands hovered over the keypad. "I have scout mobility on the radar. The blocker is online and working optimally, so they shouldn't have seen us. That's the only way they could have worked out we're on the way." He paused and looked at her, one eyebrow quirking. "Unless..." He stopped once more.

"Yeah, unless Meredith is right and they knew we were on the way. In which case, the entry point will be immaterial. What will be more important now is just how quickly I can fly this bucket to the contact point." She finished the thought, and her gaze swung to Raven. "How much harder can we push this shuttle, beyond what we're doing now?"

"I expected that and have worked on tweaking every system to run on minimal power, so I can reroute the excess to the thrusters. I also ramped up a few things, including the secondary generators, while we were working on it. I believe we can safely increase its speed by around thirty-seven percent and perhaps as much as forty-five, but that's then going to affect its maneuverability and structural integrity."

"Okay, structural integrity is going to be the biggest issue then. Increase the shielding and speed as much as you can, safely. Drop everything down to boost it except the enviro. Maneuverability is my domain, just tell me what systems you bleed before you do it, so I can compensate. There are some systems I can manage without, but give me a heads-up first, right?"

He nodded, then she let him go back to his calculations.

"Chowd? I need my seat back, and make sure your weapons

systems are primed in case they're needed," she said. "Any viable alternatives are pretty much gone now, so we follow the original entry plan. Just with a bit more speed."

She sucked in a deep breath and focused as she always had, but in the back of her mind was the refrain *Do what you have to and remember you're expendable.* She pushed the thought away. Now wasn't the time to dwell on self-destructive thoughts.

Once Chowd vacated the pilot's seat, she slipped in, pulled the belt over her shoulders, and engaged the safety locks, regaining control of the shuttle. Chowd and Raven both made alterations at lightning speed, giving her extra thrust as she worked to compensate and push the shuttle faster toward the planet. It loomed now large on her viewscreen and a moment of disquiet bloomed.

"Jemma? You okay?"

She gulped, realizing she'd somehow radiated her fear to Raven. "Yeah. I'm good." Jemma checked the radar to see the blips of the scout ships closing in. "Boys, it looks like we have incoming. Chowd, you ready back there?"

"When you are, Jem." His words were grim, and she focused on the scout ships that headed toward them.

"Time to rock and roll. Hold on tight!" She pulled the throttle stick to the side and rolled the craft as the first shots were released toward the heaving shuttle. "Get the bastard, Chowd!" she yelled, and pulled the craft back to level before tugging the nose sharply up. The exchange of fire was narrow in her focus, and she heaved and bullied the shuttle through a range of moves.

Up. Down. Around. Faster and faster while Chowd used the weapons with great accuracy. The craft took a hit and shuddered. "Damage report, Raven?" Her stomach tightened, and her palms grew damp. Her fingers cramped on the throttle stick, but she held on, firmly waiting for the information.

"Minimal. Shields took a five-percent knock starboard, at sector seven-A." His voice steadied her. She focused again. This time was harder; knowing that the ship was limited and already flying beyond its original design concerned her, but they were committed with a job to do.

They'd already taken out four of the ships thanks to Raven and Chowd's work, and she was quietly thankful they weren't spooks. She knew they couldn't take them out, no matter how well she and Chowd had altered the shuttle.

A hiss sounded and she sucked in an unsteady breath; the debris was causing issues with the trajectory they had to travel. "Focus on the lead ship, Chowd. It seems to be spearheading the attack."

Chowd grunted in response as she checked the radar.

"Fuck! This one's being difficult and I can't change course easily now. Get a lock on the bastard, Chowd." She pulled the stick again, and the ship creaked as she twisted it.

Chowd fired off again but missed the ship. "He's moving around too much, Jemma, and the computer is struggling to lock on. Raven, can you get a manual lock using the radar?" Chowd's voice was harsh and strained.

"Yeah, working it now...got it! Sending it to you now." She heard him muttering behind her as they worked to lock onto the scout ship.

"Got it!" Chowd called as they watched the ship in front of them disintegrate.

"Last one then," Jemma called back, having finally gotten behind it. It moved up and down, left and right. "Got a lock yet?" she demanded once more.

"Nearly...there...just...a little more! Yes!" Chowd fired, clipping the right wing of the scout ship. "*Barsha*! That should have taken him out. Going again. Jem, can you pull her starboard... now!"

She pulled once more on the stick, and Chowd took the shot. For a second, she thought it had missed and prepared to pull to the port side, then a ripple moved through the ship as it lit up, jagged lights rippling along the hull as it ignited from within then splintered, pieces of craft spinning out into space.

"Well, that was a brief and intense flurry of excitement. Raven, I need a full damage report. Chowd, how are the weapons going?"

"I'm stabilizing the starboard shield at seven-A, and we had thirteen-percent damage to the rear shield. That I can possibly get to around six percent, but I would need to do a physical repair to get it up to full rate again." Raven's voice sounded tense, and she looked around briefly. He hunched over his console, hands moving fast as he made the necessary changes to the shield formats.

She smiled for a moment. God, he looked cool as a cucumber still, unlike her. She pulled her flight suit under the combat jacket away from damp skin. During the brief skirmish she had sweated on each move the shuttle had made.

"Weapons systems are good. The modified laser banks are running at optimum." "Good. Raven, can you grab me a water tube from the cooler box?" She waited as he unstrapped and moved to the back of the cabin, watching the slow and unhurried movements. Once he had handed it to her, he gripped her shoulder momentarily, and she accepted the quick kiss on the forehead. "Thanks," she mumbled.

He squeezed once more then moved back to his console.

Flipping the tab on the top of the bottle, she took a long pull of the water then slipped the bottle into the holder, wiped her face, and rechecked the computer. "Entry in ten minutes. Make sure you're strapped in and ready to go. It's likely going to be a bumpy ride." With that, she once more grabbed the controls and corrected the path of the shuttle toward her projected entry point. The shuttle flew toward the atmosphere, and she checked and rechecked her speed. Minor adjustments kept her mind and hands busy as they edged closer, the planet looming before her red and somehow menacing.

She held the throttle tightly, matching it in time to the movements of the shuttle, washing off the speed of the entry, each movement no more than the gentlest nudge. The glare of the heat waves washing over the shields was almost blinding in their shimmering intensity, and the shuttle shuddered with the speed of entry.

"Come on, baby, this won't take all that long if you cooperate," she crooned to the ship as she started another small turn, each movement employed to slow the flight of the shuttle just enough to keep it from disintegrating as they entered the atmosphere.

The gray-tinged clouds of the lower atmosphere peeked just beyond the mesosphere. "Raven, how wide is the mesosphere again?" Her voice was still cool, knowing that this was one of the easier aspects of the mission.

"Two-hundred-seventy-five kilometers," he answered, his voice strained as he kept altering the shields to allow for the external strains on the small craft.

"Okay, so we don't have a lot of time for re-entry this way. Chowd, I need you to start running those figures for fuel usage now. I need to know how much of a whiff will be left in this baby by the time we hit at the new speeds we factored. Don't forget to compensate for changes to the shields. Raven, send him the current shield data now. We're going to need it as soon as we clear into the tropopause."

"Sending the data now." Raven's voice sounded rough and it scratched at her mind like fingernails on a slateboard.

Jemma turned her attention back to washing off the speed, knowing it would take a number of hypersonic split-S maneuvers to get them down safely. Sure, they could go faster, but given the damage the shuttle had already taken, it made more sense to get the shuttle down slowly with as little damage as possible, but still with enough speed that the Ru'Edan couldn't easily follow them via trackers.

Her stomach clenched; they still had to get through the canyon. She knew that would test her skills to the max. Her thoughts were interrupted as the shuttle shuddered violently, each movement magnified, and she kept watching the information scrolling over the datascreen.

The longer they took, the more the chance of being located on radar, but the faster they traveled, the chance of more damage to the shuttle's integrity. It had to be one or the other. Shield integrity came first, she reminded herself. She swiped at the beads of sweat that rose over her face.

"Come on, baby, not too much longer," she crooned once more, watching the altimeter showing the rate of descent. Her attention split between that and the data on the shields Raven kept sending her.

Raven broke into her concentration. "Jem, about ten thousand meters to the upper stratosphere."

She once more began the zig-zag movements of the shuttle, and finally she entered the cloud banks.

"Eight thousand and falling quickly."

She grabbed the bottle of water, took a quick pull to wet her dry mouth, and stashed it back into the holder.

"Six thousand and falling quickly." His voice grounded her, and she continued her movements over the keypad. "Shields and hull looking good."

"Okay, we're about to enter the mesosphere. Hang on, as once we are in that, we'll start preparations to pull into position to enter the canyons." Her voice was breathless as beads of sweat pooled on her nose and chin. The gauges showed the speed of her descent, and she fought to pull up the nose of the shuttle. "We've entered the mesosphere! Right, boys, let's get into position."

Suddenly, once more, the cabin was a hive of activity, with voices calling out their position, bogey checks, and shield diagnostics. Her hands moved fast as she altered the course of the craft with as much speed as she could while fighting the crafts natural shimmy.

"We have to enter the canyon at the exact location we plotted." Her words helped her to focus while centrifugal forces pushed them back into their seats.

Suddenly they were through the clouds and the ground grew larger by the second. The shuttle bucked wildly as she pulled and pushed it through the air, the engines whining loudly and warning lights flashing. She ignored them, knowing there was only one chance to bring them out right where they needed to be. The crevasse loomed, growing larger and larger as they hurtled toward the ground.

Jemma pulled the throttle back, and the engines screamed in distress. Her heart thudded in her chest, beating a wild tattoo while her skin itched, prickling at the sweat that was pouring down her face.

"Come on, just pull up a little bit." Her voice was hoarse as if she had been screaming, her shoulders ached as she fought the shuttle into submission, each move feeling like pushing concrete blocks across sand.

Their entry point to the canyon, no more than a fissure, rounded and weathered by nature, was just ahead. The rocky red chasm continued to rush toward them as she used every ounce of skill to keep them in the air. Closer the point loomed, getting larger, then finally she skewed the ship, shooting inside the rift then pulling up, fighting and pushing the craft to do exactly what she needed it to do.

The canyon sides came close enough to the craft that the wings pushed the air onto the walls, causing rocks to fall behind them. An outcrop loomed before and Raven called out, "Clearance less than one meter wing side, Jem."

She felt her face move into a grim smile as she waited until the last second and tipped the craft slightly.

"*Barsha*..." The word escaped from Chowd behind her, amazement coloring his tone. There was no time to respond, though, as they shot through the opening, her eyes on the altimeter and ahead to the once-more-narrowing canyon walls, striated reds and browns dotted here and there with jutting boulders.

Below them, raging blue water crashed wildly, sending up plumes of spray that coated her forward screen. Once again, Jemma tilted the craft; this time a creak and groan sounded as she scraped the side of the walls. Her stomach dropped, but she didn't let up the speed. She couldn't.

"I can't bank too much, otherwise we run the risk of being located by their radar." Her voice was tight, her grip on the ship's stick sliding a little as Jemma struggled to control the ship. Their balance had been affected by the damage to the wing. "Chowd, how much further to our designated rendezvous point?" Her chest heaved with the exertion of pushing and pulling the craft, making it submit to her demands.

"Twenty-five kilometers. Jem, it looks like there's one more major narrowing. I'm not sure we're going to be able to get through without being detected." His voice betrayed his concern.

"How far from away is it?" she asked as the craft brushed against the side of the canyon, causing a wobble. She fought the craft once more, demanding it bend to her will, but each time they glanced the rough canyon walls, the craft became a little less maneuverable. It was only a matter of time until the craft would be unflyable at their present speed.

"Five kilometers."

"Fuck! I wish we had known before." The words escaped from between clenched teeth. "The terrain here is unsuitable for mining exploration and housing due to the rapidly changing landscape. It seems that this is a new narrowing. Probably an outcrop that's dropped."

Squinting through the view she caught sight of the new narrowing of the canyon. She could clearly see where it had been formed from a falling piece of canyon wall. She glanced at the altimeter, calculated at lightning speed, and dropped the craft.

"*Barsha*!" She bit out the word as she pulled the craft just below the mass of boulders and dirt held in place by the existing walls.

They flew underneath the massive chunk of red rock, caught precariously between the walls of the ravine. The sky grew dark for just a moment, then they were rising once more.

"We dipped below the deck. Check to make sure we weren't seen, Chowd." She pushed the craft harder. "Raven, I need more speed. Increase the thrusters." Her gaze peered ahead, watching the cliffs whip by. "Chowd, how much further?"

"Ten kilometers. Nine. Eight. Jemma, ready to land in five. Four. Three." "Disengaging main thrusters. Five hundred meters to landing point...and..." Her hands raced over the controls as she brought the forward thrusters online to slow the shuttle while her body jerked. The bite of webbing at her shoulders had them screaming.

Tossing plumes of dirt covered the forward screens even as she toggled the landing gear to drop into position. Jemma engaged the undercarriage air thrusters so they hovered above the ground then slowly descended.

"Landing now." She decreased the thrust as they dipped toward the ground, and finally, with a soft jolt, they landed.

Her heart was thudding as she sat exhausted and wrung out in her seat. They achieved the first part of the mission successfully, she told herself. Her eyes closed as she gulped in air, and for a second, all she heard was blissful silence and all she saw was darkness. It wasn't quite long enough to recharge her batteries for the next phase though.

"Good job, Jemma. Now let's get going before they find us here. We have a hike to get to the bunker and we need to make sure we set up the perimeter security for the shuttle." Chowd's voice filled the air, pulling her back to reality.

Jemma undid the belt and headed for the rudimentary sanitary unit. She splashed her face after using the convenience then hauled the door open. Raven stood outside the door, quickly pushed her back in, and closed it again.

"We only have a minute." His voice was rough but warmed her. His lips connected with hers in a brutal kiss briefly before he pulled away. "*Barsha*, that was some flight! You aren't just good, you have a magic touch." Raven kissed her once more, this time softly. "We won't be able to do this again for a while, so promise me...promise—" His voice roughened as his eyes pierced her, the blue depths deepening. "—that you'll be careful. No stupid chances. Chowd and I can look after ourselves. You need to look after you." His eyes entreated her to listen, to promise.

Her hands gripped his, pulling them from her shoulders. "Raven, too much is at stake now. I will take care, because you promised me forever, so make sure you do too."

An urgent knocking on the door interrupted them. "Come on, you two, we need to get moving." *Chowd.*

She gulped, accepting that the next few hours could be the most dangerous of her life. She felt Raven pull away and straightened her flight suit under the cumbersome battle jacket once more as he opened the door. Chowd waited on the other side, holding two backpacks in his hand, a faintly amused expression on his face.

"Wait until you finish your mission, then you can lock yourselves away for however long you need." He grinned. For a second, she was sure she caught him winking, but it was gone as quick as a flash. "We need to move." With that, he pushed the packs into Raven's waiting hands and turned, opening the shuttle door and striding out.

They hurried after him down the ramp, then she turned, pressed the remote retraction button for the ramp, and waited for it to seal the ship. Finally satisfied, they stepped back, and she deployed the shields that should stop anyone from finding and getting in. Without a word, Jemma slipped the remote inside her boot, and turned.

Chapter 15

They'd been walking for hours when the bunker came into sight, the burn of two suns baking the ground as they trudged over the rock-strewn track. Every now then, a small rock fall would occur, showering the ground with dirt and pebbles. They'd slide against the walls, until they were sure there was no danger, then would head back out, moving as quickly as possible.

Jemma's mouth was dry and dusty before they resumed their trek, and she took a swallow of water, letting it settle in her mouth and drying the membranes that were parched.

At the entry to the canyon, a small crevasse hid them from sight as they watched two guards lounging by the entrance, joking. It shocked her to see how much they looked like her. Sure, she'd known they were humanoid with gray skin, but seeing them closer thrust home just how much they could all benefit if they could finalize the peace treaty.

She cast a look at Chowd. His eyes squinted, and for a second, a mushrooming cloud of worry filled her. *What if this was an elaborate set up?* She shook herself. No, she trusted Chowd. Raven trusted him too, and so did all the other members of the crew. It was a fanciful notion and so unfair to him.

As if he could read her thoughts, his eyes flicked to her. "I owe them no allegiance, Jemma. I'll do whatever it takes to ensure the Earth Empire is successful in their negotiations." His words were terse, and she was ashamed of her thoughts.

Raven placed a hand on his shoulder. "We know, Chowd." Jemma placed her hand over Raven's.

Chowd smiled then swung back to the front of the cavern, pulling a weapon from the leg holster he wore. "We need to get out there. Raven and I will head around the back. You need to cover us. Once we take care of the guards, we can see about getting inside." His voice was once more businesses-like and she breathed deeply, reading that he understood her concerns.

On silent feet, he and Raven were gone, sliding along the edge

177

of the canyon walls. The light was fading, making it easier for them to keep to the deep shadows, and the black of the uniforms merged into the dark, grayish red of the rock at this point. Raven and Chowd crept behind the guards in tandem, clasping hands over mouths so that no sound escaped. She watched as with ruthless efficiency they dispatched the bodies. Then hefting them over their shoulders, they moved quickly and silently toward her hiding place.

A matter of seconds was all it took, and they were back, dropping the bodies with a barely audible thud behind a large boulder. Her stomach revolted for a minute, and she looked at Raven. He and Chowd had already bent to the task of stripping the dead guards of the combat uniforms and helmets they had worn. Moving speedily, they stripped off their own clothes, and in the gloom she watched as Raven quickly donned one set.

Let's go, he mouthed after they had applied skin color and inserted the contacts in their eyes. They moved into the now empty posts. At first glance, they would look like any other guard as they slouched into position. Jemma waited in the shadows behind Raven, watching silently.

Silence.

So far no one knew they were there. She hoped like hell it stayed like that and that they couldn't hear the thudding of her heart. She was sure it would give them away, but she controlled her breathing, her gaze darting back and forth, watching. A creak and groan of metal filled the air, and she shrank further back. Footsteps. It sounded like just one person shuffling toward Chowd and Raven.

A young girl came into sight. "Dinner," she said as she thrust two heaping plates toward them.

Chowd grabbed the girl, her eyes large with fright. Jemma could see bruises on her skin. "Time for fun first." His voice was guttural. She'd never heard him speak like that and watched with horror as he pulled her toward him. The girl seemed to shrink back, as if she knew what to expect, and Jemma realized he was about to molest her.

Hot bile rose in her throat, and a whimper escaped and Jemma bit the mound of her palm. He bent his head, and the girl's eyes flicked open, with terror and fear. Jemma noted the girl's hands, knotted in the skirt she wore, and her torn blouse and dirty, bare feet. Her clothing was little more than rags, and Jemma surmised that the girl had been there when Crick Sur Banden had attacked and taken over the bunker. It horrified her to realize that the girl not only probably slaved in the kitchen, but also in the beds of the rogues.

She watched and suddenly noticed that the girl relaxed. She nodded her head, and Chowd motioned her forward. "Get her to the crevasse quickly, then we can get inside." His eyes held some distant thread of hurt, and she realized he'd seen and heard her reaction. Shame washed over her as she pulled the girl toward the hiding place, moving quickly into the shadows and towing the girl behind her.

She pulled the girl into the small hiding place, placing a finger against her lips. "Stay here, and whatever you see or hear, don't come out until you see us. Right? Promise?"

The girl sniffled and nodded. "And most of all, remain silent."

The girl looked at him once more and slowly nodded again.

Jemma slipped back to her spot behind Raven. She desperately wanted to speak and apologize to Chowd for her belief that he would hurt the girl but knew she couldn't for fear it would give them away. Anger at herself boiled through her veins. She should have known better than to think he would act like that.

Chowd motioned with his hands to follow silently, and she did. They padded through the doorway and into a small anteroom. She noted the reinforcing immediately, a dull gray metal that curved overhead, and even more underfoot the blood that washed the walls, a coppery-brown tint. The scent of stale blood remained though. Her stomach heaved as she followed the two men through the door at the other end and into a large corridor. The smell and feel of death seemed to hang all around the building.

Voices drifted from left and right, some rowdier than others, and chuckles and yells filled the air. Chowd once more signaled that they should move swiftly to the left at the small junction ahead, and they moved fast. Time was precious. They had only moments before discovery, and they had several tasks to accomplish.

Chowd and Raven took position, pushing up against the wall, while she assumed a defensive position, keeping an eye ahead, gun firmly in hand. Chowd's hand flicked.

Once more, they moved together around the corner, silently flowing onward. She followed and checked down another hallway and was surprised to see yet another corridor at the end and one in front of her. *The place is a labyrinth!* She looked back; they were midway along a corridor that mirrored the one right ahead.

Raven and Chowd moved forward, communicating with hand movements, and she followed their directions and took up the rear position. With the two dealing with the corridors, it was up to her to ensure no one crept up and surprised them. Terror sparked along her nerves as she moved as silently as she could in her heavy boots and controlled the sound of her breathing, only expanding her lungs as much as she needed to.

Her ears ached as she strained to hear noises over the raucous calls from the door at the other end of the corridor. The creak and groan of the bunker's dull metallic plating roared, and she shivered.

Creak. Surprised, she spun around to see Chowd opening a door. Gun ready, she watched as he quickly inspected the room then motioned to them to enter. The door closed with a snick behind them, and she looked around.

Jemma inhaled. "Raven, you need to shut down their shields, enable the locking systems on the barracks and disable the security systems. Be quick. We only have minutes now before they realize the guards are missing."

Chowd turned and looked at her. She opened her mouth, and he lifted his hand, his smile sad.

"Jemma, I am what I am. You've not been with the *Elector* long enough to know me. Your fears are natural and normal, especially in a combat situation. Perhaps when this war is over, you'll come to see me as Raven does. I bear you no ill will though. The girl had to believe what I was doing initially, and it would have been easy for you to think the same given the circumstances." He smiled at her then turned back to Raven. "I have to get to the communications point. Once you close this down, get to detention and find the infiltrator. Her name is Kera Aarens, and she will recognize you with the code *Reiver Arch*." He nodded quickly then, motioning Jemma to move to the side, opened the door and was gone, the door softly closing behind him.

She lifted her gun once more and trained it on the door. She turned briefly to look at Raven. He grinned at her then reached into his backpack for a tool kit. It was hard to turn away and not concentrate on the sounds he made. But she did.

There was an occasional clack as Raven worked, racing time to disable the shield. When he dropped a tool with a clunk, she nearly hyperventilated.

No one came. The door remained closed, and she continued to breathe in and out, eyes narrowed on the handle of the door.

My hands are steady. Jemma couldn't say why that surprised her, given what she'd managed in the long gone *Raptor*.

When a grunt sounded behind her she gasped and whirled, her gaze colliding with Raven's. He was levering up off the floor and smiling. "One job down."

She let out a breath and watched him gather his tools and stash them in a small cupboard, out of sight.

"According to the layout we have seen, detention should be next door. I'll go first. Okay?" His eyes glittered, and she nodded.

He quietly opened the door and looked out, his hand waving her forward as he clicked the door shut. He motioned to the door next to the one they had just come out of, and she assumed a position back-to-back with him.

So far so good, she mused as the quiet click of the door sounded loudly through the corridor, then she turned her head, watching Raven in action. As she'd seen Chowd do, he entered, gun forward, gaze flicking here and there before he motioned her forward.

The room stank. Wafts of who knew what, filled the air, making it oppressive. Cages lined the walls; at least seven as far as she could see, some of them spattered with blood and excrement, but no one inhabited them. Her stomach roiled, threatening to expel anything that was in it. Raven was beside her in a minute.

"Don't breathe deep. Open your mouth and take shallow breaths. That will help." His hand touched her shoulder. "You're doing great, Jem. We just need to find Kera then get to Chowd. Hopefully we can bag Crick Sur Banden while we're at it."

"No mean feat, that," she said, her tone dry.

He patted her shoulder, "We already have most of the personnel locked down in the barracks."

"What?" She looked at him.

He tugged her close. "I took care of that while I worked on the shielding systems. Now we just need to neutralize the rest, grab a couple of spooks, and get out of here. See? No problems." He smiled at her.

If only it was that simple. Jemma knew exactly what he was doing—lifting her spirits and making their mission as easy as he could. She worked a smile onto her face, but knew he wasn't fooled when he frowned. "What?" he asked.

"If she isn't here, then where could she be?"

"The schematics have me thinking there's a room toward the back, near the communications center. I think we need to check down that way and see what we can find." His hand lifted from her shoulder, and she felt the loss keenly. She cast her gaze around the room. "No one should be held like this."

She gestured to the restraints on the bars.

"We don't. But the rogues don't follow any acceptable forms of imprisonment. When this is over, we can raise this with the captain and Admiral, but right now, we have to get the job finished." He looked into her eyes, captured her gaze, and smiled slightly. "Come on, we don't have a lot of time."

He held out his hand, and she grasped it, allowing him to pull her back to the door. She cast a last glance over her shoulder, burning the memory into her brain, before she looked forward.

Raven opened the door quietly, and they slipped outside. The danger was acute now as they moved closer to the main areas within the bunker. Somewhere nearby there had to be a secondary hidden exit, and the closer they moved toward it, the more chance they would be found. He moved around the corner silently, slipping against the wall and motioning her to do the same. The first door on the right would take them to the kitchen, and they moved slowly. Inching forward, while the proud head of rivets scraped her back.

Every few steps, Raven would glance at her, checking to ensure she was still with him. Once she returned his small nod, he'd move on again. At the door, he held his fingers to his lips and opened the door just a crack, but enough to let her scan within, then he waved her forward.

Within was an enormous, cavernous room. Women stopped and looked up, fear evident in their faces, until Jemma touched one finger to her lips. She glanced around and noted no guards.

"Are you all prisoners?" The words were out of Jemma's mouth before she could stop them.

The woman nearest her rose, and Jemma backed off, gun at the ready. The woman looked at it and said simply, "Yes."

Jemma looked around. There were probably thirty women, each in various states of recovery, some sporting bruises, others clutching ripped and torn clothing to their bodies. They cast worried looks toward Raven.

"He's with me. We need to find a girl. Kera. Does anyone here know where she's being kept?" Her voice was whisper-soft as she moved forward. The woman backed off, flinching as if expecting a blow.

"She's kept in an interrogation room. They needed the medic to patch her up, as Crick Sur Banden has plans for her." Her gaze darted around. "He's going to make her his concubine. Unless his son turns up first, so I hear anyway." The woman obviously thought that she was safe to talk to, Jemma mused.

"Where's the interrogation room?" Raven's voice filtered softly through the room. He wiped at the coloring on his skin, human tones peeking out of the gray. The women surged forward, and Raven had to hiss at them to stop. "You need to be quiet, otherwise they'll know we're here."

They stopped, and many looked fearfully over their shoulders. The smell of fear and stale sweat permeated the air.

"We'll show *her*." Another woman stood, obviously pregnant, her face swollen with dried blood crusted in her hair. "But only if you will get us out of here." The woman limped forward. "I don't trust you, but we can get her in on the pretext of taking food." The woman waited, belligerence in her eyes, but Jemma noticed the shake in her hands.

"No—" Raven was about to protest, and Jemma stepped forward.

"She's right. There's more chance I can get in safely, and Kera will most likely come with me more easily than you. I'll be back soon." Jemma ushered the heavily pregnant woman forward and watched as she grabbed a platter then limped toward the door.

"Wait!" One of the other woman stepped into her path, and Raven moved forward. "They'll know if she's dressed like that." Her voice dropped to a whisper, and Jemma looked back at Raven, who nodded his head.

"Fine, change clothes with her then." The woman gestured toward another with long, dark hair and around the same build as her. Jemma stripped down quickly, handing Raven her combat vest and flight suit. The woman stripped, handing over her clothes. Jemma noted the bruises on her legs and back and nearly wept for the women, who had obviously been so mistreated.

It took a will of iron to act normally. None of them could afford discovery now, and any sympathy might result in a break down. which was something they weren't equipped to deal with.

Another of the women came forward to wipe grease into her hair, making it stringy, and another came forward with soot from the burned coals and wiped it over her face and hair. When they stepped back, she turned to see Raven's eyes glinting with danger in them.

He touched her face briefly. "Take care." He smiled at her, but it didn't reach his eyes. Once more, her heart swelled with love for Raven. They stood in silent communion for a moment as she watched as the woman crept to the door and inched out. "I have to go."

He inclined his head and Jemma followed the woman, gun concealed in the folds of the torn dress. They crept down the corridor together past one door then another, sliding against the cold, metal walls so that they would seem submissive if anyone saw them.

They reached the third door, and the woman grabbed her hand. "Follow me. Don't say anything. Just keep your head bowed if anyone comes near." The woman looked at her with determination in her eyes, and for a second Jemma saw a formidable woman.

"Right." With that, the woman before her changed, adopting a quiet and downtrodden posture as she made her way through the door.

"Excuse me, medic, but the meals are being served and I bring the woman's." She edged forward, and under her eyelashes, Jemma scanned the room. Only one man. A slight medic she thought. *Excellent.*

He sneered at the woman as she laid the food on a bare table. "You filthy creature."

Anger grew in her belly like a red-hot ball of flame. The reins stretched...

"You will bring it to me, you stupid human." He raised a hand to hit the woman, his gray skin mottled with rage, and something snapped inside Jemma.

Shoving away from the wall, soundlessly, Jemma lifted her weapon. The fury she'd banked leant her speed as she grabbed his shoulder and wrenched him back. He lifted both arms to stop her, and her gun clattered to the floor.

"Stupid human bitch!" The snarl filled the air, and they wrestled. Her hands tugged and shoved until she caught his chin. "I'll kill you, after I use your body."

Reaction took over. "No way. You won't do this ever again, and not to me." With one tremendous heave she wrenched.

A crack resounded and the body turned limp. His head sagged at an unnatural angle. She let go, and the body slumped to the floor. Jemma realized what she'd just done.

"Oh God! I killed him."

She'd snapped his neck just like a twig. For all of a minute she felt sick at what she had done, but the pregnant woman watched her without a smile, just grim acceptance. "He would have done what he said. He's done that to others."

Her words jolted Jemma more than anything else that had happened. She bent and grabbed her gun, replacing it within the torn folds.

Then Jemma turned around and there, on a wooden platform, lay a woman. At least, she guessed that was what she was. Layers of grime and blood covered her hair, and bruises marred her skin. Heavy chains weighed down her fragile body, and Jemma moved forward. The woman seemed to be barely breathing.

Jemma moved close to her, leaned over, and whispered, "*Reiver Arch.*"

The woman started, her eyes springing open, then tears began to trickle down her thin face. Jemma reached for the locks holding the restraints.

Chapter 16

Chowd moved forward. He knew where the kitchens were located and knew that the communications room needed to be somewhere nearby. There was only so much space left in this corridor. He opened one door and peered in. A great room. Thank *Eshra* it was empty, but he saw from the bowls on the table it wouldn't be for long. *So little time left.*

He focused on the task ahead—disabling the communications center before the *Elector* could make an attempt on Crick Sur Banden. In his experience, his father trusted very few of his foot soldiers.

He would have preprogrammed a communiqué to send out, so speed was of the essence. He knew, from his communications with others, that his father's use of Xeradax was causing him to be paranoid, even more than before, so he'd constantly be expecting a threat. It would be no mean feat to capture him, as he'd always surrounded himself with his most trusted warriors and advisors.

Chowd withdrew from the great room and tracked further along the corridor. He'd never wanted to be this close to his father again—unless it was to stop his plans. But if this was the only way to free the poor humans taken prisoner and to regain control of the Alpha Star Colony, then by *Eshra*, he would take pleasure in it. Another door loomed, and he carefully laid an ear against it. Silence within. *Excellent.*

He cracked it open slightly and checked the room. Empty. Sliding inside, he secured the door. Better to be sure that they couldn't get in. He spied the second door instantly. It obviously led back into the great room, and he moved quickly, making sure to secure the locks.

At the central desk screen he hovered, looking for any traps before turning it on. He smiled as it booted, but the smile melted away as the password screen blinked. *Barsha!* He entered every one he'd ever known.

Access Denied!

No! There had to be a hint. His fingers flew over the keypad, but the same message flashed. He tried again. Something started to whizz and whir on another desk screen, and he quickly made his way over, his gaze flicking over the screen. Data flowed but made no sense.

Then the knowledge flared. His father had obviously linked the two machines with an automatic message transmission code. He needed to stop the distress call to his troops. They didn't need a strike force arriving right now, when they were about to complete this part of the mission.

Chowd entered every override command that came to mind, but nothing worked. He could read the screen but not break the encryption. *Barsha!* He needed Meredith here. He warred with himself at bringing her in, but there wasn't a choice. Either he got her here now, or the mission would have to abort.

He touched the communication badge and breathed deep. "Chowd to *Elector*. Emergency sequence—Charlie-Hotel-Oscar-five-one-seven-Zulu. We have a problem. I need Meredith here to break an encryption module." He pulled his fingers away from the badge. It was only a matter of time before they knew there were intruders.

Suddenly a haze appeared before him, flickering. In a heartbeat, Meredith stood before him, her face grim. "Where is it?"

She didn't spare words, moving swiftly to the desk screen he indicated behind him. She knelt in front of it, watching the information scroll. He could see her eyes watching the data. Suddenly, she pushed away.

"Where's the central console?" she demanded.

"Here." He turned it around for her to see.

"Grab me a chair and watch the doors. Judging by what I am seeing, they'll know in the next few minutes that we're here."

More than that, he hoped they hadn't tracked her transmission. They might get away with one person he hoped.

Meredith bent her head to the keypad and started entering codes, her mouth a tight line, and a frown formed between her perfect brows. She muttered unintelligible phrases to herself as she worked. "Central code needs to be...aha, using the Zulu Zulu Tango encryption process."

He pushed a swiveling chair toward her, and she pulled it close, leaning first a knee then slowly lowering herself into it so that the flight suit firmed against her rounded buttocks. The beat of his heart raced. He wrenched his eyes away.

He heard her working, the tap of keys rattling until she suddenly she sighed. He turned swiftly to see what was wrong and spied the amusement that lit up her face. Her lips lifted in the corners, and her eyes glittered with triumph.

"Gotcha!" It was a jubilant whisper. She levered herself up from the chair, and he watched her body unfold.

"Did you break it?" he said quietly, and looked toward the door. It rattled. *Barsha!* Someone wanted in. Time was up.

"Oh yeah, and I put a couple of little extras into the message." She grinned then stopped as she noted the rattling of the door.

"We need to get you out of here." He indicated to her that it was time to transmit. She nodded, and he watched as she put her hand toward her commbadge.

"*Elector*, transmit me now."

He waited, listening for the acknowledgement. Static filled the air, and he looked at her, horrified.

"They've jammed the signal again!" He tried his. "Chowd to *Elector*. Transmit Meredith now!" Static filled the air again. *Barsha! I have to get her out of here. Now. Before they find her.*

He wouldn't let them take her. "We're trapped if we stay in here. I need to get you out and get to Raven and Jemma."

The words had just burst out when the door splintered open. He raised his gun and fired.

The minute Jemma left something changed in the kitchen. Raven didn't know what or how, but suddenly the room became hostile. The women jostled toward him. The atmosphere in the room cooled.

Their eyes glittered, and he shifted his weight, prepared to take whatever action was necessary. These women were damaged, and he had no intention of causing them any harm, but he'd do whatever it took to survive, because otherwise Jemma had no buffer against Crick

Sur Banden and his rebels.

He lifted a hand slowly, watching their eyes watching his movements. "Wait. We're here to liberate you. But to do that, we need your help. We're here from the Empire. I'm the engineer on the *Elector*."

They stopped.

He swallowed. He needed them on his side. Without their help, the alarm might yet be raised, putting all of them in jeopardy. He stepped closer, and a larger woman crowded in.

"How do we know? It could be just one more lie. Like the lies they used to gain entrance." Her words were terse and delivered with force. Some of the women nodded. Others grunted in agreement. She was obviously one of their self-appointed leaders.

"It's hard to prove it right now. Jemma...the woman I'm here with? She's a combat pilot attached to the *Elector*, and our security officer is somewhere here as well. We're going to liberate this bunker and get to Kera. We've locked down the bunker already. We just don't know how many of the men are still at liberty around here." He willed them to understand and pulled his hands away from his guns, lifting them palms up so they could see he posed them no threat.

The leader turned her head and started whispering and gesticulating to the others with her. His heart thudded. Jemma shouldn't be too much longer now. He needed to get her and the infiltrator, Kera, away from here, meet up with Chowd, and attempt to capture Crick Sur Banden. Not to mention get his hands on a spook. Standing here arguing with these women was a waste of time. Frustration welled inside him. Couldn't they see he was trying to help them?

He looked back toward the door once more. Where was Jemma? How long could it take to get the woman and get back to him? He prayed nothing had gone wrong.

Jemma grabbed the chains, yanking them off the woman as quickly as she could. "Can you stand?" Her breath caught as the woman stood, wobbly and obviously still in pain, but determination clearly sparking in her eyes.

"It hurts, but so long as you get me out of here, I'll do anything you ask." Her voice was low, the words passing from between gritted teeth.

Jemma reached over, hauled her arm over her shoulders, then swung one arm around the woman's waist. She would need to give her maximum support to get out of there. She turned to the other woman. "I'm going to need your help. We need to get her over to the door, then you're going to have to support her while I check the door. Can you do that?"

The pregnant woman nodded furiously. "Yes. However, you need to be quick. The men who're free still will be heading into the great room at any time now for their meal, and once they realize the others haven't arrived..." The words tapered off.

"Yeah, I see. We'll need to get back to the kitchen."

They hurried as quickly as they could, supporting Kera between them.

"Tell me your name," Jemma said to the woman, "so I can call you." Reaching the wall, she leaned Kera against it, pushing the other woman toward her and motioning for her to support Kera.

"Rodi. Rodi Van Doren. My husband was the overseer here."

"I'm Jemma. Raven and I are from the *Elector*. We plan on getting everyone out of here and liberating this base." She smiled briefly at Rodi, then turned back to the door, laying her ear against it. Listened.

Nothing. She breathed out, then in, centering herself again. She cracked the door open slightly and peered through the opening. No one. She opened it wider, gun ready, as her eyes and body moved side to side, scanning the area.

The corridor remained empty. Finger to her lips, she gestured for them to move forward. Rodi was awkwardly trying to help Kera stay upright. She reached over and grabbed Kera's arm again, shouldering as much weight as possible. They inched forward slowly and quietly. They made it to the first door and could hear voices and noises, some raised in what she thought sounded like anger. Adrenaline coursed through Jemma's body, and she indicated that they needed to move faster.

Are we about to be found out? She certainly had no intention of sticking around to find out. On they went until they reached the door to the kitchen. Carefully opening it, she pushed inside to see the women up against one of the doors with an armed guard in front of them. Many of the women were cowering. Raven stood quietly, pushed up against the wall, and another guard had his gun trained on him.

Her heart stopped for just an instant.

The door to the great room stood open, and the klaxons started to wail. Pushing the women behind her, she weighed her options at lightning speed.

Save Raven? Or attack the man holding the women? *There was no argument.*

She swung toward the one holding Raven in place. His captor's head had swung toward her as she opened the door, and seeing his chance, Raven thrust his arm forward. The other guard turned, and the women lurched forward, falling upon him, their arms raised, and the guard cried out. Then ceased.

A shot rang out, and the women screamed. Some fell. Jemma ran toward Raven, who fought to overpower the guard. She had screamed to Rodi to close the other door when another shot rang out. Burning fire touched her side, streaking through her body, and for a moment, gray blurred the edges of her vision.

She turned. Her body screamed as her movement jarred whatever injury she'd sustained. Jemma raised her arm, her body convulsing as a lightning jag of agony arced through her, but even though her arms shook, she aimed at the guard who'd shot her.

Before her disbelieving gaze, Rodi dashed across the room, grabbing a chair and hauling it back. *She's going to hit him with it.* Her mind whirred like a wheel in mud, slow and ponderous. *Rodi's pregnant, weaker than I am.*

The guard saw Rodi and lifted his gun once more, sighted, and the dot appeared near Rodi's eye.

"No!" Jemma must have screamed, because he turned just enough for her to move the dot of the laser pointer into the middle of his yellow eye.

Jemma squeezed the trigger, listening for the *phzzt* as the laser cut through the distance between them. He spun sideways, sprays of red flying against the walls and on Rodi. He dropped to the floor and lay still.

Another Ru'Edan arrived at the door. Jemma yelled at Rodi to get back and squeezed off another shot. The women behind her screamed, Rodi yelled at her, and the klaxon continued its wail, consuming her with the cacophony of noises. Her head spun.

She gripped her side. Blood soaked her hand, and she lifted it to see it—scarlet against her pale hand—and smelled the copper as it filled the air. Her stomach lurched. *Shit. I've been hurt worse than I thought.* She stared at her hands until more yelling filled the air. This time, though, when she raised her head, Chowd and Meredith filled the doorway.

Her body seemed to float, lighter than ever before. The gray tinge filled her vision again. Suddenly Raven hunkered beside her, his arms around her.

"Sorry, Raven. I tried. I really did..." She felt boneless, and her knees started to buckle. She closed her eyes as the blackness descended.

* * * *

Raven had seen the shot as he dodged the guard. His hand balled into a fist as he pulled his arm back. A roar of anger escaped him as Jemma's body jerked slightly and shock spread across her face.

Crack! His fist connected with the guard's face with an audible crunch. Blood spurted from the guard's nose. He pulled his other arm back and swung. He used every bit of fear and anger to push his hand toward the guard's lower chest. He gained ground and moved forward, determined to get to Jemma. She stood there looking like an avenging angel, the dress she wore now coated with her blood.

His foe reached up to protect his face, and Raven wrenched at his gun, his own having been taken by one of these when he'd been detected. The butt felt unfamiliar in his grip, but he held it tight and met each defensive move with another far more accurate blow.

The guard responded by pulling back. Raven held on, wrenching at the gun while his other hand delivered another stunning blow to the face. The guard was now dazed and lost control of the gun. It clattered to the floor, lost beneath the seething mass of humanity.

He kicked the guard in the kneecap as the women spilled over from their fight with the one who had them against the wall. He heard Jemma yelling, but his vision tunneled. The guard went down heavily, and Raven pressed the trigger, finishing the fight. Barely seeing the Ru'Edan fall still, Raven moved forward to Jemma.

Her face was now colorless, her lips tinged blue. She wavered on the spot, and he heard her whisper, "Sorry, Raven. I tried. I really did..." Her voice died away as her eyes closed.

"*No!*" he screamed, clutching her still body to his. He looked to Chowd and saw the horror on his face mirrored.

"Get the women and get out of here. Once you're outside the bunker, you should be able to raise the *Elector*. Get her to the SurgiTech suite. I'm taking Meredith and heading to find Crick Sur Banden and hopefully whatever they are using to jam the signals." With that, Chowd turned, pulled Meredith back through the door, and disappeared from view.

Raven looked down at Jemma, her breathing shallow, and he noted the blood still seeping from her side.

"Don't you leave me now. You promised me." He wasn't aware of the seeping tears, only that he scooped her up and held her close. The whisper of her breath was thin and urgency filled Raven. "Hang on, Jemma."

He headed to the door. "Follow me!" he yelled, setting a rapid pace, hoping they would get out without meeting any other guards. Time was of the essence. He had to get help and fast.

He didn't look around to see how many followed, just hoped

that they would. Down the corridor he ran with Jemma in his arms, turning the corners unerringly. The light at the entrance shined, the golden glint of moonlight filtering through the door. They had just reached the entry when a voice called for them to stop.

Screaming. The women were screaming. He looked back to see them descend on a single guard, heard the grunts and screams. Indecision warred, but Jemma needed help. That kept him moving.

Once outside, he sucked in an unsteady breath, while he checked her heart rate. Uneven but still there. It would do until he could get her to Elara. Raven laid her gently on the ground. "Just another minute or two, Jemma. Then Elara will look after you. She'll fix you."

The pregnant woman who'd helped Jemma waddled over, then helped the younger woman she clutched to the ground. With an oomph she dropped down beside him. "You need pressure on the wound. Call your ship. I'll help." She tore another strip off the rags she wore and pushed down firmly.

He raised a shaking hand to his commbadge. "*Elector*, this is Raven. Get Jemma to SurgiTech now. She's hurt. There's a woman with her."

The badge crackled and popped, but he heard "Transmission set to begin. Direct to SurgiTech." Grayson's voice. In a haze, Jemma and the captive they'd rescued, Kera, disappeared from view.

He turned and saw the women huddled in groups. "There's a young girl. We left her in the crevasse," he said, his voice hoarse. He wanted to get back to the *Elector* and be with Jemma. He felt the loss of her keenly, but she'd have told him to finish the job first. She'd be right. So instead, he pointed to the canyon. "Over there. Someone should find her and bring her back."

The squark of a communicator blared and eyes settled on him. "Raven."

Grayson's voice shimmered through the comm. "We're about to transmit some guards down. Stand by."

The shimmer began again, and three burly security officers stood in front of him. He nodded to them, feeling old and sick. He turned and headed back inside the bunker. The gun in his hand shook from the hate boiling inside him. He moved down the corridor and caught sight of a Ru'Edan skulking in the shadows ahead of him. Raven broke into a run. *I'll get this one!*

The Ru'Edan looked back, raised his hand, and fired a small gun, then set off away from him toward the end of the bunker with in limping spurt of speed. Raven twisted as the laser fire surged past him, hitting the wall with a thwack. He followed the Ru'Edan, pounding his feet down the metal floor.

"Stop!" he screamed, but the Ru'Edan warrior paid no attention. He reached another doorway, stopped, and swung around. Raven ducked as another flash of laser shot toward him, this time hitting the wall beside his head.

He let off a round that missed and swore in frustration. The Ru'Edan reached out, opened the door, and moved through at speed. Raven ran to the door, pushing and heaving against it until it finally splintered, rage giving him a strength he normally lacked. He pushed his way inside just in time to see the Ru'Edan warrior disappear through another door at the end of the room. This time he kept running, with Raven behind him.

"Bloody labyrinthine base!" His chest ached but he kept running.

Raven used the door as cover to look around. Another door! He snarled. It stood open, and he heard thudding from the other side. He pushed away, his heart pounding as he followed out through the door.

A spiral metal staircase led up and Raven followed. "Surely...not too...much...further." Beyond his sight, a whine built. Loud and the walls trembled. "*Barsha!*" It was the sound of an engine.

The stairs led to a dock, where rows upon rows of Phobos spooks sat waiting. Just as he reached the plascrete, he caught sight of a battle shuttle rising as the dock doors closed. He squeezed off a shot. It twanged on the shields but with no real effect.

Raven backed off just in time to see the thrusters spew fire and smoke as the ship shot out of the cavernous opening and into the night.

Thudding behind him had him raising his gun once more, but just as he was about to call to the person running up the stairs, he saw it was Chowd and Meredith. He dropped his gun.

"They got away." His chest heaved with exertion. "Only just, but they still got away. *Barsha!*" He dropped to his knees and cradled his head, back bowed. His body protested against the mad dash he had made, but he pushed that aside. "Jemma. I need to know how Jemma is." He felt one hand, then another, on his shoulder.

"Meredith found the jamming device. We can transmit." Chowd's voice was strained. "Wait. The women. Outside. A security team transmitted in." His voice was defeated, and he felt unutterably weary. His head remained bowed, his eyes closed, fear beating in his heart. "I'll see to them. Chowd to Elector. Transmit Raven directly to SurgiTech."

He closed his eyes and let them take him wherever they would, so long as he was with Jemma.

✪ ✪ ✪ ✪

Her eyes opened slowly. *God, how I hurt!* The white light hurt her eyes, and she screwed them up, moaning quietly. A rustle to her side made her turn slightly. Her side pulled, and she sucked in a breath at the sudden lancing pain. A soft hand lay on her arm, and she opened her eyes. Raven, his face tired and drawn.

"*Barsha*! You gave me such a fright!" His voice was thick with emotion, and his eyes shined with tears, making their blue sparkle. His hand unsteadily rose to her face, pushing sticky strands of hair aside and stroking the skin. She could feel his fingers, gentle and looking for reassurance.

"I'm sorry. I tried to stay safe. I really did." Her voice broke, and her eyes burned. She felt the tears softly roll down her face, hot and wet. She tried to raise an arm and struggled. "They were going to hurt you. I couldn't let that happen. If I lost you, I'd be nothing. Just empty."

A set of muffled footsteps interrupted. "I see my patient is awake and you've already upset her." Elara stood looking down at her, looking relieved. "You caused me a great deal of worry. Worry we really didn't need." She moved forward, laying her scarred hand on Jemma's arm for a minute. "Raven. I need five minutes with Jem, then she's all yours." Her tone was kindly but firm, and Raven rose from the seat without an argument. He moved wearily to the door.

"I'm going to shower and change, then I'll be back." He turned and left them to it. "Well, Jemma. I've never met anyone who can get into as many accidents and life endangering situations as you." Amusement colored Elara's voice. "By the time we got you here, you were going into shock caused by blood loss. We had to use all our stored plasma supplies for your blood type." She worked quietly, checking her handscreen as she spoke. "All I can say is thank heavens we've now perfected the enzyme activated plasma, so it didn't matter what type you were. Apart from that, we had to stabilize you before we could treat your injuries, but thankfully the shot missed most of your vital organs. You did nick one of your kidneys, but we have used nanite therapy to rebuild the damaged tissues."

Elara stowed the device in her pocket and sighed.

"The long-term damage is negligible, but your recovery will be longer than you're used to." She smiled at Jemma. "You should be able to leave here as early as tomorrow. Mind you, after several days here, you may be feeling a little weak."

"Days?"

"Yes, three days." Elara pressed a button, and the bed moved to a reclining position. "This is a good start to get you a little bit upright. I have someone just outside the door who wants to see you, so I'll leave you to it. When Raven gets here, he can stay until you go to sleep, then tell him to go to his cabin. He's been messing the place up ever since he transmitted back." There was a fondness to her voice, and she stooped down to quietly whisper, "I'm really pleased to see you back in the land of the living." Then she swirled and was gone, the spot filled by a person who looked vaguely familiar.

It took a minute of hard thinking, then... "Rodi. That's your name, isn't it?" The woman came forward, smiling and nodding, her stomach now flat. Oh God, what had happened? "Your baby?"

"Born two days ago. She's making remarkable progress, though she'll need time in a humidi-crib. She was early. The doctor said it was the stress, but lucky for me your people were able to help. She's all I have now. My husband, Rayhan, was killed when the Ru'Edan overran the bunker. I'm so thankful to the crew of the *Elector* and particularly you. I need to name her, and I wanted to call her Jemma. After you. Jemma Reyna Van Doren. Do you mind?" She stood in the doorway looking anxious, her brown hair bound back in the traditional hairstyle of the miners, fingers twisting as she waited for the answer.

"I'm honored. But I didn't really do anything other than my job."

"No, you were the one who risked everything for your man and us. I'll never forget what you did for me and my babe. The *Elector* will have a place in our tales of the history of Alpha Star Colony, too, for the warriors it carries. Already they are singing songs about the victory wrought by so few."

Jemma felt her face flame. "Well, I really don't know about that. But I'm deeply honored. Will I get a chance to see her before we leave?"

Rodi looked at her. "I brought you a holo-pic, because we weren't sure of when you would wake and when the *Elector* would move. Captain McCord said it depended on the orders the *Elector* received." She grimaced. "I would also like you to be her care mother."

"Care mother?"

"It's a mining expression from years ago. The care parent, in her case, care mother, steps in if the parents perish. Because we started to open so many new frontiers, many died on planets, asteroids, and moons and had to have someone to stand in to care for their children. I want you to be Jemma's care mother because you're a strong figure. Please?"

Once more Jemma felt uncomfortable. "Yeah, I guess. When you put it like that," she mumbled. A quick grin from Rodi then Jemma looked up, and in the open doorway was Raven. She smiled at him, and Rodi looked behind her.

"Ahh, I should leave you be. I'll leave my details with Elara. She will know how you can contact me." With a quick squeeze of her hands, Rodi was gone and Jemma was left alone with Raven.

"So, how is little Jemma today? Did Rodi give you an update?" He surprised her by seeming to know exactly what was going on.

"You knew?" she gasped.

"Yeah, she was brought in because she was so early. Elara had Rodi and the baby here for twenty-four hours to stabilize then transferred them to the Alpha Star Colony Infirmary. Rodi asked after you, and once Elara explained your position, the only way she would let us transfer her was to promise that once you regained consciousness, we would let her come back to see you." He sat down beside her. He looked better than he had.

"How long were you here?"

"Most of the last few days. Duvall let me take leave so I could be with you. He and Mellissa filled in when Elara made me go back to the cabin. You know what? I never knew 'Lara had a mean left hook."

She laughed, even though it made her side ache, at the idea of Elara threatening, let alone hitting him.

His face softened, and a warming glow started right inside her, filling up all the empty spaces that had never been filled before. "Raven? Do you remember you said we would talk when I was ready? I'm ready to talk now. I want forever with you." She reached over and touched his hand. "No one else will ever fulfill me like you do, or even understand me. But I'm ready to find what there is waiting for us. Now." She smiled at his stunned expression. "So, what do we do next?"

He swooped in, kissing her fast and hard. "When you get out of here, we'll make this official. I'm not letting you change your mind." His voice was thick with emotion. "I want to be with you forever too." His hand slid over the tears that leaked from her eyes.

"I want that too. It took seeing that guard going to hurt you to remind me that I've been a fool. Now that I know what I have, there's no way I'm ever letting you go." Her words were hard, and he dropped his hands to lace them through hers. "Forever." It was a vow.

Epilogue

They stood on the bridge of the *Elector*, waiting for Duvall to complete his preparations. He was thoroughly flustered as he stood there in his best formal uniform, finding the rites on the desk screen. Jemma chuckled silently to herself. Here they were, Raven and herself, waiting for him to perform their communing ceremony, and Duvall was the one as nervous as a virgin.

She wore her best ship suit, now that her personal effects had been transferred from the *Star of Ishtar* after its arrival some days before. Raven stood quietly by her side, a grin on his face.

Not too many days before, Duvall had carpeted her for the inappropriate relationship with Raven, and here he was joining them forever. She looked at Raven, and his eyes twinkled.

Neither had wanted a big deal in the ceremonial halls on Earth. The *Elector* was their home and the crew their family in every way that counted.

As far as Jemma was concerned, no other man could ever live up to Raven. His blond hair and blue eyes had caught her attention from the beginning, and no matter how much she had fought against her desire, it kept coming back to her in waves. The rocky road they'd traveled together had made them stronger.

She smiled softly, looking at Elara and Mellissa. The ceremony would not have been complete without them.

Duvall cleared his throat, and they turned to look at him. "Raven Fraser, do you promise to continue in a communion with Jemma Cardnew, to keep her safe, to respect her, love her, and protect her for all the days of your life?" The words that would bind them together resonated within her soul.

"I will always do so." Raven looked at her. His eyes shining with triumph. He smiled as he held her hand.

"Jemma Cardnew, do you promise to continue in communion with Raven Fraser, to live with him, to love him, to share your joys and your sorrows with him, and to protect him, for all the days of your life?"

"I will always do so." Her voice was soft but firm. Never had she wanted anything more. Never had she hungered for the connection they were forming. Her heart swelled and threatened to choke her as her eyes burned.

Elara brought forward the equipment to mark them with the visible evidence of their communion, and they laid their arms out to accept the final step in their union.

Jemma had always been alone before. She had always kept herself aloof from everyone around her, protecting herself from the potential fallout of relationships. Never trusting or forming long-term connections. Now here she was, a part of a family. The senior crew of the *Elector* would always be there for her and for Raven forever.

They nearly had him. He sat in his shuttle, his anger boiling in his chest. His ground crew and pirates were gone, captured on that piece of dirt, Alpha Star Colony, and he swore viciously. How could this happen?

He grabbed the pipe. He needed his Xeradax, needed it now, but his supply had been left behind. He puffed on the fireweed in the pipe, sucking it in as if his life depended on it. He was lucky to escape. *But at what cost?*

He'd lost his concubine, he'd lost his pirates, and he still didn't have his son. His hand curled in anger. "Dirty humans!" he raged. "No better than the insects that eat the fodder!" His gray skin turned a mottled red.

He would need to plan and regroup. Thank the Mistress he had the shuttle on standby under the guard of his second-in-command. If not for that, they would have caught him in his own trap.

Once more he reeled. How could they have infiltrated so quickly and so efficiently? He had known they were coming, had been prepared for them, but they had arrived early and undetected. Was there someone inside his rogues? Had they found a quicker way to travel?

"Someone had passed on the information of how to beat them." He nodded at the thought. "It had to be, otherwise how could they have surprised me?" Perhaps the time had come to mete out some traditional Ru'Edan justice.

He grabbed the mead in front of him and took a long draught. That was it. Find the one who passed on the information. Make them suffer. Make an exhibit of them. Others needed to learn and see. He smiled. Feral teeth showed in widened lips against a gray skin tone. Yes.

Retribution. Seek and make them suffer. Teach them a lesson.

He pushed back into the shuttle seat and thought, planned, and smiled.

STAR OF THE

FLEET

Chapter 1

"We should be disembarking you soon, Commander."

Kera slumped down in the seat, watching through the porthole as the small shuttle pulled alongside. Its dark gray mass loomed ever closer to the freighter and the area she was waiting in. The bumping and grinding of the vessels joining caused her tiny duffle bag to jostle against her feet. The noise of the extending walkway did little to alleviate the ache still churning through her abused body or the dull pounding in her head. Even after weeks of therapy, the lingering traces of the abuse remained with her.

The medics and SurgiTechs had worked hard to heal the torn, damaged bones and muscles below the surface, allowing her to regain full use of her limbs. More often than not now, she moved without the streaking pain flashing through her system. But too long in the same position meant some muscles still seized every now and again, and she grimaced as two weeks of freighter travel proved that rule true. The techs had assured her though, in time, that too would cease. She hoped it would be sooner rather than later as she rubbed her left hip.

After Elara, the SurgiTech on the *Elector*, had pronounced her fit enough to travel back to Aenna and on the admiral's orders, Duvall McCord had quickly arranged her ride on a commercial freighter. Since the incursions of the Phobos pirates, the ship had to wait to join a guarded flotilla, and one wasn't going to be there for some time if they didn't take the only available opportunity.

As usual with those of Duvall McCord's ilk, there had been strings pulled to ensure she was out of the way—and on her way back to the base, whether she wanted it or not—with as much speed as possible

The last five weeks had been grueling. While the bruises had faded and finally disappeared from her skin, and the bones, broken over months of torture, had knitted, it was the injuries laying below the surface of her mind that still caused her emotional pain. Her memories visited her as nightmares each time she slept.

When she arrived at the base, Gustav Elphin would be there

waiting, of course. As an admiral, Aenna was where he belonged. She closed her tired, aching eyes, and a vision of him rose behind the tightly closed lids. For a long time, he had been the fleet captain aboard the *Star of Ishtar*. In the last few years, his promotion to admiral had put him behind a desk, much against his own desires, she was sure.

Kera had been a raw recruit when she first met Gustav. Not long after his most trusted crew—his nephew Chowd, Grayson Myatt, and Duvall McCord—had left the *Ishtar*. These three were now members of the highly decorated *Elector* crew, quietly considered to be the best of the best.

From the first moment she had spied the admiral, she'd sensed the loneliness emanating from him. Not just the kindred feelings of a lost soul, but something deeper. Over time she came to recognize that indefinable emotion. It tied into the deeply sensual pull on her senses, making her want a future that remained out of her grasp. The yearning for a physical connection made the situation, from her perspective, so much harder to bear. Especially when he had, by action, shown her his preference for being alone.

Kera knew the dragging pull of loneliness. Since the death of her husband, Martin—in a sortie against Crick Sur Banden's own rogues—she had felt as if part of her was lost. And nothing could fill the void. At least until Gustav.

She knew he experienced the inexplicable connection too. Every now and then, she had met his gaze and read that knowledge of loss and pain in his blue eyes. Then he would pull back and shut down his emotions to become the senior officer again. Each time he did, the hurt cut a little deeper. Kera grimaced. Now she was about to meet the shuttle which would pull her back into his world.

Both excitement and dread coursed through her at the prospect of seeing him once more. She yearned to be near him. It was as if she'd been starved of the oxygen she needed to breathe and he would give that back to her. But Kera worried he might cut her loose again and shut down on her emotionally, as he always had. That was, if he did anything at all about their nonexistent relationship.

The uncertain emotional situation was the major reason she had taken a role with the diplomatic corps on the Ru'Edan home world.

The need to escape the memories, of an encounter he obviously didn't remember, drove her mercilessly. She had always weighed his responses with the certain knowledge that her feelings had never changed. Even when the pain of his apparent rejection sat heavily on her shoulders.

The clank and whirr of the airlocks roused her from those depressing memories. Kera waited impatiently, watching as the heavy metal hatch swung open to reveal a young man, probably in his early twenties. She stood, shouldering her bag.

The ensign saluted her crisply, his flight suit freshly pressed. She had to suppress a small laugh. He was perfect in his uniform from the precision combing of his blond hair to the tips of his shiny deck boots. *Did I ever look so young, so eager?* The thought startled her. Since when had she become cynical about youth?

"Ma'am, if you'll follow me. The captain requests your presence on the bridge."

His step backward—on the clanking deck—was regulation length she noted with a silent snort. The sound of his heavy boots rang through the almost empty bay.

She turned around, giving a small smile to the waiting crewmember of the *Merry Darling Girl* who had accompanied her. "Thank your captain once again for his assistance and forbearance."

His reply was a quick nod.

Turning, she stepped over the lip of the open hatch and walked the few steps through the secondary airlock. Kera listened to the rattle and bang as it swung closed behind her and the hatches lock sequence lights changed color.

"Ma'am, err, Commander Aarens? My name is Ensign Preston, and it is my duty to ensure that on this run your needs are adequately addressed. Would you like me to take your bag?" His voice was earnest, and once more, she looked at the young man.

"Thank you, Preston. Yes, take my bag and show me to the bridge."

He swooped in, grabbed the half-empty bag, and sped off along the corridor. Obviously new out of the academy, she mused as they moved down the dingy walkway. The lights flickered and an acrid, oily smell tainted the air.

The compact shuttlecraft was not one of the newer, sleeker models and was obviously used for transporting goods along with the occasional sentient species. The drab gray walls were dinted and pitted with age, and she wondered idly who the captain in charge was. A metal door clanged, and she looked forward to the bridge, revealed through the opening hatchway. Kera stopped momentarily before dipping her head and slowly stepping through, entering into the waiting silence.

"Commander Aarens? Captain Alverson. I'm glad you made it safe and sound. Those freighters aren't built with military staff in mind. They don't meet our needs too well, but you're now safely back in the Admiralty's hands. Take a seat and buckle in."

His ruddy face, portly figure, and the shock of white hair reminded her of the ancient myth of Santa Claus, a tale she had read during her time at the academy. She grinned inwardly at the whimsical thought. Finding an empty spot in a taped-up seat, Kera pulled the belts around her body and heard them snick in their locks.

"It's a two-day run to the Admiralty from here," he told her, his loud voice booming over the bridge.

The sounds of the engines thrummed around the cabin. Vibrations grew underfoot as she waited and watched, the unhurried movements of the crew quietly reassuring her that she was leaving this hellhole. She listened to the low drone of voices surrounding her. The captain gave the command to pull away, and the force involved thrust her hard into the seat as they moved away from the freighter. She didn't glance back.

The shuttle docked in the large hangar used for Admiralty and official visitors. There were other hangars, but she had never needed to enter them. She dragged herself out of the craft and took a look around. Years had passed since she'd last been at the Admiralty base on Aenna, but it hadn't changed much.

The movement of ground crews reminded her of the schools of fish she had seen on the remnants of the Great Barrier Reef in Australia. Colorful swarms moved over the shuttles as she stepped onto the plascrete flooring. Red suits for the engineering staff, yellow for the general maintenance workers, both interspersed with the gray ship suits.

The cacophony rising up as announcements blared over the speakers hurt her ears after the relative quiet and calm she had enjoyed for the last few weeks. Each bay filled with a seething mass of people trooping on and off crafts while alarm lights whirred, signaling incoming shuttles and outgoing mini-transports. She turned, once more shouldering her duffel, and headed for the doors leading to the inner offices.

"*What...*" An itch on her back irritated, warning her of potential danger, and she lifted a hand to the back of her head and scratched lightly before swinging slowly around. It was instinctual, the need to scan the hangar. To find who watched her. With so many people swarming, if someone was watching her, she couldn't detect them.

Kera shrugged her concern away. Here in the bay, anyway, she was relatively safe, and she felt certain they were merely watching, but she'd be more aware from now on. She refocused on her task and walked toward the large glassed doors.

Entering the quiet reception center, she waited for the officers behind the desk to acknowledge her. The subtle blues and grays of this zone combined with plush carpeting had a calming effect after the manic movements and noises of the hangar bays.

Five women operated the counter, and other people sat in readiness for appointments. Each receptionist, carefully groomed with perfect hair and uniforms, served a section of the reception area. Well-manicured too, Kera noted. She thought the dark-haired woman might be the oldest of the staffers, not that she'd call any of them anything other than young adults. Reading the woman's nametag *Lieutenant Pamilla Trillo*, Kera guessed her age at maybe mid-twenties. Her rich chestnut hair, neatly tied up behind her head, showed the long line of her throat, and her regulation uniform plastered itself against her trim form. Trillo tapped her fingers against the desktop as if Kera was wasting her time.

"Commander Aarens, reporting to Admiral Elphin."

"Ah, yes. The admiral is expecting you." Trillo pointed to a long hallway leading left. "Follow the corridor to the room at the end and present your credentials at the office."

The woman turned away in dismissal. Kera didn't like the objectionable manner of the younger woman but had to accept she had been dealt with both swiftly and efficiently. Pivoting, Kera made her way down the corridor, noting the wood panels and discreet nametags adorning them. From beyond some of the doors, she detected muted voices.

Her long legs ate up the distance, moving over the deep carpeting, which silenced her footsteps, until she stood in front of the door at the end of the hallway. Nerves skittered through her stomach like a hive of bees. She knew he would ask about her health, the mission, and what had occurred on the Alpha Star Colony, if not now, then soon. She hoped the questions came later, when she was able to talk of the experience without emotion.

Laying a hand on her stomach, she drew in a deep breath, attempting to steady herself. The ache inside her chest didn't settle though. Instead it grew as she fought against the fates which kept putting her in his path. Get it over and done with, she told herself. Kera placed her hand on the scanner, and once the light flashed green she entered the room.

The door shut behind her, and she quickly took in the office, adorned with real wood furniture, more deep carpeting, and quiet, piped-in music. Two women looked up at her from the desk, a question in their eyes. The blonde, tall and rail thin, smiled, a brittle veneer of interest overlaid...with what? Kera couldn't make sense of the waves of negative emotions emanating from the other, red-haired woman, not when her own were so churned up. So she pushed it aside to consider later.

"Can I help you?" The blonde's voice, perfectly modulated and educated, grated on Kera's ears.

"Commander Aarens. I was told to report to the admiral."

She waited while the other woman, dark-haired and younger,

clicked on a button and spoke so quietly it could almost be a silent communion. Her eyes grew wide as she stared at Kera, then swiveled away.

"Yes, sir. We'll send her straight in." She spun her seat back to face Kera. "The admiral will see you now." She pointed toward a wall retracting to reveal an office.

There he was, sitting behind an imposing desk, looking older and more careworn than she had ever seen him before. She stepped forward into the room and heard the panel slide shut behind her.

"Kera! Thank the stars you're safe." He stood, but she remained by the door.

He stopped, obviously sensing her cool and uncertain response. The smile faded from his lips. It hurt to see his eyes lose the sparkle and become flat blue orbs, but she needed to remember all the other times he could have taken a chance on a relationship instead of cutting her off.

Kera dropped the duffel to the floor. "Permission to sit?" She kept her tone level and professional. He was the senior officer, after all, and she needed to hold on to that thought.

Gustav nodded, and she moved toward the seating. His gaze followed her as she moved, and she wanted to reach out to him and wipe away the traces of stress on his face. Instead, she curled her fingers into a fist, welcoming the small twinge of pain where her fingernails bit into the palm of her hand. This was business. Nothing more and nothing less was imaginable from her behavior.

The air around Kera, wound tight and brittle, betrayed her current state of mind as much as the sight of her body. She was more slender than before, with hollows at her cheeks, and while not gaunt, what was missing was the softening of her features. Her eyes carried a distance and chill Gustav had never seen on Kera. The green depths froze him out. He couldn't detect any long-term signs of damage from the torture she had experienced. But he itched to strip the clothes off her to check, needing to be sure she'd healed. The impulse shook him to the core.

Duvall McCord had kept him apprised of her physical condition while she recuperated on the *Elector*. However, once she'd recovered enough to board the freighter, there had been total silence. He didn't like that. But he was an admiral with a role to fulfill.

How well I understand the restraints of my position, he thought sourly. It kept him from acting on the emotions clawing at him all the time, especially the one telling him Kera was his woman. Instead, he observed radio silence and stewed. His staff had been confused by his slightly irrational behavior during the last months.

Now she was here, vital and alive. He ached to touch the soft, satiny skin of her face. He cleared his throat instead of acting on his desires. "Good to have you back, Commander. How are you feeling?"

He winced at the question, thinking soberly that while she seemed fit enough, dark shadows remained in her eyes. Her beautiful, rich brown hair was tied up in the severe bun she always favored on duty. Her flawless skin was paler than usual. He didn't need to see evidence of the bruising, having already received and reviewed the holographic images Duvall had sent him. Her condition when Raven and Jemma had found her enraged him even now.

"I'm fine, Admiral. The SurgiTech aboard the *Elector* cleared me to take a leave period. However, I believe I'm well enough to report for duty." Her eyes glinted, and for an instant, he wondered if she meant to disagree with her placement here.

He knew she would argue the medical leave, but he could stonewall until a satisfactory evaluation arrived showing she'd recovered enough to resume duty. He needed her fully recovered before she took over the grueling position she'd accepted.

She had such a fiery temperament. But the one particular hot-blooded trait that had drawn him to her over time seemed muted. The vitality she normally exuded warmed him, and he craved her heat, even now, after all these years. He wanted to see that temper flare within her again.

"Commander, you will remain on medical leave until I have received a clearance from our resident ST."

She started to rise, the lines at the sides of her mouth tightening, and on top of his desk her knuckles turned white. He waited as she drew herself back, tensing like she was ready to argue the point. "With all due respect—"

"No, Commander," he cut her off. "This is a routine requirement, and you know it. Besides which, you need to log in with the accommodation section and obtain a billet. So I have no doubt the time will be welcomed."

Her eyes flashed against her pale skin. She sat back in the seat, obviously understanding this was not an argument she needed. "Sir. Yes, sir."

He understood she wanted to fight his decision, and the urge to grab her and tell her why he'd brought her back here raged within him. He contained his anger as reality of the distance she hid behind slammed into him. He held on to his patience. With time, he hoped to breach the armor she'd erected around herself.

"You've also been transferred to the Admiralty on security detail. The current commander is taking leave. He will arrange to complete the official handover in the next day or two. Once you've effectively taken control, we'll be required to meet and discuss a particular case I want you to investigate. You will also contact SurgiTech to arrange an exam, allowing you to resume duty." He kept his words quiet and controlled, dismissing her.

"Sir, I need to be back in the field—"

"*No.*" His voice was decisive and firm, stopping her outburst. His gut churned. It felt like every word he had spoken had built a brick wall between them. This one more insurmountable than the one which already existed. "I need your completed report on my desk before 1500 hours."

She reached into a pocket of her suit and pulled out a micro-disk. Leaning forward, she placed it on his desk. "My report is complete. I had five weeks of nothing to do." She raised her chin and looked at him. "Sir." The last word she chewed out, cold enough he visualized ice dripping from her lips, and that almost shattered his control. "If that is all, sir?"

He nodded, and she stood, a small gasp escaping. He half-rose.

Even as she tried to deny the truth she still experienced pain, and he wondered just how much. He needed to know she was ready to resume her role as a security officer. Sending her in, unprepared and only half- recovered, wasn't an option. Her eyes flicked to his, as if daring him to say something. He subsided, watching her heft the bag, and with a smart salute, she left.

That went well. He slammed his fist on the desk, watching as the disk she had presented him jumped in response. *Barsha!* Even after nearly ten years, he still wanted her. The tortures of being near her, but unable to be with her, would never end, not if they continued this way. He closed his eyes and breathed deeply in through his nose, before exhaling.

Gustav pushed the defeatist thoughts aside and focused on his work once more. He pressed the communications center, giving orders to his staff.

Chapter 2

She's arrived. Jerrold grunted to himself as he made his way across the plascrete. His master's concubine had arrived at the Admiralty and remained under surveillance.

He'd only caught a quick glimpse of her in the hangar, but enough for him to be positive of her identity. His legs propelled him forward. Crick Sur Banden had always rewarded them well for the information they gleaned and passed along. He and his few associates here would share the spoils received in return for the information. But first, he needed to relay the information back and find out what Crick wanted done next.

Jerrold passed the officers' billets and sneered. "Cunts."

He headed to the laborers' apartments located at the end of the long plas-glass tunnels. As he shuffled wearily to the building he thanked the stars his shift was finally over. Now he needed to confirm what her new posting would be and where. He wondered if he could use the information as leverage. Would he be able to act against the admiral now? Pay him back for his actions as a captain so many years ago.

He spat on the plascrete flooring, watching the spittle fly through the air and land in a blob on the ground. The admiral. The one who had busted him down from petty officer to a grunt when the admiral first took command on the *Star of Ishtar*. Jerrold knew his personnel file was stamped *Embargo on Promotion*. It alone was the reason why he was here now on Aenna, this filthy, forgotten rock in the middle of an asteroid field, working in a hangar crew as a basic grunt.

"I'll get even yet," he vowed.

The panel opened beneath his scanned palm, and he moved inside the dingy apartment, shutting the door firmly before commanding the locking system to engage. He didn't want anyone coming in while he sent his transmission. Not even his associates, though he doubted they would. Stuck-up bitches, they were. They refused to discuss anything until he cleaned himself. As if they weren't the same as him. Infiltrators.

Under the bed, a small box filled with stashed supplies such as emergency food bars waited. He snatched it up. Investigators didn't usually check these boxes, something he had learned in his years of training. Pushing a hank of greasy hair away from his face, he rooted around in the box until he reached the base, and jerked up the false bottom.

Holding the communicator in his dirty hand, Jerrold checked the blocker—a small black box which kept his furtive communications undetectable—that he kept beside it and sent the transmission. Texts were quicker and easier to send and only required a single blocker, unlike vid-trans. He waited until the unit's light returned to a dim, green glow before he turned off the transmitter and stashed it back in the box. No use waiting for a reply; it would take a few days.

For now, he would need to update the others on the status of the transmission sent. "Those bitches just get in the way."

Jerrold closed his eyes, envisioning himself back on a shuttle or freighter and off this lifeless rock. A trio of women naked and on his bed ready for him. Better yet, he imagined them tied up and available for his pleasure. His liberation from this ugly, dirty, little life was coming and he'd live the life he was meant to enjoy, rather than the existence he endured. The thought made him hard and engorged, and no one could satisfy him as much as himself. Smiling, he stripped his pants off and rubbed his erect shaft, baring his teeth in pleasure.

Chapter 3

O rders in hand, Kera moved quickly toward the stores where she planned to grab her communicator badge and extra uniforms. She had already received her billet details; a small one- bedroom unit in the senior officers' lines. She was surprised at the bright, sunny yellow colors. Military apartments usually ran to dull grays or blues. So it niggled at her that the rooms were decorated with her favorite color, and that gave Kera pause.

She focused instead on how to requisition furnishings—until redeployment anyway. Or not, she thought with a sour laugh, depending on what openings became available within the Admiralty. Since she'd been working with the diplomatic corps as a security officer on the Ru'Edan home world, most of her belongings were shipped to the embassy apartment complex. She groaned, thinking of the pretty cushions and images she had collected to fill her unit. She had to hope they'd salvaged her items after a new officer had moved into her place. Perhaps they'd packed her items away? All she could do was wait and see.

New communicator in hand, Kera contacted the SurgiTech bay, hoping they'd find a way to fit her straight in. Thankfully, it was quiet and she arranged to meet with the senior attending officer. He was amazed at her progress, assuring her there was no reason she couldn't immediately resume duty. His promise to write the necessary report for the admiral within the shift made her feel a little more sure of herself. She wouldn't consider the niggling doubts she still harbored that her injuries would stop her from working. Or that in the back of her mind there remained the fear Crick Sur Banden's men would come looking for her. After all, he'd wanted her as his newest concubine, a role she feared and remained sure he still wanted her to fill.

Kera returned to the ST suite several hours later and collected the report before hurrying along the drab gray tunnel and up the echoing steps leading to her apartment. She quickly scanned the surrounding area as she reached for the handle before letting herself in and wondered what pre-prepared foodstuffs were available for ordering.

The door swung open beneath her fingers, the scanning pad already disengaged. Clenching her fingers, she swallowed even as her mouth dried with concern. Silence greeted her from inside, and she moved her hand to the gun belt she always wore slung around her hips. Kera grasped the butt of the slender EM-4 laser pistol, sighting as she hunted around in the gloom for any sign of the intruder.

"Hello?" Kera called. Stupid! Alert the intruders that you've worked out they're here.

Kera rolled her eyes at herself. *A rookie mistake.* She had become rusty at her job, and that only made her angrier.

"In here." Gustav's voice filtered out of the room beyond, and she closed her eyes. Gustav was here, in her apartment. *Barsha!* She hadn't expected his arrival this evening. Indeed, she'd planned to put together her case for immediate reassignment to Earth, or one of the other major staging points, either as Head of Security or a similar role.

She cursed her bad luck as she stepped into the darkness. "What are you doing here?"

"Waiting for you, Kera."

A light flicked on. She ignored the glass of wine he held out toward her and watched his face. *Why is he here?*

"Admiral. Is there something I can help you with?"

His face stiffened at her words, just like the rest of his body. His smile died away, and she could see the yearning in his face along with intense loss.

"Kera..."

Her heart thudded rapidly. Could he hear the way her heart was thumping so loudly, moving faster than usual at his presence? Even across the room, she was sure he'd be able to.

"Kera, I need to talk to you."

"Good. You've just saved me requesting a meeting with you, *Admiral.*" With a decidedly professional tone, she let the words drop between them. Kera reached into the pocket of her flight suit before stretching out her hand and giving him the small disk the medic had given her.

He took it, a puzzled look on his face. "What is this?"

"Those are the results of my scans and my medical clearance."

She smiled tightly. "That means I can return to work as early as tomorrow."

"Kera...don't rush back. You were badly hurt..." He seemed flustered and at a loss for words. For an instant she fought the need to hold out her hand and take his, to offer him some comfort. The genuine concern in his voice pierced her heart. With ruthless strength, she shoved the crushing pain aside.

"Admiral, if there's nothing else, I'd really like to go to bed. It's been a trying day." She wasn't sure how much longer her control would last. The urge to fling herself into his arms screamed through her system.

"Kera!"

She closed her eyes as the pull in his voice reached out to her like a physical entity. *No! He's used all his chances, and it's time for me to move on.* "Gustav, you chose this path of distance. Not me. You put this space between us." The words escaped, sounding strangled, and her eyes burned.

For the first time since her return to Aenna, her own lack of self-assurance made her weak and vulnerable. Staying with him, day after day, seeing him and ignoring the emotions welling in her chest, would become a consuming ache. One she couldn't bear to deal with.

"Please, Gustav. Please leave. Now."

Kera opened her eyes as the sensation of movement in the room intruded on her pain. He touched her face as he walked past, and a spark of electricity arced through her body. She flinched away from the sadness in his face. Desolation coursed through her at the sense of loss she experienced. But she had to wonder what the loss was really of. Friendship? It had been so much more and yet a lot less than that, Kera conceded. It couldn't possibly be the chance at a lifetime of love. He'd never allowed anything more to develop.

Gustav nodded and left the room without another word.

Her heart broke again, shattering into tiny, sharp pieces. This time, she wasn't sure she would be able to put it back together.

Chapter 4

Kera dressed with care, clipping her identification disk to her heavy, dark uniform. Then she twisted her hair into a knot, securing the length at the back of her head. "This feels more like me." She patted the coil with a smile.

Her newly grown long hair hid the multitude of marks and scars at the back of her neck, at least when they weren't covered by the collar of her uniform. She turned slowly, looking at herself in the mirror. The dark circles under her eyes remained, reminding her of the nights tossing and turning as she relived the months of captivity. Kera was pleased that the bruises had faded away though. She refused to let what happened to her stop her from living her life though.

"I don't look half-starved and wild now." Kera spoke quietly as she ran a finger along the side of her face, pleased the gauntness and hollows of her features had filled in once more.

With a sigh, Kera turned away from her reflection; she still had a long way to go before she looked as good as before. Not that I want to look my best for him, she told herself. But somewhere deep within her psyche she knew she lied.

Turning swiftly on her boot-shod feet, she grabbed her holster, checking the charge in the small silver pistol before fastening the well-worn leather around her waist. "Come on, Kera. You're going to be late for your meeting with *him*." She knew being late was never acceptable with Gustav, so she hurried her movements.

Simon Beckett, the commander in charge of base security, had met with her the day before, handing over final responsibility for station's safety. She had a sneaking suspicion his intentions of returning to this particular command were nonexistent. The post wasn't the most sought-after position, even if the placement ranked highly within the Admiralty. After all, apart from their duties, opportunities to recreate and participate in social activities were naturally limited by Aenna's hostile environment.

Kera knew she was capable of running the security command post, yet she felt a level of concern centered on his final comments.

As he left the office, Beckett passed on some concerning intelligence: short transmissions were leaving Aenna for unknown recipients, and they believed it had been going on for some time.

Picked up accidentally, these communications continued to be untraceable because access to the correct tracking equipment remained unavailable. Admiralty believed for such a low-level threat, as the one to Aenna posed, the request for better equipment rated as overkill. In the face of such resistance, the security officers hadn't managed to find the point of origin, except knowing the point was somewhere on Aenna.

She would need to investigate the threat more fully, but not now. The intelligence niggled away in the back of her mind as she moved around the quiet room. It was imperative that she sift through the available material before drawing any further conclusions.

Her immediate concern was the meeting with Admiral Gustav Elphin. The man who made her burn with a passion she had never before experienced. Not even during her short marriage with her long-dead husband. Gustav had avoided his attraction to her for years by ignoring it. But the zing of connection hadn't been imagined by her. She'd caught his long looks and the subtle indicators when he didn't realize she was watching. At least until that fateful night, then he'd forgotten about it and how he'd made her feel. She didn't want to feel attachment to him anymore, because the emotions just hurt too damn much.

Hefting the still-hot coffee, she took a sip from the disposable cup. Even after all those years had passed, she remembered her one indiscretion with him clearly. However, he didn't remember, and for that she would be eternally grateful. Dealing with the fallout would be the final indignity, but the knowledge remained, quiet in the back of her mind, never shared.

Both of them had imbibed a little too much on the night he'd announced to his closest crewmembers his promotion to admiral. She'd been aboard the *Star of Ishtar* for five long years, crawling her way up the ranks to the second-in-command of the security division. During which she had come to feel respect and something deeper for Gustav.

The announcement that he would take six of his most trusted crewmembers with him stunned her as her name was added to the list. The celebrations of that night still loomed bright in her mind. Those present had enjoyed the fine ales and wines laid out, some too much. At the end of the evening, after everyone else had drifted away, she'd sat there with him talking before insisting he should retire for the night.

How she wished she had taken her own advice.

Kera tried to cease the roll of memories coming to mind but couldn't. They kept tumbling along, and she relived her emotions once more. Oh stars, even now, remembering the fine taste of him made her breath hitch and her skin burn with need.

Together, they zigzagged to his cabin, and she tumbled with him onto the bed. "Kera, you're a fine officer and a finer woman."

"Captain..."

His finger, unsteady but warm brushed against her lips. "Shhh. I want you. Right now."

The ache in her belly and the fast beating of her heart, the press of his hot lips against hers, the touch of his hands, warmed her. He flicked open the jacket, revealing her shirt. Kera's heart beat like a rapid tattoo, thud-a-thud.

With exquisite tenderness, he pulled her down to him, his mouth roaming over her heated skin as he stripped her with shaking hands, murmuring words of love against her flesh.

Their legs tangled and the heft of her feet intruded. Dammit! *Kera had no intention of making love in shoes. She rolled only to pull off her boots, but when she turned back to him, he lay still, his eyes closed tight.*

"Gu... Gustav?" Kera chanced the use of his given name as she laid her hand on his shoulder.

He didn't move. "Sir?"

He'd passed out. Kera redressed hurriedly, leaving him there, not looking back. What had she hoped for?

Nothing, she reminded herself with a dash of anger. He had made it clear that he wasn't seeking a life partner. He never spoke of lifelong relationships except to state they stopped a man from achieving his full potential. She'd heard that a time or two when he'd spoken to Duvall.

"I'll bet he doesn't have any recollection of the night." Muttering under her breath didn't make her feel any better. Neither did mulling it over in her mind, but the memories continued to rise.

That night had been the only time he'd touched her in any way that could be called sexual. From then on, she'd vowed to never let him close to her.

Once arriving at the Admiralty, she looked for an escape from her own personal hell. Eventually Kera accepted a post in the diplomatic corps, based on the lesser Ru'Edan home world of Re'Erdant. Her work began ostensibly as a guard while she really strove to infiltrate their Senate. Gathering information to help the Empire form a long-term peace.

She had immersed herself in the position, telling herself she loved the work. She'd lied to herself though, because in truth, accepting it meant she was far away from Gustav. "Look how that had turned out." She snorted, taking a long drink of the deep, rich coffee before throwing the empty cup into the trash.

Heading out the door, Kera ensured it locked behind her with a snick, and the palm plate turned a dull red. Her steps rang as she hurried to the stairs, taking them two at a time. She moved through the tunnels, toward the administration block, with an energy that still came from those burning memories.

Once inside the clear plas-glass tunnel leading to the Admiralty offices, she debated whether to go to her office or the admiral's. *Get the torture over and done with, then you can head to your office for another coffee and unwind.* If her luck held, perhaps there would be something waiting to take her mind off the encounter.

With a snort, she hurried along the eerie, cold corridor, reaching his office. Kera scanned the area before swiping her hand over the palm plate and entering. The two women she'd seen before waited inside. The dark-haired woman—Allison McIntyre, according to her nameplate— gazed at her steadily.

"I'll just check with the admiral, Commander. Please wait." The woman buzzed the admiral on the communicator. She nodded once before touching a button and indicated to Kera to make her way through the opening door.

Moving forward, Kera entered into what she was coming to think of as the Lion's Den, and waited until the door slid closed. "Admiral, you requested to see me?"

He nodded slowly and pointed to a chair. Kera gripped the arms of one of the wooden chairs and let herself sink into its soft padding, pressing against the firm cushion of the seat.

"Commander, I'm not going to waste time with unnecessary banter." He spread his hands out, making the point. "By now, you'll be aware this base has a problem. An incident occurred in the last year that put one of our senior cryptologists in danger."

Kera waited, her mind mentally flicking through the files she'd perused.

"I'm aware of the incident, though..."

"She made her way to me and I arranged for her escort to a safe location. She's subsequently been deployed to the *Elector*. Her work centered around the decryption of the communications of Crick Sur Banden."

Kera nodded, having heard some of the gossip relating to the near capture of Meredith Gentry.

"We...*I* believe that we have a nest of infiltrators here. I need someone with the ability to investigate and shut that threat down."

She nodded again, listening intently. Beckett had shared some of this information with her.

Gustav shuffled papers as he spoke. "Beckett's been looking into this issue, but with little success to date. All the teams I have brought in to assist have also been unsuccessful. As you're aware, we're moving into a delicate stage of negotiations with the Ru'Edan ruling the Senate and the current ceasefire. I need this dealt with now." He looked at her closely.

"Beckett has apprised me of certain details. In fact, he found evidence of the transmissions but is unsure of their origin. I believe, however, that we may be able to decode the wave pattern the perpetrator used." She breathed deeply, taking a moment to gather her thoughts. "I spent last night looking at the instances of transmission, and based on my assumptions, I believe another is due any day. I've already begun a strategic targeting of interceptors." She let that settle between them. He sat quietly, as if waiting for what she had to say next before drawing any conclusions, so she continued, "I also believe there is a pattern of sending and receiving. Although, as we are unsure of the information contained within these messages, I will be briefing your personal security team and ensuring their vigilance."

Kera watched for signs of emotion. As always in his work mode, Gustav was cool and collected.

"If there is an effort to breach the Admiralty, I believe it will come soon and possibly be aimed toward you, as the head of the base. While we wait for movement from the infiltrators, I think we should also scan the records of all enlisted members based here, as well as officers and ancillary staff." Kera stopped, looking him in the eye. "It can be run through the systems in security, in case anything new pops out, and my people can act with immediacy."

She watched his face cloud, but he nodded his acceptance. She pulled out her small palm unit and entered the information, beginning the security runs while he waited.

"Kera..."

She glanced at him. "Admiral?" Kera smiled, aware she sounded official and businesslike. She placed the unit in her pocket, waiting for him to continue.

"Kera, have dinner with me tonight."

The words stopped her cold for an instant. "We aren't here to discuss this. Now, if I may be excused—"

"No. Kera, please. Have dinner with me so we can find some sort of resolution to this mess." Her heart thudded at his words. "Please. Nothing more, just a dinner between two old friends."

Kera didn't really want to give in but found herself nodding.

"2000 hours in my suite?" He couched it as a query, but somehow it felt more like an order. He touched a button on his desk, and she heard the whoosh of an opening door behind her.

"Yes, sir." She rose and walked out of the office, the door closing soundlessly at her back.

✪ ✪ ✪ ✪

Picking through her wardrobe, Kera tried to decide what to wear. The admiral commanded her presence for dinner, perhaps to smooth out the kinks in their professional relationship, though how that could happen she didn't know. She hoped he would avoid any personal discussions. But for now, she needed to prepare for the ordeal of the night ahead.

Her formal uniform lay discarded on the bed, replaced once she arrived at her apartment by a flight suit and a range of more casual pieces of clothing that she had collected on her trip back to Aenna. "Oh, come on, Kera. It doesn't really matter what you wear."

In truth, her uncertainty about what to wear kicked up a notch with every outfit she discarded. Nothing seemed like it was the right look. Casual didn't feel appropriate, but then what if she turned up in the formal uniform and found him in civilian wear? A flight suit seemed somewhere in-between, but what if he dressed formally?

With a snort of disgust, she pulled off the latest choice and tossed the clothing onto the pile filling her bed before stalking naked to the small bathing room. The shower jets engaged, and warm water sprayed her body, helping to release her pent-up tension. "Damned foolish behavior! What are you *thinking*?"

Having a water-recycling unit employed on Aenna meant she could only shower briefly, but it helped wash away some of the concerns flying through her mind. She lathered with an economy of action then let the warm water wash away the gentle foam. She reached out to disengage the head of the unit and stepped out to dry herself.

"If you keep doing this, you're going to feel worse when you arrive and find him in whatever he has on." Feeling disgruntled, Kera dropped the towel onto the drying rack and headed back toward the room. Pulling underwear off the bed, she dragged it on before reaching for her better ship suit. "The uniform will keep a distance between us." She snorted with self- disgust as the words filled the air.

She slipped her feet into her favorite boots, scraped her hair back into a ponytail, and palmed the security disk and communicator.

Gustav's suite was two floors above hers, so Kera headed for the stairwell, taking the stairs two at a time. Hurrying on stairs allowed her to take advantage of the benefits of the cardiovascular exercise while saving time so she reached his floor in next to no time.

Kera checked the corridor and then looked for his door, marching up to it and swiping her hand over the panel. It silently slid open to reveal a masculine room all black and blue with silver accents. She wandered in slowly, automatically listening for the door shutting behind her.

"I can see this is something I'll have to talk to him about." She let her words echo.

"What was that?" Gustav entered the room, his hair wet and tousled. She felt a lump wedge low in her belly, burning with intensity as the punch of desire kicked in.

"Well, you really shouldn't enable access to just anyone. You need to get into the habit of first checking to ensure they are who you think they are." Her voice was higher pitched than usual; she hoped he didn't notice. She needed to focus on her job, but how could she when the sexiest man alive had just joined her in the room?

At one point, after he'd left the *Ishtar*, he'd said his security staff had goaded him into shaping up. At the time she'd shrugged that off, because to her he'd had a nice physique. In hindsight, she realized it probably had more to do with his need to connect with his crew. Now here he was, trimmer and leaner, and she was ready to melt into a puddle at his feet. His shirt was partially open, and she could see that beautiful, bronzed, hairless chest of his. His casual pants molded to the lines of his firm body, and she felt herself steaming up. *Maybe this isn't such a great idea.*

"Come on through to the lounge and I'll grab you a wine. White?" He smiled at her, and any ideas of an easy night fled at the sight of his blue eyes. New lines sat at the corners. Funny, she hadn't noticed them before. Kera nodded in answer to his question, and he gestured her through to the living area.

The smell of freshly cut flowers filled the air, and she breathed the scent in. Kera could hear him pouring her wine, and when he returned she gratefully accepted the glass he handed her. "Thanks."

He pointed to the seats, and she lowered herself into the comfortable cushions, thinking they would be the perfect place for seduction.

"How was your day?" His voice was mesmerizing. It washed over her like a wave, caressing her heightened senses like a sensual massage, and Kera felt the tension seep away.

"It was good. I was able to start setting the net to catch the infiltrators. Talked with the senior officers and we all agree there must be several to be able to get into the cryptology labs undetected, and continue to get the transmissions out without detection." She wondered if she should share the sensation of danger she'd experienced in the hangar the day she arrived. She shrugged inwardly; it had seemed so amorphous at the time, so she kept that to herself.

"You checked the senior officers thoroughly?" His words were lazy, and she felt herself relaxing fully. Sitting in the relative quiet, glass of wine in hand, Kera concentrated on his words and the topic.

"Yeah, everyone checked out as expected. I called in some favors from the diplomatic corps."

"Excellent. Now, how is your wine?"

She laughed at the change of conversation. "Great. Spicy, but refreshing." She grinned, and he smiled back. Her heart melted just a little more.

He was sitting near her, close enough that if she reached out a hand, she'd touch him. She fought the urge to forge the physical connection though. *I'm here to talk work.* If only she could remind her heart of that.

✪ ✪ ✪ ✪

The food was served before a memory surfaced and a spark of devilry emerged. "You cooked?"

His eyebrow rose. "You already know the answer to that!"

She smiled. "Well, I suppose I shouldn't be surprised. After all, I can't cook either." Since both of them had spent the majority of their adult lives working for the Admiralty aboard various vessels, they never needed to learn how.

"Yes, I know, having to cater even a dinner like this is a sad, sad thing to admit." His deep, throaty laugh filled the air.

The veal piccata was followed by a chocolate mousse cake which melted in her mouth.

They talked about aspects of her role and his requirements of the position. The cares and concerns of experience and position skittered away. He made her laugh at some of the funny antics he'd had to deal with since she left Aenna.

"Of course, the ensign opened his mouth. He had no idea who I was and started repeating all sorts of nonsense about the admiral being a pain in the ass. How he wouldn't let the head of his section take leave and generally didn't understand how hard enacting the changes would be and more so if he wanted them in a hurry." His eyes twinkled with mirth. "Needless to say, once the staff pointed out who I was, he didn't know where to look. He couldn't apologize fast enough. Poor kid blushed for a full ten minutes. That made me laugh." He smiled at her.

"Yeah, you always were a big ogre!" Kera groaned. Her stomach hurt from laughing so hard, and she had to press a hand against the dull ache.

His eyes sobered. "You okay?"

"What? Oh, yeah. You shouldn't let me laugh so much." She caught her breath. Gustav continued to look at her as he leaned forward, topping off her drink again.

"It's good to have you back, Kera."

Her stomach curled, rather like a somersault. *Not now. Oh please, don't open this topic.*

"Yeah, certainly better than my previous circumstances." She took a deep breath. "It's nice to be back here, even if I was only here for a couple of months." She shrugged, hoping to head off the discussion he clearly wanted to have.

"Why did you go? You could have stayed. I would have liked you to stay." His blue eyes searched her face with intent, and she wondered if he waited for a specific answer.

"I don't want to discuss this, Gustav. That was a long time ago."

Kera let her eyes stray from his, fidgeting with her wine glass.

"It isn't for me though. After you left...I worried about you. Then you disappeared and I... Let's just say I didn't handle the situation too well."

Her eyes focused on his face once more. She had the uncanny feeling he was trying to say something without speaking the words.

Hope warred with the experience of desolation once more. How she wanted that to be the truth. But too many years of hopes dashed made her wary of looking for something that didn't exist.

The burn, low in her belly, in reaction to his words turned hotter. She wanted to stop the conversation, to get up and walk away, but she couldn't. His eyes held her in place; the emotion in their cool depths called to her soul. "Gustav..."

"Kera, please. I need to understand. Why did you leave?" His voice was both soft and compelling.

"I left because of something which took place on the *Ishtar*." She knew the minute those words slipped out he would want to know everything. She turned away, her eyes stinging and her chest tight with the years of pain.

"The night of the farewell? The night I passed out on you?" The words were full of rough emotion. She turned back, the frown on his face confusing her.

"You remember?" Her whisper was full of pain, and he winced slightly. Anguish nearly bent her double.

"I dreamed about it for a long time afterward. Touching you and kissing you. I needed to be sure, but you left so fast. So I spoke to the purser when the *Ishtar* docked here. He saw us leave the officers' mess together that night. *Very much together* as he put it. It was then I knew it wasn't a dream. Kera..." He stopped, a ruddy glow creeping over his face.

He remembered, and he hadn't said anything.

Well, that firmly puts me in my place, doesn't it? Time to get out of here before I embarrass myself further. Kera started to push away from the table, the lump in her chest crushing her, making it difficult to suck in the breath her lungs screamed for.

✪ ✪ ✪ ✪

Gustav stood, but let her stand. She seemed so shell-shocked by his words. Her jerky movements while attempting to push away from the table had broadcast the depth of her inner turmoil.

"Kera, if I had remembered before, I would have said something." He reached out an unsteady hand, hoping she would listen enough to understand his situation. "Wait. Please."

Her eyes were bright with unshed tears. "I think it's time I left, Admiral." The rasp of her words made him cringe with pain.

Damn, she's freezing me out again. He needed to tell her everything. Only one last gamble remained though—if his attempt would work or not lay in the lap of the gods. At least this time he had a chance to do everything possible to rectify the mess of his own making. Time to roll the dice.

"I dreamed about you every night. I wanted to make you burn in my arms every time I saw you," he said. She stopped at the doorway, shoulders stiff, and he pressed on. "I wanted you so badly, but I couldn't get past my own inability to comprehend anything beyond my career. Or to understand the hurt my actions would cause you."

She shuddered, reaching an unsteady hand to the door handle. His stomach clenched and roiled. The taste of bile crept up his throat at the knowledge of how deeply he'd hurt this generous woman.

"You could have found a way. The stars knew, I kept trying to reach you. Each time I tried, you cut me dead," she said, her head bowed. Her words, so thick with emotion, speared him. He closed his own burning eyes.

What a mess I've created! "I thought that I had to be focused on my career. I always believed I was doing the right thing. Not once did it occur to me that I would feel so alone, or that in doing the right thing I would hurt you too." He opened his eyes and shrugged, knowing his words sounded like a pale, weak excuse, but he refused to give her anything less than the full truth now.

"Why? Why didn't you *ask* me? I was always honest with you." She continued to face the door, one hand flung out to clutch the doorjamb, as if she needed the support. Need chewed at him to support her, physically and emotionally, but it was clear she wouldn't welcome his touch. "Why didn't you give me the chance to have my say?" The anguished words fell between them.

"Kera, I'm sorry." His feet moved, against his better judgment, as he stretched out his hands. When he touched the cloth of her flight suit, she shrugged him away, turning around with anger and fury clear on her face. Her fists clenched tightly, and her lips compressed, little white strain lines apparent around her beautiful mouth.

"You know what? Sorry just isn't good enough for me. You've had years to turn this over in your mind. This is the first time you've acknowledged any feelings to me. It's not like tonight is the first time you knew how I felt. You've known for a long time. Years." She straightened, pushing back shoulders that still shook. "So, that's where the situation ends. I can't do this anymore. Not with you. From now on, we are commander and admiral. Nothing more and nothing less." She made a cutting sign with her hand. It slashed through the air, illustrating her deep anger. It felt as if he had been physically cut by her movements.

"Kera..."

"No. I'm leaving." She swiped her hand over the palm screen, turning back just once, her face pale and tight. "Make sure you lock this. Just like your heart." With that last sharp shot, she left, not waiting for the door to slide closed.

Gustav stood there, watching the door. His heart had been thoroughly trampled, and he rubbed the aching spot where the damaged organ lay shattered.

The man many hailed as one of the greatest strategists in the Empire couldn't say or do the right thing with the one woman he'd wanted for so long. He shook his head. Tomorrow, in the cold light of artificial day, he would roll it over in his mind. Perhaps with a clear head he would find some way, something to save the situation.

He turned slowly, emotional exhaustion dragging at him. Heading back to the table, he picked up his half-empty glass. Gustav stared at the red wine glowing under the lights before carefully placing the glass back on the table. Alcohol would offer nothing except a temporary escape.

Chapter 5

Jerrold had apprised the others of the information. The woman heading their team, bitch though she was, had seemed pleased with the intelligence he'd already gleaned.

Turning, he noted the jerky movements of the ashen-faced commander as she scurried away from the door of the admiral's private quarters. Her emotional state told him something unpleasant had occurred. He smiled, knowing Crick would be pleased with this report.

Remaining in the shadows, Jerrold followed her down the hall, his feet silent on the treads. His long hair caught on the stucco of the wall, and his skin felt abraded from the bite of the gritty surface through his thin uniform.

He smiled as he formulated his latest communiqué in his head.

Crick would no doubt wish them to move swiftly and head off the threat to his plans. The woman needed to remain uninvolved. Best of all, the person who'd suffer would be the admiral. The one who had made sure Jerrold had no future in the Admiralty. How he would regret that once everything they worked for came to pass.

At her quarters, he saw the palm plate on her door glow red, indicating she was already inside, and he swung away. *Nothing more to do tonight.* And with that thought he turned back to the doorway leading out of the building. While he made his way to his own dingy apartment nearby, he allowed his mind to wander to the food he would eat after he found release. That need *always* came first.

Excitement zinged through his blood, and he gripped the printed image in his pocket. Her picture would offer enough incentive for his pleasure that night. He laughed, feeling his erection moving against the cheap clothing as he entered his apartment block. Slapping a dirty hand to the palm unit, he shoved his way inside and tore at his buttons.

Chapter 6

Kera moved down the stairs, dashing at the few tears which had escaped with the heel of her hand. Her eyes burned as the pain in her chest ballooned, threatening to choke her, but she held the sobs inside. She wouldn't lose her dignity here, where anyone might hear her despair and share the news. No, she would wait until the relative safety of her apartment encompassed her. Even so, thoughts of Gustav's deception skittered through her mind, and she tried to slam the mental door shut.

He knew but never said anything. He experienced the same emotions, and even knowing her feelings, his decision was to push them...push her away without even considering her needs or asking her thoughts. That was unconscionable to her.

With eyes blinded by tears, Kera made her way to the door. Fitting her palm over the reader, she waited for the panel to turn green then lurched unsteadily inside. The door whooshed shut behind her, and she let go of her tenuous hold of the grief ripping through her entire body. Great heaving shudders and sobs rent the air, scorching her throat and eyes.

"Nooo..." Kera slumped to the floor, the cool of the tiles battering her senses as much as the hot tears, and she rocked back and forth against the door. The sobs quieted, spent of emotion, her body and mind welcomed the numbness gradually invading. "I'm not going to stay here. I can't." Not now, she couldn't.

She would finish her short-term placement and consider a transfer to anywhere else. She would take a position somewhere safe, where she could rebuild her life far away from Gustav. She clambered to her feet, struggling as if old and brittle.

With a groan, Kera stripped off her clothes, moving slowly. As she clumsily stumbled through the echoing rooms, she thought about options. "I've got a job to do, and I'll find the infiltrators and see them apprehended. Then I'm going to build a new life." The words didn't help though; instead, she welcomed the cold emptiness filling her chest. Kera didn't want to experience the hurt, anguish, and betrayal so she embraced that empty feeling.

She pulled her exercise clothing over her body before retreating to the lounge. Grabbing the holographic glasses from the small table, Kera fitted them on while reaching for the matching holographic laser sword—which snapped to life in her hand. She would work off the aftermath of her meltdown in front of Gustav in a hot, sweaty fight session.

The unit winked to life, placing her in the training center, and Kera prepared herself. Rolling her shoulders, loosening the muscles of her legs, she watched as the holographic attacker came at her swiftly. She sidestepped the telegraphed blow. Her opponent launched at her, and Kera felt the zing, generated through the unit, sing in her arm as sword met sword. Sparks flew as they touched, and she grunted.

Again and again she met the resistance from the opponent, and she relished the burn in her muscles. He came at her again, swords locking onto each other, and with a tremendous heave, Kera sent him flying backward onto the safety mats. Rolling her shoulders, loosening the tense muscles, she waited. The opponent stood, a grimace on his features.

A communicator buzzed and Kera gave a short command. The hologram stilled as she ripped the goggles from her head. Snatching up her communicator, she tossed the holographic sword on the chair.

"Aarens. Go ahead."

"Transmission received. We're working on pinpointing the location." Commander El Jarad's voice filled the air, and she smiled. The holographic scene be damned. She had a better way to work off her anger and frustration. *A real opponent.*

"Keep running the scans. I'm on my way." She turned long enough to snatch up the black laser sword she preferred for close combat, together with the laser pistol. She pulled her ID lanyard around her neck before slipping through the door. Kera paused long enough to ensure it locked and then set off at a lope along the darkened passages of specially toughened plas-glass toward the security offices.

Looking out through the plas-glass she saw the twinkling of stars even as the bulk of smaller asteroids crowded around the artificial atmosphere dome. She'd read the dome had been erected when

Admiralty had relocated to Aenna.

Her footsteps were silent as she neared the security station. Kera slid her ID over the unit, and once the door slid open, she entered the office. A sense of calm reigned throughout the rooms as she moved toward El Jarad's door.

"What have you got for me?" she asked.

The muted colors of his monitor highlighted his alien features. His gray tentacles quivering, his green fingers plying his estrad keyboard fitted for his numerous, gnarled digits. She was thankful the Admiralty had mandated that everyone speak the Earth Basic language.

"Incoming transmission received at 2100 hours. Encoded to Alpha-two-four-four." He scowled, and his gray-green eyes followed the scrolling information that glowed before him.

Kera pulled a seat over next to him, easing down and watching the screen. "Okay, can you pinpoint the receiver?"

"Yeah, the general laborers' quarters. Somewhere in the middle."

"*Barsha*! You can't get a better reading that that?" She eyed him, and he stopped what he was doing.

"Commander, there is only so much this technology can do. If we had a working STAD, we might be able to get a closer reading."

"I've been out of this for a while. STAD is what?"

"Standard Tracking Audible Device. We've been working on the next generation for the last couple of months, but we're not sure it's quite ready to deploy."

"I've heard of them." Kera frowned. "Hang on, you have one here?" She peered at the Estvanian before narrowing her eyes.

"Actually, we have two. Both are prototypes of their generation. Why?"

"Because I think this would be an excellent time to trial them. What's their range?" Kera pulled out her palm unit, bringing up the schematics of the building as El Jarad watched her.

"What?" His eyes widened with surprise, and she huffed in frustration.

"When we have an advantage, we have to use it. Now, the range?" She tapped her foot on the floor.

He turned back to his unit, and she watched as he slowly entered a search string, and then turned back. "If we place the units here and here," he said, pointing to two central points, "we should get enough coverage."

Kera nodded. "Fine. You know who to ask, so get those decoders in place, and I mean tonight. Make sure no one is aware of your people installing them. Oh, and add me to the list of data streams straightaway."

She stood abruptly, turning away from the Estvanian, and strode out of the room, heading for her office. Thoughts lurched around in her head as she plotted and planned.

Entering her office, Kera slammed the door shut. "If I have El Jarad cobble the system together, thereby avoiding use of any comptechs, we can bypass any possible data-stream tapping. If I can keep working this, keep a lid on the information and employ a secondary team, running bogus investigations, I might be able to deflect them." She murmured the words to herself, pleased with the plans she made.

❂ ❂ ❂ ❂

The coffee hit her system, dark, rich, and potent. Kera inhaled the scent as she scrolled through the reports on her desk screen. Weariness dragging at her senses, eyes blurring every now and again as she sipped the brew. A yawn escaped, and her head dipped once more.

Her tiny personal communicator buzzed, and she glanced down. *Him. Again. Ignoring the admiral doesn't make him go away. More the pity. I'll answer his hails soon.* "Not yet though." She let the words whisper into the silence of her office. *How did he even get this communication address?* Kera pushed the thought away. If Gustav truly needed help, he'd use her Admiralty issued communicator.

Since the transmission hours ago, she hadn't rested. Time was of the essence. Three hours on the lumpy couch in the office with a handscreen didn't constitute as downtime. Her back still twanged a little as a result, and she needed to change. Sitting in the smelly exercise clothes she'd worn when answering the hail the night before was unpleasant. Kera wrinkled her nose. Maybe if she headed back to her apartment, showered, changed, and grabbed something to eat she would feel better.

At the thought of food her stomach rumbled, and she checked the chrono on her battered desk. 0800 hours! Kera scowled at the monitor as she logged out and stood up. She twisted and stretched before checking her laser sword and pistol were secure at her waist. Collecting the communicator, she moved slowly down the corridor and out of the security offices.

The early shift crews filled the walkway, making their way toward checkpoints. Kera squeezed between the bodies, catching some interested glances and feeling self-conscious in the slim-fitting clothing. She kept moving toward the building looming ahead.

The door to her apartment in sight, she closed her eyes, and a wave of vertigo washed over her, her stomach churning with hunger and exhaustion. Kera swiped her hand over the plate. The door slid open, and she stepped in. She looked up to see the admiral waiting in her living area.

Nooo! The protest screamed in her head, but she was a commander and he was her superior, so she squared her shoulders and met his gaze. "Admiral? Is there something I can help you with?" She congratulated herself for being smooth, efficient, and professional.

"Kera. I heard about the transmission. Is there something—"

"No, Admiral. The situation is under control. I will contact your office to arrange a meeting later today so I can brief you. However, I need to change, so if you don't mind..." She glared at him and noted he had the grace to blush and appear uncomfortable. Something twigged in her mind. "Where is your security detail, Admiral?"

His mouth quirked. "Well, since I'm only here in the quarters—"

"Admiral, I know you've been instructed to make full use of the security detail until this problem is neutralized." She cut him off. "Now, I will contact them and have them escort you to your office immediately." She moved her hand toward her communicator. He stepped forward, surprising her.

"Please, Kera, just give me a minute to explain."

She shook her head. She wasn't ready to listen to his excuses. Not right now while she felt raw. "I need to change and get back. There are so many—"

"You can escort me." His words were quiet.

"Excuse me?" *What?* Her, escort him? Let him wait, while she showered and dressed? "I don't—"

"It's the perfect solution."

His words had her shaking her head slightly. She wanted to argue, but the knowledge he spoke sensibly ended her argument.

"Fine. Wait here. I won't be long." Her stomach chose that time to gurgle with hunger, and she rolled her eyes as her body conspired against her. "*Barsha*! Have you eaten? Because I've been in the office since 2300 hours and I'm hungry. Can you order breakfast while I dress? That way we can get out of here quickly."

Without giving him a chance to answer, she turned away and strode toward the bedroom. Kera muttered under her breath while her pulse quickened at his proximity.

She closed the door and leaned into it, the reassurance of the metal cooling her slightly fevered skin. She could strip down now and walk out to him and safely be assured he would accept what she offered. Her blood pulsed in her veins, the thought arousing her.

She shook her head. Not the right time, and definitely not the right man, she reminded herself. That didn't stop the wanting though. Pushing away from the door with both hands, Kera headed for the bathroom.

A quick shower and change of clothes would improve her state of mind. Such a shame she couldn't give in to her urges, she told herself.

Gustav sat down, jiggled his feet a little, then stood back up. He cast his gaze around the empty apartment. No pictures or personal items filled the space. Funny, she'd always decorated with photos and bookpads on the *Ishtar*.

He touched his communicator and ordered their breakfast, instructing it be delivered to the apartment. He imagined Kera beyond the door, peeling the skin-tight exercise pants and top off. The first flush of arousal crept through his system, tightening his body and causing his heart to thud double time.

"Don't be an idiot. She made her thoughts clear last night. She doesn't want you anymore." Hearing the words aloud didn't help him. *I still want her.*

Closing his eyes, his imagination took another giant leap as thoughts of skin, bared for his touch, rose behind his closed lids. He swallowed hard as the sound of water running met his ears. He pictured her in his mind: long limbs climbing under the water, her supple hands gliding over every inch of bare skin, soapy bubbles caressing her naked length. His arousal, confined within his pants, jerked at his thoughts, and he breathed heavily.

"Don't think about her." Gustav tried to banish the image of Kera's naked body from his mind. But the sounds continued to emanate from beyond the door, and a thin trickle of sweat snaked down the back of his suit, itchy on his burning skin.

Gustav stepped as far away from the door as possible, not wanting to listen to the arousing sounds from beyond. He moved with an uncoordinated gait, and he wiped away the sweat dotting his upper lip, while blood rushed through his veins. His heartbeat accelerated even as he damned himself for being foolish.

The water turned off with a reverberating hiss, followed by the clunk of the water hammer. He forced his mind to concentrate on the situation with the infiltrator and not on the towel currently sliding over Kera's naked form. She will find them, he reminded himself.

He hadn't realized she'd returned to the security offices until he had arrived at her apartment, hoping to catch her before she began the day. Then he'd buzzed her, several times, through the comm channels, but she didn't respond, making him worry that something had happened. When she'd finally come through the door, the weariness was clear on her face, and there were shadows under her eyes, but even so, she still looked amazing.

Gustav recalled the first time he'd seen her, new to the security detail aboard the *Star of Ishtar* and widowed less than six months. The sadness in her eyes was the first thing that drew him in. It hadn't hurt that she was also sexy, he reflected with honesty. Her curves had been outlined in the flight suit, her eyes piercing with intensity. While addressing the new crewmembers, his focus kept returning to her. Her hair had been tied back in a bun, showing off her long, lean neck and strong chin that she'd raised—warding off an emotional blow, his mind offered. *One against the world.* He'd found the strong woman who'd faced great challenges appealed to him.

He remembered her drive and the way she'd been determined to make the most of her opportunities for advancement. She'd excelled in martial arts while aboard the *Ishtar* and had shown an aptitude for security and leadership. Those qualities had been the catalyst for her moving through the ranks, not at a meteoric rate, but slowly. She'd taken on extra duties and made choices that showcased her character and abilities. Of course, her amiability also helped, as other crewmembers found her approachable too.

Not overtly, and he doubted even consciously, she had drawn him like a moth to a flame. His awareness of her had been instant, and as she had emerged from her grief, he could tell she found him intriguing. He'd detected it in her shy smiles and soft glances. But he'd kept to his time-honored theme of no emotional ties. When he finally reconciled himself to any possibility of creating a relationship, he had made the worst mistakes in the book.

That damned night. He clenched his fist.

She'd been everything he wanted, and while he might blame the alcohol for dulling his senses, he knew placing all the blame on the alcohol was unfair. He'd wanted her. Badly. Enough to lose his head as his inhibitions dulled and slipped away. In turn, because of his actions he'd lost her before they'd had a chance to find out what the relationship might become.

Gustav shook his head. How could he possibly expect her to come back for a second round?

Kera had frozen him out once they'd reached Aenna, and that initially puzzled him...until he'd remembered. She had only stayed a few months, distant and cool, before taking on the diplomatic posting.

Losing her left him both empty and alone.

Now she was back, and once more he let *that* encounter become a wedge between them. The anger and anguish in her eyes the night before told him her emotions were still raw. He exhaled heavily, sitting down once more on the hard furnishings of the falsely bright room. The yellow on the walls mocking with its gaiety.

Placing his elbows on the table, he let his head drop into his waiting hands and thought about options. He needed to make her see that he had learned from the mistakes he'd made.

The chimes of the door alerted him, and he sat upright. As if she'd been listening and waiting, the door to her bedroom opened and Kera marched out, piercing him with a stare. "Stay right there."

He subsided, unsure and uncomfortable with her giving him orders. But she was the security expert, and he already ranked on her problem list. He didn't want to climb any higher than he already was.

"Ahh, thanks so much." Her voice filtered from the room beyond, and he listened to the drone of someone else talking. The door shut, and the voices stopped. He waited for a moment Then she returned, exiting from the kitchen door, holding a tray. "So, you ordered it for here?"

He couldn't tell if she was upset or not, but she indicated the small table and pulled the holo-goggles off it as she started to put the tray on the black-grained surface.

"I thought you would have arranged something in the mess." She exhaled. "I suppose we have a few minutes to eat, but I'm expecting an update from the crew, so I need to get back quickly."

He watched her pull the covers off the steaming dishes, grab a fork, and started on the frittata. She didn't sit down, but moved constantly while she ate.

Gustav groaned inwardly, taking a bite of the hot food and a drink of the cool juice. She clearly didn't want to spend any extra time with him. Gustav placed his fork down. Kera speared the last piece of food and lifted it to her lush, pink lips. He glanced away, a lump forming in his chest as his groin twitched again.

He reached over and grabbed a denta-tab from the tray. "You know, I read somewhere they used to have to use brushes to clean teeth. Imagine how much time that wasted. Thankfully, now we're more civilized."

She smiled thinly, grabbing the other denta-tab. "Yeah, just imagine. Now, if you're ready, I'll get you to your office. Oh, and from now on, Admiral? Don't wander around without your detail. Until we get the infiltrator situation dealt with, we don't know what they'll try."

Chapter 7

Kera's coffee cup needed refilling often as she read the reports coming in throughout the day. She noted the team had the STAD devices installed, and she waited to evaluate how well they worked. Of course, more to the point was *if* they worked. She had a sense of surety, not just based on intuition as much as the frequency of the communications, that another would come soon. Hopefully today. She drummed her fingers on the desk.

The results of the decoding weren't great. If she had Meredith Gentry here, she'd probably have them decrypted already, but as she needed to manually hack the message the work wasn't that simple. Her frustration mounted. She checked the chrono on her desk screen. *Barsha!* She was supposed to meet with Gustav—no, she reminded herself firmly, not Gustav, the admiral—in ten minutes.

Standing, she brushed down her uniform before clipping on her pistol and communicator. She grabbed the sheaf of prints so she could give the hard copies to him. Kera worked to soothe her ruffled nerves, taking a deep breath before stepping away from her desk.

Her walk was purposeful as she called out to the assistant by her office. "Heading to the admiral's office, Eve. Not sure how long I'll be gone. I'm on comm though." Her words sounded firm and calm, and Kera congratulated herself as she walked away from Eve's desk, working her way through the maze of privacy cubicles and into the main corridors. She moved through the complex, past the reception desk, flicking a disinterested gaze at the women operating it as she headed up the corridor toward his office.

A flash of her identification across the screening unit opened the door soundlessly. The two female personal assistants sat at the desk beyond, just as they had previously, and the darker- haired assistant raised her head.

"The admiral will be with you soon, Commander. Please take a seat." The words were quiet, and Kera wondered about the atmosphere between the two women. She noted the blonde glance at her swiftly, and Kera was pretty sure the woman was trying to freeze her with the cold stare.

Sitting in one of the hard chairs against the wall, Kera placed the printed file on her knee as she scanned the room. Last time she'd only filed away impressions. Now she had time to look and explore. The quiet blue walls held images of ships, with the *Star of Ishtar* featured prominently. She smiled as she realized they were all ships he'd served on.

The door to his office slid open, and Gustav strode out, not noticing her, and Kera followed his movements with her gaze, fascinated by his air of command. "I want those reports, Marina. Today."

The blonde woman raised her eyes, lips flattened with fine, white lines bracketing them.

She nodded. "Yes, Admiral."

He turned and saw Kera sitting in the seat. "You're here to see me?"

Kera rose. "I've got those reports you requested, Admiral. If you're ready?"

He nodded and indicated she should go before him, watching while she stood, then followed her into his office. "Kera, I'm aware you're working on decoding the communication. How's that going?" He sat down, and Kera laid the prints on the desk.

"Not so well. They're using a hybrid code, which is causing us some concern. We thought we'd found the key yesterday, but when we moved through the report, we noticed the dates didn't match." Kera sighed, venting her frustration. In the three days since she'd seen Gustav, they'd worked like demons, hacking at the code and looking for some way to break it. "If we could get Gentry..." She lifted her eyes to meet his.

"No. She's working with Duvall and his crew. I can't recall her at this point."

"Fine then. This is what we have." Kera pulled the first page out, laying it on his desk. "Here is the message received three nights ago. We can break sections of the code, but not all of it. This is what has been decoded so far." She pulled a second sheet from the pile.

Gustav bent over the page, and he grunted before raising his head, his gaze meeting hers. "What do you think?"

"Based on our current intelligence, I'm sure something is going to happen. It's just the what and when we can't work out. I am expecting another communication soon." She pulled yet another sheet from her stack and carefully placed the papers in front of him. "We're basing our assumptions on this record here." Kera tapped her finger against the file. "Communications are between three and six day intervals. There is no way they could detect our use of backup servers to work on the problems though, so we do have a tactical advantage. I ordered a number of desk screens, sequestered from the Ultranet system, so there can be no trace of what we're doing."

Kera rubbed her hand over her eyebrow, hoping to massage away the tightness that lay beneath. She could feel his cool eyes on her while she waited for his input.

"Do you think your work is being monitored?" His words were gruff, and she shrugged tiredly.

"At this stage? I think it's fair to assume someone is in a position to keep track of our progress. That's another reason I have a secondary team working on a bogus aspect of the investigation. If we can keep them off our tail while we work on the decoding and continue to monitor for transmissions, we at least have hope." Kera sat back in the chair, watching him pore over the papers she had presented. Her fingers itched to move the lock of hair falling over his face and to wipe away the tiredness in his eyes.

He lifted those blue orbs to her. "What time did you start this?" His query startled her as much as the softness in his face.

"What? Oh, sometime around 0400 hours. The team is working all hours at the moment to find the infiltrators." She shrugged again. She didn't want the complication of knowing he was concerned about her.

"Tired people miss things. You need a break." His words were quiet, and she reared back.

She wanted to yell at him, anger rising in her chest, but she spoke with a professional calmness. "Are you saying we aren't doing our job?"

He waved a hand at her. "No. All I'm saying is that you're tired.

It's there in your eyes, and you clearly have a headache. You need to rest." She wanted to argue, but knew he was right. She needed a break.

"I can't. Not yet." She swallowed, knowing she needed to warn him. Had to make him understand. "Admiral? I'm concerned. I think they're planning something big. I need to ensure, at this point, you don't go anywhere without your security detail." She knew he often went without them, and a bubble of fear rose in her chest. He had to listen this time.

"Come on, I don't—"

Kera cut him off mid-sentence. "Yes, you do. Please."

He looked at her with a calculating expression. "Only if you promise to call me Gustav, like you used to when we were alone, and you have dinner with me once this is over and discuss this mess between us."

She stared at him. *What? That isn't fair.* "Admiral. Please, this isn't something to joke about." Her words were thin, and she waited for his reaction.

He smiled! "Agree to those conditions and I promise faithfully."

Kera gritted her teeth. "*Barsha*! All right. I don't want to though. So be clear, it's only under duress that I'm agreeing."

Maybe she could find a way out of that agreement down the track, but right now, she had him where she wanted him, and that was all that mattered.

"Fine!" she growled the word, but he didn't look triumphant, more sad. She wanted to call back her acquiescence before reminding herself of the mess that had come before. "Permission to be excused? Gustav?"

She understood he was troubled by her unwilling acceptance, but he nodded, and she rose. *The sooner I'm out of here, the better.*

Chapter 8

Both Marina and Allison had left for the day after Gustav shooed them out, seeking the silence which now prevailed. Under normal circumstances he'd consider them efficient, but Marina's perpetual bad mood—especially since his comments in front of Kera of needing the report finished earlier in the day—seemed worse. Of course, his assistant didn't cope well with other women, a fact he learned early on in their association. Her ability to work with Allison seemed to be based on the fact Allison's lover was also female. Therefore, Marina didn't consider her colleague competition.

Marina had worked out quickly that Kera held a special place in his heart and now expressed her deep anger with him. For years he had rebuffed the woman's advances, not that he ever encouraged them. She made it clear in more ways than one she would welcome an interlude; the way she spoke to him, handled matters, and those secret smiles she sometimes bestowed. He huffed with frustration.

Now her barely concealed animosity any time Kera's name was raised built to a level he couldn't ignore. Allison also confirmed, quietly, Marina's refusal to talk to Kera. "Perhaps I should consider adding Marina's name to the list of possible transfers." Gustav made a mental note and continued packing away for the evening.

He grabbed his palm unit and the micro-files to take them back to his suite. He needed to work on reviewing the ships' allocations. He was tossing around the idea of not calling the security office to arrange for an escort when a loud bang on the outer door alerted him to something odd going on. He grabbed for his laser pistol only to remember that he had left it in his suite. "You damned fool, why didn't you listen to her?"

This time the bang was louder, and he knew something had been smashed to the floor. A surge of adrenaline raced through his system. He lunged for his door control, sweat trickling down his shirt as the door slid shut, creating another obstacle. But he knew the barrier in here was weak—being more for show than security.

Gustav depressed the communicator and called Kera. Her voice sounded tinny through the small device. "What's up, Admiral?" Before he spoke, a third and even louder bang filled the air. "Gustav? Are you okay? Where are you?" Her voice turned urgent.

"Office. I'm fine for now." He kept his gaze on the door, knowing it would only hold for so much longer. He hoped she had reinforcements with her and would arrive soon. The walls shuddered slightly under the impact of whatever they were doing on the other side.

"On my way." The sounds of scraping and then exertion echoed through the communicator. Her breath coming in measured puffs told him she was running as she spoke.

He moved around the desk. If they got to him, he refused to be taken cowering like some half-witted, local yokel. *I'm an admiral. One who wears the uniform with pride, and if they do gain entry through the door, then I'll look every inch an admiral.* Gustav straightened his jacket, tugging on the cuffs as he sat down.

He waited for what seemed an age, though he was sure only a few minutes passed. Another bang resounded, and a crash, louder this time, followed by...silence.

His communicator blared again. "Admiral? Gustav?" Her voice came through the device breathless and strained.

"Where are you, Kera?"

"At your door. Open up now and be prepared to move fast."

The sound of voices rose in the background as he grabbed his micro-files, shoved them into a pocket, and slapped the door lock button.

She stood there, chest heaving and face glowering. "We need to get you out of here now." She grabbed his hand tightly and his fascination with her kicked in again. This was a side of Kera he'd never experienced before, not in this sort of situation.

A breather mask was shoved into his other hand, and he grabbed onto the plastic, checking she also gripped one.

"What's going on?" he asked. Now she had him jogging down the plush corridor.

"Not now," Kera answered tersely before pushing him into the arms of his security detail. "Get him stowed in my office and don't let him wander." She pulled the hidden blast door shut as she disappeared back inside the office area.

"What's going on?" he asked again.

Anger mounted as the officers ignored his demand, propelling him toward the security suite and into Kera's small, dingy office. Two burly guards assumed a sideways position at the front of the door, arms crossed over their broad chests, and he glanced at the large laser pistols at their hips.

"I demand to know exactly what is going on." He didn't yell, but they still winced at the tone of command before sharing a glance. One of the men left the room.

"Admiral, my partner has gone to check clearance on what we can tell you at this point.

Commander Aarens gave us very specific instructions pertaining to your safety."

Gustav didn't much like those words, but he understood exactly why Kera made the decision. Keeping a lid on the situation meant a calm base. He didn't like the idea that she was in the thick of it though, and him not knowing if she was safe had him climbing the walls.

The second guard returned with a grim smile on his face. "We are authorized to explain what happened. Commander Aarens responded to your call for assistance. While she made her way to you, she sent out an urgent request for assistance. On arrival, she noticed gas-based explosive canisters had been deployed. As we were accessing your office, another call came in alerting us to a range of chemical explosions occurring in another part of the compound. Commander Aarens felt that you should be brought here, as it is a safe haven, until such time as an all-clear is given." The monologue now delivered, the guard stepped back, taking his previous position in front of the door.

A chemical attack? On a base like Aenna, that could mean certain death for a large proportion of those living here. The Admiralty had discarded the idea of building more defenses at the heart of the Empire. Now Gustav knew the Admiralty had become complacent. Rage surfaced, white-hot inside his chest. He wanted to find the perpetrators and knew Kera would ensure just that. He hoped it would be soon enough to save everyone.

Once this incident was dealt with, he would arrange a full overhaul of the security systems. The other admirals wouldn't like it, but too many lives were jeopardized. He glowered at the desk screen ahead of him, not liking the conclusions he drew.

How many more distractions were they planning to throw at them? Kera made her way to the office with slow footsteps. Weariness washing over her, a tide pulling at her senses. Her head pounded and muscles ached. She reached the entry and swiped her hand over the palm reader.

The two guards stood ready, pistols in hand until assured of her identity, and she nearly laughed as a bubble of hysteria bloomed in her chest. She controlled herself, knowing it was a byproduct of the adrenaline which kept her going. The panic she'd experienced earlier knowing he was under attack had nearly swamped her. Even now, her stomach roiled and her heart thudded wildly at the memory of racing to his office. She had barely contained her anger that someone—a person on the base—had dared to threaten him. The thoughts were distractions she couldn't afford.

She dismissed the guards with a nod and then a jerk of her head to indicate the door. They left without a sound, making sure the door closed behind them.

"Well, Gustav, I think the problem is deeper than we imagined. The canisters contained a cyanide-based compound. Thankfully, the ones we've located were faulty and didn't explode. If they had, the projected loss would have included the hangars and all the staff contained within, and to be clear, we are talking hundreds, not to mention the catastrophic media nightmare that would have ensued. Officers are being deployed, combing the entire base right now, for other canisters." She sat down, letting her body slowly relax, and placed her feet on the chair opposite. Closing her eyes, she listened to him rise and move around the desk toward her.

"You could have been killed in there tonight." His words were gruff, but she let them flow away as she worked to release the tension in her body. Focusing inward and with slow breaths she worked on relaxing tense muscles. The techs' work on teaching her relaxation techniques had paid off.

"Yeah, but so could you. Let's be clear, this was totally opportunistic. What does concern me though is the lack of planning. This means they're likely scared and we're running them into the ground. A scared operative can be among the most dangerous when cornered." She kept her eyes closed. The headache she fought without success grew more aggressive behind her eyelids as she worked at soothing her body. Hoping for an extended period of quiet. "Can you pass me a couple of the pain-tabs in my top drawer?"

She listened to the rasp of the drawer opening then closing again. He dropped the small tablets into her palm. "Drink this. The water will help wash them down." Gustav pressed the flask into her hands, and she gratefully swallowed the pills.

"Thanks. Now, where was your security detail, and why, after our discussion, were you on your own? Again?" She knew she really didn't want to hear the answer, but it had to be asked.

Her stomach roiled, and the throb of blood pulsing in her veins beat loud. She was sure he would detect the sound in the small office. Kera never wanted to experience such fear again; of not being sure of his safety. But she'd be damned before she told him that.

"Marina isn't happy with me at the moment."

She cracked open one eye. "Marina? She isn't happy with you?" The words dripped with sarcasm. Because of Marina she'd had to drop everything and rush to his office? Because of Marina, he'd been on his own? She didn't like his receptionist, not one bit. Her petty jealousy put the entire base at risk. But why, in all heaven, had this issue been allowed to arise? "And what does Marina being unhappy have to do with the situation?" Kera waited for an answer while her ire rose.

"Marina has issues with understanding we don't have a relationship. Since you turned up here again, she's barely speaking to me and certainly isn't attending to the details of her role...effectively."

He sounded almost defeated, and Kera sat up straight in the chair.

"So she left you without your security detail? Didn't contact them to inform my people that you were alone? *Stupid woman.* From now on, they will be stationed in your office, full time. We are running a sweep-through now, and then I'll arrange a team whose sole role is to ensure the safety of your office. Another team will remain with you around the clock. Until this issue is resolved, you need a personal protection unit at all times. I placed a requisition to headquarters on Earth for more sweeps and officers to reinforce our current deployment. Once aware of the situation, they put up no argument."

She dropped her feet down as her communicator squawked again.

Her sigh betrayed her lethargy, but she answered the hail. "Aarens."

Kera kept her answer short, but she didn't have the energy to waste on diplomacy. She yearned for the end of the day—not that it would end for some considerable number of hours, she realized. She still had to ensure every area was safe from the poison-filled canisters and get her crew back for debriefing. Then she'd need to make sure the admiral had full-time protection.

"Commander, we have information you're going to want to view. Immediately, I'm thinking."

She knew exactly what the hail from El Jarad meant. Elation swept through her. "You cracked it?"

"Yes. Can you meet us in the conference room?"

"The admiral and I are on our way." Kera turned toward Gustav. He might be disheveled, his uniform slightly askew and his hair mussed, but he still looked delectable. She focused carefully on her work. No time for sexual thoughts, she told herself. "Come on. They've cracked the communiqué."

Kera didn't look back to check whether he followed, although she remained aware of how near to her he was. She always found his nearness energizing. In fact, right now the zing of his proximity was immensely welcomed. She wanted to inhale the scent of him; the way it made her pulse leap and her senses to move into overdrive was more than welcome. Now that he was safe again, she yearned to stop and throw herself at him, but there wasn't time. And she certainly wouldn't do that in front of her team. So she continued marching down the hallway and into the small conference room. The team she had working on the data was present but subdued.

"So, we're here. Tell me what you found in the communiqué."

Lieutenant Daviston, a small, wiry woman in her late fifties, shut the door. "I don't think you're going to want anyone outside this room to have access to this information." Daviston's blue eyes, shaded by heavy black brows, scowled at Kera. Disquiet rose together with mushrooming panic.

"Why?"

"Because it's about you and the admiral." Her voice was both gruff and apologetic.

Kera stepped forward, pulling a seat out, and sat down alongside Gustav. Her head pounded harder, and she lifted a shaking hand to rub over her sore, dry eyes. "Go on then."

"Okay, so we're aware they used a hybrid form of their regular encoding. What we did is work backward to find the actual code devices used so we could then apply that to the communication."

Kera nodded, understanding the concept. "Yeah, I got that part." She just wanted them to spit the information out.

"Well, we're all aware that you were held prisoner, and we gathered Crick Sur Banden is more than a little upset that you were... retrieved by the crew of the *Elector*. The information shows he is looking for a way to get you back and to get even with the admiral here by doing so."

Her stomach threatened to heave up its contents at the information, and she pressed an unsteady hand to her belly.

"Commander Aarens—"

Kera cut off Daviston as she turned to Gustav. "He isn't going to succeed this time. I won't be taken again." She turned away from him but accepted the reassurance of his touch on her hand, which she gripped. Hard.

"They have been instructed to arrange a distraction, at which time their operative would make an attempt to take control of either one of you. They named the operative in the communiqué as Pamilla

Trillo."

Kera reached for her palm screen. "Who is Pamilla Trillo, and what position does she hold?"

"Pamilla Trillo, Lieutenant. Currently the most senior officer attached to the reception unit." The information rolled across the screen on the wall, and Kera looked at the image.

"I've met the bitch before. I want this operation to be watertight. I don't want to see so much as a bead of sweat escape on this mission. Now, someone get me a list of known associates, her hours of duty, and known haunts. Let's make this quick. I want this one, and I want it soon and clean."

Chapter 9

Silence surrounded Kera as she lay on the bed. Gustav had put up a hell of an argument that they should pool the already stretched resources by sharing the security detail and she should stay with him. After all, his suite did have two bedrooms. Damn him. His argument had been well considered, and she hadn't found the energy to dispute his words. So here she lay in the spare bedroom of his suite. Not where she wanted to be, not at all.

She turned onto her side, punching her pillow, unable to sleep. He was only in the next room. It would be so easy to go in there and climb into his bed. Kera knew he still wanted her. In all honesty, she wanted him too.

Her side cramped, and she rolled back, thoughts spinning inside her head as a knot of need gnawed at her belly. Her body responded to the thoughts, her nipples tightening and warmth spreading within her. She groaned. "This is such a bad time to be feeling these things."

Rolling again, she grabbed the spare pillow, shoved it in front of her, and tried to rest against the downy softness. Her hip protested, and she rolled back once more, more than a little aggravated at her body, herself, and most of all her thoughts. She flung her arm over her face and prayed for respite from the feelings churning within her. How long could she keep up the stoic attitude if her own body kept betraying her?

"I need a drink." Swinging her legs over the side of the bed, she padded to the door and headed to the small kitchen. She had stationed the guards outside the suite, so she was startled to see the light shining.

Kera slid her hand to her hip, and she realized she wasn't wearing her pistol. She damned herself a thousand types of fool while scanning the room for a weapon. A large paperweight caught her eye. *Hmm, that should be enough to act as a cosh.* She plucked it up, testing its heft.

Kera snuck through the doorway and cast a quick glance around, only to drop the paperweight. It hit the floor, clattering before smashing into shards.

"Gustav! What in *Eshra*'s name are you doing?" She kicked

herself mentally as she took in the glass of milk and plated sandwich he held—or had held until he jumped. The dish fell to the floor, smashing on the tiles and mixing with the shards of the paperweight.

"*Barsha*! Kera! What are you doing up?" He reached down to pick up the mess scattered across the floor. The door burst open, and the security guards entered, laser pistols ready to fire.

"It's all right, men. The admiral wanted a midnight snack and then dropped the plate." She smiled as she hunkered down onto the floor, helping him collect the broken shards and bits of food, noting when the door closed again.

As they tidied up, she let her gaze scan him. In his nightclothes, he looked better than ever. The shirt pulled tight over his defined chest, and the drawstring pants meant his heated flesh was only a single tug away. The urge to pull him closer and investigate those lean lines raced like quicksilver thrumming in her veins. Kera clenched her fingers against the need curling in her belly.

"So Gustav, you hungry?"

His eyes flashed before roaming over her body, and for one second she saw the desire in them as his nostrils flared. "Something like that. What about you?" His blue eyes captured her attention.

"I couldn't sleep. Thought I might grab a drink." She was aware she only wore light clothing and no underwear. The thin shirt shifted over her nipples, causing them to constrict and the nubs to become more sensitive. She knew he watched them through the shirt. Her pants itched with the soft material sliding over her aroused flesh.

"I'll make you a drink. What do you want?" His voice was gravelly, and the muscles at the side of his face ticked.

"Actually, I think a glass of wine wouldn't go astray right now."

He smiled, and her heart tripped in her chest. "Sounds like a plan. Why don't you go through to the living area and I'll bring them in."

Padding away, she went into the living room and sank into one of the seats. Gustav followed her quickly, carrying two glasses of blood-red wine.

"Here." He handed her one, and she gratefully accepted the cool crystal then took a small sip. The smooth liquid slid over her tongue with an explosion of flavors.

"You always knew how to pick a good wine or three. This one is nice. Peppery." She smiled at him and set her glass down. "Look, we need to sort this mess out between us."

He nodded. "You're right, of course. I want you, and you want me. So, where's the problem, apart from some very poor choices on my part in the past? Which, I might add, I most sincerely regret."

Kera closed her eyes. A rustling sound came from nearby as she inhaled deeply. "I don't think we should—"

His lips touched hers, cutting off her words. When she opened her eyes he leaned away from her. How did he move so fast?

"That one is just the teaser. I want the whole dessert." Gustav leaned in again, sweeping his arms around her, and Kera arched into his touch. His mouth opened over hers and—heavens preserve her—she opened to his searching tongue. Sparks of electricity raced between them. It felt like coming home and ecstasy all at once as every nerve quivered with hunger.

She moaned as the kiss deepened. Slid her hands up his shoulders, fingertips gliding over his skin, and she felt the muscles ripple beneath her questing touch. His fingers burrowed under the back of her shirt, skating over bare skin, causing her to quiver with sensation.

Gustav pulled away slightly, raining tiny kisses over her face and neck. A haze of desire settled over her, filling her body with warmth. Her breasts ached and moisture pooled between her legs, making her squirm.

"I've wanted you for so long, Kera. Let me touch you," he groaned. The words stopped her cold, and sanity rose.

"No." She pushed him away, although her body continued to betray her with the heave of her chest and her nipples budded under her shirt. "We can't. *No*." Her voice was husky, and she took in his heavy lids over somnolent eyes. The rapid rise and fall of his chest filled her sight.

He opened his mouth, but she cut him off, laying a finger on his lips. He sucked it into his mouth, causing a frisson of sensual excitement to thrum through her system.

"Neither of us is thinking clearly at the moment," she said. "To be fair, after last time, I want to be sure I've considered all the aspects fully before I agree to anything."

He growled low in his throat, letting go of her finger. "I need you to forgive and accept me, Kera."

"Gustav, this isn't about forgiveness or acceptance. This thing between us is bigger than that. It's about being prepared and honest—with ourselves and each other. We both made mistakes last time." The words tumbled forth, and she felt the lightening of her spirit as she spoke. "I should have stayed. Should have told you what happened and not run away when I realized you didn't remember. And you should have told me or asked me what happened." She shook her head as he gazed at her. Judging by the arrested expression on his face, he was stunned by her short speech. She waited, hoping he would understand what she was trying to say.

"Then, what do you want from me?"

"I want us both on the same page, and I need you to commit fully this time. Until you can do that, we can't be together. There's too much history, doubt, and hurt for either of us to do anything else."

He nodded silently, and she hoped he understood.

"I'm going to retire. I suggest you do the same so we'll be ready for whatever arises in the morning." She murmured the words and reached for her glass as he moved back, allowing her to stand. Kera softly smiled at him before she turned and headed to the bedroom. It was certainly going to be a long night.

Chapter 10

Jerrold waited as the two women entered, looking around to ensure no one saw them. Anger emanated from the blonde bitch. He understood anger and hate. The young girl, dark- haired and in her mid-twenties, followed the other in like a puppy. Her perfect figure, pert breasts, and firm ass made him salivate.

They sat down, avoiding the bed, and he grinned inwardly. What he wouldn't give to get both of them—no, perhaps not the blonde—in his favorite position.

The bitch in charge opened her mouth to speak, and the other girl, Pamilla, shook. He followed her movements, watching the motion of her breasts. *A mighty fine body indeed.* His own stirred once again as she exhibited a weakness that so aroused him.

"I don't know why you took such a stupid risk. We could have been exposed," the blonde said to the girl.

"I agree. Exposure is the last thing we need at the moment," Jerrold concurred.

"No one was there, and I thought the time was right." The little girl's voice was thin as she worked to explain her reasoning, but the sneer on the blonde's face cowed her. The girl sniveled, and tears slid down her cheeks. "I didn't think... I mean I didn't expect—"

"No. There's the problem. You weren't thinking at all. Your ill-conceived actions put us all in jeopardy, and all the years of planning and preparations too." She glared at the girl.

Jerrold sat back. He didn't find bossy women exactly stimulating, but the other girl, sitting and shrinking...yes, a piece of that would suit him fine.

"I have nothing to say to you," the blonde woman continued. "Wait for my summons, and do not contact me until I call for you." Her finely manicured finger pointed at the door, and the young woman, Pamilla, left the room with a shuffle full of uncertainty.

He continued to wait. There was more to come. He felt the knowing all the way to his

bones.

"That last transmission named her directly. She's no longer an asset to our plans. You need to neutralize her and the threat she poses to our operations. Not tonight though. Tomorrow." She nodded as if carrying on a private conversation in her head. "Contact me when the next communiqué arrives." The blonde stood, shaking out her skirt as if dislodging any dirt that may have amassed on it—from simply being in his apartment—before leaving.

As the door shut behind her, he started to mutter. "Too high and mighty by far. No, that little piece of ass is more my style. Perhaps I should give her a little prod before I am done."

But now he was hard and ready, exhilarated as he released his turgid length from the confinement of his pants. The pleasure of his plans spiked through his system once more as he started rubbing.

Morning came too quickly, and Kera rose from the bed, seeing the abandoned wine glass on the bedside table. She stretched without feeling any benefit from the small amount of sleep she had finally managed. She rooted through the pile of clothes Daviston had grabbed from her apartment and grimaced at the tiredness that dogged her every move. A quick shower would help, she thought, before getting back to work.

Kera stripped quickly, dropping her nightclothes onto the soft coverlet before heading to the bathroom, the cool air playing over her nude body.

The mirror hung on the wall, and she looked at herself dispassionately. There was some scarring over her torso, but her breasts were still firm and high. Undamaged too, she was pleased to see. She turned her back and glanced over her shoulder. Gustav hadn't found the scars on her back when he'd touched her skin, and she wondered how he would react to the sight. "Kera, it's foolish even concerning yourself with those kinds of thoughts."

She climbed into the shower stall and gave the directions for a warm shower, hoping the water would let her shrug off the last of the 'morning after the night before' miasma. She soaped quickly. The soft touch of her hands over her body and the sluice of the water over naked skin made her tingle. Since coming back here and seeing Gustav, she had been in a constant state of arousal. And it was quite disconcerting.

Giving the command for the water to shut off, Kera stepped out and toweled herself dry. Pulling on her clothes, she turned up the collar on her black suit and tamed her hair into her usual efficient bun. Fastening the thick tresses into place with a small clip.

She grabbed her black, leather pistol holster and communicator and hunted around for the scuffed, black boots. She spied them in the corner and was getting down on one knee to pull them up when her communicator squawked.

"Aarens."

"Commander? Are you on your way? The team is already assembled and waiting."

She swore in every language she knew. "Yeah. Just grabbing some things and I'll be on my way." She stuffed her feet into her boots and headed out the door. "Gustav?" she called, and he popped his head out from the kitchen.

"What?" In his hand was a nutrition bar. She plucked it away with a grunt and took a bite.

"I gotta head out. The team is waiting for me. Your security detail will escort you to your office and remain with you. I'm grabbing Venturs now to go with me." She was uncomfortably aware of his gaze on her.

"Take care, Kera." His voice was gruff. Grabbing her, he dropped a quick kiss on her lips before letting her go. "You'd better get a move on."

Flustered, she backed away. "I'll catch up with you later," she said, turning for the door. Outside she shook her head then pinned the waiting security officer. "Venturs, with me."

She took off jogging down the stairs and out of the building, ignoring the people who moved out of her way.

"The team is already gathered, so we should be able to get straight to it," she said.

The office suite lay ahead, and they hurried through the maze until reaching the conference room. They quickly snatched up the body armor an officer held out to them.

"Commander. I have a team in place who will enter Trillo's apartment, another will make their way to the reception area, and smaller teams in her usual haunts. I believe, based on her patterns of behavior, we'll find her still in the apartment preparing for the day. We have added extra members for that detail."

Kera nodded to the officer running through the plans in a calm and unhurried manner. This was a good crew, and she was happy to leave them in charge for the most part.

The personal aspect to this case made her determined to be present at the arrest, even if she didn't participate. Kera expected her men to banter as they had done before, but today they prepared mutely, pulling on body armor and safety helmets. The teams broke up and headed to their designated points, and Kera trailed Daviston to the door, pushing on her helmet.

"Commander, I take it you mean to be there at the apartment?"

Kera nodded to Daviston, who shrugged and pulled on her own equipment. "Daviston, you're in charge. I just need to—"

Daviston laid a hand on her arm. "I understand, Commander.

They swung out the door together, and she noted the team carried laser pistols and stun grenades. Kera quirked an eye at having grenades on a space port but said nothing. Daviston would run this operation in whichever way she deemed appropriate.

Filing in behind, they jogged toward Trillo's apartment building, moving in silence toward the sixth door on the third floor. Members cut off the access to stairwells, and another ran a security override on the lift beside her. Her heart rate increased as, without a word, the team surged forward, demanding access. They overrode the door commands and gained entry into the dim interior of the small apartment.

The officers, laser pistols in hand, cleared the rooms with shouts until they reached what she imagined was the bedroom. Commands of "Get down!" filled the air. Kera moved forward into the small abode to see Trillo in uniform lying on the floor. Her long, brown hair fanned the ground around her, but she didn't say anything, just lay there scowling.

"Get her to the secure processing unit. We'll be there shortly," Daviston's voice cut through the air.

Three security officers flanked the woman, marching her quickly out the door, her wrists bound with sonic cuffs. The rest of the team began to turn the apartment upside down, looking for evidence of her involvement and her co-conspirators.

❂ ❂ ❂ ❂

Kera watched the interrogation on the closed monitor system in her office. She wouldn't get in the way. Daviston was running an excellent line of questioning, as Trillo, not so smug now, looked limp and exhausted. She also looked more than a little fearful, which Kera found interesting. So far, all they'd retrieved was the name of a low-level drone, although she was sure there were others on the base. Any unnamed plot members were in better positions to create havoc and the potential to destroy the base on Aenna. The cup of coffee in her hand had turned cold, and Kera pushed it aside.

A young ensign appeared at her elbow. "Ma'am? El Jarad sent me to tell you we have a problem."

She closed her eyes. *When don't we have a problem these days?* "What now?" Kera couldn't keep her frustration from her voice.

"Umm, Commander El Jarad told me to tell you your gut instincts were correct."

That information was another blow. Someone had been monitoring the computer systems. "*Barsha!*" The word erupted from her as she rose, stalking past the young man.

This was the final straw. Monitoring their communications systems meant the infiltrators had the knowledge, all the way along, of what was going on in the security corps. At least they'd set up a network of desk screens off the Ultranet. Thank the stars for her planning and cynicism.

She reached El Jarad in his office, and he smiled. This time she considered the jagged teeth and the agitated movements of his tentacles. "You were right, Commander. I managed to find the worm-file here." Taps from his gnarled fingers showed the offending file.

"Have you pinpointed the origin of the file?" She bent closer to the screen, looking at the changing face of the data, the sending and receiving of information through the system.

"Not yet, but if I were to bet, there is someone with both access to the high-level files and the knowledge to build the worms involved. Has Trillo named anyone?"

She nodded absently, still studying the screen. "Yeah, a low-level drone. Jerrold Rolls. Works in the main hangar bay. I'm planning to run a cross-reference on his file, but the team is heading out to pick him up soon. There's enough information so he can't wiggle out of the charges. But we need to take him within his apartment so we don't create the mass hysteria the news of the infiltration could cause."

"Ah, if only you were Estvanian. I would take you for my Alpha-mate." He grinned once more, delivering the line she knew he tried on every male and female in the unit. "We Estvanians enjoy our mates to be skilled at reading others."

"Alas, for my pains, I'm but a humble human." She smiled at him. "Great work, El Jarad. Keep me apprised of any further findings."

Kera stood, making her way back to the interrogation room, watching through the viewing portal for a time before heading back to her office. She needed to meet with Gustav and let him know the outcomes and developments in the case. Now that they had definitive knowledge of the holes in the systems, they would need to plan a way to plug them from the inside.

This sort of information she should deliver personally, she told herself before snorting. That was only half the story. From this point on, she needed to ensure that everyone working the case avoided the Ultranet and potentially the communicator systems.

She addressed the guard on duty. "Let Daviston know I'm meeting the admiral, if she's looking for me."

The guard she'd personally chosen for herself shadowed her back to the office while she grabbed the prints and palm-screen. At the door, she stopped at her assistant's desk. "Eve, we're heading to the admiral's office. Daviston knows and so do you. It's not for general knowledge though."

She moved swiftly toward Gustav's office, wondering impatiently if Marina was still working there.

A number of journalists waited in the reception unit. Voices sang out with queries regarding the arrest of Trillo, but she refused to answer any questions. Kera pushed her way through the throng. One of the journalists got too close, and she nearly lost her pile of prints. She gritted her teeth and kept going, but something in the back of her mind worried her about the sudden appearance of journalists on Aenna. How had they known?

Kera entered the quiet corridor and headed toward his door. She waved her ID over the viewer, and the door slid open easily. As before, Allison and Marina sat in the office. She groaned at finding the woman there. *Damn! She's still a thorn in my side!*

"Allison, I'm here to meet with the admiral. I need about half an hour of his time."

Allison had no time to answer as Marina launched a verbal attack. "You want to see the admiral, do you? Right, and it's about the case? Yeah, you just want to jump him, that's all. But you can't. He was mine first." The woman bared her teeth, lunging around the desk, and Allison quickly moved out of the way of the jealous blonde.

Kera's guard moved forward, but she thrust the prints into his hand. "Stay out of the way and look after my files."

She would show Marina once and for all that she was sick of histrionics and petty jealousy. Of the childish silent treatment and total lack of respect. Not to mention that she was challenging a senior officer.

Kera rolled up her sleeves. "Fine, you want a piece of me? Come on, try it. I've had enough of your time-wasting, stupid stunts." Kera took a stand, legs slightly apart, and clenched her fists.

Marina's eyes widened, and her mouth opened, but apparently she had lost the power of speech. Clearly no one had ever stood up to her like this, Kera thought smugly.

"Now, let me tell you something, Marina. I'm here in pursuit of my duty as the commander of security. I have no tolerance for vacuous, jealous women like you. Neither does the admiral. You couldn't catch him because you don't have enough class, and you sure as hell aren't woman enough to keep him." Kera stepped back, observing the guard watching with a huge grin on his face. "Get her out of here. I'll let you know when I'm ready to leave."

She turned and stopped, shocked to find Gustav lounging against the doorway with his arms crossed, a small smile on his face.

"That show was quite entertaining." He glanced at her.

"Yeah, well, sometimes you've just got to deal. Now, I need to update you. Are you free?" She brushed away the stray hairs which had escaped the bun.

"For you? Always." He smiled again, and her traitorous heart skipped a beat as she preceded him into his office.

Chapter 11

Kera sat down with a groan, waiting for the hail telling her the time had come to get Jerrold Rolls. Information continued to scroll across her palm screen. She would be pleased when they finished dealing with the mess. Kera brushed a stray hair aside as Gustav walked into her office.

"Tired?" he asked.

"I've been more awake, to tell the truth. It seems like security has remained busy since I arrived." She shrugged. "You don't really want to come with us when we apprehend Jerrold Rolls, do you? I'd prefer you stayed in your office under guard."

"No, I'm coming. Do you know, I don't even remember him? I couldn't have picked him out of a line-up until you showed me his ID image and file." He shrugged, frowning at her. "I read through the report you prepared and don't even recall the incidents. They were among so many I dealt with on the *Ishtar*, yet from what you've concluded it had such a significant impact on his life."

He sat down in the chair opposite her, seeming a little haunted.

"I made a few mistakes that have taken years to come back and haunt me, and this is one. But the worst was the one I made with you."

His sad eyes and words tore at her, but now wasn't the time to discuss their situation.

Instead, she reached out to grasp his hand, offering support, and was surprised when he held on. "You know that, don't you? I never meant to hurt you. I wanted you...dammit, I still want you. The hunger never goes away, Kera. Tell me you understand."

"Yeah, I do. Now isn't the time to talk about it, and there isn't a lot of privacy here. We should discuss this somewhere quiet and uninterrupted." She smiled, hoping to soften her words. He returned the look, and the tension in her muscles started ebbing away.

Kera returned her attention to the palm screen as the hail came. "Okay, we have to move. Gustav, remain with your guard at all times. Take no chances and follow every instruction given by my people. Stay safe, otherwise I'll kick you from here to Earth and back." Kera stood up and watched quietly as he smiled and rose from his seat.

"Yes, Mother!" He laughed it off, but she felt uncomfortable having him along.

She slung body armor toward him, which he caught deftly. Kera reached for her own, shrugging it on, all the while watching him. She checked her laser pistol and holstered her laser sword as well before walking over and checking to make sure his armor was on correctly. He quirked an eyebrow at her sword, and she shrugged. "I don't like being without it."

Kera led the way toward the assembled team and ensured Gustav remained in the middle as they hurried carefully up the tunnel to the apartments where Jerrold Rolls lived.

"Our operatives observed him entering ten minutes or so ago, and he hasn't exited yet. We believe he might be expecting another communiqué tonight or tomorrow, so we doubt he'll be leaving," Daviston said quietly. "This needs to be as clean as possible. With the admiral here, there can be no mistakes, otherwise we could end up with a dead top man."

Not going to happen. No way would Gustav face injury, even if she had to defend him personally. She would take a bullet for him.

They entered the building quietly, looking for civilians and the uninvolved. A couple waited, open-mouthed, before one of the officers led them away to a safe point.

Several heavily armed officers peeled off to guard the stairs while another disconnected the lifts in silence. Quietly, they trooped up the stairs, brushing the walls as they went, attempting to blend in as much as they could with the dark, shadowy doorways. First floor, second, and finally the third. Each officer prepared themselves, and Kera waited as they moved into position outside the doors and in the hallway.

Looking over her shoulder, Kera checked that Gustav was covered. The door behind him opened and a woman emerged, her face angry, and Kera knew what was about to happen. *Damn! What part does she play in this plot?* Seeing the laser pistol lifting and the stream of light emerging from its dark muzzle, Kera launched forward. A guard took the full shot to the leg and went down hard. Yelling and screaming filled the hall, and she heard Daviston give the command to move.

Ignoring everything except the need to protect Gustav, she screamed for him to duck. He did, but time seemed so slow that Kera was sure the blonde woman would get another round off and Gustav would be hurt, or even killed. Kera raised her pistol to fire, noting dimly that her hand shook. There was a recognition of fate in the other woman's eyes. She knew Kera would shoot.

Kera grunted as searing pain lanced across her arm like fire. Jerking back, she brought her pistol back into position and aimed. Her vision narrowed on the target. With the touch of her finger on the cold metal, her opponent flew backward among a spatter of dark red blood through the open doorway to rest on the tiled floor. *Still; lifeless.*

The smell of burned flesh filled the air, and a dribble of blood oozed from the hole in the woman's chest. Kera's heartbeat raced, and her stomach churned as she turned, needing to know where Gustav was.

"Gustav!" she screamed, moving forward while keeping an eye on the body on the floor. Hearing a wild commotion rising behind her, she looked over her shoulder.

This mission was now FUBAR, and she was boiling mad! Doors opened, and residents peered into the corridor, taking in the shocking scene before shutting them again. Kera continued to move forward; the team would have to deal with Rolls as she checked Gustav, who lay on the floor, his eyes wide and his face so damned pale.

There wasn't a hint of blood on his uniform, but still she searched with worried eyes, aware her emotions were spiking when she most needed to keep her head in the mission. "Stay here with the guards. I'm going in to check the apartment and make sure it's clear."

"You're not going by yourself." He levered himself up, but she pushed him back down with one hand.

"Of course I'm not going by myself." She flicked a hand at the guard beside her. "You, come with me." Kera glared at the other before letting her tongue fly viciously. "Keep him safe, or you'll wish you ended up like her." Then she was up, surging forward, checking for a pulse in the woman she had dropped like a stone. "Dead."

Kera waited for the hit of satisfaction at the outcome. There wasn't one. With this woman dead, there'd be no opportunity for interrogation. They'd have to rely on whatever they found in the apartment.

She straightened and peered into the gloom. "I like right and high, stay to my left and let me take point."

She didn't wait for the guard to accept her directions but moved forward in silence, her gaze flicking from side to side, and her chest pounding.

"Clear!" she called one room after another, anger present in her voice as she moved. "Nothing!" Kera growled as she made her way back through the apartment to the doorway.

Gustav sat waiting exactly where he had fallen, and they took in the commotion down the hall. She noted the suspect had been pulled from the other apartment. His black, greasy hair, which she guessed had been tied back, now flew everywhere around his gaunt, lined face as he fought against the restraints. Kicking and screaming, spittle foaming around his mouth.

The man—Jerrold Rolls, she reminded herself—spat at one of the guards, who wiped his visor clear with a gloved hand. One of the other officers took a foot in the groin, and she winced in sympathy as he hit the deck, rolling and writhing. "That had to hurt," she murmured.

Others came in to reinforce those struggling to hold their wild captive. Kera waited for the officer in charge of the mission to join her.

"I'm going to need both these apartments searched thoroughly," Kera said. "Someone had information of the investigation, and my gut tells me it's either our dead woman or the man. If there were many more involved, we'd likely have started hearing whispers. It's not something you can easily keep quiet. You need to canvass every resident on this floor. Look for any known associates. Be thorough, these charges have to stick." Kera waited quietly for Daviston's agreement before turning back to Gustav. "Come on, let's get out of here. I need a shot of coffee, and I bet you do too."

He nodded to her wounded arm. "And you need that attended to."

She rolled her eyes but agreed.

Chapter 12

Kera yawned and stretched, the action pulling on tender muscles. "Fuck!" She'd forgotten about the wound.

She continued writing the reports, hating the tedium of the job, but knew it was necessary in order to file the infiltrator situation away as completed. Pamilla Trillo became most cooperative once she realized Jerrold Rolls was in custody for questioning and would feed her to the lions. In response her charge was downgraded to assistance in treason.

The completed searches yielded enough ammunition to put the two main perpetrators away for a long stretch. Somewhere nasty, Kera thought while continuing to enter data. "Perhaps Vega 4." She grinned at the thought of the penal colony that was so far from everywhere that even the guards detested it.

In Trillo's apartment officers found a number of key passes allowing access to nearly every section of the base. Written records, decoders, and most importantly, dossiers of her partners had turned up as well.

She kept typing, tapping and adding the findings and recommendations for changes in the Aenna base security systems. The recent incidents backed up her recommendations. The attack on the admiral's reception center, the lack of vetting of arrivals on base, and now the plot that her staff had foiled. Clearly the base needed a higher level of defense.

Kera rubbed her wound, willing away the ache, as Gustav entered her office.

"How's your arm?" His eyes were soft and flicked over her body like a caress.

"Feels like I've been shot. But the pain is going away, slowly." Kera shrugged. "What are you doing here? I thought you'd be tied up with Admiralty business for some time yet." She waited, hoping this was more than a medical status visit. In those seconds when she thought he could have died, everything had become clear. Dwelling in the past wasn't the way forward; it would just stagnate her and her future.

"Ah. So what can you tell me?"

Kera grunted. "You might as well sit down while I update you. Jerrold Rolls has had a vendetta against you since the incident on the *Ishtar*, as you know."

Gustav nodded. "And?"

"Well, I've yet to figure out how he wangled the job here, but it could be something to do with our mystery blonde, Refugia Augenstein. She's been in a position of authority and has a hand in personnel. I'd be willing to bet she had something to do with it." She stretched her back, trying to work out a crick. "She had extensive computer hacking skills. We found her little spy- in-the-ceiling cameras that she had placed in the entries to the apartments. That explained her awareness of our entry to the building."

Fury welled. The stupid woman almost cost her Gustav. Kera cursed the woman again. At least her security officer would make a full recovery; immediate attention by the medics, once the danger passed, had ensured that outcome.

"I'm now finishing my report, which includes a full overview of everything from the personnel department to the reception desk duties. I also want to retrofit keypads to the office doors, and further reinforce them. That way, each office becomes a safety bunker."

"Well, that's certainly thorough. I was thinking, we should do something about dinner and call it a day. You aren't personally handling the investigation, so you can leave now." Kera opened her mouth, but he raised a hand. "Nor do I think you should be. We're both too close, and from what you've gleaned, Crick Sur Banden wanted you back, something that will never happen on my watch. Jerrold wanted revenge on me for finding him guilty of unconscionable conduct, something you wouldn't countenance." She waited as he shrugged those broad shoulders of his, and a shudder of sensual awareness jolted her. He was right, on so many levels. She was too close to this investigation, and she had to let others handle it.

"All right." Kera pushed away from her desk.

Standing quietly, she took his outstretched hand. In her mind, the act assumed the importance of a lifelong promise. Gustav smiled, pulling her into his arms, and his mouth descended on hers. Hot and intoxicating.

The tickle of his breath captured her senses, and she opened them to accept his caress. His tongue touched hers briefly as she was crushed against his chest. When he lifted his head and raised a hand to her face, she shivered. Her nerve endings whirred into overdrive at the feather- light touch against her skin.

"Gustav." Kera nestled closer. A sense of contentment flowed deep within her.

They stood quietly for a moment until he pulled back, smiling with a quiet light of satisfaction in his eyes.

"Let's get out of here." She smiled once more, grabbing her holster and strapping the leather about her waist. Picking up the micro-disks, she pocketed them, even though she had an inkling she wasn't going to be achieving a lot that night. At least not work-wise, she told herself with a grin.

Kera picked up the plates from the dinner they'd shared. Gustav stepped behind her, encircling her waist before covering her breasts with his hands. "Tell me if you don't want this," he whispered in her ear.

Kera arched back. "I want this. I want you."

His fingers flicked her erect nipples softly as his warm, wet lips touched the back of her neck. Gustav turned her, hands light but insistent, and she faced him. Those cool blue eyes of his blazed. "I need to tell you...I love you."

She melted in his arms as he continued.

"I should have told you already. I adore your strength of character, I adore you for your mind, and I love your body." He interspersed his words with hot, quick kisses, his mouth raining down on her face, her lips, and her eyes. Kera shivered in his arms as he pulled at her clothes before diving his hands beneath her shirt to touch warm, bare skin.

"I have loved you for the longest time, Gustav. Even when I

thought you didn't want me."

His face shined with triumph before he dipped in for another kiss. With aching slowness, he slipped his hands back down to grip the sides of her shirt. "Let's get rid of this."

Kera raised her arms, giving him access, as the shirt was pulled up. Their gazes locked until the material slid over her face.

"Beautiful," he muttered as he thrust the offending material away from him and lifted his hands to the pale-blue bra she wore.

He cupped her breasts through the cloth and kneaded. Her heartbeat faltered for an instant before a new, faster rhythm began.

Kera reached for the small buttons of his shirt, the metal cold beneath her fingers. She twisted the disks back through the loops that held the shirt closed. With each deft twist, more of his bronzed flesh and scorching heat was revealed. Alive and warm beneath her hands.

Gustav dragged his palms back down to her midriff. Feather-light touches skimmed her sensitive flesh, and she shivered as he found her scars, tracing them.

"What they did to you..." His voice shook, and she ran a finger across his lips.

"It's nothing now. He won't hurt me again."

She found the hard muscles of his arms and caressed them with her hands. The kiss scorched her mouth and tongue, before his lips skated over her jaw and down her arched throat.

Her moan was filled with desire and need left her quaking, her heart thudding a quick tattoo. His body was hard and urgent against hers. And Kera burned for his touch as the molten heat of his kisses reached her collarbone.

Her knees melted under the onslaught, and she gripped his shoulders to support herself. Gustav slipped hard, firm arms beneath her, lifting her against his chest. The shock of skin on skin stole her thoughts. Twining her fingers at the nape of his neck, she held on as he moved with controlled grace toward the bedroom.

Kera barely registered the dip of the satiny coverlet beneath her bared skin, as his eyes, no longer cold, burned her with a shining intensity. Gustav released the clasp of his belt, then the buttons of his pants. Heaven help her, she wanted to reach out and take over. As if reading her mind, he smiled while pushing the pants down, over lean hips, to stand naked before her.

His cock now released from the confines rose to his abdomen, reinforcing the urgency of his need. Kera resisted the urge to reach over and fondle it.

"You're overdressed." His words were smoky, and she shivered once more as he moved toward her. He reached behind her to unclasp her bra before he stripped back the straps, freeing her breasts to his view and the kiss of the cool air. "You are so beautiful. I'm looking forward to tasting those strawberry tips."

She closed her eyes. And as his fingers started pushing at her pants, she lifted her hips.

Gustav joined her on the bed, looming over her, looking into her eyes. "If any of this makes you uncomfortable, say so."

She knew he alluded to her capture. He bowed down his head, touching his lips to her breasts, opening over them and suckling at her. With aching slowness he slid his fingers over her belly to find the curls that lay at the apex of her thighs. She gasped as tremors began to rack her body.

Kera flung her head back, the electric sensations rippling through her. His caressing fingers, mouth on her breast, and then his skin moving against hers made her writhe with passion. She grew damper and hotter against his bare flesh.

"Gustav!" The cry was broken, and he lifted his head, settling back on his knees. He dipped his fingers ever lower, barely skimming her flesh. "I need to touch you."

He smiled at her with passion-filled eyes. "Not just yet, my beauty. I want to give you pleasure and watch you explode." She made to sit up, but he extended a muscular arm, stopping her. "Stay there."

He gently rubbed the moist flesh between the folds of her sex. Touching the nub between her legs, teasing and tormenting with a gentleness that wound her higher. She jerked beneath him as he found the secret entry, working back and forth over the sensitive lips. His face hard and ruddy with desire.

"I love that you're so wet for me." His words came out as little more than a growl in the almost silent room.

Gustav slid one finger within her hot, wet core, and she closed her eyes, moaning at the feeling. She welcomed the sensation of him touching her this way. He kept his movement slow as a second finger joined in.

"More!" Her voice turned thready as he increased the pace of the thrusts.

"I'm going to make you explode, and then I'm going to do it all again," he said, his voice a tattoo beating in her mind while with magic fingers he touched her intimately. His thumb rubbing the hooded bundle of nerves.

His moves came faster and wilder, his lips returned to suckling at her until, with a hoarse cry, she orgasmed. Her body milked his fingers and her heart beat wildly. Boneless, she lay still, basking in the afterglow of her climax.

A tide of red washed over him, arousal blushing his skin, and she sat up with slow, deliberate moves. "My turn now." Meeting his lips with hers, she skimmed her hand down his body until she found his cock.

Kera encircled the shaft, squeezing lightly before pulling away and dragging her index finger over the already wet slit. His hips moved against her, before she raised her mouth, and he grunted.

"I want to suck you, to ride you and take all of you, deep within me." Kera pushed him back, her mouth roaming over his stubbled chin and down his throat as she flicked her fingers over his brown nipple. "Lie flat for me."

She waited as Gustav settled down on the bed, his eyes searching hers while she lowered her head to his shaft. Blowing slightly against the flared tip, she watched in fascination as his erection jerked. She skimmed the top softly with a finger and then dipped her head to him, opened her mouth, and savored the satiny hardness and the salty tang of his body.

She teased and licked, hearing his heaving pants, and welcomed the thrust of his hips. She knew he was moving closer to orgasm. His hands caught her head, stopping her.

"Not like that. Not the first time, Kera." He pulled her up toward him, and she reveled in the feel of his body so close to hers.

His mouth ravaged hers, his touch scorching as he positioned himself below her. She felt the head of his cock between her legs and cried out as he moved against her sensitized skin. He felt so hot, and she welcomed him.

He lowered her, impaling her as she took him into her body. And Kera gloried in the way he assuaged the ache deep inside her. Gustav gripped her hips tight, keeping her still as he made a throaty request. "Not yet. I want to watch your eyes. I want you to see mine."

Aching with the need that consumed her, burned her, she opened her eyes and saw the same need and desire in his. Slowly, so slowly, he withdrew then slid back in, filling her fully again. She cried out with the sparks of pleasure, his hands toying with her breasts, and she heaved for breath, needing to move on him.

"Oh, Gustav!" Her body tightened, and Kera knew she was close, already. "Gustav!"

"*Let go.*" He grunted the words, moving his hips faster. Each slip and slide wound her higher and closer toward her looming orgasm. "I'll be with you. Let go."

She flung her head back, and awareness of the world fled as waves of ecstasy filled her. She heard him groaning as he joined her, pumping his seed deep. She was held suspended within the pleasure, before slowly slumping forward. His arms folded around her, their hearts beating fast, their bodies damp but replete.

"I love you." The words were whispered against her temple as she relaxed and floated away.

✪ ✪ ✪ ✪

Consciousness reasserted itself as Gustav lay back with Kera safe in his arms. Her warm body pleased him on both a sexual and emotional level. He needed one more promise from her, and he worried slightly.

Will she say yes? Should I ask her?

"Kera?" he whispered, and she nodded groggily.

"Gustav? Again? Already?" Her bemused tone made him laugh.

"No." His laugh died away. "I have a question though."

She raised her head, and he saw the worry in her eyes. "What?" She tugged away a little, and he felt the distance which might so easily come between them.

"C'mere." He pulled her against his body so her head lay on his shoulder. "I need to ask a serious question."

She frowned but snuggled back against him.

"I need to ask..." He stopped. *Is this the right time?* He didn't remember ever experiencing nerves like this, but he needed her, and he had to be sure she felt the same need.

"Gustav?" He could hear the concern in her voice. Looking at the ceiling, he took a deep breath before plunging forward.

"Kera, I know you Communed once before. But would you consider doing so with me?" He breathed deeply, hoping she would accept. He'd pushed her away once and—

"It's about time you asked. Of course I will."

His heart stopped for an instant, and he closed his eyes. His heart restarted, this time beating hard and fast. He was so full of love for the woman in his arms.

"Good. Then no more leaving me. Ever. You'll stay here, in my arms." With that, he pulled her closer, letting his mouth descend on hers.

About Imogene Nix

Imogene is published in a range of romance genres including paranormal, science fiction, and contemporary. She is mainly published in the UK and USA due to the nature of her tales.

In 2011, Imogene Nix was born at the Bondi ARRA (Australian Romance Readers Association) Conference. Returning from the conference enthused, Imogene sat down and worked tirelessly for three months culminating in the book *Starline*. This book became the first in the Warriors of the Elector series. In fact, she has completed six entire series. Imogene has successfully been contracted for twenty-five titles and self-published three others under this pseudonym. She has also completed another three and is, like many of her contemporaries, seeking homes for these books—with at least one likely to be self-published once ready.

Imogene is a member of a range of professional organizations, including Romance Writers of Australia (where she holds a committee position as the Public Relations). She is also a member of Romance Writers of America, FFP (Fantasy, Futuristic, and Paranormal) Chapter of RWA (US), Australian Romance Readers Association (ARRA), Science Fiction Romance Brigade (SFRB), Dark Siders Down Under (the Australian Paranormal, Fantasy, and Futuristic Chapter of RWA), Erotic Writers of Australia, and Queensland Writers Centre and most recently Romance Writers of New Zealand.

Imogene's Website: www.imogenenix.net
Reader eMail: imogene@imogenenix.net
Newsletter:
eepurl.com/cp-bZD

Books by Imogene Nix

Blood Secrets *(Totally Bound Publishing)*
1. The Blood Bride
The Illuminated Witch
3. The Sorcerer's Touch

Celtic Cupid (*Totally Bound Publishing*)

1. Blame The Wine
2. A Stranger's Embrace
3. Revenge On Cupid

Reunion (*Beachwalk Press*)
1. War's End
2. The Assassin
3. Executing Justice

The Plan BioCybe
Tangled Webs (Sex Love Aliens 1)
Covert Webs (Sex Love Aliens 2)
A Bar In Paris
Hesparia's Tears
The Chocolate Affair
Tomorrow's Promise
False Webs
A Sapphire For Karina
Falling In Love Again

With Suzi Love
Self Publishing: Absolute Beginners Guide